"NOW YOU WILL BE MADE READY."

Then the speaker stepped to the left, revealing the ugliest specimen of Plated Folk Jon-Tom had ever seen. Its body was long and thin and flattened from head to thorax. It was also the smallest of the Plated Folk in the chamber, barely three feet long. So was the tightly curled ovipositor-like tube which protruded from the base of the bulbous abdomen. It curved up over the insect's back and head. The hypodermic tip quivered in the air a foot in front of the creature's head.

Jon-Tom found he was breathing fast as he searched for a place to hide.

"Listen, you don't have to do this," he told the speaker, his eyes following that wavering point. "I'm not going to give you any trouble. I can't, without my duar." He wasn't ashamed of the hysteria rising in his voice. He was genuinely terrified of what was in essence a three-foot long needle.

"There is no need to struggle," the speaker assured him.

"You're not sticking that thing in me!" Jon-Tom leaped to his right, not caring anymore if the guards used their swords or not.

They did not have the chance to react. As soon as Jon-Tom moved, the stinger lashed down like a striking cobra . . .

Also by
ALAN DEAN FOSTER

THE SPELLSINGER SERIES

Spellsinger

The Hour of the Gate

The Day of the Dissonance

The I Inside

The Man Who Used the Universe

Alien

Clash of the Titans

Krull

Outland

Shadowkeep

Starman

Published by
WARNER BOOKS

ALAN DEAN FOSTER

THE MOMENT OF THE MAGICIAN

A Warner Communications Company

WARNER BOOKS EDITION

Hardcover edition published by Phantasia Press

Cover design by Don Puckey

Warner Books, Inc.
666 Fifth Avenue
New York, N.Y. 10103

 A Warner Communications Company

Printed in the United States of America

First Printing: March, 1985

10 9 8 7 6 5 4 3 2 1

For Tim Hildebrandt,
A good friend and a fellow journeyer
Through the lands of Never-Never...

Timeful Desert
Crestleware
Redrock
Village of the Enchanted Folk
Snarken
Crancularn
Orangel
Cities
Forest
Hills

Muddletup Moors
L'Bor
Malderpot
Timswitty
The Bellwoods
Beach
Yarrowl
Clothahump's Tree
River Tailaroam
Polastrindu
Bahamanian Encounter
Duggakurra Hills
Glittergeist Sea
Wrounipai
Quasequa
Lake Region
Mountains
Swamps
ORIOLO

I

"And I say Oplode should give way!"

The speaker, Asmouelle the tamandua, stood before the narrow wooden oval that was the Quorum table and glared at his colleagues. His nose was damp and glistening, and so was the table. Most everything stayed damp in Quasequa, a city built on numerous islands in the middle of the Lake of Sorrowful Pearls. Causeways joined the islands together, and each isle sent its duly chosen representative to argue for it in the Quorum.

This afternoon the arguments raged hotter than the air outside the Quorumate. The members were debating the selection of an advisor in matters arcane and magical.

The unexpected challenger for this mystic position sat and brooded in a chair at the far end of the Quorum chamber. Reluctant attendants saw to his needs. They were afraid of the newcomer. So were several members of the Quorum, though none confessed such unseemly fears openly.

Two members openly supported the challenger, but not out of fear. Kindore and Vazvek saw a chance to better themselves by striking a bargain with the newcomer for their aid. The rest of the

Quorum regarded this naked display of sycophancy with disgust.

And now Asmouelle appeared to have joined them.

The tamandua sat down. Domurmur the lynx rose and spoke dispassionately. "And *I* say this wanderer has yet to prove himself capable of anything stronger than bad breath." His paws rested on the ancient table, which was as black and shiny as a bottle of oil.

Kindore responded with an insult of some subtlety, and once again the debate dissolved into chaos. It ceased only when Trendavi raised a hand for silence. He did not stand. Long experience had taught him that it was not necessary for a legislator to jump up and down like a toy in a box to make a point.

The aged pangolin squinted down the length of the table, studying the challenger silently for a moment. Then he nodded to his left.

"Oplode the Sly has been principal advisor in arcane matters to the Quorum of Quasequa for nearly thirty years. Skillfully and well has he served. The city and its citizens have profited much from his advice." Trendavi showed scaly palms. "As have we all."

Words of agreement rose from the members while Kindore and Vazvek were conspicuous by their silence. The newcomer said nothing.

"It is true that this Markus person"—and Trendavi gestured toward the individual in the solitary chair, who sat smiling to himself as if at some secret joke—"has demonstrated to the Quorum nothing more than a facile tongue."

Now the newcomer stood and approached the black table. "Since you credit me with it, let me use it, friends." The towering form of his personal body-guard moved to stand close to the door. "Can I come nearer?" He smiled pleasantly and even Domurmur had to admit that this Markus the Ineluctable, as he styled himself, could be downright ingratiating in manner when he so desired. Especially for a human, a species not noted for its social graces.

Trendavi nodded. All eyes focused on the newcomer as he moved close.

For his part, Markus the Ineluctable sensed antagonism, fear, curiosity, and some open support among the members of the Quorum. He would concentrate his efforts on persuading those who seemed to be wavering. Of the ten, he could count on three. The two who openly feared him he could ignore. He had to persuade at least two others.

And he had to move carefully lest he panic them all. It was too early to press his demands. His position was uncertain in Quasequa, and despite his powers, he had no wish to raise a formal alliance against him. Far better to make friends of them than enemies. Of a majority, anyway.

"I've come here from a faraway land, a land farther off and stranger than any of you can imagine."

"So you've claimed." Domurmur had become something of an unofficial spokesman for Markus's opposition. "All that you claim is difficult to believe."

"Yet much of it is proven by my presence, isn't it?"

"Not necessarily," said Newmadeen, preening her whiskers casually. One of her long ears was bent forward in the middle, a sign of beauty among the hares.

Markus turned away momentarily and coughed. He did not need to cough, but he didn't want them to see the expression on his face. He didn't like being called a liar. Calming himself, he turned to face them again. Newmadeen he didn't reply to, but he would remember her. Oh, yes, he would remember her. Markus the Ineluctable never forgot an enemy.

"Why not?"

Cascuyom the howler shrugged. "There is nothing unique or remarkable about your person. There are many humans living in Quasequa. All species mix freely here. Or you could have come from any one of several neighboring lands with denser human populations. Your humanness is proof of nothing."

Markus stepped up to the table, enjoying the way several of the members shied away from him. "But I'm no mere human! I'm not your usual mortal. I am a magician—*the* magician. Markus the Ineluctable! I have powers you cannot comprehend, abilities you cannot conceive of, talents you cannot imagine!"

"A mouth big beyond belief," Domurmur whispered to the beauteous Newmadeen.

Trendavi cleared his throat, spoke thoughtfully and, he hoped, with some degree of neutrality. "You must think quite highly of your skills to come straight to the Quorum to challenge the faithful and talented Oplode without first passing time as an apprentice. For the nonce I will credit you with boldness instead of ignorance. Whether Oplode will be as forgiving remains to be seen." He nodded toward the salamander seated in the advisor's chair off to his right.

Red-orange blotches decorated what was visible of Oplode's back. He wore a single garment that resembled a raincoat. It was not close-fitting. No salamander could wear anything close to its skin because its natural bodily secretions would cause the material to stick.

Oplode's long tail flicked nervously back and forth. What he'd heard of this Markus the Ineluctable hadn't pleased him. Now that he saw him in the flesh, he liked the man even less.

Still, he'd held his peace because protocol demanded

it. Not that his personal opinion would be accepted as evidence. The selection of chief advisor to the Quorum was purely a matter of business. He would have his turn in due course. So he continued to sit quietly, ignoring the debate as best he could while trying to still the twitching of his tail.

Markus was talking on. "I can do things you won't believe by means of a magic you've never encountered before."

"More talk," said Domurmur, slapping the table with a paw. Markus grinned at him.

"I suspected it would come to this. You want more than talk from me."

"That'd be nice," said Domurmur sarcastically. "We've had to contend with applicants whose loquaciousness far exceeded their abilities before."

For an instant, it seemed as if Markus the Ineluctable was about to lose his temper. His barely concealed rage didn't faze Domurmur. He was made of sterner stuff than some of his colleagues.

"Yes," said Oplode suddenly, unable to contain himself any longer. "Let's have an end to this talk!"

All eyes turned to the chief advisor as he rose from his seat. The glow bulbs hanging by their single strands from the curved stone ceiling pulsed a little brighter as the salamander stood. It was his spelling which provided their soft, steady light. The servitors flanking the doorways whispered expectantly among themselves. Attendants and Quorum members alike could feel the power flowing from the old wizard, could sense that he was completely involved in what was taking place.

About the challenger there was no such perceptible aura of strength. There was only the air of mystery and feeling of alienness he had brought with him from the moment he'd stepped into the chamber.

That, and the regal bearing he affected, which somehow seemed not to fit.

Nor was his actual appearance particularly impressive. He was tall for a human but not spectacularly so, round of countenance, and crowned with less fur than most. In hand-to-hand combat it was unlikely he could have defeated any of the Quorum with the exception of old Trendavi, for he displayed a considerable paunch above his belt line.

The forthcoming battle would not be physical, however. Oplode approached the Quorum. "I see no reason to oppose a challenge. Indeed, I could not turn it down if I wished to. Nor is there any way you can choose between us without a contest of wills. The people of Quasequa deserve to have an advisor who has proven his abilities." He sighed deeply, looked resigned as he smoothed the slime on the back of his hands with a fold of his voluminous robe.

"I have demonstrated my fitness many times before and expect to have to do so many times again." He cocked an amphibian eye toward the newcomer. "Have you any objection to a public contest?"

"Here and now suits me fine." Markus fairly oozed confidence. "I'm a little new at this kind of duel. Do we need seconds?"

"I think not. In any event, my assistant Flute is quite young and I would not want him subjected to mystic influences that could injure him at a delicate stage of his development."

"Aw, I wouldn't do that." Markus turned. "Prugg, no matter what happens you stay there and keep out of the way. Understand?" The huge bodyguard nodded once and backed away from the table. He was not completely impassive, however. Like everyone else in the chamber, he was curious to see how his master would fare. He was even a little worried. After all, Oplode was the most noted wizard in the land. It was simple for his master to overawe the peasant folk with his magic, but outwitting Oplode would be another matter entirely.

Markus the Ineluctable seemed anything but intimidated, though. He grinned and gestured expansively toward the salamander. "You first."

Oplode did not smile. "Food is vital to the health of all. No food is more important to the people of Quascqua than the fish that swim in the lakes around us." He slid back his sleeves, cleared his throat, and his words rolled through the chamber.

"The bounty of the lake
I bid you all to share
Your hungers may you slake
With meat beyond compare
For while I advise Quasequa there will be
No nutritional dystopia
But always instead if you look you will see
An ichthyological cornucopia."

Quorum members and servitors alike watched with the fascination of children as a small, glowing blue-green whirlpool formed in the air above the floor. You could smell the lake water as the vortex hummed. Then the fish poured forth, falling head upon tail, until there was a heaping mound of flopping, bouncing weewaw lying in the middle of the floor. Weewaw, the hardest to catch and tastiest of all. And Oplode had brought forth this expensive and improbable feast with a wave of his hands and a few words.

The wizard spoke only when the last fish had tumbled to the stones and the whirlpool had vanished. "Can you so readily insure the supply of food to the citizens of the city?"

Markus frowned a moment. Then his grin returned. He raised his hands above his head, the fingers pointing outward. His black cape fluttered behind him. The Quorum members strained to listen, but those with good hearing could make no sense of the newcomer's words. Even Oplode, who could hear the incantation clearly, did not understand. The words were strange and sharp.

Sense they might not have made, but there was no denying their effect. A bright green glow appeared before the table. A few of the members shifted nervously in their chairs, and Markus casually assured them they had nothing to worry about.

The glow expanded and thinned. Markus looked smug as the glow formed a floating rectangle above the floor.

It was an aquarium without sides. Magic alone held the water in place. Swimming to and fro within the drifting section of lake was a whole school of weewaw, suspended before the Quorum.

"I don't know about the rest of you, but I hate waste. Wouldn't it be better to get your fish one at a time and keep the others fresh for the taking?"

Oplode muttered something and his pile of dead weewaw vanished. Markus did likewise and the floating aquarium also disappeared, save for a few misplaced drops which stained the floor.

"Well brought!" said Kindore, only to have his colleagues shush him. Oplode glared at the flying squirrel, then turned his attention back to the smiling Markus. They had determined one thing already.

His challenger was for real.

"It is not enough to feed a population in times of difficulty, stranger. One must be able to defend them as well." Again he lifted an arm, made sinuous motions in the air.

"Let those who threaten
beware, beware

We will not fight
with air, with air
We mold our weapons
with care, so there
Be metallurgical might!"

Fire this time, bright and hot. The Quorum members shielded their faces as the set of armor coalesced before them, melting out of the flames. Sword, shield, and long spear accompanied it. The fire cooled and flickered out.

Notorian moved from his seat to inspect the newly forged weapons. He hefted the sword, tapped the armor with it.

"Fine instruments for fighting."

"For one fighter, yes," Markus agreed readily. "For a trained warrior. But what of the ordinary citizen? How does he, or she, defend the community?"

Once more he raised his hands, once again he intoned an invocation none could comprehend. This he concluded by swinging his cape around in front of him, to form a funnel in the air.

There was a tinkling sound as something fell from the base of the funnel. Then another, and another. It became a metallic clashing as the flow increased, until the flow of knives was a shining waterfall pouring from the bottom of the cape.

Notorian the wolf picked one up and tested the edge. "Finest steel I've ever seen," he declared to the stunned Quorum. The rush of metal continued until Trendavi finally raised a hand himself.

"Enough!" Markus nodded, let the cape swirl back around his neck. As he did so, the clanging waterfall ceased. The floor of the Quorum chamber was awash in knives of every shape and size. Markus kicked a few of them aside and bowed.

"As my employers wish." He swept a hand out to

encompass the armory. "A gift to the Quorum and to the citizens of Quasequa, my adopted home."

"They're only knives," Cascuyom muttered.

"You'd prefer swords?" Markus asked him, overhearing. "Or maybe something more lethal still? Like this." He threw his left hand toward the ceiling. A burst of lightning flew from his fingers to shatter the pole holding a banner across the table. Splinters and fabric tumbled onto the Quorum. Markus grinned as they fought to extricate themselves while maintaining their dignity.

"Something more impressive?" he inquired.

"No, no, that will be quite satisfactory," harrumphed Trendavi, trying to untangle himself from the fallen banner.

"You can feed and you can destroy," snapped Oplode, "but can you create?"

Again the salamander's hands moved in time to his mouth.

"Jewels of the earth
Scarce and profound
Gems of great worth
Come forth from the ground
Rise here to please us
To tempt and to tease us!"

Crystals of blue and yellow, of rose and lavender began to take shape in the center of the table. They seemed to grow out of the wood, catching the light as they developed, throwing back delightful colors at the enraptured members. By the time Oplode concluded the incantation, the entire table was encrusted with crystals. A smattering of applause came from the servitors gathered along the walls.

But Markus the Ineluctable only smiled wider as

he moved his fingers against one another. The applause for Oplode turned to awed whispers.

Flowers began to appear, growing out of the naked stone of the walls and ceiling. Exotic, alien blossoms that put forth the most exquisite smells. A blaze of color and fragrance filled the Quorum chamber to overflowing.

You could see the opinions of several members of the Quorum begin to shift in Markus's favor.

"Satisfied yet?" Markus asked them. "You tell me which of us is the more powerful magician."

"A magician is a trickster, not a wizard," said Oplode.

Markus shrugged. "I prefer magician. I'm comfortable with it. I've always called myself a magician. As for my 'tricks,' they seem just as effective as your wizardry. Had enough?"

"There is one more thing," said Oplode slowly. "You have shown what you can do for others, but can you do for yourself?" So saying he pointed a red-and-black arm at Markus's face and uttered an incantation so powerful the words cannot stand repeating. A slight but steady breeze sprang up, rippling the fur of the onlookers, and the glow bulbs grew dim. No one in the chamber dared to breathe, lest a fraction of that energy latch onto them and turn them to dust.

As they stared, Markus the Ineluctable began to rise from the floor. He put his hands on his hips and considered his levitation thoughtfully, then nodded appreciatively in Oplode's direction.

"Hey, not bad. Not bad at all." Then he raised one hand and murmured something almost indifferently.

Oplode the Sly, Oplode the clever, Oplode the principal advisor in matters arcane and magical to the Quorum of Quasequa, vanished.

Shouts and cries from the servitors, mild panic

among the more impressionable members of the Quorum as Markus settled gently back to the ground.

"What have you done with him?" Domurmur's teeth were clenched, but he knew when he was overmatched. There was little more he could do than ask. "Where is he?"

"Where is he? Well now, let me think." Markus rubbed his chin. "He might be over . . . there!" He pointed sharply toward a far doorway. Servitors stationed there scattered, dropping a platter of fruit behind them. Markus turned, inspecting the chamber.

"Or he might be . . . under there." A couple of the members of the Quorum inadvertently peered under the table, hastily sat up straight in their chairs when they realized how easily the newcomer had manipulated them.

"But he's actually probably right . . . here." Markus the Ineluctable removed his black hat, turned it upside down, and tapped it once, twice, a third time. Out plopped a dazed and very disoriented Oplode the Sly. Disdaining Markus's proffered hand, the salamander struggled to his feet and backed away, shaking his head and trying to regain his bearings.

From the Quorum came a rising cry in support of Markus.

Oplode ignored it, stared narrowly at his opponent. "I don't know how you did that, but of one thing I am certain: it was no clean wizardry."

"Oh, it was clean enough," said Markus smugly. "Just a mite different from what you're used to, that's all. Are you afraid of something different, something new?" He turned to face the Quorum. "Are you all afraid of something different, even if it's better than what you've been used to?"

"No," said Trendavi quickly. "We are not afraid of what is different, or of what is new. We of Quasequa pride ourselves on accepting new things, on promoting innovation." He gazed sorrowfully in Oplode's direction. "It is my recommendation and I hereby move that the Quorum officially nominate Markus the Ineluctable to the position of chief advisor to the Quorum on matters arcane and magical, and I furthermore move that Oplode the Sly, who has served us so well lo these many years, be retired from the post with a vote of thanks and an official commendation to be decided upon later."

"Seconded!" said a pair of voices simultaneously.

And that was that. It was done, over, and Markus stood smiling, arms crossed before him as his supporters gathered around to congratulate him on his victory and those who had opposed him moved to offer grudging words of acceptance. A few would have offered their condolences to the defeated Oplode, but the salamander did not linger. Instead, he left quickly and with dignity, still a bit shaken from the manner in which Markus had handled him, but in no way cowed or beaten.

It was dark in the wizard's study. But then, Oplode preferred the dim light and the dampness. His rooms were situated at the edge of the Quorumate Complex and below the water line. Ancient stones held back the warm water of the Lake of Sorrowful Pearls while allowing a pleasant dampness to seep through. Thick moss, red as well as green, grew on the stones and ceiling. The furniture was fashioned of stone or boram root, which resists rot.

Glow bulbs dangled overhead, their magic lights dimmer than usual, the weak illumination a reflection of the wizard's uncomfortable state of mind. Oplode stared steadily at one flickering bulb as he lay in his thinktank. The stone basin was filled with freshly drawn lake water rich with lichens, mosses, light blue hot pads, and minute aquatic insects.

Altogether, the rooms constituted a benign and thoroughly salamandrine environment.

But as Oplode lay on his back, his arms crossed over his chest, his tail gently agitating the water, it was plain to see he was disturbed. Tending the crackling fire nearby was a much smaller and younger salamander, well aware of his master's unease. Flute wore the cloak of an apprentice. He was stouter than Oplode, marked with black spots instead of red, and his expression was anxious. His feathery pink gills lay flat against his neck as he waited patiently for Oplode to arise. A sad day. He knew what had happened in the Quorum chamber far above. Everyone in the city would know by tonight.

Finally Oplode rose from the basin, shifting easily to inhaling air instead of water, and declared portentously, "This thing must not be allowed to happen!"

"Your pardon, Master," said Flute softly. "What must not be allowed to happen?"

"I have lost. There is nothing that can be done about that. Nor do I deny the strength of this newcomer's magic. He is a valid wizard, or magician, or whatever he chooses to call himself. A manipulator of the unknown. But it is not his abilities I fear; it is his intentions. Those I comprehend even less than his magic."

He walked over to stand before the fire. Flute moved to the table and checked the settings for supper, then to the stove on which a big pot of caddisfly stew sat boiling. He stirred it carefully. One had to have a delicate touch with the dish or the nests within would become soft and stringy and would lose the delicate crunch so beloved of gourmets.

"Nor do I like the attitude of his original supporters on the Quorum," Oplode went on, staring into the fire. "Kindore and Vazvek. Those two opportunists would throw in their lot with anyone they thought might help them turn a profit. And Asmouelle and some of the others have the spines of worms. With so much support, there is nothing to stop this Markus."

"Stop him from doing what, Master?"

"From doing whatever he wishes to do. He is chief advisor to the Quorum. A prestigious position and one which would satisfy most. But not him, I think. I saw that much in his eyes. That is not sorcery. That is thirty years of experience, Flute. No, he wants more. I fear, much more."

"Evil designs, Master?"

"Flute, I have lived long enough and dealt with those in power often enough to recognize the hunger for power when it manifests itself on the face of another. I saw it in the face of Markus the Ineluctable as I left the Quorum chamber. He conceals it from the others, but he cannot hide it from me.

"Did you know, Flute, that the great joy of living in Quasequa is that we have never had a single ruler? No kings here, no presidents or emperors. Only the Quorum, which functions in a kind of constrained anarchy. It suits us, we Quasequans.

"This Markus will think otherwise. He will see weakness where we see strength. And it does have its vulnerabilities, our system, particularly when some are ready to grovel at the feet of the first would-be dictator who comes along and declares himself."

"You think he means to announce himself absolute ruler?"

"I wish I could be certain, but I can't." Oplode absently cleaned his left eye with his tongue. "In any event, I am no longer in a position to stop him."

"Is his magic so much stronger than yours, Master?"

"It was today. On another day"—he shrugged slick shoulders—"who can say? But there is no denying his power. If I only knew the source he draws upon..." He broke off and moved to the table, the frustration sharp on his face.

Flute reached for the potholders. "Supper, Master?"

"No, not yet." Oplode waved him off, his mind working intensely. "If I could only be certain of his intentions, of his motivations—but where humans are concerned, nothing is obvious, nothing is certain."

"What if he truly is more powerful than you, Master?" It was not a disrespectful question.

"Then we will need the assistance of one who can deal not only with strong magic but with strange magic."

"There is one more talented than you, Master?"

For the first time that day, Oplode smiled slightly. "You have seen but little of the wide world, my young student. It is unimaginably vast and rich with wonders and surprises. Yes, there are wizards more powerful than I. I am thinking of one in particular. One who is wise beyond all others, knowledgeable beyond comprehending, stronger even, I think, than this Markus the Ineluctable...I hope. One who is brave, courageous, and bold, an inspiration to all other wizards. It is he whose help we must have: Clothahump of the Tree."

Flute frowned, turned away so that Oplode could not see the skepticism on his face. "I have heard of *him*, Master. Truly it is said that he is wise and full of learning, long-lived and powerful. However, I have yet to hear it said of him that he is brave, courageous, and bold."

"Well," Oplode retreated somewhat, "I confess some of it may be rumor. But his ability is proven fact. You know that he was largely responsible for the recent defeat of the Plated Folk at the battle for the Jo-Troom Gate."

"I have heard many versions of that battle, Master, some of which were less flattering to Clothahump of the Tree than others. It is told that he was there at the critical moment, yes, but to what degree he was involved depends on which storyteller you are listening to."

"Nevertheless, he is the only one powerful enough to help us. We *must* seek his aid. He cannot refuse us."

"How will you inform him, Master?" Flute gazed sadly at the supper that was on the verge of overcooking. "Shall I prepare the pentagram for a traveling conjuration?"

"No." Oplode rose from the table. "This Markus might be strong enough to detect it. And there is no guarantee of its working, given the distance the conjuration would have to travel. Clothahump's home lies a long way from Quasequa—and I am getting old. It has been a long time since I attempted a traveling conjuration over such a distance."

Flute was shocked by this admission of weakness but fought not to show it. Truly the loss of today's contest had weakened not only his Master's stature but his confidence as well.

Or perhaps Oplode the Sly was merely being properly cautious. Flute preferred to think that that was the case.

"We must have a messenger," the wizard muttered. "A reliable messenger. One who is used to traveling far and fast and who will not be afraid to leave the familiar country that surrounds the Lake of Sorrowful Pearls." He thought a moment longer before nodding to himself and looking up at his apprentice.

"On the Isle of Kunatweh, the furthermost of the four high islands that form the eastern part of the city, in the place where the fliers congregate, lives a raven named Pandro. Bring him here to me. Make certain that none see you. I will explain what he must do. Although I have never had reason to use one such as him before, by reputation he is brave and trustworthy. Again I tell you to take care in your going and returning. It is said that this Markus already has spies roaming the city and reporting back only to him.

"Although he defeated me today, he strikes me as no fool. I am sure he still regards me as his most dangerous rival. In that he is right," Oplode muttered grimly. "I sense and see what kind of individual he is and so am unalterably opposed to having him in a position of power in the city I love so dearly. I believe he must know my feelings toward him, and in any case, such as he will leave nothing to chance. So he will have this place watched. At least you can slip out without being seen. I do not believe anyone else knows of my private entryway."

"When do I leave, Master?"

"Now." The wizard hesitated. "Have you eaten?"

"It does not matter, Master. I can eat anytime."

"No," Oplode said firmly. "You may need all your strength. First we eat."

They did so, the meal passing largely in contemplative silence. Then Flute secured his waterproof cloak snugly around him and moved to the arched alcove on the far side of the room. The arch was an inverted bell fashioned of tightly chinked tile. A pressure spell invoked by Oplode kept the lake water out.

Flute climbed the stone steps until he could look out onto the black water that lapped against the wall of the bell. He readied his gills, fluffing them out with his hands, and dove into the water.

A couple of fast kicks carried him well out into the open lake. He did not surface but swam hard and unerringly for the four high islands of the east. Like the other isles that combined to form the sprawling city of Quasequa, they were connected to one another by causeways, but this was not the time to walk openly on city streets.

It was time for stealth and for clinging to the dark bottom of the lake.

II

Oplode sat in his robes of office, a thin, narrow upswept cap balanced on the middle of his slick head, and regarded his visitor. Flute stood quietly by the front door.

The raven wore the kilt of his clan, colorful material striped with green, purple, and red. His vest was lightly spun lavender. A single gold chain hung round his neck to rest against his chest feathers. He rubbed the underside of his beak with a flexible wingtip.

"Let me get this straight, now, sorcerer." He was studying the papers Oplode had handed him. "You want me to fly north along this route, turning slightly west here, to deliver this message." He shuffled the papers, held up one filled with writing instead of diagrams. "It goes to an old turtle named Clothahump who lives in"—he checked the map briefly—"this major tree here. For one hundred coins." Oplode nodded.

"That's a helluva long flight," Pandro said.

"I had heard that you were not afraid of long flights."

"I ain't. I ain't afraid of anything, least of all a little long-distance traveling. But considering how quiet you're being about this, and the amount you're paying me, well, no disrespect, Master Oplode, but—what's the catch?"

Oplode glanced at Flute, then sighed and smiled down at Pandro. "It would not be right for me to keep it from you. You must know what you are about, as well as its importance.

"You must have heard that another has assumed my position as chief advisor to the Quorum."

"Sure. It's all over town. This Markus fella... what's it to me?"

"Good Pandro, I have reason to believe that this newcomer intends ill toward our great city. But I cannot convince the members of the Quorum of that. They would think I was making accusations out of bitterness at my loss. And I cannot move against this Markus by myself. I need help. This Clothahump that you will seek out is the only one who can help us.

"The 'catch' is that this Markus the Ineluctable is crafty as well as skilled in the arcane arts. You are sure none saw you arrive here?"

"As sure as we can be, Master," said Flute. "I took every precaution."

"Then, good Pandro, there may be no catch. But be ever alert as you wing northward, for this Markus is not stupid. If he believes you are aiding me, it could be dangerous for you. If he did see you arrive here, or sees you depart, he may try to stop you from completing your journey."

"Is that all?" The raven rested his wingtips on his hips for a moment, then rolled up the message and the map and slipped them into his backpack. "Then there's nothing to concern yourself with, Master Oplode. There isn't another flier in Quasequa who can stay in the air for as long as I can on as little food as I can. Anybody he sends after me, *if* he sends anyone, I can outfly." He flicked his beak with a wingtip.

"See here? Been broken twice in fights. I can take care of myself and I'm not worried about anything this Markus fella might send up after me. If it flies, I can outrun or outfight it."

"It is good to be confident. Overconfidence is dangerous."

"Don't worry. I'll use my good judgment, sir. I've a mate and three fledglings to take care of, and you can bet I'm coming back to them. That's stronger motivation than your hundred coins. Relax. I'll get your message through."

"Can you fly at night?" Oplode asked him.

"Night, day, the air's all the same to me whether it's light or dark out. But if you'd feel better about it, I'll leave tonight."

Oplode smiled. "Feel better, I would. The night must be a friend to us all, now." Flute nodded solemnly.

"As you wish, sir."

"Caution above all," Oplode counseled him. "This Markus has spies everywhere. Even among the fliers."

"I'll keep it in mind, sir. Once I'm clear of the lake district I should have free flying all the way north. Besides, I know all the good fliers and fighters in the high islands. I don't think any are in this fella's pay."

"I was not worried about your cousins," Oplode said darkly, "so much as I was concerned about what this Markus might call forth from another, more sinister sky to challenge you."

"Can't spend all our time worrying about the unforeseeable, can we, sir? At least I can't. I suppose that's your job." He tapped his head. "Anyway, anything I can't outfly or outfight I can sure as hell outsmart."

"Then be off with you, owner of an unseen cloud, and hasten back to us safely."

Pandro started for the doorway. "You can bet on that, sir."

* * *

"A raven, you say?" Markus the Ineluctable was listening with only half his mind to what the mouse was telling him. He was too busy enjoying the splendor of his new tower quarters, the finest that the Quorumate Complex could offer.

"Yes, wise one," said the mouse. It had a tendency to stutter, a condition made worse by its proximity to the powerful and much-feared new chief advisor to the Quorum. "It flew s-s-straight away from the l-l-landing where Mossamay Street and the wizard's c-c-close join."

"Which direction did it take?"

"It f-f-flew north, wise one. Few city fliers live to the n-n-north."

Markus turned from contemplation of an exquisite wood carving to stare at his bodyguard. The mouse barely came up to his hip. "Prugg, what's your opinion of this?"

Prugg was very big, very strong, and not very bright. Despite his size and strength, people had a tendency to laugh at him. At least, they used to. Since he'd become Markus the Ineluctable's personal servant they'd stopped laughing. Prugg was just intelligent enough to realize this. He was very grateful to the magician. Markus made him feel comfortable, even though he understood very little of what his new master had to say.

But he didn't have to think anymore. Markus did all his thinking for him. Prugg found thinking uncomfortable. And nobody laughed at him anymore. He was respected and feared. It was a new sensation and Prugg found that he liked it. Markus understood him, understood his needs. Prugg responded with devoted, unquestioning service.

So he considered the question carefully before replying. "It is true that the lands to the north of the city are not as thickly inhabited as those in other directions, Master."

"What's the land to the north of here like?"

"Open forest where live peoples who do not pledge their allegiance to the city or to any other government, Master. North of that is the Wrounipai, the first of many swamps all connected together that run from west to east. They cut us off from any lands that lie still farther north."

"And what about those lands?"

"I do not know, Master. I have never been there. I do not know anyone from the city who has ever been there."

"And that's the way this bird was heading when he left Oplode's place." Markus turned his full attention on his spy. "You're certain of that?"

"Y-y-y-y-for sure, wise one! I am certain of it. He f-f-f-flew straight away from the wizard's neighborhood. I followed him with my eyes from the rooftops nearby."

"Okay, but how can we be sure he was on a mission for Oplode?"

The visitor moved nearer, anxious to ingratiate himself with the magician. His whiskers trembled as he whispered.

"The wizard Oplode has a young assistant named Flute. I s-s-saw him conversing with the raven before he took off for the north." Markus was nodding absently, admiring the polished hardwood inlay of the table behind him. A single chair rested against the table.

It needs something, he thought. A gargoyle or demon or some such carved atop the chair. Something to draw the visitors' eyes upward. For that matter, if the table was going to serve as a desk, it had to be up on a dais. He'd have to get some carpenters in here and get them started on the alterations he wanted.

He was aware of his spy standing hopeful and silent by his legs. "That's it?"

"That is all, w-w-wise one."

Markus nodded, glanced toward Prugg. "Give him a gold piece."

"Thank you, wise one!" The spy was unaccustomed to such largess, but Markus had always believed in paying his help as much as possible. Otherwise you ended up with garbage working for you, ready to sell you out to the first high bidder. Even if he was overpaying for this particular bit of information, in so doing he was buying himself a valuable servant forever.

The mouse took the coin; skittered quickly away from the ominous, silent shape of Prugg; and did some admirable bowing and scraping as he retreated from the magician's room.

When the door was closed once more, Prugg turned to his benefactor. "What will you do now, Master?"

"What would you suggest?"

Prugg strained. Thinking hurt his head. "There are faster fliers than ravens, Master. I would send them after this one. Better not to take chances. Kill it."

"He has nearly a full day's head start," Markus murmured, "but I agree with your suggestion." Prugg smiled proudly. "I will send fliers out after him, yes, but I will not hire them. I will conjure them forth to do our bidding."

"Yes, Master," said Prugg admiringly, waiting to see what the magician would do next.

What Markus did was to assume a wide stance in the middle of the room. The floor there had been cleared of all furniture and decoration. Prugg moved to one side for a better view. He found it astonishing that Markus required no special chamber in which to perform his wizardry. Nothing but a clear floor and plenty of arm room.

As always, Markus mumbled the incantation. Not that Prugg would have understood the words any better than Oplode, but Markus the Ineluctable took no chances with his secrets.

The room darkened perceptibly and the air grew very still. Prugg would have been able to see better with glow bulbs, but Markus would have nothing of Oplode's around him and insisted instead on using simple torches for illumination.

Then a faint whine became audible, alien and harsh, rising slowly in volume. Prugg strained to see. In the center of the room, in front of Markus, shapes took form. It was as the magician had said: fliers, but fliers akin to none Prugg had ever heard tell of. He found himself backing away. They were far smaller than he was, but ugly and threatening to behold.

Markus, on the other hand, seemed delighted by their appearance. They danced and whirled over his head as he guided them with words and hands.

"Beautiful, beautiful! Better than I dared hope for. If only I could've called them up as a child. Ah, well, Prugg, it takes time to master the art. See, they're just as I described them!"

The demons continued to pivot and spin over their master's head, roaring exultantly and gnashing their long teeth. In the enclosed space the din was deafening.

They had no faces, Prugg noted.

No eyes, nostrils, external ears, or visible mouths. Only those mindless, clashing teeth. Fangs without jaws. Prugg found he was shaking. There were worse things in the world than one's own nightmares.

"To the north!" Markus cried, pointing with one

hand. "There flies the raven named Pandro. Where he's going I don't know, but see that he doesn't get there. Go!"

One by one, in single file, the faceless demons tore through the open window. Only when the last of the growling chorus had faded into the light of mideve did Markus drop his hands and return to stand behind his desk.

"About this chair, Prugg. What I want you to do is—" He stopped and stared at his bodyguard. "Are you paying attention?"

The huge servant forced his gaze away from the window where the demons had taken their leave and back to his master. Markus was speaking as though the conjuration had never taken place. It was all so matter-of-fact, so ordinary to him, this calling up of otherworldly powers.

Truly Prugg was fortunate to have him for a master.

It was a lovely warm day, the air thick with humidity but not oppressively so. Below Pandro the trees had closed in, shutting off sight of the ground. He was already well north not only of Quasequa but of its outlying villages and satellite communities as well.

Rising thermals allowed him to glide effortlessly over the dense tropical forest. Since departing Quasequa he'd stopped only once, and that briefly, the previous night to catch a bit of sleep. Then up before dawn for a fast breakfast of fruit, nuts, and dried fish and on to the north.

In his mind he reviewed the landmarks he would pass on his way to the distant Bellwoods, a forested region that was little more than rumor in Quasequa. Oplode assured him such a place existed, just as he assured him the great wizard he was to deliver his message to existed.

If he was real, Pandro would find him. He'd never

failed to make a delivery yet, and this morning he was feeling particularly confident. He felt so good he skipped his usual midday snack, preferring to cover as much territory as possible. Thus far the journey had proved anything but dangerous. He'd assured his mate before leaving that it would be more in the nature of an extended vacation than a difficult assignment. So far it had developed exactly as he'd told her.

Then he heard the noise.

It was behind and slightly above him and growing steadily louder as he listened. At first he couldn't place it. More than anything, it sounded like the droning he imagined the fliers of the Plated Folk might make. But those historic enemies were likewise little more than rumor in Quasequa. Pandro had only seen drawings of them, the fevered sketches of far-ranging artists with more imagination than fact at their disposal.

Hard-shelled, gray-eyed relatives of the common bugs and crawly things that inhabited the woods and lakes, they were. None had penetrated as far south as Quasequa. He certainly never expected to see them in person. Yet when at last he was able to look back and make out the shapes pursuing him, he was startled, for they certainly looked like the representations he'd seen of the Plated Folk.

The reality as they drew nearer still was worse. They were not minions of the Plated Folk but something far more sinister. Similarities in shape and appearance there were, but even the Plated Folk had faces. The demons overtaking him had none. They were hard-shelled but utterly different from anything he'd ever seen before. Nor were they fliers like his cousins, for where there should have been beaks he saw only hungry, razor-sharp, strangely curved fangs.

No matter how he strained he couldn't outdistance them, and they closed the space between with terrifying ease. Hoping to lose them in the trees, he dove for the crowns of the forest. They followed easily, closing ground still more when he reemerged from the branches. He dipped and rolled and dodged, employing every maneuver he could remember, sometimes vanishing among the foliage, sometimes doubling sharply back on his route before rising again to check the sky. And the demons stayed with him, inexorable in their pursuit, malign in their purpose. For Pandro they meant only death.

One veered just a little too near the mass of a giant tocoro tree and smashed into the bark. Glancing backward, Pandro was relieved to see it fall, spinning and tumbling and broken, to smash into the ground below. There was still hope, then. Demonic visitors his tormentors might be, but they were neither invulnerable nor immortal. They could be killed.

Six of them had fallen on him. Now there were five left. But he couldn't continue the battle at this speed. All the diving and dodging among the trees was wasting his strength at a much faster rate than mere flying. Yet having tried to outrun them and failed, he didn't have much choice. He had to keep to the woods.

One of his pursuers swooped around the bole of a forest giant, only to find itself caught in the grasp of a huge, carnivorous flying lizard. Blood spurted as the two combatants tumbled groundward, unable to disengage. The lizard was stunned by the ferocity of the much smaller creature it had caught, while for its part the demon was unable to break free from sharp talons. They struck the earth together.

Four left, Pandro thought wildly. His heart was pounding against his chest feathers and his wing muscles ached. One of the demons was right on top of him, and he had to fold his wings and drop like a stone, plummeting desperately toward the ground only to roll out at the last second. Even so, curved fangs slashed at his left wing in passing, sending black feathers flying.

He checked the injury as he climbed cloudward. The wound was superficial, but it had been a near thing. Too near. And his assailants seemed as fresh and untired as when they'd first attacked. He had to do something drastic, and soon. He couldn't keep dodging them forever.

Once more he drew his wings in close to his body and fell earthward. As though of the same mind, the four demons followed in unison, screaming at him.

Again he rolled up and over before crashing, but this time he landed behind a chosen tree. His pursuers split and came at him from two sides. The first one went over his head, the second missed him on the right. The third went straight for his throat and crumpled itself against the tree, teeth flying in all directions as the head shattered. The fourth turned away to reconsider.

Pandro pushed air as he flew back toward Quasequa, hoping they wouldn't see him and intending to make a wide curve back northward once he'd lost them. Looking back over his shoulder he spotted two of them skimming low over the treetops, hunting him in the opposite direction.

But where was the third surviving demon?

He turned just in time to duck, but the teeth bit deeply into his neck and back, barely missing his face. Blood flew with his feathers. The clouds began to swim in front of his eyes, blotting out all the blue sky. He felt himself falling toward a green grave.

Good-bye, Asenva of the saucy tail, he thought. Good-bye fledglings. Good-bye worried wizard, may your skin never be dry. I tried my best. But you didn't tell me I would have to fight demons.

The first tree reached up to catch him. He hit hard.

Prugg enjoyed the expressions that came over the faces of Kindore and Vazvek when the demons returned. The two members of the Quorum made protective signs in front of their faces and all but hid beneath the master's cape. Markus let them quake in terror for a few minutes before assuring them they were in no danger and that the faceless fliers were his servants. Even so, Vazvek did not emerge from behind the magician until the demons had settled one at a time into waiting wall alcoves.

As soon as he was sure they had fallen asleep, Prugg approached them. He did not want to show fear in front of the Quorumen, but he feared the master's magic nonetheless.

"Go on, Prugg," said Markus helpfully. "They won't hurt you. They won't move unless I command them."

Prugg studied the trio. True to the master's word, they ignored him. They were not very big, especially for demons, but those curved fangs were very impressive. Prugg ran a finger over one and still its owner did not stir.

"Only three of them," Markus murmured. "I wonder what happened to the other three." He shrugged. "Doesn't matter. I can always call up more." He turned to face his supporters.

"What do you think, Kindore? Should I bring them back to life and have them dance in the air for you?"

"No, no, no, advisor," said a badly shaken Kindore. He pulled at his thin coat, working to refasten the buttons which had come loose as he'd scrambled to avoid the demons. "I have never seen demons like that."

"How many demons have you seen?" Markus grinned at the squirrel. "They're harmless now. We can resume our discussion."

This was done. When Markus's questions had all been answered, he gave the pair his orders. Not advice, orders. Markus the Ineluctable had already moved beyond making suggestions, and Kindore and Vazvek hastened to carry out his bidding. Things were moving rapidly now, and the master was pleased.

He dismissed them, watched with amusement as they retreated quickly, and then walked over to inspect his now-silent aerial servants.

"Only three." He rubbed a forefinger across his lower lip, then gestured at the last demon in line. "See, there's blood on this one's teeth."

"I saw, Master."

"But whose blood? Could it be demon blood?"

Prugg strained but could not come up with a quick reply.

Markus looked pained. "You're slow, Prugg, you know that? Real slow."

"Forgive me, Master. I know that I am stupid. But I try."

"That's okay. I don't keep you around for your wit. You may as well know that it can't be demon blood because there is no blood in any of these creatures. Just as there is no life in them. They only live at my command. They're not sleeping, Prugg. They're dead. Until I choose to give them life again. Therefore it stands to reason, doesn't it, that this is the blood of the black messenger?"

"Yes, that must be so," agreed Prugg. "Yes, the black flier must be down, along with whatever messages he carried from that slimy bad loser, Oplode."

Prugg looked pleased. "Can I tell the old wizard his servant has been killed?"

"No, Prugg, you cannot. Nor will I tell him. Let him squat in his bath believing his messages are going to be received. Let him think his trusted messenger ran out on him. Let him stew those possibilities over for a while. It will keep him out of our hair for now." He smiled thinly. "I have a lot to do and I don't want to have to waste time worrying about the salamander."

"What's wrong with him?"

Pandro heard the words faintly through the black haze that was the inside of his head. There was a moment during which he thought the words might've been part of a dream, a bad dream he'd been having. Then more words, different, a little more intelligible this time.

"How the hell should I know? Do I look like a physician?"

"You always did look like something escaped from a hospital," countered the first voice. "One where they treat mental problems."

"Shut up, you two. I think he's coming around," commanded still a third voice.

The voices went away again. It occurred to Pandro that perhaps they might be waiting for some kind of response from him.

"I... can hear you okay, but I can't see you. I'm blind."

"He's blind," said one voice, not in the least sympathetic.

"Have you tried," said the third voice, a little more gently, "opening your eyes?"

Pandro mulled this over. "Why, no. I haven't."

"Try," the voice urged him.

Pandro blinked, discovered he was lying on a crude

platform built between two branches high above the forest floor. The foliage around him was swarming with the graceful, swift shapes of fellow fliers. They had one thing in common: every one of them was considerably smaller than he was. None stood more than a foot high.

Two of the three who were staring down at him wore blue-and-black kilts with bright chartreuse vests, while the third was clad in a kilt of white and yellow with a pink vest. This attire was subdued compared to their natural coloration, which was brilliant and metallic.

At first he had a hard time telling them apart. They hardly ever stopped moving, darting in front of him, behind, making erratic loops around the branches, arguing constantly with each other, and occasionally flitting overhead to sip from one of the huge tropical blossoms that burst forth from the tree.

Shoving backward with his wingtips, Pandro sat up, winced in pain. His wing came away from the back of his neck unbloodied, however. If he hadn't turned at the last instant, the demon would have bit him in the face. The image that produced in his mind made him queasy all over again.

"Where are you from? . . . What are you doing here? . . . Who are you? . . . Why the neck chain . . . ?" The trio threw one question after another at him and didn't wait for replies. One of them was tapping him on the shoulder as it spoke.

"Take it easy," Pandro pleaded. A quick inspection revealed that the surrounding trees were filled with tiny homes and traditional covered nests. "My turn first. Where did you find me?"

One of the querulous hummingbirds drifted in front of Pandro, fanning his face with wings that were sensed rather than seen. It nodded to its right.

"You came down over there." Crimson flashed beneath its bill. "Busting branches all the way down. Wonder is that you didn't bust your skull."

"Some others tried to."

"Oh ho!" said another, whose throat was blue as an alpine tarn. "A fight! If it's a fight they're looking for..." He curled the tips of both wings into fists and glared belligerently at the sky, looking for someone to sock.

"Watch your blood pressure, Spin," said the third bird. He was slightly less hyperkinetic than his companions.

"Watch your rear." The bird dove on him, and the three of them went round and round in the air, jabbing with feet, wings, and beaks. When they finally separated, Pandro saw that no harm had been done. None of them was even breathing hard. Two buzzed upward for a sugary drink while the third regarded the injured visitor sorrowfully.

"That's the trouble these days. Nobody knows how to have a good fight anymore."

"I know civilization's in a bad way," Pandro agreed dryly, "but it's going to be worse if I don't carry out my mission."

"Hot damn, a mission!" He danced all around Pandro as the raven stood and tested his wings. Emeralds flashed on his tiny chest.

Except for a few missing feathers and the naked scar that ran from the back of his neck downward, Pandro seemed to be intact.

"Yes, a mission for the wizard Oplode, former chief advisor to the Quorum of Quasequa."

"Never go into Quasequa," declared the hummingbird, shaking its head and forcing Pandro to duck back to avoid the swinging bill. "Nothing going on there. Talk about *dull*."

"Cousin, to your kind, everything is dull. Are the

rest of us responsible if you happen to live at a speed twenty times faster than anyone else's?"

"No, you're not," said the one called Spin. "You can't help it if you're slow and boring. The whole rest of the world is slow and boring."

"It's liable to get exciting real soon," said Pandro grimly. "Some weird human's taken over as chief advisor in Quasequa. This Oplode's worried about what he might do. The newcomer's a powerful magician, and Oplode doesn't seem to think much of his plans." He had a sudden horrible thought, and a wingtip went to his chest. When he clutched the vial containing the messages, he relaxed. The demons had ripped off his backpack, but they'd missed the chain and vial hanging around his neck. A good thing he'd taken care to put the messages there for safekeeping.

He eyed the sky. "I guess they think they got me."

"Who thinks they got you?" asked Oun, the second hummingbird.

"The demons. They must've been sent after me by Markus the Ineluctable, that new advisor I just told you about. Oplode warned me to watch out, but there wasn't anything I could do. They were just too fast for me."

"Demons, wow!" said Spin. "About time we had a decent scrap." He turned to his two companions. "I'll go find Wix and the rest of the gang and we'll—!"

"Hold on a minute," said Pandro. The hummingbird pivoted in midair. "You don't want to go looking for these things."

"We're not afraid of anything that flies."

"I'm sure you're not, but these were different." He shuddered, remembering that cold, barren contact on the back of his neck. He made a chopping motion with one wing. "And they've got teeth, not just bills. They'll take you apart."

"Condor crap!" snapped the second hummingbird, darting through the air and striking out with lefts and rights at imaginary opponents. "We'll pull their wings off! We'll—!"

"Do nothing of the kind," said the spokesman for the trio, "because there aren't any demons around."

Oun's crimson chest feathers flashed. "There aren't?"

"Seen any demons lurking about? Either of you?"

"Well, no." Both looked abashed and finally landed on the platform. "Not actually." Spin lifted slightly. "But if Pandro here could lead us to them..."

The raven shook his head violently. "Thanks, but I've got a job to do. Anyway, if they were still looking for me, I'm sure you would've seen them by now. They brought me down, but they didn't kill me." He flexed long black wings and rose from the platform. No damage to the vital shoulder muscles. Considering that he'd recently missed death by inches, he felt pretty good.

"Listen, thanks for your help, but I'd better be on my way. I'm beginning to share some of that salamander's concern about what's happening in the world."

"Phooey," muttered Spin, "who cares what some old wizard thinks?"

"Some might," said the third flier thoughtfully. He stared at Pandro. "Fly high, cousin, and don't look back."

"Don't worry." Pandro rose skyward. "And while I'm gone, consider this: Oplode the Sly believes that this new wizard may have evil designs that extend even beyond Quasequa. Perhaps even to your forest."

"Then he better not come here," hummed Spin, darting and jabbing at the air, his wings a blur. "Flying demons or no flying demons, we'll send him running without his tailfeathers."

Pandro's voice was faint now with distance. "He doesn't have any feathers. I told you, he's a human."

Spin settled back onto his branch. "A human. Now what would a human want with us?" He shrugged, turned to his companion Oun. "What say we go round up Wix and the rest and have ourselves a good punch-up anyway?"

"Yeah, sure!" They zoomed toward the next emergent.

The third member of the trio held back and struggled to grasp the import of the raven's words. Then he shrugged and flew off to join his friends.

That's the trouble with being a hummingbird. One's attention span is so damned short.

III

"But I *know* that she loves me!" Jon-Tom spoke as he paced back and forth in the turtle's bedroom. There was plenty of headroom even for his lanky six feet two inches because Clothahump had thoughtfully expanded the internal dimension spell another foot.

For that matter, the entire tree was filled with rooms that shouldn't have been, thanks to Clothahump's wizardry. The turtle wasn't engaging in any wizardry now, though. He was lying on his plastron among the mass of strong cushions which served him as a bed, his arms crossed under his horny chin. Only his eyes moved as he followed the nervous progress of the upset young spellsinger.

"You know, I was once in love myself, lad."

That revelation was sufficient to halt Jon-Tom in his tracks. "What... you?"

Raising his head, the turtle peered indignantly at the tall and tactless young human through hexagonal-lensed glasses.

"And why not me?" He looked suddenly wistful. "It was about a hundred and sixty years ago. She was quite attractive. The colors and patterns in her shell reminded one of flatly faceted jewels, and her plastron was smooth as polished granite."

"What happened?"

Clothahump sighed. "She threw me over for a slick-talking matamata. I believe her tastes were rather kinkier than mine." His attention snapped back to the present.

"So I am speaking from some experience, my boy, when I tell you that this Talea does not love you. Besides which, you are a spellsinger with a promising future and can do better. She is nothing but a petty thief."

Jon-Tom didn't turn away from the wizard's gaze. "It's not her profession I'm interested in. She saved my life and I saved hers and we love each other and that's that."

"It is *not* 'that' or anything else," argued the imperturbable turtle. "I do not for an instant deny that she is brave and courageous. I wish I could also add that she is thoughtful. Brave and courageous do not automatically translate into love, however. As for thoughtful, if she were that and she did indeed love you, she would be here now."

Jon-Tom looked uneasy. "Well, you remember how she is. Flighty, high-strung, nervous, especially around you."

"Me? Now, boy, why should she be in the slightest nervous around me?"

"You are the greatest, most powerful sorcerer in the world. You make a lot of people nervous."

"Do I? Dear me," said the turtle, "I thought I only made a lot of people irritable. Take my advice, my boy, and put her out of your mind. She will interfere with your studies, which you neglect as it is." He brushed dust from one of the bed pillows and frowned. "Have to get Sorbl to clean this place up, if I can corner the little sot long enough to put a dirt hex on him."

"Damn it, I know that she loves me!" Jon-Tom

spoke with unaccustomed intensity. "I know she does. I can feel it. She's just...she's just not quite ready to make it permanent, that's all. She needs more reassurance, more encouragement." He stared at the wood chips carpeting the floor. "Of course, that would be easier to do if I had some idea where she is."

"You'll never get a wild type like that to settle down." Clothahump removed his glasses and squinted through one eye as he gave them a perfunctory cleaning, then set them back on his beak. "Why not just marry her and then go your separate ways? There's so much world left for you to see."

"I want to see it all with her." An uncomfortable pause followed. Then Jon-Tom moved to the bed and knelt before it. "Look, you're the greatest wizard alive. Can't you help me?"

Clothahump shook his head, wrestled himself into a sitting position, and crossed his arms over the compartments in his plastron.

"I must say it is hard to refuse the requests of one of such perspicacity. I only wish you could find a more stable possibility for a mate."

"Talea's the one I love."

"What about that Quintera female you brought over into this world?"

Jon-Tom swallowed, turned, and walked away from the bed. "Why bring that up? You know it's a sore point with me."

"Why? Because in the end she preferred that sophisticated hare Caz to you?" Clothahump shook a warning finger at him. "That's what comes of projecting your own desires onto someone else. She may have been your physical ideal, but mentally and emotionally she was neither...and neither is this Talea."

"No!" Jon-Tom whirled on the bed. "Talea's the

right one. I'm sure of that, even if our relationship is developing a little, uh, slowly. Come on, Clothahump, I know you can help if you want to."

"With what? You want me to mix you up a love potion to slip into her drink?" He shook his head. "I don't deal in those kinds of petty emotionally manipulative devices and you know it. If that's what you want, go to the chemist in Lynchbany. I'll give you a prescription, but I won't mix you anything myself. You'll be wasting your money, though. Ninety percent of that stuff's no better than what you can buy over-the-counter."

"I don't want your potions or prescriptions, Clothahump. I want your wise, sage advice."

"Really? All right. Get a haircut."

Jon-Tom moaned. His hair was only shoulder-length. "Not here too. Or do you have a prejudice against fur because you've none of your own?"

The turtle looked down at himself. "My, my, so you've noticed that, have you? I can't imagine how one so observant hasn't been able to win the undying affection of the woman he thinks loves him."

"It's not a question of 'winning,'" Jon-Tom muttered. "This isn't a war."

"Isn't it now? Dear me! Perhaps after your first two hundred years you'll learn to adjust that view."

"And don't lay any of that 'venerable ancient' shit on me, either! I want your advice, not your sarcasm."

Clothahump peered over his glasses. "If you want to learn what love is all about, my boy, you'd better learn to handle sarcasm."

Jon-Tom shifted to another tack. "I've been working on a song for her."

"If you think you can spellsing her into love with you, my boy, then you—"

"No, no, just a friendly little song to show her how

I feel about her. I've always been better at conveying my emotions through music. Want to hear it?"

Clothahump muttered under his breath, "Do I have a choice?"

Jon-Tom walked over to the corner where he'd set down his duar and picked up the peculiar, double-stringed instrument. He caressed it lovingly. It had brought him through some tough spots, that duar. It, and his ability to make magic with it, however erratic and unpredictable.

"Just something to put her in the right mood," he assured Clothahump. "I've been trying to remember what she likes so I can sing about it the next time we meet."

"Sing about a rich drunk lying alone in an alley," Clothahump suggested.

Jon-Tom ignored the gibe. "I remember her telling me one time how much she liked roses. She said they were pretty. She'd never use the word 'romantic.' Talea's not the romantic type. But she said she liked their smell and the way they went with her hair. So I've been trying to think of a song about roses. It wasn't easy. It's not the sort of thing my favorite musicians like to write songs about, and I have to be careful or I'll wind up with that amazonic tigress I told you about.

"Anyhow, I finally settled on this. I'd like your opinion of it."

"Hold on a moment, boy. I want none of your hit-and-miss spellsinging in my home. If you feel the need to practice, do it outside."

"Oh, it's all right." Jon-Tom found himself a seat on a strong shelf. "It's just a little tune. I'm not going to do any spellsinging."

Clothahump eyed him warily. "Well, if you're *sure*..."

Jon-Tom smiled confidently at him. "Sure I'm sure. What could be dangerous about a song about something as innocent as roses?" He let his fingers fall lightly across the first set of strings, then the second, adjusted the control for tremble ever so slightly.

The chords floated through the room, soothing and mellow, not nearly as sharp or discordant as Jon-Tom's heavy metal favorites. Clothahump relented.

"All right, boy." He moved as far back on the bed as he was able. "If you're certain you know what you're doing and have everything under control."

Jon-Tom smiled reassuringly and began to sing. The music was lovely, but that didn't relax Clothahump. He was watching and listening to more than the melody.

Sure enough, there it was: an intense red glow near the foot of the bed.

"Boy, see there, I told you . . . !"

But Jon-Tom wasn't listening to his mentor. He was transported to the kingdom of love by images of how Talea would react to this song, composed specially for her by the man who adored her.

The intense, blood-red ball of light hung in the air, throwing off red sparks as Jon-Tom's voice rose passionately. Clothahump waved anxiously at it and was pleased to see it fall to the floor and disappear.

He let out a relieved sigh and narrowed his gaze as he waited for Jon-Tom to finish his song. So he did not see the branches that sprang forth from beneath the carpet of wood chips. They grew with astonishing speed.

Jon-Tom concluded his chorus and looked proud. "There, you see? Nothing to worry about. I've been working hard on my control, and I think I've gotten it to the point where I only conjure up what I want to." His expression changed to one of curiosity. "That's funny. I don't remember your planting anything at the foot of your bed."

Fearing the worst, Clothahump tumbled forward to peer over the edge of the bed. Growing out of the floor was a small, nicely pruned collection of thin branches. As they both watched, some two dozen American beauty blossoms erupted from the naked twigs.

"Hey, how about that?" said Jon-Tom, delighted. "Now I ask you, what girl could resist that?"

"Well," Clothahump said reluctantly, "I have to admit that's quite a charming little bouquet you've called up."

Jon-Tom hefted the duar. "I didn't even get to the second chorus. What color would you like this time? How about a nice canary yellow?" He sang again, and this time the second bush appeared sooner than its predecessor. It was also twice as tall and, sure enough, heavy with fragrant yellow blooms.

"Nothing to it. I told you I've been practicing my control."

Clothahump stared at the bush. "Good. Then you can stop it now."

Jon-Tom's jaw hung a little slack. "Uh, stop what?"

"Stop it from growing."

"But I have stopped. I'm not singing anymore."

Clothahump pointed. "Tell it to that rosebush."

Indeed, it didn't take especially sharp vision to see that the bush was continuing to expand. It was almost up to the roof. When it hit the ceiling, the branches began to spread out sideways, throwing out shoots and blossoms in every direction.

"No sweat. I'll just sing the final chorus. That ought to finish it." He proceeded to do so, the words falling gentle and sweet on the now heavily aromatic air of the bedroom.

It had absolutely no effect on the fecund rosebush, which continued to spread out across the walls. Having covered ceiling and sides, branches began to fill the room, crisscrossing and occasionally running into one another. Some of the stems were now as thick as birch trunks. The room was shaking.

"That's enough, boy!" Clothahump was hemmed in against the headboard of his bed. Jon-Tom was trying to edge his way toward the near doorway, had to duck as two sapling-thick branches boasting three-inch-long thorns tried to block his exit.

"I... I don't understand. I'm not singing anymore."

"You bet your ass you're not, lad." Clothahump struggled with one drawer in his plastron, finally yanked it open. "Got to lubricate these one of these days." The drawer finally popped open and he rummaged around inside himself. "Hope I can stop it before..."

"Before what?" wondered the thoroughly distraught Jon-Tom as he stumbled back from an encroaching branch. It vomited a three-foot-wide blossom in his face, and the burst of perfume made him dizzy.

"Before these damned things start growing out of *us*," Clothahump shouted at him.

His path to the door blocked, Jon-Tom scrambled across the floor toward the only remaining open section of the room... Clothahump's bed.

"Maybe I overdid it a little bit."

"My boy, your powers of observation and your innate ability to intuit the blatantly obvious never cease to amaze me. Ah, there!" He removed a small box from his plastron, shoved the drawer shut, and opened the box. From within he selected a pinch of white powder and leaned forward.

> "Roots and shoots and cellulose
> Blossoms that be profane
> Dwell in lands of malathane

Make thy xylum comatose
Dry up thy tannic stain!"

He threw the powder into the advancing thorns. It evaporated. The cluster of branches seemed to shudder, to slow...and finally, to petrify.

They were surrounded, engulfed by beauty. Jon-Tom felt sure he was going to throw up.

He took a step toward the door which led into Clothahump's laboratory, found he couldn't move more than a few inches off the cushions before swordlike thorns pricked his legs. He retreated back onto the bed.

"Sorry," he whispered morosely. The smell of roses was overwhelming.

Clothahump sighed, gave him a fatherly pat on the back. "That's all right, lad. We're all a little overconfident now and again. You were right about one thing, though. If your ladylove were here, I've no doubt she'd be impressed with this little floral tribute of yours...if she wasn't cut to ribbons first. I will say this for your spellsinging: you don't seem able to do anything in a small way." At least a thousand blossoms of all shades and hues kept them imprisoned on the bed.

"There's nothing basically the matter with your spellsinging, my boy. But you are going to have to work at moderating your enthusiasm a bit." He eyed his bedroom appraisingly. "An impressive, though difficult to deliver, bouquet."

Tucking his head down inside his shell until only the crown was visible, he slid off the bed and waded out into the brambles, quite safe from the thorns. They couldn't penetrate his body armor, but neither did he have the strength to force a path through them. Finally he gave up and returned to the bed.

"It's no good, lad. I'm neither as young nor agile as I once was."

"How about a spell?"

Clothahump's reply to that suggestion was tart. "You spelled this jungle up: *you* unspell it."

Jon-Tom's fingers twisted against each other. "I don't think I ought to try that."

Clothahump looked dazed. "What's that? What's this? Some small hint of humility? How gratifying. Today we pass another signpost on the road to wisdom." A powerful, resonant voice interrupted his sarcasm.

"THERE'S SOMEONE AT THE DOOR!"

"Drat, that's the bell," the wizard groused. "Why am I blessed with visitors who have such wonderful timing?"

They waited patiently on the bed. Minutes later an uncertain voice called to them from the vicinity of the doorway.

"Uh, Master?" They could just make out the four-foot-tall shape of Clothahump's apprentice standing in the opening. For a wonder, Sorbl sounded almost sober this morning. That was something of a magic itself.

"There is someone at the door, Master."

"We know that, you idiot," said Clothahump with a grimace. "We heard the bell too. *Who* is at the door?"

"He says he's come a long ways on a mission of great importance, Master."

"Don't they all."

"His name is Pandro. He's a raven and he says he comes from a city named Quasequa."

Suddenly Clothahump was more interested than indifferent. "Quasequa, you say? Well, I have not heard from anyone in that distant land in some time. I recall mention of a young sorcerer of some promise, a fellow name of Oplode, who was trying to set himself up in business down there."

"That's who's sent him here, sir!" said Sorbl excitedly. "This Pandro says it's most urgent."

"Oplode, yes, that was the name. Though I can't be certain. My memory's not what it used to be. I'll see him, though." The turtle's tone darkened. "You will *not* offer him any liquid refreshment stronger than fruit juice!"

"Master, I? Do you think that I . . . ?"

"Yes, I do. Now, shut up, see him comfortably in, and inform him I'll be along directly. Then go to the storage bin outside the parlor. Inside you'll find some large wood clippers. Bring them back here and cut us out of my bedroom. Then, while we are listening to this visitor's tale, you may take the remainder of the day to prune around my bed."

The owl let out a resigned sigh. "As you direct, Master." A brief pause, then, "Would it be improper of me to ask what happened here?"

"Not at all. You should find it instructive. This minor botanical catastrophe sprang from the heart of our young spellsinger here. He is in love, you see. One would tend to say he has a green thumb. The actual problem, however, lies with the protuberance which arises from between his shoulders."

It was a mild enough reprimand and Jon-Tom fought to accept it gracefully. Lest he do additional damage, he forced himself to put all thoughts of the beauteous Talea aside and concentrate instead on the potential import of whatever this far-ranging guest might have to say.

Clothahump's spell-sharpened shears soon cut a tunnel to them through the tangled growth, and the two of them were able to crawl to freedom.

"A good job," the wizard complimented his apprentice. "Now clean out the rest of it, but leave those pink blooms over there, the ones under the window.

They're rather attractive, and that part of the floor's always damp anyway."

"Yes, Master." They left him hacking away with the shears at Clothahump's bedchamber.

The raven awaited them on the guest perch which had been installed by Clothahump for the comfort of winged visitors. He might have come a long ways, but he didn't look particularly fatigued to Jon-Tom. Of more interest was the bruise on his forehead, the feathers missing from one wing, and the ugly scar which ran down the back of his neck. The wounds looked recent, and Jon-Tom wondered if they had anything to do with the raven's reason for coming to the Bellwoods.

If Clothahump noticed any of this, he gave no sign, preferring instead to stare grimly at the widemouthed glass from which the raven was sipping decorously.

"What's that?"

"What's what?" said the raven uncertainly, looking up as they entered. "Oh, this?" He gestured with the glass. "A drink, and nice and strong, too. I sure as hell needed it. Thanks to your—"

"I know who to thank," rumbled Clothahump dangerously. "He did not by any chance have one himself? Just to prove that he could be a proper host?"

Before the raven could reply, the wizard had whirled and was clomping angrily back toward his bedroom.

"SORBL!"

Jon-Tom and Pandro eyed each other uncomfortably for a couple of minutes until Clothahump returned.

"I'll be lucky if he has my bedroom cleaned out by nightfall, and he'll be lucky if he doesn't cut off one of his own feet in the process. I'll deal with him later." He calmed himself as he gazed over at his guest.

"Please pardon the interruption. Now then. Your name is Pandro and you come from far Quasequa?"

The raven put his glass aside on the shelf that was attached to the perch. "That's right, sir."

"That is quite a journey."

"Tell me about it." Pandro fluttered to the floor and hopped over to stand close to them. "Keep in mind that I'm just a hired messenger. I'm not completely sure what this is all about. I could tell you what I know, but I imagine these documents I was instructed to deliver to you will explain what's going on in my country much better than I could." He removed the papers from the cylinder hanging from his neck chain.

"These come from Oplode, former chief advisor in matters arcane and mystic to the Quorum of Quasequa."

"'Former'?" Clothahump peered at the messages through his thick glasses. "Um." He turned to read silently.

Jon-Tom tried to make conversation. "What happened to your neck?"

Instinctively, a wing felt of the recently acquired wound. "I was attacked while on my way here. Someone or something wanted to make sure I didn't make my delivery."

"Who attacked you?"

"Demons," Pandro said with admirable casualness. "Faceless demons. Gray and black they were, with long curved teeth and no eyes."

It wasn't the explanation Jon-Tom expected, and he was more than a little taken aback. "You don't say."

"They *were* demons," Pandro insisted, mistaking Jon-Tom's surprise for disbelief. "I know a demon when I see one, let alone when it tries to take my head off."

"I wasn't disputing you," Jon-Tom replied.

The raven studied him with interest. "You're the biggest human I've ever seen."

"I'm also a spellsinger," Jon-Tom told him proudly.

Clothahump spoke without looking up from his reading. "That he is. If you want to see a demonstration of his powers, have a look in the next room over."

"It doesn't matter. It's not very impressive," Jon-Tom said hastily. "This wizard Oplode: you work for him?"

"I was only hired to make this single delivery. I'm not in his regular service, if that's what you mean."

Clothahump concluded his perusal of the papers with a noncommittal grunt. "This doesn't sound too serious, even though Oplode's language borders on the hysterical. Certainly not important enough to warrant my personal attention. Still, if he feels he needs help, I suppose it is incumbent on me to provide some." He turned back to face the raven.

"This new advisor, this Markus the Ineluctable Oplode refers to: have you met him?"

Pandro shook his head. "I just run a small messenger service. I don't get into the halls of the Quorumate Complex much. No, I haven't met him. From what I've heard, not many have. Keeps to himself a lot. But there are plenty of stories about him. And about his peculiar powers."

"And he's a human?"

Pandro nodded. "That's what they say."

Clothahump examined the papers again. "A human who claims to have come here from another world?"

Jon-Tom felt suddenly faint... but not so faint that he couldn't interrupt with anxious questions.

"Another world! Tell me, does he sing his magic, spellsing like I do, or use a musical instrument when he's exercising his powers?"

Pandro flinched, taken aback by the gangling young human's unexpected enthusiasm. "Not that I've heard, sir, no. It's said that he whispers his spells so that none can hear him. I haven't heard anyone mention music."

"It is not used," said Clothahump, "or Oplode would have mentioned it in his communication. The rest he does confirm, however." He was watching Jon-Tom carefully. "A human magician who claims to have come here from another world."

"It's possible," said Jon-Tom excitedly. "Don't you think it's possible? It happened once, to me. Why not to another?"

"All things are possible. However, just because you have a good heart and good intentions does not mean that this new visitor is as good and kind as yourself, or that he even comes from your world. The plenum is full of other worlds."

"That's right," said Jon-Tom, momentarily downcast. "I got so excited I forgot about that."

"In fact," the wizard went on, still eyeing the papers, "from what Oplode says, this Markus appears to be sadly lacking in the social verities. Oplode is not only afraid of what the newcomer has done; he is even more afraid of what he may intend to do next. As for the visitor's magic, it is powerful indeed." He folded the papers.

"This is none of my business. I'm not one to insinuate myself into another wizard's difficulties. Oplode admits that this Markus defeated him in a battle of talents. These 'fears' he alludes to may merely be a reflection of his own disappointments. And he speaks only of worries and concerns, not of any actual threat. I see no reason for such panic.

This Markus hasn't instituted any sort of reign of terror or inquisition or anything so boring since assuming Oplode's office, has he?"

"No sir," Pandro admitted. "As far as the average citizen is concerned, nothing's changed. At least, not insofar as I've seen. Of course," he added thoughtfully, "I *was* attacked on my way here, and the forest where I encountered my assailants is not noted for having a large demonic population."

"I wouldn't know," Clothahump murmured. "I am not familiar with that part of the world. What do you think of all this, Jon-Tom?"

Sorcerer and spellsinger discussed the matter while Pandro stood and waited quietly. While hardly an experienced judge of wizardly qualities, if asked, he would have had to confess that Oplode was whistling up the wrong trunk if he expected to get any aid from this bunch. The apprentice who'd ushered him inside was an obvious drunk, the turtle showed signs of senility, and the tall human struck the cosmopolitan Pandro as something of a hick.

Still, surely Oplode the Sly knew what he was doing in sending here for help. And what *was* it they were arguing about?

"I'm telling you, this guy's from my own world, from my home!" Jon-Tom was saying. "He's got to be. Transported here by accident, just like me."

"There have been no recent disturbances in the ether as there were when I brought you over," Clothahump told him.

"Maybe he crossed over in a different way. Do you know of every path between the dimensions?"

"No," Clothahump admitted, a mite huffily. "As I said before, all things are possible. All I am saying now is that there is nothing to suggest that this Markus the Ineluctable came over from your world. For one thing, according to Oplode, this fellow seems to have been practicing his magic for quitc a while, whereas you discovered your spellsinging ability purely by accident and only after you had been in this world for some time. Furthermore, all this blather of coming from another world may merely be typical wizardly showmanship, an attempt to cow and overawe impressionable Quasequans. There are many humans in this world, as you well know. This Markus may not be a transdimensional traveler; he may be nothing more than a slick talker. Remember, my boy, that your materialization here was an accident."

"Maybe this isn't an accident," Jon-Tom argued. "Maybe some wizard from another world has found a way to cross over on his own."

"As I recall, there are no wizards in your own world."

Jon-Tom slumped. "I know. But maybe he was something else. Maybe he's an engineer like you thought I was, and he can make magic here by reciting engineering theorems, or something. The point is, *I've got to know.* Don't you see, Clothahump? If he got through on purpose, by design, maybe he can return home the same way. Maybe with the two of us working together we can manage a way home for both of us!"

Clothahump was nodding. "That is how I thought you would react to this information, my boy. Well, it's only natural that you should be excited. I certainly will not stand in the way of your finding out."

IV

Pandro had been silent long enough.

"Look here, I'm not at all sure what you two are talking about any more than I knew what Oplode was talking about. Like I said, I'm just a messenger." He gestured with a wingtip toward the papers Clothahump held. "One thing Oplode did tell me, though. He said that if this Markus is truly from another world, then it must be a place of evil and darkness." He eyed Jon-Tom uneasily.

"And you say you're maybe from the same place?"

"Maybe. We've no reason to believe that yet," Clothahump replied.

"Well, he's sure peculiar-looking, but according to the descriptions I've heard, mighty different from this Markus the Ineluctable."

"What's he supposed to be like?" asked Jon-Tom eagerly.

"Definitely human. Tall, but much shorter than you. Fat, and older. Not much fur left on his head."

Jon-Tom was nodding. "He *could* be an engineer from my world."

"And it's said he still wears the clothes he was wearing when he came into our world."

"Tell me about them, describe them! Does he wear

jeans—pants of rough blue material? Or maybe a suit, something with a long V-shaped opening in the front, with a white shirt underneath, and maybe a long strip of material tied around his neck?"

"No," said Pandro thoughtfully, "the description that I heard was somewhat different. I was told he dresses entirely in black of some slick, finely woven material, with a black cape to match, and a strange black tower atop his head, and a spot of petrified blood he keeps always over his heart."

"That doesn't sound very familiar," Jon-Tom replied slowly. And he'd been so *positive!*

"From another world, perhaps, but not necessarily yours," Clothahump told him. "Interesting. Not necessarily dangerous, but interesting."

"Even if he is from your own world, sir," Pandro told Jon-Tom, "I wouldn't plan on him helping you to get back to wherever you're from. From what Oplode says, this magician helps no one but himself."

"Maybe because he's frightened," Jon-Tom suggested. "Maybe if by working together, the both of us can return home, he'll turn out to be much less threatening."

"If you can get him to leave, regardless of how you help yourself, sir, all of Quasequa would be grateful." He hesitated. "Oplode did not say as much, but there are rumors that this Markus has plans for doing away with the Quorum and installing himself as an emperor or king or something. That would be a disaster for Quasequa. We have no tradition of powerful, single rulers. I think what Oplode the Sly is saying is that now is the time to stop the newcomer before he can put any evil designs into effect."

"*If* he has any such intentions. That may be nothing more than your employer's paranoia at work."

"That is something Oplode felt you would sense,

sir. He said that you were wise and knowledgeable, brave and bold."

Clothahump removed his glasses, spoke while cleaning them. "Even as a student, I recall this Oplode being somewhat of a stickler for accurate descriptions."

"I wish I could tell you more, sirs, but I am only a messenger."

"You've done better than could have been expected of you."

"So you will send help?" asked Pandro hopefully.

"Certainly I will."

"You'll come yourself?"

"I will send help," Clothahump said firmly. "You may convey that message to Oplode. I'm sure he expects some sort of reply, and that should cheer him. As for specifics, I prefer not to divulge my methodology to the hired help."

"I understand, sir," said Pandro, bowing and finishing his stiff drink. He set the glass aside and headed for the front door. "Any other messages, sir?"

"Sorbl. *Sorbl!*" Clothahump yelled. "Never mind. I'll do it myself." The door swung inward at the flick of his hand. It was a tiny magic, very minor wizardry, but it impressed Pandro nonetheless. A good impression the raven would carry with him all the way back to Quasequa.

"No, no other message. Tell Oplode if he feels the need to convey additional information to me to send you back again."

"Oh, no, sir! He may send more information back to you, but I won't be bringing it. I've had enough of wizardly goings-on. Humans from other worlds, faceless demons, no thank you, sirs! I'll inform him you're sending help down to Quasequa and I'm sure he will be heartened by that, but if he wants to thank you he can do it himself. I've had more than enough of such doings. Never again."

"Don't you mean 'nevermore'?" Jon-Tom asked him.

Pandro eyed him oddly for a moment before bowing a last time. Then he left, closing the heavy wooden door behind him.

"Hope for the better rather than for the worst," said Jon-Tom after the raven had taken his leave. "I'll start packing our supplies."

Clothahump coughed softly. "What do you mean 'our' supplies, my boy?"

Jon-Tom halted in mid-stride. "Now, wait a minute. What about all that business about your being 'courageous, brave, and bold'?"

"Dear me, is that what he said?" Clothahump was studying the ceiling. "I thought certain he said 'courageous, brave, and *old*.' Because that is an accurate description. In any case, I'm certainly not about to leave my work here to embark on some long hike simply to salve the injured feelings of a deposed wizard. As I said, this hardly sounds to me like a crisis."

"No crisis, eh? Some evil sorcerer from another world throws a colleague of yours out of office and is scheming to take over an entire city with who-knows-what eventual aims in mind, and you don't call that a crisis?"

"It's not *my* city, and I'm not the one who's been deposed. As for Oplode the Sly's being a colleague, I've never worked with him and know of him only by reputation."

"That's one hell of a cold attitude."

"I would rather say realistic. However, I did say I would send help, and so I shall. You are so convinced that this Markus the Ineluctable is from your world that I wouldn't think of putting off the day of that meeting by so much as an hour. I would only slow you down, my boy." He indicated the duar Jon-Tom cradled against his side.

"You can handle anything that comes before you. You now know enough of this land and have mastered sufficient of your spellsinging skills to extricate yourself from any minor difficulties." He grinned. "Should this Markus turn out to be as belligerent as Oplode feels, you can always threaten him with a bouquet."

Jon-Tom gave the wizard a sour look. "What would I do without your confidence and support?"

"Oh, I support you, my boy, I support you. Your talent is developing nicely. I merely try to keep a close watch on the diameter of your head, lest in a dangerous moment of overconfidence it grow too large.

"Oplode desires speed in this matter and so do you. I would be an encumbrance to you both. I am quite confident of your ability to manage this matter on your own."

"What if he's not from my world?" wondered Jon-Tom, suddenly thoughtful. "What if he is some strange demonic being in human guise? That raven's description of his attire and his attitude, those don't make him sound much like an old friend from back home."

"Then you must deal with him as the circumstances dictate," the wizard told him firmly. "I can't wet-nurse you through maturity."

"I'm already mature."

"Then act like it." He winced. "Besides, my arthritis is acting up."

"Funny how your arthritis always seems to act up whenever there's a long journey to be taken."

"Yes, it is peculiar, isn't it?" Clothahump admitted without batting an eye. He lumbered toward his bedroom, peered through the doorway. "Ah! Sorbl has excavated my bed. I can hear him shearing away in there. Presumably he is not so drunk that he has cut off either of his wings." He raised his voice. "Sorbl! How are you managing in there, you useless befeathered sot?"

"I am tired, Master," came the faint reply from somewhere deep within the thorny brambles. "These vines are tough." A pause, then, "Can't you just magic them away?"

"Perhaps I could, but I did not acquire an apprentice so that I might engage in menial labor. Besides, a little exercise is good for the system, especially when that system is overloaded with ethyl molecules."

"With what, Master?"

"Liquorish magical symbols."

"Not me, Master! I would never—!"

Clothahump closed the door to the rosebush-ridden bedroom, shutting off Sorbl's too-emphatic protestations of innocence. He turned back to Jon-Tom, peered up at him over steepled fingers.

"Oplode has a reputation for exaggeration, my boy, and all salamanders are notoriously paranoid. I know that you will enjoy the journey to Quasequa. It will be a long but pleasant trip. The city itself is rumored to be most beautiful, constructed on a series of islands out in the middle of a body of water called the Lake of Sorrowful Pearls. If I were a hundred years younger, I would not hesitate to accompany you."

Jon-Tom was nodding knowingly. "Sounds delightful. In fact, it sounds a lot like our recent relaxing vacation jaunt to distant Snarken."

Clothahump shifted his eyes away from the tall youth. "Ah, any excursion can be dogged by unforeseen bad luck." He cleared his throat self-consciously. "This time you will encounter no oceans to cross, no morose moors to traverse. Merely shallow tropical lakes and lagoons, such as the one on which Quasequa itself is constructed. A land of moderate temperatures and quiet beauty. A veritable paradise compared to these cold Bellwoods. Often's the time I've thought of traveling there with an eye toward retiring in such a place."

"You'll never retire. You like your reputation too much."

"No, I mean it, my boy. Someday I will consider it seriously. Perhaps when I turn three hundred."

"When you hit three hundred I hope I won't be around to see it."

"Yes, your unquenchable desire to return home. Perhaps this Markus the Ineluctable will turn out to be helpful."

"You're just trying to make me feel better about going off without you, but you're right. I'd go anywhere, under any conditions, if I thought there was a chance I could get a little closer to home."

"And what of Oplode's concerns?"

"Maybe he exaggerates, just like you say. If this Markus *is* from my own world, I'm sure that if the two of us can get together and chat for a while, he'll be as happy to see me as I will be to see him, and we can work something out."

"And if he's not of your world, and Oplode does not exaggerate?"

Jon-Tom took a deep breath. "In that case, I've got my duar. If it comes to a battle of sorceral skills, I think I can handle anything." *Except my own mistakes,* he added silently to himself.

"Good for you, my boy! That's the spirit! Maintain that attitude and I'm sure you'll have things in Quasequa sorted out in no time."

Jon-Tom looked uncertain. "There is one drawback. I can't make a journey like that all by myself. Oh, I understand if you don't feel up to coming along or don't feel it's necessary, or whatever. But I won't risk a trip like this all by my lonesome. I know that flier wouldn't have guided me. Not his job, and fliers get bored having to hang back with us land-bound types. That much I've learned. What about making use of public transportation systems along the way?"

"A good thought, except that there aren't any, my boy. There is no commerce between the Bellwoods towns and Quasequa. All trade from Lynchbany and Timswitty and the like goes to the Glittergeist Sea or Polastrindu."

"Then I'd like to have an old buddy accompany me."

Clothahump shook his head sadly. "I wonder that your choice of company does not otherwise mirror your normal good taste."

"I just feel comfortable with Mudge around. He's clever with words, knows the customs and ins and outs, is good with weapons, and is reasonably trustworthy so long as I keep an eye on him round the clock and don't let him get his paws on the expense money."

Clothahump shrugged beneath his shell. "It's your neck, my boy. You choose your own companions."

Jon-Tom frowned. "The only problem is, I haven't the slightest idea where he's to be found. Last time I had to track him all the way up to Timswitty. Since Quasequa lies in the other direction, I'd lose a lot of time if I had to hunt through the Bellwoods in search of him." He finished on a hopeful note.

"I agree. And don't give me that innocent-apprentice look. It doesn't have the slightest effect on me. However, if you will insist on having him with you..."

"I wouldn't insist," Jon-Tom said quickly. "It would just make me a lot more confident about the whole business."

"Very well, very well. I will see what I can do. I will

attempt to locate him and explain that he is wanted here.

"As for yourself, you'd best begin preparing for the journey. Fill your backpack with care, make certain you have ample spare strings for your duar, and try to get a good night's sleep. I will be able to discuss this matter of your 'friend' with more certainty tomorrow morning."

"How long do you think it will take for you to locate him and give him the message?"

"We will just have to wait and see, my boy. We will have to wait and see."

Jon-Tom arose the next morning still excited by the prospect of meeting someone else from home, someone who might be able to help him get back where he belonged. It wasn't that Clothahump hadn't been good to him. In his own distinctive, demanding fashion, the wizard had gone out of his way to make the displaced human feel welcome.

Nor had his sojourn in this land been uneventful. Quite the contrary. But he was more than ready to return to the calm, familiar life of an anxiety-ridden pre-law student in Westwood, CA.

He washed his hands and face in the wooden basin that grew from one of the tree's inner walls, wondering not for the first time what kind of intricate magical spell could provide indoor plumbing within the dimensionally expanded trunk of an oak. After drying himself and dressing carefully, he went through the contents of his backpack.

It held jerked meat, dried fruit and nuts, a selection of medicinal herbs and potions, a small metal box holding the few Band-Aids and pills he'd had on his person when he'd been sucked into this world, a change of underclothing, and a small assortment of toiletry items and personal effects. Packed to bursting, it was heavier than it had been when he'd set out on a previous journey to distant Snarken. On that trip Clothahump had informed him he would encounter towns and villages in which to purchase food and other necessities. The land between here and Quasequa, however benign, was apparently a good deal less urbanized.

That meant living more off the land. Well, he'd always enjoyed camping out, and if Clothahump's description of the country south of the river Tailaroam was accurate, it should be a relaxing experience.

First breakfast, then he'd ask if the wizard had succeeded in locating Mudge. Probably he'd have to meet the otter somewhere. A couple of quick hellos, and off they'd go, traveling at a brisk but unhurried pace southward, enjoying the clear weather while reminiscing about—

A terrible scream split this image and pushed everything else into the background. It pierced the thick walls of living wood, was followed by a second and third. Each howl was more horrible than its predecessor. Jon-Tom's skin prickled.

His first thought was that Markus the Ineluctable was everything Oplode feared and more, and that he'd somehow tracked the course of Pandro the raven and had sent his faceless demons to do away with any potential allies the flier might have made contact with. Jon-Tom grabbed his ramwood staff and rushed for the next rooms.

He flicked the concealed switch in the wooden shaft, and six inches of sharp steel emerged from the base of the staff. If only he wasn't too late and whatever had entered the tree hadn't gotten ahold of Clothahump! The screams continued, but their intensity had fallen somewhat. They seemed to be coming from the vicinity of the kitchen. He turned down a narrow hall, keeping his head low, and bounced off a wall, then skidded to a halt just inside the dining area.

Clothahump sat in his reinforced chair next to the table that grew out of the floor. He was spooning ground fish and water plant from a steaming bowl. A tall glass of murky, aged pond water stood nearby. Heat rose from the iron cookstove where Sorbl labored diligently over two bubbling pots and baking bread. As he watched, the owl dropped from the perch welded to the front of the stove, slid a couple of fried mice out of the oven and slipped them between slices of fresh bread, and began to munch on his own breakfast. The bread smelled delicious.

At the moment, though, his thoughts were not on food. Instead, he stared openmouthed at the construction which had appeared in the middle of the floor.

It was a cage, and not a very elegant cage at that. Six feet tall and three or four square, it seemed to hover in midair a foot or so above the kitchen tiles. It had six sides instead of four. Instead of bars, thin threads connected top and bottom. They did not ripple in the heat of the room. They did not move at all.

Not even when the berserk, spitting, squalling creature caged within chose to bang against them with its body. It bounced off as if the threads were fashioned of inch-thick steel. It used its shoulders because its arms were tied to its sides. In fact, the occupant of the cage wore a mummylike cylinder of heavy rope that encased him from ankle to neck.

"Good morning, my boy," said Clothahump cheerily, as though nothing out of the ordinary had occurred. "Have some breakfast?"

"In a minute." Jon-Tom put his staff aside. He moved into the kitchen and walked slowly around the hovering cage, never taking his eyes from it.

With a finger, he tested one of the threads. It refused to move no matter how hard he pushed or pulled on it. He had to pull away fast because the bound creature inside tried to bite off his finger. Sharp teeth just managed to nick his skin. He sucked on the thin cut.

"I'm sorry, Mudge," he said, "but I didn't have anything to do with this."

"Oi now, didn't you, you stretched-out offspring of an otherworldly bitch? You slippery sliver-tongued bastard. Of course you didn't 'ave nothin' to do with it, you and that calcified lump of solid bone wot calls 'imself a sorcerer."

Clothahump ignored this tirade and continued to slurp daintily at his meal.

"Don't give me that crap, mate! You and 'im 'ave always been in league with one another against me. Don't try to deny it! 'Tis been that way all along."

Jon-Tom continued to suck on the finger his friend had attempted to amputate, spoke quietly. "He was just supposed to find you and send you a message." He turned to face the wizard. "You were just supposed to send him a message."

Clothahump considered, the spoon halfway to his mouth. "I did send a message, my boy, and you were correct in your concerns. He was quite a distance away, in a town near Kreshfarm-in-the-Geegs."

"It weren't far enough!" Mudge howled. He tried to sit down, but the enveloping ropes prevented the maneuver, and he had to settle for leaning up against the threads. "Seems it'll never be far enough to get me away from you two arseholes! It won't stop me from tryin', though. I'll never stop tryin'!" He glared accusingly at Jon-Tom.

"Why, mate? I thought after that little sea voyage I 'elped you out with we were even up."

Jon-Tom found himself unable to meet the otter's

gaze. "We were . . . as far as that particular trip was concerned. Unfortunately, something new has come up." He tried to smile. "You know how highly I value your company and assistance."

"And you want good old 'appy-go-lucky Mudge along to 'old your bleedin' 'and, right? Or maybe to push you along in your pram?"

When Jon-Tom didn't reply, the otter turned his attention back to the kitchen table. "Untie me, you disgustin' ball of reptilian corruption, or when I get out of 'ere, I swears I'll shove you in on yourself and cement up all the openin's!"

"Now, now." Clothahump dabbed delicately at his mouth with a linen napkin. "Let us remember who we are talking to."

"Oh, I know who I'm talkin' to, all right. The world's master meddler. I don't care anymore, you see? So I can say wotever I want. Turn me into a snake, turn me into a worm, even turn me into a bloody 'uman. See if I care. Because you've gone too far this time, the two of you, and I've *'ad* it! I'm not goin' anywhere." He nodded in Jon-Tom's direction. "Especially not with 'im. Not across any oceans, not into any fights, not to the local market to buy chestnuts. Nowhere, nohow, no way!"

Jon-Tom switched to rubbing his bitten finger. "Ever hear of Quasequa, Mudge?"

The otter frowned down at him. "Qua wot?"

"Quasequa. It lies far to the south of the Bellwoods. Exquisite country, a beautiful tropical city built out on a vast lake. The kind of place an otter, it seems to me, would find downright paradisaical."

"Charming, friendly inhabitants," Clothahump added without glancing up from his meal, "who know how to make a stranger feel at home. Especially, I am told, the ladies."

Mudge seemed to waver, but only for an instant. Then his determination returned.

"Oh, no, you ain't goin' to smooth-talk me into it again. Not this time. I know 'ow you two operate, I does." He nodded again toward Jon-Tom. "This one's 'alf solicitor and 'alf devil. Between the two of you, you could sell ice to polar bears. No, I'll 'ave none of it this time. Do what you want to me."

Jon-Tom approached the cage, his best professional smile fairly lighting up the dim kitchen. He was careful, however, not to get within biting distance of his best friend.

"Aw, c'mon, Mudge. One more time. For old times' sake. Be a friend." The otter didn't reply, stared stolidly at the far wall.

"I know you're upset right now, and I can understand why. I sympathize, really. I meant it when I said I had nothing to do with bringing you here like this. I was going to come out and meet you, but Clothahump decided that it was important to try and save time, I guess, so he brought you here this way without telling me of his plans."

"Time. Let me tell you somethin' about time, mate. Do you 'ave any idea where I was when 'is sorcerership there yanked me out of reality and into nothingness? Do you 'ave any idea what five minutes in Chaos is like?"

"There are somewhat smoother methods of generating the transition," Clothahump murmured, "but they take too much time."

"Do they now? Time, wot? I'll tell you about time." A wistful expression came over his face. "There I was, sittin' in Shorvan's Gambling Palace in downtown Toothrust... which is a good place for a gambling chap like meself to be... 'oldin' twelve of a kind. Twelve of a kind!" He almost broke out sobbing, but managed to restrain himself.

"And the pot... there was enough gold in that pot, me friends, to set me up for three, four years o' comfort. So I'm gettin' ready to make me play, see, because I know wot the score is and that the one chap with a chance to stop me 'as to be bluffin' because 'e ain't 'oldin' diddly-squat in 'is paws. This bum's a foxie with no moxie, see? I can read 'is bloomin' whiskers, and I know I've got 'im beat, I know I do! So I push in all me chips, a great galumphin' pile won at great labor and pain, and wot do you think 'appens to me and me twelve of a kind, eh? Wot?" Jon-Tom said nothing.

"I'm jerked bodily into Unfamiliar Chaos, which ain't no garden spot, I can tell you, and then finds meself bound up like a B&D 'oliday gift in this bloody cage so's that tuft o' blotchy, moth-eaten feathers over there can tell me that I've been summoned hence because *you,* mate, needs me 'elp on one of your forthcomin' suicidal excursions."

Jon-Tom glared at Clothahump, who appeared not in the least distressed. "You did say, my boy, that you wanted his company on this journey. If anything, I expressed a dissenting opinion."

"I said that I wanted his help, his willing help."

"Best not to waste time," the turtle harrumphed, "debating semantics."

"If you don't want to waste time," Jon-Tom said, "why not send us to Quasequa the same way you brought him here?"

"It's not quite that simple, my boy. Bringing and sending are quite different things. The spells are more complex than you can imagine. Bringing takes enough out of you, and I am not at all adept, I confess, at sending. If I were better at either, I'd bring this Markus person here. That would simplify everything, wouldn't it? Unfortunately, I cannot do that. I was only able to manage this recall because of your strong association with this creature and—"

"Who're you callin' a 'creature,' you fat-brained..." Mudge hesitated, latched onto a new thought. "Wait a minim. Who's this 'Markus' you're talkin' about?"

"Someone I have to talk to," Jon-Tom explained. "In beautiful Quasequa."

"Ain't nowheres as beautiful as a gamin' room with a big pot o' gold lyin' in it waitin' for the takin'. Twelve of a kind. The draw o' me life." He looked back to Clothahump again. "The least you could've done, your sorcerership, was to 'ave brung me 'ere first-class instead of economy."

"I am not one to indulge in frivolous, unnecessary expense."

"Right, guv, and I'm sure you travels steerage every time you transpose, too. At least let me out o' these blasted ropes!"

"Yes, I believe I can do that, now that you have calmed down somewhat and decided to act halfway civilized. All that screaming and cursing, tch." He mumbled something under his breath.

Nothing happened. "Well," Mudge asked, "is that it?"

"Not quite. You have to sneeze."

"Oi, I do, do I? Just like that? You think sneezin' on cue's as simple as talkin'? As simple as drawin' to twelve of a kind? Right then!" He inhaled sharply, tickled his nose with a whisker, and blew messily in Jon-Tom's direction. No question but that his aim was deliberate.

The ropes turned to dust at his feet. He stood and rubbed his arms to restore the circulation.

Same old Mudge, Jon-Tom mused, cleaning himself up as he inspected his old friend. The otter boasted a new vest of gray shot through with silver thread together with matching silver-and-black shorts.

His new boots were bright metallic blue. The familiar longbow and quiver of arrows were slung across his back. On his head rode the same battered green felt cap. New feather, though.

"That's an improvement, guv'nor. Now 'ow about this bloomin' cage?"

"What cage?" asked Clothahump with a half smile. "There is nothing barring your path save a few flimsy threads."

"Few they may be but flimsy they ain't. Don't think I 'aven't tried." He pushed out with a hand, casually, and several of the threads snapped. He had to rush to jump clear as the wooden roof started to collapse on top of him. Then he was standing unrestrained on the kitchen floor staring at what up until a moment ago had been an impenetrable prison but was now nothing more than a couple of blocks of wood lightly linked together by a few cloth threads.

"The only thing worse than a bloody wizard," he mumbled, "is a bloody wizard who likes to play jokes."

"I do not play jokes," declaimed Clothahump with dignity. "Such mundane exercises in plebeian amusement are beneath my stature." He coughed lightly. "I do admit to some slight subtle sense of humor, however. At my age you pass up no opportunity for some mild amusement.

"As for your late lamented twelve of a kind, for that I am sorry. I have reason to believe that the wizard Oplode the Sly, whom you travel to visit, will be willing to reimburse you fully."

"Yeah, that's wot you always say, guv."

"In any case, you will surely have the run of lovely, exotic Quasequa, whose climate and virtues the poets extol beyond—"

"Oh, come off it, guv'nor, I've 'eard all this before." He sniffled once. "Twelve of a kind." A glance up at

Jon-Tom. "You know 'ow long a player waits for a 'and like that, mate?"

"No, I don't. I thought the most you could get in a game was four of a kind."

Mudge mulled this over. "I can see we're talkin' different games 'ere, mate. You wouldn't understand, then." He turned to face Clothahump. "Right then; this brotherly dabbler in the back o' beyond may or may not pay me for me time and trouble, but wot about me own 'ard-earned money I put on the table? Wot about the loss o' me gamblin' stake? Or don't you think you're responsible for me losin' *that*?"

"I am not responsible for your gambling debts," said the turtle slowly, "but I agree it would be wrong were you to suffer the loss of your own money on my account."

"Well now, that's more like it." Mudge looked surprised and somewhat mollified. "You know, guv, if you wouldn't treat me like an old 'ammer and saw all the time, I might be a mite more inclined to participate willingly in these charmin' little diversions you and the 'airless one 'ere come up with. Quasequa, wot? Never been there, 'tis true. Wot is it we're supposed to do there?"

"Check out a new chief advisor to the local rulers, a newly arrived wizard who calls himself Markus the Ineluctable," Jon-Tom told him.

"Sounds straightforward enough to me." His gaze narrowed and darted back and forth between Jon-Tom and Clothahump. "You're sure that's all, now? You two wouldn't be concealin' somethin' from old Mudge, now would you?"

"Certainly not," said Clothahump, obviously insulted.

"Would I do something like that, Mudge?"

"I don't like it. You two are too chummy. I feel safer when you're arguin'." He focused on the turtle.

"Wot's the land like between 'ere and this Quasequa place?"

"Tropical, friendly, largely uninhabited and unspoiled. I would be coming along myself if my arthritis were not acting up. That, and the fact that this is really a minor business, precludes my accompanying you."

"There's something else." Jon-Tom put a comradely hand on Mudge's shoulder. The otter moved out from under it, but at least he didn't try to bite. "This Markus the Ineluctable claims to have come from another world. If he comes from my world and the two of us strike up a friendship, it's a chance for me to get home. Maybe for both of us to get home."

"Well now, that would be worth the journey, to see the last of you, mate, though I don't know as 'ow I could stand more than one of you otherworldly twits in the same place at the same time. Nothin' personal, but if you get back to your 'ome, maybe I can get back to 'aving a normal life o' me own."

"A normal life," said Clothahump dryly, "rich with thieving, fighting, wenching, and being in a condition verging on permanent inebriation all the time."

"Yes, that's wot I said," agreed the otter blithely, missing the wizard's sarcasm entirely.

Clothahump eyed him sadly. "I fear there is no hope for you, water rat." He looked suddenly thoughtful. "I was led to believe that the most you could hold in a game of artimum was eleven of a kind."

"I thought artimum was a spice," said Jon-Tom.

"A spicy game of chance, my boy. Spices are involved as well as dice and cards." He gave the otter a shrewd look. "You didn't, by any chance, cardamom your hand?"

"Oh, wonderful!" Mudge threw up his hands and beseeched the heavens for understanding. "I'm snatched away from the biggest winnings of me short life so's I can be accused o' cheatin' by someone who wasn't even there."

"Did you cardamom your cards?" Clothahump persisted.

Shaking his head, Mudge turned to Jon-Tom, put a hand around his waist. "Right then, mate. Long as our course 'as been determined, we might as well be on our way. Sooner we gets there the sooner we can start 'ome, right?"

"Might as well wait another day, since I've saved so much time what with Clothahump bringing you straight here. We can leave tomorrow morning." He was taken aback by the otter's sudden enthusiasm.

"Let's 'ave a chat then, must be a lot you 'ave to tell me, and I've plenty to tell you." He eased Jon-Tom toward the doorway.

"Twelve of a kind." Clothahump was rubbing his lower jaw and gazing speculatively after the hurriedly departing otter.

Mudge made sure to close the door behind him.

V

It was raining when they departed the following morning. Mudge appeared to have undergone a complete change of heart and was all but pushing Jon-Tom out the door.

"No reason to wake 'is nibs," the otter told him, smiling reassuringly. "Let the poor bugger 'ave 'is rest."

"Tell me about this game called artimum. I've heard of it before but I don't really know how—"

"Now don't *you* start, mate. Tell you about it when we're well on our way. Wouldn't want anyone else to get the wrong idea about old Mudge, would you? Besides, there's more interestin' tales I've yet to tell you. Did I mention yesterday about the vixen in Tenwattle who...?"

The rain slid off Jon-Tom's waterproof iridescent lizard-skin cape, which he kept well over his head, while Mudge merely placed his felt cap in his pack to protect it. Other than that he ignored the rain, for otters are as comfortable soaking wet as they are bone dry.

Heavier drops rang some of the bell leaves which gave this country its name, but for the most part the trees were quiet. A tendaria rested on a nearby branch. The blue-and-puce flying amphibian sat with its mouth agape and head back as it collected rainwater in the flexible sac attached to its lower jaw. It would carry the fresh water back to the clay-sealed nest it had made in the trunk of some hollow tree and add it to the growing basin therein. In time the female of the species would lay her eggs in the nest. The young flying amphibians would eventually hatch and mature in the protected pool, remaining there until they were old enough to fly and breathe air.

"Really, Mudge, don't you think it's about time you gave some thought to altering your life-style?"

"And wot's wrong with me life-style?"

"For one thing, you couldn't exactly call it productive. You're a sharp guy, Mudge. Yet you choose to spend your life as a wastrel."

"I calls it freedom, mate. And it's a challenge walkin' the fine line between the legal and the debatable, leavin' it to everyone else to guess which side o' the line you're on, on any particular day." He winked broadly. "Of course, the trick o' such livin' is to 'ave one foot on each side o' the line at all times, and to be able to dance back and forth without gettin' caught on the one side or the other. Never a dull moment."

"I know it's an exciting way to live, but it doesn't seem to have much of a future to it. I'll bet you don't even have enough put aside to pay for a decent funeral."

"Funeral? Hell, mate, I know them that spends their 'ole lives worryin' about 'ow they're goin' to be buried. The goal o' their life is death. 'Ardly seems worth livin' at all. Might as well slit your throat and miss out on all the worryin'."

"Go ahead and make light of it, but there'll be no one to cry at your funeral. No pallbearers, no mourners. Or do you think your thieving acquaintances will take the trouble to show up?"

Mudge shrugged. "I don't worry about it none, but I do know there'll be at least one there to weep for me passin'."

"Yeah, who?"

"Why, you, mate," and the otter grinned up at him so infectiously that Jon-Tom had to turn away lest Mudge see his own smile.

"Maybe, just maybe, but I still think you could do more with your life."

"Plannin' takes all the surprise out o' life, mate. Me, I'd rather take it as it 'its me, even if it sometimes 'its kind o' 'ard."

They marched on, arguing about life and meanings and directions. Mudge cited chapter and verse from personal experience—always frenetic, often foul, but never dull. Jon-Tom countered with quotes from everyone from B. F. Skinner to Woody Allen. None of his arguments had the slightest impact on the free-living otter.

They passed the glade where the footprints of M'nemaxa still showed as deep depressions in solid granite; passed through dense, familiar woods; and finally emerged on the banks of the river Tailaroam. Westward the great river tumbled and churned on its way toward the distant Glittergeist Sea, while far off to the east lay the impressive range of mountains known as Zaryt's Teeth, which gave birth to the Tailaroam's tributaries.

Their immediate concern was the broad section of fast-running river directly in front of them. It flowed from east to west, and their course led due south.

"How do we get across?"

"As for me, mate," Mudge told him, "I'd as soon swim it in a couple of minutes. I'd enjoy it more than these past days' trek." He glanced around, searching the shoreline. "If we can find a nice dry log, I'll give you a push across. Wouldn't want 'is nosyness to think I weren't takin' good care o' you."

They hunted for and found a suitable log. Jon-Tom sat astride the fallen tree with his long legs stretched out in front of him, clinging to the otter's clothing and his own belongings while struggling to balance himself as Mudge pushed out into the river. Fortunately, the otter's sense of equilibrium was better developed than his own. Every time it looked like he was about to tip over, Mudge adjusted from behind. They arrived on the opposite shore of the Tailaroam without Jon-Tom's getting his toes wet.

Mudge climbed onto the sandy bank, shook himself off, and then lay down in the sun until his slick fur was completely dry. As soon as he'd dressed, they started south along a well-trod and easy-to-follow trail.

Soon they found themselves in the Lower Duggakurra Hills, a landscape of rounded boulders worn smooth by the action of wind and rain. Thick brush thrived in pockets of dark soil between the rocks. Already they were starting to leave behind the larger conifers that dominated the expanse of forest called the Bellwoods, and the tall tropical hardwoods of the lake region would not put in an appearance for some time yet.

Jon-Tom took his time breaking camp the following morning, quenching the embers of their campfire and scattering the ashes. Time was important, but he didn't want to arrive in Quasequa too exhausted to think.

The trail had grown more and more obscure the deeper they'd penetrated into the rocky terrain, so he wasn't surprised to see the confused expression on the otter's face when Mudge returned from scouting the path ahead.

Or was there more there this morning than just confusion? He rose, kicked the last splinters of smoking wood apart, and brushed dust from his hands.

"Something wrong? If it's the trail..."

"'Tisn't that, guv. It's...well, you'd better come and 'ave a looksee for yourself."

"A looksee at what?"

Mudge said evenly, "I think the ground ahead's on fire."

Jon-Tom swallowed his ready retort as he saw that the otter was in dead earnest. Hurriedly he slipped into his backpack and followed his companion southward. Mudge underscored the seriousness of his claim by not talking as they marched.

Sure enough, as they topped a small pass between the boulders, Jon-Tom could see vapor rising off to the left. It was only after they'd hiked another mile that he could be certain it wasn't smoke.

Mudge could see the difference, too. "Sorry, mate. I turned back to camp before comin' this far. That ain't smoke from no fire. 'Tis steam."

"That it is," Jon-Tom agreed, "but what's the source?"

They found out when they crested the next rise. Stretched out before them was a most wonderful panorama. Hot pools of varying depth and hue bubbled and growled in the cool of morning. Steplike terraces of calcium carbonate climbed the rocks, each one like the entrance to a sultan's palace. Steaming water cascaded down them from hot springs above, constantly adding to and altering an already spectacular sight. Brown-and-yellow bands of travertine enclosed emerald-green basins. Everywhere could be seen the blue, green, and yellow of heat-loving algae.

"Just like Yellowstone," Jon-Tom murmured. "I feel privileged to see this."

"And I feel like a moron," muttered Mudge. "'Earth on fire' indeed!"

"Don't feel bad. It could look that way from a distance." Jon-Tom removed his backpack, then his shirt, and started on his belt.

Mudge eyed him curiously. "Now wot are you up to?"

"I haven't had a hot bath since we left Clothahump's tree."

"A hot bath. Now there's a novel idea."

"Find yourself a cool pool if you want to join me," Jon-Tom told him, slipping his pants down his legs. "I enjoy hot water, Mudge. Keep in mind that I haven't got your insulating layers of fur and fat."

"Wot fat?" snapped the indignant otter. "I ain't fat."

"It's a subcutaneous layer and it's there to keep you warm when you're under water."

"Sounds bloody disgustin'." Mudge lifted a flap of skin from his left arm, eyed it as though seeing it for the first time. But he was damned if he was going to sit and watch while Jon-Tom enjoyed himself. The water in the pool the human had chosen was much too warm for his taste, but another nearby was pleasant enough. Stripping quickly, he dove into the natural basin, found he had to float. The sand at the bottom was too hot to touch.

"A hot bath. You 'umans are burstin' with weird notions."

Jon-Tom didn't reply. He was too comfortable, drifting on his back in the warm water, listening to it bubble and tumble down the hillsides surrounding them. There were no geysers in evidence, suggesting that this was a relatively calm thermal area.

"Back where I come from," he told Mudge lazily, "there's a tribe of humans called the Maori who live in a place just like this. It's called Rotorua and it steams all year round."

Mudge sniffed, paddling across the surface of his

own pool. "It ain't for me, mate. Give me a nice ice-cold mountain stream to go swimmin' in any day. Though this stuff does," he admitted, "clear out your sinuses." He dove in a single flowing motion, a graceful curve that belied the presence of a stiff backbone.

As he did, something struck the water just behind him.

Jon-Tom stood, the heat of the bottom sand tickling his feet, and tried to see what had entered the water aft of the otter's submerging backside. As he stared, something went *spang* against the boulder behind him and flew to pieces. Some of the pieces floated. He picked them up and identified them instantly.

When Mudge broke the surface again, it was to see his companion huddled in a narrow cove formed by overhanging rocks. He paddled toward the adjoining pool. "Wot's up, mate?"

"Didn't you see?"

"See wot?" Mudge frowned, pivoted in the lukewarm water.

"It went right over when you dove."

"Wot went right over me when I dove?" Something whizzed past his right ear and he jerked around sharply in the water, his eyes wide. "Cor, somebody's shootin' at us!" He ducked just in time, and a second arrow struck the water directly behind him.

He emerged as if shot from some subterranean gun, leaping completely over the stone barrier separating the two pools, and swam over to huddle next to Jon-Tom. Their weapons and clothes lay on a nice, dry slope on the opposite side of the water, in a sunny spot completely devoid of cover.

"We'll 'ave to make a run for it, mate." Mudge spat out warm water. "We can't just squat 'ere and let 'em pick us off." He took a deep breath and started to submerge.

Jon-Tom grabbed him by the fur on top of his head and pulled him up again. "Hold on a minute." A half dozen arrows whizzed past, far overhead. "Listen."

High-pitched squeaks sounded from thc far ridge. More arrows went past. None landed near the nervous bathers.

"Maybe they're not shooting at us." He paddled out just far enough to see around the rocks beneath which they were hiding, trying to follow the flight of the arrows.

Sure enough, moments later other cries and shouts came from that direction, and several small spears arced past overhead, retracing the path of the missiles which had initially panicked the two travelers.

The shouts and screams grew steadily louder, and soon both groups of combatants revealed themselves. The opposing war parties clashed in the middle of a single natural causeway which wound its way across the hot springs. Spears, stones, and arrows filled the air, flying through the steam. Mudge and Jon-Tom strove to make themselves as inconspicuous as possible.

There were a few gophers and moles among the fighters, but the large majority on both sides were prairie dogs ranging between four and five feet in height. They slashed and stabbed with quick, short movements, their high-pitched battle squeaks rising above the hiss and rumble of the springs. They fought with a determination and ruthlessness that Jon-Tom found appalling in such, well, *cute* creatures.

There was nothing comical about the carnage they wreaked on one another, though. Body after body tumbled into the steaming water, limbs flew through the air as swords made contact, and the perfect clarity of the springs was soon stained dark by the blood of the fallen.

This went on for the better part of an hour before

the war party on the left began to retreat. Their opponents redoubled their efforts and in minutes had gained complete control of the causeway. They fanned out over the opposite hillside, dispatching those of the opposition too weak or badly wounded to join their comrades in flight. They did so with a matter-of-fact bloodthirstiness that chilled Jon-Tom despite the surrounding hot water.

Something pricked his shoulder and a voice sounded from behind them.

"You two there. Out of the water!"

Jon-Tom turned. Four of the victors stood looking down at them. The one holding the spear on him wore a helmet fashioned from the skull of an opponent. It was bright with beads of many colors, trade trinkets, and dangling feathers. An elegant barbarism, Jon-Tom mused. It was a perfect frame for the expression beneath it.

"Hiya, guv'nor," said Mudge cheerfully. He spread his paws in a gesture of innocence. "See, we didn't know there was goin' to be a punch-up 'ere, we didn't. We were just 'aving a spot o' bath, and we—"

The one with the skull headdress shifted the point of his spear so that the tip hung in the air an inch from Mudge's nose.

"Right you are, mate! We're comin', we're comin'." He climbed out and Jon-Tom followed him.

Their captors backed off a bit, intimidated by Jon-Tom's unexpected size, and allowed them to march over the causeway to retrieve their clothes. Eyes turned among the rest of the victors as the peculiar pair passed among them. High-pitched queries followed their progress.

"Where'd you find these?"

"Down in one of the pools."

"What were they doing there, you suppose?"

"Spying, I wager."

"A good place to spy from, *if* that was their intention."

"Mighty big human, isn't it?"

"Doesn't look so tough to me."

This steady exchange between the four captors and their colleagues continued until a cluster of older prairie dogs clad in real armor approached. The newcomers were led by one white-furred oldster who was taller than Mudge. His helmet was of brass, with holes cut on top for ears and curved slats to protect the bulging cheeks.

"I'm General Pocknet," he said in a curious but no-nonsense tone. "You two don't belong hereabouts."

Jon-Tom wasn't about to argue with him. "We're travelers, just passing through on our way south."

"South?" The general frowned. "There's nothing to the south of the hills."

"The city-state of Quasequa," Jon-Tom told him helpfully.

"Never heard of the place," replied Pocknet, shaking his head. His jowls and whiskers quivered.

"Still, that's where we're headed." He nodded toward the bloodstained causeway. "Looks like your troops won."

"We won this day, yes."

"Glad to hear it."

"Don't try and ingratiate yourself with me, man. We have settled our differences with the Wittens for another month. Then we must fight again to see who retains possession of the springs."

Mudge was frowning as he tried to understand. "Let me get this straight now, guv. You lot 'ave this same little argument regular-like every month?"

"Naturally," said the officer behind Pocknet.

"You two honestly don't know what is happening here, do you?" said Pocknet. Man and otter shook their heads in unison. Pocknet gestured across the water.

"Over there is my home, the land of Pault." He turned and pointed up the hill pimpled with the bodies of the Wittens. "Beyond this rise lies the territory of Witten, our hereditary enemy. We fight the good fight on the first day of every month."

"For fun?" asked Jon-Tom hesitantly.

"A typically human conceit. Of course not for fun. We fight for control of this." He indicated the valley of hot springs with a sweep of one hand.

"Wot do you want with a bunch o' boilin' water?" Mudge wondered.

The general eyed him distastefully. "Civilized folk know what to do with heat. It cooks our food, cleans our clothing, pleases us in many ways. Whoever controls the bridge controls the Mulmun, and whoever controls the Mulmun controls the springs."

"Uh, pardon our ignorance," said Jon-Tom, "but what's the Mulmun?"

The general was shaking his head. "It's true; you two are ignorant, unsophisticated travelers, aren't you?"

"That's us, your generalship," agreed Mudge readily. "Just a couple of innocent dolts bumbling our way southward."

"That remains to be determined. You've said where you are going. Where do you come from?"

"From the north, from across the Tailaroam. The forest known as the Bellwoods," Jon-Tom told him.

"That would explain your evident ignorance of civilized matters," the general agreed. "But I suspect this pretense of innocence is nothing more than a clever ruse. Obviously you were spying for the Wittens." A circle of spears closed in tight around Jon-Tom and Mudge.

"Hey, let's 'old on a minim 'ere, guv'nor! We were

just 'aving ourselves a spot o' bath is all, wot? Didn't know shit about this Wittens-mittens-Smault business, we didn't!" One of the encircling soldiers touched him with a spear, and Mudge turned to glare angrily at him. "Poke me with that again, short whiskers, and I'll put it where the sun don't shine."

A senior officer leaned forward to whisper in the general's ear. "Your pardon, sir, but their stupidity appears genuine to me. I honestly believe they have no idea what the Mulmun is."

"Hmmph. Well..." General Pocknet nibbled one curling whisker and squinted at the two strangers. "You are an odd pair, no denying it. Too odd even for the Wittens to employ, perhaps."

"Oddest pair you ever set your bloomin' eyes on, guv," Mudge assured him readily.

"I may have erred in calling you spies. Yes, you happened to be bathing in the springs, purely out of ignorance of reality, only to find yourselves caught in the middle of a battle."

Jon-Tom let out a sigh of relief as the spears withdrew slightly. "That, sir, is just about the size of it."

The general waved the spears aside completely. "Let them have their weapons." He moved to stand close to Jon-Tom, staring up at the much taller human. "Since you are not our enemies, I guess you have to be our guests."

"General, sir, if it's all the same to you, we'd just as soon...umph!" He grabbed himself and looked angrily at Mudge, who'd quickly elbowed him in the ribs. Mudge beckoned him close, and Jon-Tom restrained himself long enough to hear the otter out.

"Listen to me close, mate. I know these tunnel-dwellers, I do. They can be real touchy about 'avin' their 'ospitality turned down."

"Oh, all right." He stood, still rubbing his side. "So we're your guests. What does that entail?"

"A good meal and friendly chatter," the general told him. "You can tell us of where you're from and where you're going." He turned and barked orders. His troops began to regroup and to fall back across the causeway. The general and his senior staff flanked the visitors, Pocknet striding along briskly with both paws clasped behind his back. An armor-bearer walked behind him, carrying the general's helmet and sword.

"Tell me now, how comes an otter and a man to be traveling together in our country?"

"Let's save that for dessert," Jon-Tom told him. "If you don't mind, I have a couple of questions of my own." Mudge was making shushing sounds in his direction. Jon-Tom ignored him.

"Can't you share the hot springs with the Wittens?"

The general smiled up at him. "You are a dumb stranger, so I will excuse the affront. You see," he said, as if explaining to a child, "there is but the one Mulmun, the symbol of the springs. That is what we fight for control of. Whoever possesses the Mulmun has the right to control the springs."

"But isn't there enough here for both communities? Can't you share?"

"Why share," replied the general, favoring him with an odd look, "when one can have it all?"

"Because it makes more sense than slaughtering your neighbors."

"But we like slaughtering our neighbors, and our neighbors feel exactly the same way about us," said the general easily.

"How do you know sharing wouldn't be better? Have you ever *tried* sharing?"

"Absurd notion. We could never trust the Wittens. Wouldn't dare to try. The minute our backs were turned, they'd cut our throats and take control of the springs forever. If any of us survived, we'd never see the Mulmun again. At least, not for another month."

"You only fight on the first of the month? Nobody ever tries a sneak attack on the other side in the middle of an off week?"

The general looked indignant. "Certainly not! What do you think we are, uncivilized barbarians? What an outrageous notion. Ah, we're home."

Ahead lay a hole in the side of a hill. The large, ornately carved wooden gate had been flung wide to reveal the well-lit tunnel beyond. A line of sentries stood drawn up in review on either side of the pathway. Other, much less spectacularly decorated entrances were visible off to the left.

The general led Mudge and Jon-Tom inside. As usual, Jon-Tom was forced to bend in order to clear a local ceiling. Once out of the sun, the gophers and moles in the group were able to remove their protective sunshades.

Before long they began to encounter noncombatants, citizens engaged in daily chores. Greetings were exchanged between civilians and soldiers. Cubs tagged alongside, jabbering at one another and occasionally pausing to engage in mock battles. Tunnels appeared that branched off in all directions.

Eventually they turned right and entered a room with a ceiling high enough to permit Jon-Tom to straighten. He pressed a hand gratefully against his complaining lower back. There were half a dozen long tables in the room, each decorated with neat, miniature place settings. Pennants hung from the rock overhead, while spears and more exotic weapons were attached to the walls. Fires burned in several fireplaces whose chimneys had to reach all the way to the surface above. Kettles and pots simmered over the flames.

"Officers' mess," General Pocknet informed them. He directed them to the head table. Jon-Tom found a cushion and tried to balance on it. The low table made the thought of trying a chair out of the question.

Females brought out hors d'oeuvres, platters heaped high with fruit and nuts. The general cracked one between his front teeth, tossed the shell into a communal basket in the center of the long table, and gnawed on the nutmeat. Soon the room was filled with sharp cracking noises and flying shells. Jon-Tom felt like a kernel in a popcorn popper.

Mudge was trying to make conversation with one of the waitresses, so it was left to Jon-Tom to engage the general.

"This war of yours, it's been going on like this, month after month, for a long time?"

"As far as history tells," Pocknet assured him. "We're quite comfortable with the arrangement, and so are the Wittens. Gives our lives continuity. All disputes between us are settled by control of the Mulmun."

"Exactly what is this 'Mulmung'?"

"'Mulmun,'" the general corrected him smoothly. He pointed toward one of the fireplaces as he cracked another nut.

Resting on the mantel was a garishly colored, three-foot-high blob of regurgitated ceramics, mostly maroon, pink, purple and glazed with pearlescent white. It was possibly the ugliest piece of sculpture, if it could be dignified by such a description, that Jon-Tom had ever seen.

"That," said the general proudly, "is the Mulmun. Whoever wins the battle on the first of each month retains it. It is the symbol of the springs. While we hold it, the Wittens may not come near or make use of the warm waters. We've held it for six months now, at great expense, but it's been worth it."

Jon-Tom considered as he chewed on the contents of a long, thin nut. The meat was delightfully sweet, which was good, because it had taken him at least four minutes to break the tough shell.

"I think I understand. If you didn't possess the Mulmun, then you'd have to relinquish your absolute control of the hot springs."

The general nodded. "We carry it with us into battle each month. Should the Wittens win, they would take it back to Witten with them and dominate the springs for a month." He chuckled, obviously relishing his opponents' discomforts. "They must be very filthy by now."

"I didn't see it during the fight."

"Do you think we'd risk putting it in danger?" the general asked him, aghast. "The possessors display it in its special container, well out of the way of the combatants' arms but up where all can see it for inspiration. It is quite irreplaceable, quite."

"Ghastly piece o' puke, ain't it?" Mudge whispered to his friend. The otter had found something alcoholic to imbibe and was draining his mug as fast as the dainty prairie lass nearby could refill it for him.

"Christ, watch your mouth!" Jon-Tom warned him anxiously. He smiled at the general. "Being a stranger here, it's not for me to criticize your customs."

"Then don't," Pocknet advised him blandly. "Enjoy your meal and be on your way. Now, tell me about your plans." He looked eagerly at his tall guest.

Jon-Tom regaled their hosts with tales of his many adventures, and the underground citizens listened politely, for all that they thought he was the biggest liar to come among them in many a moon. None, however, denied the amusement value of Jon-Tom's rambling prevarications, and they applauded politely at the conclusion of each anecdote.

The dinner also featured some live entertainment.

Several captive Wittens were dumped in the center of the room, hauled erect, and tied to stakes so that the ladies, when not serving the tables, could pull the unfortunate prisoners to pieces. Jon-Tom found that this diminished his appetite considerably. His hosts seemed to find it uproariously amusing.

Several times Mudge had to lean over and warn his friend to keep his opinions to himself. You don't insult true believers in the middle of their own church. Besides, hadn't they seen worse outrages in their travels? Tomorrow they could leave, none the worse for the experience.

So Jon-Tom smiled thinly and made a show of enjoying himself. There wasn't a damn thing he could do about it anyway. The "entertainment" over, everyone repaired to their respective bedchambers. Their hosts even managed to rig a bed of sufficient length for Jon-Tom to stretch out upon.

Comfortable though it was, it didn't lull him to sleep. Instead, he lay wide-awake, thinking hard about all he'd seen and heard during the day.

The situation existing between Witten and Pault, two communities of similar size and population, was intolerable to a civilized human being. It was worse than intolerable: it was sickening, disgusting, a sin against common sense! It ought not to exist. It must not be allowed to continue.

Since no one else seemed to give a damn, Jon-Tom resolved quietly to do something about it himself.

VI

It was pitch-black inside the burrow when he decided it was safe to move. A good five hours had passed since they'd retired, and, Jon-Tom reasoned, most of the underground community should be resting soundly.

He fumbled along the wall until he encountered one of the ubiquitous oil-soaked torches each hall and room was equipped with, struggled with his flint until it sprang to life.

"Mudge." He moved quietly toward the otter's bed. "Let's go, move it. We're getting out of here. We're going to help these people whether they like it or not. Mudge?"

He put out a hand, feeling for the otter's shoulder in the dim light provided by the torch. It went all the way down to the mattress. The covers came away with a yank.

"Well, shit," he muttered, swinging the torch to inspect the rest of the room. No sign of the otter sprawled unconscious on the floor. Nor was he asleep in the bathroom, or in the hall corridor outside.

No one bothered him as he stood thinking furiously in the passageway. Could the reluctant water rat have run out on him this early in their journey? Knowing

Mudge, that kind of desertion couldn't be ruled out. Or was he off somewhere within the subterranean town, carousing with newfound buddies or gambling his shorts away?

Tough. He should've stayed with his companion. Anyway, the otter was a superb tracker. Jon-Tom was willing to bet he could find a vanished friend with ease. Let him stay behind if he wanted to and do his own explaining. What Jon-Tom had in mind was bigger than either of them, something that should have been done in this part of the world a long time ago. Fortunate chance had given him the opportunity to correct a monstrously maintained wrong.

In the darkness he struggled to retrace his steps. Down a hall, and sure enough, there off to the left was the dimly lit and now-deserted officers' mess. The dishes had been cleared from the long tables. Lingering embers still glowed and popped in the three fireplaces, sending smoke up to the surface world above. Not a soul in sight.

He tiptoed across the floor between two of the tables until he stood before the central fireplace. None of the locals could reach the mantel, but it was an easy stretch for him. The Mulmun was heavier than it looked.

Back quickly out to the hall, and then he was running at a steady pace up an ever-ascending slope, the Mulmun tied to his belt and concealed by his flapping green cape.

There were sentries on night duty, a pair of wide-eyed and fully awake gophers. They recognized the guest.

"Evenin', sor," said one courteously. "You're bein' up kind o' late for a day-dweller."

Jon-Tom tried to bend to his right to hide the bulge at his waist. "Can't sleep."

"A sensible attitude," commented the other guard approvingly.

"Thought I'd go for a walk." How convenient, he thought, that the voluminous cape also hid his backpack. Its presence wouldn't square with a brief evening stroll.

The guards weren't in the least suspicious, however. Jon-Tom backed around them, smiling brightly. "Just a quick little look around. Got to be back early to wake my friend."

The sentries exchanged a glance. "That's funny, sor. Your companion went off toward the springs 'bout an hour or so ago."

"What? My friend? Are you sure?"

"No otters livin' in Pault," said the first sentry. "Had to have been him, right?"

"I guess so. Yes, it must've been him. That's certainly interesting. The sly little cuss neglected to mention it to me. I will have to remonstrate with him, yes indeedy. I know. I'll bet he went for a moonlit swim. Sure, that's it."

"He didn't say anything to you?" Suddenly the second sentry seemed more than casually curious. "That is odd."

"Oh, no, no, not really," Jon-Tom assured him as he continued backing toward the exit, now tantalizingly near. "He does things like this all the time."

"Funny time o' night for a day-dweller to be takin' a bath," the guard went on.

"You know these water rats." Jon-Tom's smile was frozen in place. "So damned unpredictable." He turned and jogged out onto the surface, leaving the puzzled sentries conversing noisily behind him.

Once out of sight he increased his pace to a run. Puzzled guards could be dangerous guards, especially if their curiosity matched their confusion.

More important, what the hell was the otter doing

at the springs in the middle of the night, and why didn't he see fit to tell his traveling companion about his plans for a nocturnal excursion? It didn't make any sense, which meant it was perfectly in character for Mudge. He paused only briefly to catch his breath and retie the awkward burden of the Mulmun.

It was certainly a lovely night for a swim. The moon was high, and pale silver light bathed the boulders and rising mist. Of the otter there was no sign, and the only sounds came from the bubbling, hissing springs.

Or was there something else? It rose and fell, but it didn't sound like water bubbling or steam venting. It issued from behind a cluster of granite spires.

Jon-Tom approached them cautiously. The sounds were familiar and yet alien. Invading Wittens, perhaps, scouting out the terrain in preparation for next month's carnage.

He peered over the top of the rocks. It was Mudge, all right. Only, he wasn't alone. Jon-Tom thought he recognized the prairie dog lady who'd been serving them during the ceremonial meal. Coquettish little sprite. She was being anything but coquettish at the moment, however. Mudge was moaning softly and she was emitting a rapid sequence of high-pitched squeaks and bleats. Some were undoubtedly too high-pitched for Jon-Tom's human hearing, but he got the idea fast enough. They weren't talking about the weather. Matter of fact, they weren't talking at all.

"Mudge!" he whispered.

"Wot the bloody 'ell is that?" The otter withdrew, only to lose his footing on the round stones and stumble head over heels. His paramour scrambled in the direction of her clothing.

The otter's sharp eyes quickly found Jon-Tom staring down at him from atop the ring of boulders. He let out a tremulous sigh.

"Bless me bottom, mate, 'tis only you. Wot are you tryin' to do, give me 'eart failure?"

"No." Jon-Tom wondered why he was still whispering. The little lady cowered off in a corner. "Get dressed. We're getting out of here."

Mudge shifted rapidly from relieved to startled. "Wot, *now*?" He began gathering up his clothes and weapons. "Ain't you got no sensitivity at all, mate?"

"I'm sorry, I didn't know. If you'd bothered to tell me your plans for the evening..."

"...You'd've tried to talk me out of 'em, guv'nor. I know you. Wot's the bleedin' 'urry, is wot I wants to know?"

"Mudge, I saw these people fight today, brother against brother, more or less. I listened to their talk and learned their sordid local history. What we've got here are a bunch of people so immersed in an ongoing bad habit they haven't the foggiest notion of how to cure themselves of it."

"Your pardon, mate," said the otter as he slipped into his shorts, "but wot we 'ave 'ere is a bunch of people who are perfectly 'appy with their lives just as they are."

"That's because they can't break out of this cycle they've slipped into. Mudge, there's plenty of hot water in these springs, more than enough to supply all the needs of both towns. It's not like they're fighting over a limited resource."

"Jon-Tom, I'm beginning to think that your brains are a limited resource, wot? If they 'aven't been able to make a peace stick between them for 'undreds of years now, wot makes you think you can suddenly up and create one?"

Jon-Tom grinned at him, fumbled beneath his cape. "Because as a third party, there was nothing to stop me from taking this."

The lady inhaled sharply at the sight of the revered Mulmun.

"This isn't a symbol of the springs or of communal contentment," Jon-Tom told him in an angry whisper, "but of stubbornness and calcification in the body politic. Now that we've taken it, they won't have a symbol, a totem, to fight for. They'll *have* to make peace."

The otter said nothing for a long time, just stared at his patently insane companion out of wide, disbelieving eyes.

"You pinched their Mulmunk, or whatever the 'ell they call the bloody monstrosity. You pinched it."

"Exactly," Jon-Tom said smugly.

"Oh, mate, 'ow I do wish you'd talk with poor ol' Mudge before embarkin' on these pet projects of yours."

"They went this way, sor," said a not-distant-enough voice. One of the guards from the entrance to Pault. The next voice they heard was also familiar. It belonged to General Pocknet.

And he wasn't alone.

"Come on!" Jon-Tom turned and raced for the causeway that crossed the springs.

"Later, luv," said Mudge hurriedly, bestowing a brief, parting nose-rub on his betrayed lover. Then he was flying over the rocks in pursuit of his certifiable companion.

Armed prairie dogs, some only half-clad, others wearing odd bits and pieces of armor, soon appeared in their wake. They were squeaking bloodcurdling threats and waving swords and spears over their heads.

"Wait, listen!" Jon-Tom held the Mulmun in both hands, raised it over his head. "Give me a chance to explain!"

"Shut up, mate!" Mudge snapped, trying to increase his short stride and secure his vest simultaneously. He prayed he wouldn't stumble in his hastily donned boots. "You can't talk to this lot."

"I have to! I'm sure once they hear what I have to say, they'll see that I'm only doing this for their benefit, so that they and their neighbors can begin to live together in peace and harmony."

"Snakeshit! I'm telling you they won't listen to you."

"They'll have to. I've got the Mulmun."

"Well, 'tis not just that which I fear disinclines them to sweet reasonableness, mate." Mudge looked suddenly uncomfortable. "See, that sweet little powderpuff I was dallyin' with back there amongst the mists 'appens to be the good general's daughter."

"Mudge! How could you? After all the hospitality they showed us, the food and the room and—"

"Don't get sanctimonious on me, you naked baboon," Mudge snapped up at him. "You're the one who stole their fuckin' symbol. If you'd been decent enough to 'ave let me in on your private reformation, maybe we wouldn't be in this little fix."

"And if you'd told me about yours..."

"You'd 'ave wot, mate? 'Ave concurred in and blessed the assignation? Not bloody likely! Cor!" He pointed ahead. "Too late, they've gone and cut us off. We're finished. That's about right, it is. Me ardor gets cooled before me body's t' get boiled."

"Wait, won't you listen? Listen to me!" Jon-Tom waved the Mulmun, prompting a roar of outrage from their pursuers.

"That's it, mate," said Mudge sarcastically, "stir 'em up good. We wouldn't want to put 'em in a position to grant us mercy or nothin' like that."

"We're not done for yet. Look!" He nodded ahead. "Troops from Witten. Their sentries must have heard the noise and sent for reinforcements."

"Snatched from the jaws o' death at the last instant," said Mudge, relieved. "You cut it too close for comfort sometimes, mate. We 'ave their bloomin' symbol. We'll be treated like 'eroes in Witten, we will. Mate... where are you goin'?"

Jon-Tom had turned right. Instead of running toward the succor and safety offered by the Witten soldiery, which quickly forced its way across the causeway, the spellsinger was racing up a side path that led to the top of the highest hill in sight. They climbed as they ran, leaping boiling waterfalls and mudpots. Wittens and Paultines glared at each other in the darkness, but they were too busy to fight one another now. Besides, it wasn't the first of the month.

"Mate, slow down, wot are you doin'?" Mudge was trying to comprehend his friend's seemingly wild, random flight while keeping an eye on their pursuit. "We can't outrun 'em all. Turn it over to the Wittens and we'll be bloomin' 'eroes. Or give it back to the ruddy Paultines, but do *something* with that ceramic abomination!"

"I intend to, Mudge," said Jon-Tom grimly. "That's why I stole it. I'm going to use it to show both groups the error of their ways."

"We'll be feelin' the arrows o' their ways in a minute. I don't know why they 'aven't tried to bring us down already."

"They're afraid I'll drop the Mulmun," Jon-Tom told him.

"Right." Mudge relaxed a little. "I 'adn't thought o' that. That ghastly thing's our insurance, wot?"

The slope increased just ahead. Water vented from a cleft in the modest cliff. Jon-Tom started climbing with Mudge right behind him.

By the time they reached the top the opposing soldiery had reached the base. Wittens and Paultines eyed one another by the light of their torches, undecided how to react to this unprecedented situation. Some wanted to fight, but for what? For the first time in memory, the all-important Mulmun rested in the hands of an outsider.

"Now, you listen to me, all of you!" Jon-Tom held the sculpture over his head. The significance of the gesture was not lost on his pursuers. In an instant, he had absolute quiet save for the hiss of water and the crackle of torches.

"I know what this is and what it stands for. So do all of you, or rather, you think you do. You believe it stands for honor and dignity and victory in battle. You're wrong. It doesn't stand for a damn one of those things. Where I come from we've had to deal with this kind of internecine stupidity a little longer than you have, and I think we've learned a few things about peace and about the futility of war."

"Give it back to us!" shouted a voice from the crowd of Paultines. It was General Pocknet. "Give it back to us and we'll let you depart with your genitals, man! As for that one"—and he gestured toward Mudge—"him I want!"

The otter made an obscene gesture in the general's direction, concealing himself as he did so behind Jon-Tom's bulk.

"No, give it over to us!" shouted the leader of the Wittens. "Give it to us and you can name your reward, man. You can wipe out the memory of six months of shame for us."

"I'll win the day for no group." Jon-Tom held the Mulmun firmly in one hand and used the other to encompass the valley of the springs in a single sweeping gesture.

"There's enough warmth and water here for all to enjoy. There's no need to go through this mad bloodletting once a month. At heart I believe all of you are good, but you've been suffering from a communal illness for a long time, so long that you've no idea how to treat it. Well, I do, and I'm going to cure the lot of you right now."

A collective gasp and not a few screams came from the mass of fighters gathered at the base of the cliff as Jon-Tom drew back his right arm and heaved the Mulmun as far out into the night as he could. One of the screams came from Mudge.

Every face turned to follow the Mulmun's descent. It seemed to fall in slow motion, turning over several times in the moonlight. It landed on an outjutting rocky snag in the center of a large hot pool and shattered noisily. The pieces disappeared instantly beneath the superheated surface.

"There!" Jon-Tom put his hands on his hips and glared down at them. "See how easy that was? Aren't you all ashamed? Now you can shake hands with your neighbors for the first time in years. Do you realize what this means? It means that yesterday was the last day any of you had to die for the use of the springs. Now you can share in its bounty equally, as you should have from the beginning." He smiled beatifically down at his audience. "Blessed are the peacemakers."

The silence he had requested before his polemic continued after he'd concluded. Soldiers from Witten glanced uncertainly at hereditary enemies from Pault. Conversation between them was hesitant at first, uneasy, but soon blossomed into earnest discussion. General Pocknet made his way through the crowd to greet his opposite number from Witten. They talked rapidly and with passion before finally shaking hands.

Then Pocknet turned to gaze upward and said clearly, with the obvious concurrence of the other commander, "Tear out their eyes!"

The cry was taken up with great enthusiasm by both groups of soldiers, who began scrambling determinedly up the steep but short cliff. Jon-Tom ducked as arrows flew over his head and spears began to land uncomfortably close.

Mudge led him down the opposite slope. "But I don't understand," Jon-Tom muttered dazedly as he ran.

"I understand, mate." Mudge spared a backward glance. "I understand that we'd better get a decent 'ead start out o' that steep spot or there won't be nothin' left to worry about understandin'." The cries and shouts of their enraged pursuers were loud behind them.

"Cheer up, guv." Mudge held onto his hat with one hand as he ran. "At least you got 'em to agree on somethin'."

"But I still don't understand," Jon-Tom murmured, also checking behind them to make certain the recipients of his helpfulness weren't getting any closer. "I did what was best for them, for all of them."

"You did wot you thought were best for them, mate, and there's a small but important difference there. But I 'ave to 'and it to you, you did get 'em workin' together. Now, shut up and run."

Utterly downcast and defeated, Jon-Tom allowed his legs to carry him along....

Night and mist helped them to shake the determined pursuit, though for a while it seemed as though the prairie dogs were going to chase them to the ends of the world. In addition, the Duggakurra Hills had given way to a low-lying marshy region thick with moss-draped trees and long-petaled flowers that moaned when the slightest breeze disturbed them. Not good country for civilized folk to be prowling around in at night, and so the Wittens and Paultines reluctantly abandoned the chase.

Insects and tiny amphibians filled the air with a steady humming and buzzing. By the time Mudge located a little hillock that was reasonably dry, Jon-Tom was soaked to the skin from wading through murky water and clinging muck. He watched as Mudge started a fire.

"Think we ought to risk that here?" He glanced nervously into the darkness. He wasn't fearful of catching cold. The night was warm and humid. But the marsh might be alive with disease-carrying insects, and he conjured up disturbing images of plague-carrying water bugs and giant leeches.

"We're safe enough now, mate, I think." The otter added a few more twigs to the fire. The green wood sputtered in protest, burning only reluctantly. Mudge eyed the surrounding landscape. "One o' your mentor Clothagrump's balmly tropical paradises, wot? This country's bloody sickenin', it is. Not that I mind the water, mind. I'm as at 'ome in it as out, and well you know it." He plucked distastefully at his filthy vest. "But it plays 'ell with a gentleman's wardrobe."

Jon-Tom sat down next to the fire and clasped his arms around his knees as he stared into the flames. He was too tired even to eat.

"I just don't understand what happened. All I wanted to do was bring them peace and harmony." He glared suddenly across the flames. "And all you wanted was a piece."

Mudge was chewing reflectively on a strip of fish jerky. "Somethin' you need to learn bad, guv, is to stop messin' in other folks' business. Ain't nothin' most folks hate worse than good intentions. Might be they'll be better off now for wot you've done this night, but that doesn't mean they'll be any 'appier.

"Seems to me they 'ad their relationship pretty well worked out. If you're goin' to 'ave a war with your neighbors, you might as well do it on a regular schedule. Everyone's prepared and ready and there ain't no nasty surprises sneakin' up on you in the middle of the night. Me, I wouldn't care for the lack o' spontaneity, but I've 'eard tell o' far less civilized ways of settlin' differences between folks."

"There's nothing civilized about it," Jon-Tom grumbled, "but I guess I shouldn't be surprised. That's typical of this whole stinking world."

It was quiet for a long time around the fire. Mudge finished his jerky, rummaged through his pack until he found another. Like any incorrigible philanderer, he always went to his assignations prepared to travel in a hurry. He waved the piece of dried fish at his companion as he spoke, using it the way a schoolmaster might use a ruler.

"Well now, mate, 'tis true I can't comment on that without 'avin' ever 'ad the dubious privilege of visitin' your world, but for the sake of argument let's just say that you 'appen to be accurate in your presumptions and that this world is stinkin' and uncivilized. That accepted, it also 'appens to be me 'ome. I 'ave to live 'ere, and the sad fact o' the matter is that you do too. So maybe you ought to climb down off your pulpit and quit prejudgin' folks accordin' to otherworldly standards. You might get along a mite better and you'll certainly save yourself a lot o' discomfort."

"I can't help it, Mudge," Jon-Tom replied softly, staring down at his hands. "It's my legal training, or maybe just my natural disposition, but when I encounter pain and unhappiness and suffering, I have to try to do something about it."

Mudge nodded back in the direction of Witten and Pault. "There were pain in that relationship, that's for sure, but there's a certain dollop o' pain in everyone's existence. Maybe even in your world. As for un'appiness, I suspect that those folks were just as 'appy and content as could be until you busted in on 'em."

Jon-Tom looked up at the otter. "But it was *wrong,* Mudge."

"Only by your standards, mate. Mind now, I ain't saying yours ain't better; only that they're yours and maybe nobody else's, and you'd better quit tryin' to impose 'em on every bunch you feel sorry or compassionate for."

Jon-Tom sighed, moved the duar onto his knees. When he flicked the strings, lonely notes drifted out over the surrounding water.

"Now wot? You goin' to try and spellsing me over to your way o' thinkin'?"

Jon-Tom shook his head. "I don't feel like spellsinging now. If you don't mind, I'm going to indulge in a little musical sulking."

He began to play without an eye toward any particular end, to play just to amuse himself and take his mind off their present predicament. Where was the benign tropical land Clothahump had told him about, the land alive with friendly people and ripe strange fruits waiting to be plucked from low-hanging branches and brilliant hothouse flowers? Not within walking distance, that was for sure. They were going to have to find a boat.

Unless he could spellsing one up. Sure, why not? His spirits rose slightly. He'd done it once before. This time he'd be able to avoid the mistakes which had plagued them on their previous water journey.

He strained for the right song, a safe and proper boat song. Mudge had been lying on his back, his paws behind his head. Now he sat up sharply, his nose twitching.

"I thought you weren't goin' to try any magic-makin'."

"We need a boat. Remember how I did it before?"

"Oi, I remember. I remember it made you fallin' down drunk for nearly a week."

"It won't happen again," Jon-Tom assured him. "I'll be more careful this time. I've reviewed all the lyrics in my mind and they're perfectly innocuous."

"That's wot you always say." He retreated behind a large tree to watch as Jon-Tom began his song.

His first thought had been of "Amos Moses," but there was no boat directly mentioned and the song possessed disquieting overtones. Another Jerry Reed ditty served fine, however. He modified the lyrics slightly, confident he could call up a fully stocked Everglades-style swamp skimmer to carry them speedily southward through the marsh to distant Quasequa.

Sparkling, dancing motes appeared in the air around him. Gneechees, the best indication that his spellsinging was working. A different light, yellow and brown, began to form a sheet just above the surface of the water.

"See, no trouble at all." He concluded the song with a Van Halenish flourish not exactly appropriate to Jerry Reed, and waited while the object solidified and took form.

It had a flat deck and bottom, just like the swamp skimmer Jon-Tom had hoped for. But as he peered into the night he frowned. There was no sign of the airplane prop that should have been mounted aft. He shrugged. A small oversight in the magic. Maybe he'd confused a verse or two. An outboard would serve adequately.

The craft bumped gently against the shore. Mudge walked down to pick up the rope attached to the bow end.

There was no inboard. There was no outboard. There wasn't even a rudder. But there was plenty of board.

The raft was fashioned of split logs. It was eight feet wide by ten long. Mounted on each side was a large, split-bladed oar that could be used to propel it slowly through the water.

"An elegant example o' otherworldly technology," Mudge observed sarcastically.

"I don't understand. I tried so hard, I was so careful." He strummed the duar. "Maybe if I tried again . . ."

"No, no, mate!" said Mudge hastily, putting his paws over bare fingers. "Leave us not push our luck. So it ain't elaborate and it ain't fast and it ain't labor-savin'. But it floats, and it beats cuttin' down green trees to try and make one ourselves."

"But I can do better than this, Mudge. I know I can."

"Best not to get greedy where magic's involved, guv. You might make it better, 'tis true. Then again, you might sink wot we 'ave, and we'd be back to walkin'. A bush in the 'and's worth two in the bird, right? No tellin' wot you might call up a second time."

As if to emphasize the otter's concern, the water at the raft's stern began to froth and bubble. Mudge raced up the sand to grab for his bow and arrows while Jon-Tom backed slowly away from the water's edge. Something was materializing at the back of the boat that had nothing to do with its locomotion or seaworthiness.

Eyes. Eyes the size of plates.

VII

They glowed bright yellow against the night, and each was centered with a tiny, bright black pupil. Then there were two more emerging from the water nearby, and another pair, until ten hung staring down at the little islet.

Trouble was, they all belonged to the same creature. Nor did they operate always in pairs. Instead they drifted with a sickening looseness on the ends of thin, flexible strands that protruded from a smoothly rounded, glowing skull. Arms and tentacles rose from around the raft. Two of them seemed to be holding the bald yellow skull in place, lest it drift off on its own.

There was a long thin slit of a mouth, dark against the glowing bulbous head. It was a strip of solidity in a mass of insubstantial semitransparent yellow luminosity. You could see swamp water and the raft and trees right through it.

"Go away!" Jon-Tom stuttered. "I didn't sing you up! Mudge, I didn't sing this up."

"Right, mate," said Mudge, his tone indicating what he thought of his companion's disclaimer. He held his bow at the ready, but what was there to shoot at? He was confident his shafts would pass clean through the apparition.

"I know wot it is, mate. 'Tis a Will-o'-the-Wisp, for certain. I've heard tell of them livin' in swamps and marshes and such places, if you can call that livin'."

"There is no such thing as a Will-o'-the-Wisp." Jon-Tom held tight to his duar as though its mere existence might protect them. "They're not living things, just floating globes of swamp gas."

"And what are you?" said the Will-o'-the-Wisp in a surprisingly resonant tone for such an insubstantial creature. "An earthbound sack of water with a few brains floating around inside one end." It nudged the raft, which was shoved halfway up onto the tiny beach. Swamp water sloshed over Jon-Tom's boots. "You hit me with this," the wraith said accusingly.

"Now, why would you go and say a thing like that, mate?" said an injured Mudge. "Wot would we be doin' with a bunch o' dead logs like that when we 'ave this nice, dry little island to spend our lives on?"

"Don't lie, Mudge." The otter threw up his hands and looked imploringly heavenward.

The Wisp floated out of the water, hovering above the tallest trees. Glowing eyeballs focused on Jon-Tom, all ten of them. Then they shifted to stare down at Mudge.

Mudge smiled ingratiatingly up at the ghostly horror. " 'E's not with me, guv'nor. I'm goin' this way, 'e's goin' that way. Now if you'll just excuse me . . ." The otter turned to dive into the water.

"I mean you no harm," the Wisp told them. "I was only curious because this"—and he nudged the raft all the way out of the water—"seemed to appear from Nowhere. Nowhere is a land my kind usually have to ourselves, except for the occasional tourist."

"It was an accident," Jon-Tom explained. "We needed some transportation, so I called this up. I didn't know you were anywhere around." He hesitated, asked, "Are you sure you aren't just swamp gas?"

"I should be insulted," replied the Wisp, "but I am not, because the fact is that I *am* largely swamp gas." To demonstrate this truism, several tentacles broke free and drifted off into the distance. They were rapidly regenerated.

"I just don't like being called swamp gas, that's all."

"No harm intended," said Jon-Tom. "We all have pet names that we dislike. For instance, not long ago someone called me a preppie. Say, maybe you can help us out. We're heading south from here for a place called Quasequa. Anything about the country between here and there you can tell us about?"

"I linger longest in Nowhere," the Wisp informed him. "Does this Quasequa lie in that region?"

"I hope not," Jon-Tom confessed.

"Then I do not know of it. But this I do know. If you go south from here, you have the great Wrounipai to cross, and that is very near to Nowhere."

"You mean there's much more o' this filthy disgustin' 'ell ahead o' us? I want to be sure," Mudge added pleasantly, "before I slit me friend's throat."

The water glowed where it foamed around the Will-o'-the-Wisp's body.

"A great deal more, travelers. Even I do not know its full extent."

"Tropical flowers." Mudge was staring forlornly at the dark water. "Compliant lasses waitin' to greet you with open arms." He turned angrily on Jon-Tom. "You know wot, mate? I always did 'ave a 'ankerin' to try some turtle soup."

Jon-Tom smiled up at the Wisp. "We thank you for that information, even if it's not quite what we wanted to hear."

"We don't always get to hear what we want to, do we?" The energetic phosphorescence curled about itself. "Now, I"—and the multi-eyed skull floated frighteningly near to Jon-Tom—"happen to like music. I heard yours. Could you sing me a little more?"

"Why, I'd be glad to."

Mudge put his paws over his ears. "Saints preserve us, not another music lover, and this one ain't even got the decency to 'ave proper ears."

The unfortunate otter was kept awake all that night as Jon-Tom sang every old Halloween song he could remember. The eerie chords drifted out over the calm swamp water while the Will-o'-the-Wisp danced delightedly in the air, tossing off sparks and glowing splinters of its gaseous self and making lowly lichens and algae flare with rainbows.

Jon-Tom couldn't remember the last time he'd had such an appreciative audience. Sadly, when the Will-o'-the-Wisp's interest finally evaporated, it did, too.

The otter's mood hadn't improved much by the time morning dawned. "Wonder if this wondrous Quasequa even exists," he grumbled. "Probably some poor fallin'-down mud-town if it does. Wouldn't be the first time 'is sorcererness 'as lied to us."

"He doesn't lie, Mudge. It's against the wizard's code to lie. He told me so."

Mudge sighed and looked disgusted. "The companions fate 'ands you." His voice rose. "Suppose this bloomin' paradise do exist? Suppose 'tis everything your 'ard-shelled instructor says it is? Wot 'e neglected to tell us before we set out on this little stroll is that there's a thousand leagues o' swamp between 'ere and there, wot? Wot a load o' wizardly crap!"

Jon-Tom looked unhappy. "He wasn't too specific about the distance to be crossed. I admit I didn't press him on the point."

"I'd like to press 'im on the point," Mudge said grimly, savoring the thought as he fingered his short sword. "I'd like to press the point right through the back o' 'is deceiving shell and use the 'ole for a—"

"Careful, Mudge," Jon-Tom said warningly. "It's not healthy to be disrespectful of a sorcerer's powers even if he's a fair distance from you."

"Frog farts! I tell you, mate, I'm gettin' fed up with these bloody surprises o' yours. For 'alf a gold piece I'd leave you now and 'ead back to the good ol' Bellwoods."

"Back through Witten and Pault? By yourself?"

"You broke their bloomin' totem, not me. Besides, I've got some unfinished business back in Pault I wouldn't mind taking care of."

"If General Pocknet gets his paws on you, he'll finish your business."

Mudge shrugged. "So I'd circle around both towns. Then 'tis back to the Bellwoods for me, back to Lynchbany and Timswitty and Dornay and real civilization. Back to..."

Even had Mudge not rambled on, it's unlikely either of them would have seen the shadow. The swamp was a world of shadows, and one more was easily lost in the shifting, diffused light. The shadow blended in completely with trees and creepers.

But this shadow was different. It moved independently of those which blanketed the island, moved with purpose and exceptional speed. They didn't see it until it was directly over them, and then it was too late.

Mudge yelled a warning while Jon-Tom dove for his ramwood staff. The otter reached for his sword: no time for bow and arrows.

Then it was gone, as quickly as it had appeared. Mudge lay panting hard on the sand, eyes wide, his sword held defensively in front of his chest even though there was nothing left to defend against. The danger had vanished along with the shadow.

In its place it left three things: Jon-Tom's ramwood staff, his sword, and a single steel-gray feather. The feather was four inches wide and two feet long. It lay motionless near the otter, the only hard evidence of something which had come and gone with blinding speed.

Mudge picked it up, ran it through his paws. The quill was as thick around as his finger. He straightened his cap, which somehow had stayed on his head during the seconds-long fight, and gazed eastward. The shadow had disappeared in that direction, carrying Jon-Tom in a single brace of impossibly big talons.

The otter considered his situation in light of his recent declarations. The raft was intact, and in addition to his own weapons and supplies, he also had the spellsinger's. He was uninjured.

Well, that was that, then. So much for one brave, ignorant, meddling, exasperating, immature spellsinger. There was no shame now in returning home. He would even report the debacle to the wizard Clothahump. Sure, he owed the unfortunate Jon-Tom that much. At least the youth wouldn't be worrying about returning to his own world anymore. As for the wizard, he would accept his student's demise philosophically, and there was no way he could blame it on the otter. It had happened too fast.

One minute Jon-Tom had been sitting there next to him, listening politely to his complaints, and the next he'd been carried off by a dark cloud. Not Mudge's fault, no sir. Couldn't have been prevented.

He loaded the raft and stepped aboard, then pushed out into the water. At last he could start living his own life, without fear of being conscripted for some lethal journey halfway across a hostile world. He could get back to living like a normal person again, could sleep soundly once more without listening for strange sounds in the night.

Certainly there was nothing he could do. There wasn't, was there? He pushed angrily against the shaft of the split-bladed paddle and wondered why his thoughts were so damn troubled....

Jon-Tom hung in the grasp of the powerful talons and did not struggle, hoping the enormous eagle which had carried him off preferred live food to dead. Because dead he'd certainly be if the bird let him fall. The Wrounipai flashed past far below.

He twisted as best he was able in the unyielding grip and examined his captor. The eagle had at least a twenty-foot wingspan. It carried him effortlessly. Like the much-smaller feathered inhabitants of this world, it wore a kilt which trailed backward over hips and tail and a vest with a peculiar zigzagging pattern of black on gray. The pattern was almost familiar to Jon-Tom, but he didn't pursue it through his memory. At the moment he was not in a position to spend much time doing a detailed analysis of another creature's clothing.

Since the bird showed no sign of stopping, Jon-Tom tried to make a detached survey of the terrain below. It was much as the Will-o'-the-Wisp had described: endless swamp and water stretching off in all directions spotted here and there with tiny islets.

A short while later their apparent destination hove into view. Some powerful tectonic disturbance had thrust a vast mass of black basalt straight up out of the earth. It was thickly overgrown with climbing trees and vines as thick as a man's body.

An opening showed in the rock two-thirds of the way up its side. The eagle dove straight for it. For an instant Jon-Tom didn't think those huge wings would make it, but the eagle just managed to squeeze through the opening without bashing Jon-Tom's head or legs against the rock below.

The opening was not a cave. It was a tunnel leading to the interior of the butte. The inside was hollow.

The eagle flapped its wings twice before touching down on one foot. It flicked its prize away, almost contemptuously.

Jon-Tom rolled over several times, feeling gravel cut into his face. He suffered the pain and chose instead to do his best to protect the duar strapped to his back. When he finally rolled to a stop he was bruised and scratched, but otherwise in one piece.

Keeping one eye on the eagle, he rose to examine his surroundings.

The hollow place was not a volcanic throat, but rather the result of some convulsive fracturing. Six-sided stone columns rose toward the distant sky. Jon-Tom had seen them before, in pictures of the Giant's Causeway in Scotland and the Devil's Postpile in California's High Sierra.

Where each column had broken, a natural perch was formed. These were occupied by numerous nests and homes. The floor of the great open shaft was a charnel house full of bones picked clean by razor-sharp beaks.

The occupants of the homes and the owners of the beaks were normal-sized avians. Not one stood more than four feet in height. With increasing interest, he noted kilts belonging to hawks and falcons, ospreys and fish hawks and vultures. They soared and swam through the air of the shaft, coming and going through the opening above and, less often, through the tunnel that had served as his own entrance. They all seemed to be talking at once. The multiple screeching was deafening.

Several of them walked or flew by to greet the

giant who had brought him with a spirited, "Hail, Gyrnaught!" Each raised a right wingtip in salute. That also struck Jon-Tom as somehow familiar, but he didn't pay overmuch attention to it. There were too many other things to try and absorb simultaneously, and he was too disoriented for deep thought.

For one thing, he was far more concerned about his immediate fate, since the giant eagle didn't appear particularly interested in eating him. Not yet, anyway. The mountain of bones which covered the floor of the shaft was anything but reassuring.

The shadow towered over him again. The eagle was not quite as impressive as it had been with its wings outspread, but it was just as intimidating.

"Stand up straight!" the eagle commanded him. Still sore and cramped, Jon-Tom fought to comply with the request.

"They say, 'Hail, Gyrnaught.' You're Gyrnaught?" A minuscule nod of head and beak. The eagle was big enough to bite him in two without straining itself.

"What do you want with me?"

"Not dinner. Flesh is cheap." He gestured with a wing. "Welcome to the Raptor's Lair. You have been brought here to serve, not to be served. *If* you prove yourself."

"I don't understand."

Again the beak dipped, this time to gesture toward the duar. "An instrument. You are a musician?"

"Uh, yeah." Somehow Jon-Tom felt this wasn't the most opportune time to explain that he was also a spellsinger. He might want to demonstrate that talent later. In fact, it was all but a certainty. The longer he could keep that fact a secret from his captor, the better Jon-Tom's chances of catching him unawares.

"I thought as much," said Gyrnaught. "I have need of a musician."

It was in Jon-Tom's mind to comment that the eagle didn't look much like a music lover, but he kept his thoughts to himself. Trying to still his trembling, he struggled to put up a bold front. The fact that he wasn't on the evening's menu helped.

"Quite a place you've got here."

"Ah, this is but the beginning." Gyrnaught was pleased. Good, Jon-Tom thought, gaining a little confidence. He can be flattered. To what extent remained to be seen. "This is only a temporary lair for my troops and myself. They are but the foam of a wave which will fly forth to dominate the whole world. Today this mountain, tomorrow the Wrounipai, later the world! The nest will reign for a thousand years!" The eagle's eyes flashed as if focusing on something only it could see, and that, too, half reminded Jon-Tom of something.

"I don't think I recognize the pattern on your kilt and vest."

"You could not, for it is not of this world. I brought it here from another place many years ago. It has taken me this long to organize just this small striking force." He made a disgusted noise. "The raptors of this world are difficult to convince of the truth."

"Really? Another world? That's interesting. See, I'm from another world myself."

The eagle's eyes narrowed. "Say you so? What were you in your world?"

"A student of law and a singer of songs," he admitted truthfully.

"I have need of song. As for law, I make my own."

"What were you?" Jon-Tom asked hastily, to change the subject.

"I?" The eagle gazed down at him proudly. "I was

a symbol. I was everywhere, in thousands of replications. In stone and steel and brass. In symbols as small as this"—and he held the two great wingtips barely an inch apart—"and in granite monoliths bigger than you can imagine. I was a symbol everywhere and all people bowed down to me.

"But," he went on angrily, "they saw me only as a symbol. They did not stop and pause and consider when they chose one of their own to be a symbol over me. From that moment on my powers were lost. I could not manifest my true self. When their substitute symbol was ground into the dust, only I, of many thousands of me, escaped destruction. While in symbols I was destroyed, in this world I found myself set free. Here I am whole again and can start the work properly, myself." He gestured at the raptors swarming through the shaft, the light dancing on their wings.

"My soldiers will rule above all others. It is destined to be so, destined for the strong to rule over the weak. We of beak and claw shall dictate to those who only can walk. It is right. It is destiny."

It all came together in Jon-Tom's mind. He'd studied too much history for it to escape him for long.

He'd seen Gyrnaught before, in metal and stone standards. Just as the eagle said. Seen him in pictures rising above obscene parade grounds, atop cold inhumane structures, a frozen caricature of evil.

"I know you," he said. "It was before my time, but I know what you stand for."

Gyrnaught looked pleased. "A historian as well as a musician. You will prove even more valuable to the nest. Tell me, then, do you know the Horst Wessel song?"

"No. Like I said, it was before my time. But I know the kind of music you want. What I want to know is, why should I sing for you? Why should I help you spread your old evil to this new world when your infection has already been cleared from mine?"

"Because if you don't, I will bite off your head and swallow it like a pumpkin."

Jon-Tom moved the duar around in front of him. "Can't argue with that kind of logic."

"Ah, you are going to be reasonable, then. That is good. If you continue to be reasonable, you will continue to live. Besides, you should be proud that the nest has need of your services."

"What is it, exactly, that you want?" Jon-Tom sighed.

Gyrnaught gestured at his fellow avians. "These are difficult to inspire. I have not yet been able to convince all of them that they are destined to rule all others, that they belong to the master race."

"Why? Because they have wings and the rest of us don't?"

"Naturally. It is only right for the higher to rule the lower. I will see to it that all the raptors of this world flock to my banner."

"There aren't enough of you. You're just a few species among many."

Gyrnaught looked smug. "We will enlist others to serve under us, and they will do the heavy dying. They will be proud to when they see what the new order is to be."

"You haven't got a chance, any more than your human counterpart did."

"He was a fool, and only a human. I am confident." That beak moved close, but Jon-Tom stood his ground. There was no place to retreat to anyway. "And now we shall see if there is truth to your words. Sing, stir the hearts of my followers, and you will live long."

Jon-Tom did so, though it stung badly. He rationalized his efforts by assuring himself he was only stalling for time. Stalling until Mudge arrived to spirit him out of this place. Then they'd figure out a means of stopping this disease that had crossed over from his own world before it could spread.

He sang all the marches he could think of. The raptors were drawn to the music, dipping low to listen. There was a screech of approval at the conclusion of each martial melody.

When Jon-Tom's lungs finally gave out, Gyrnaught put a friendly wing over him. Jon-Tom felt suddenly unclean.

"You did well, musician! Put aside your otherworldly, primitive moral conceits and join me. I am not ungrateful to those who pledge their lives to me."

Jon-Tom wanted to tell the eagle precisely what he thought of him and his totalitarian philosophy, but he had sense enough to shrug and say instead, "Maybe you've got something here. Maybe it could work in this world if not in the one we've left behind."

"That's the spirit." Gyrnaught patted him on the back, nearly knocking Jon-Tom down. "The others moved too fast and became insane. But I am not insane, and I will not force my wing. Our advance and conquest will be patient, but inexorable. This time the cause will not fall." He looked around.

"Over there is a small cave. A good place for you, unless you would prefer a higher perch."

Jon-Tom let his gaze travel up the vertical walls of the shaft. "I'd never get up or down. I think I'll stay close to the ground."

"A poor, earthbound creature. But you see, with me, you can fly! In truth, good singer, you will be able to lord it over your fellows. Think on that."

Another crushing pat and Gyrnaught walked off to talk with his underlings.

Smooth, Jon-Tom thought. He has the charisma down pat. The odor of the charnel house was powerful in Jon-Tom's nostrils, an echo of similar, greater slaughterhouses from his own world's recent history. That could not be repeated here, *must* not be repeated.

But he had to be careful. Gyrnaught was no fool. He would listen carefully to anything Jon-Tom might sing until he was more confident of his pet human's loyalty. So he had to be careful until he could do something.

He just wasn't sure what.

One thing struck him forcefully as the days passed within the shaft: the ease with which Gyrnaught had taken control of the minds and spirits of this world's raptors. They drilled efficiently on the ground and in the open air overhead, seemingly having readily abrogated their traditional independence in favor of Gyrnaught's rule. It just wasn't like them, according to those Jon-Tom had met in his travels.

One day he asked an osprey about it. To his surprise, the bird informed him that when left to themselves, the hawks and falcons and other birds of prey often questioned the wisdom of Gyrnaught's philosophy. They weren't sure they really wanted to conquer the world. But in his presence they were helpless. The force of the eagle's personality and the strength of his arguments overwhelmed any hesitant opposition. Furthermore, anyone who questioned it was never seen again. So there was no organized opposition to his plans.

The osprey left Jon-Tom much encouraged. Maybe they weren't confident enough to oppose him, but at least not all of the raptors had signed over their souls to Gyrnaught. That uncertainty could be exploited, but not gradually. Gyrnaught would surely trace any such dissension to its source, and that would be the end of Jonathan Thomas Meriweather.

No, it would have to be fast, a sudden collapse of will if not outright opposition. Trouble was, all the songs he knew were full of life and delight and fun. He didn't know any music darker than the martial bombast Gyrnaught himself favored. Nor could he think of anything potentially disruptive which would work fast enough. And he didn't think he had much time. His renditions of old marches were quickly losing their edge as his own disenchantment manifested itself, and Gyrnaught was getting suspicious. One day soon the eagle might decide to go hunting for a new musician.

He was sitting in his private alcove on the bed of straw that had been provided for his comfort, chatting with a small falcon named Hensor.

"Tell me again," he asked the raptor, "why you all follow Gyrnaught so blindly and willingly. Because he's bigger than the rest of you?"

"Of course not," said Hensor. "We follow because he is smarter and knows what's best for the rest of us. He knows how to make us act as a single talon able to strike death into the hearts of any who oppose us."

"Yeah, but nobody's opposing you."

"All oppose us. All who do not bow down to the rule of the master race."

"Well, suppose everyone else did bow down to you?"

"They won't." Hensor spoke with confidence. "We'll have to knock it into their heads. Gyrnaught says so."

"I'm sure he's right, but just suppose, just for a moment, that everyone did bow down to you. Then what?"

"Then we would rule without bloodshed. Except for the inferior races, of course, who would have to be disposed of."

Jon-Tom felt a chill but continued politely. "Who would rule?"

"We would, the raptors would. Under Gyrnaught's enlightened leadership, of course."

"I see." Jon-Tom shifted on the straw. "Suppose all this comes to pass, suppose you conquer the whole world under Gyrnaught's direction. Then what happens?"

"Well..." Hensor hesitated. Evidently Gyrnaught's orations hadn't sought that far into the future. "We wouldn't have to work. Others would do our fishing and hunting and gathering for us."

"Then what will you do?"

"Why, we will rule, naturally."

"But you already have everything you require."

"Then we'll get more."

"More what? How much food can you eat? How much wood do you need for a house or traditional nest?"

"I...I don't know." The falcon shook his head, rubbed at his eyes with the flexible tip of one red-feathered wing. "Your questions hurt my thoughts."

"I know what you'll do, and I'll tell you." Jon-Tom peered quickly outside. Gyrnaught wasn't around. Probably off drilling troops somewhere. "You'll get bored, that's what you'll do. You'll sit around doing nothing until your feathers fall out and you can't fly anymore. You'll look like a bunch of chickens."

"Take care," Hensor warned him. "Some of my best friends are chickens."

"Well, you know what I mean. Laziness will result in flightlessness."

Hensor's confidence returned. "No it won't. Gyrnaught's drills will keep us strong."

"Strong so you can do what? No, once you've conquered everyone else, you'll get bored and soft because you won't have anything else to fight for, and defeated people will see to all your needs. Raptors are born to hunt. Without any need to do that, you'll all get flabby and flightless."

"You confuse me."

"Oh, I don't mean to do that," Jon-Tom assured him immediately. "Heavens no. I'm just concerned, that's all. You're all such strong fliers now, I'd hate to see you waste away."

"What do you suggest?"

Jon-Tom moved close, spoke in a conspiratorial whisper. "There'll be one of you who'll never get fat and lazy because he'll be too busy making sure the rest of you stay in line. Those that don't, of course, are liable to end up on his dinner table."

Hensor looked shocked. "No, that would never happen! Gyrnaught would never do that."

Jon-Tom shrugged. "He'd only be following his own philosophy. The strong rule, the weak perish." He hoped he was having some impact on Hensor because the convoluted reasoning was beginning to make him a little dizzy himself. "There is a solution to the problem, though."

"What?" asked Hensor eagerly.

"It's simple. Everyone must be equal. None of the master race must be any less the master than his neighbor. That's only fair, isn't it? That way everyone will have to maintain himself in optimum condition for fighting."

Hensor's expression showed that this notion of all chiefs no Indians was new to him. "Gyrnaught wouldn't like it," he replied slowly.

"Why not? If you're all members of the master race, shouldn't you all have an equal part in ruling the lesser races? He'd still be the prime leader, but you'd all be leaders together. Isn't that how it's always been among the raptors?"

"Yes, that's true," Hensor agreed excitedly. "We could all be leaders. We *are* all leaders." He turned and spread his bright red wings. "I must tell the others!"

Jon-Tom retreated to the depths of his alcove and went through the motions of rearranging his few belongings. Before too much time had passed his attention was drawn outside by a rising din. He smiled to himself as he turned to peek out of the cave.

Something a mite stronger than an animated discussion was taking place among the soldiers of the master race, high up in the air of the central shaft. It appeared to involve a majority of them, in fact. In the midst of the discussion was a large gray shape, dipping and swinging its wingtips in what looked very much like fury.

Soon it was raining feathers. They were of many sizes and colors, and Jon-Tom amused himself by gathering a few and stuffing them into the lining of his cape. As the screeching and angry squawking continued, he casually picked up his duar and strolled toward the path leading to the tunnel. No one paid him the slightest attention, since everyone was fully involved in determining who was qualified to be a leader and who was not.

Apparently Gyrnaught was having some difficulty sorting out this business of multiple leadership, and the offer to make him prime leader wasn't sufficient to satisfy his ego. There was only one leader here, one master! His heretofore obedient soldiery was vigorously disputing this position.

Jon-Tom reached the lip of the tunnel, spared a last backward glance for the argument which had freed him, and then hurried into the passageway. He was almost to the exit when a very large hawk swooped down from a hidden perch near the ceiling to challenge him.

Jon-Tom hadn't expected a guard. This one had

an eight-foot wingspan and gripped a long pole tipped with four sharp points in both flexible wingtips. Jon-Tom was more fearful of its natural weapons. Beak and talons could tear him apart.

"Where are you going, musician?"

"Just getting a little air," Jon-Tom told the guard, smiling thinly. He glanced over his shoulder, eyed the hawk significantly. "Aren't you going to join the discussion and put your application in?"

"What discussion?" The hawk's bright eyes never left him.

"The one where everybody's going to determine who's a proper member of the master race and who isn't."

"I am the sentry," the hawk told him. "That is enough for me to be."

"But everyone else is—" The hawk cut him off by taking a step forward and jamming the sharp spikes against Jon-Tom's belly. Jon-Tom retreated. The hawk followed, prodding him backward.

"Haven't you heard about the discussion?" Jon-Tom asked lamely.

"I'll find out later."

"But everyone's a master now, everyone's a leader."

"I'm only a sentry. I think maybe we'd better talk to Gyrnaught about this. I don't think you're allowed out to 'get a little air.' There's plenty of air in the lair." Again the spikes pricked Jon-Tom's gut, forcing him back another couple of steps.

He was on the verge of panic. Unarmed, there wasn't a chance he could overpower this determined guard. In a little while Gyrnaught might whip his fracturing reich back into shape. When he did, Jon-Tom had a hunch the eagle would do some interrogating. Then he'd come looking for his pet musician, whose clever songs wouldn't save his skin from being slowly peeled from his clever body.

"Can't we talk this over?" he pleaded.

"Nonsense. I can't discuss things with a member of an inferior race because it would—" The hawk stopped in mid-sentence. He pivoted slowly, and as he did so, Jon-Tom saw something like a quill protruding from the back of his skull. It wasn't a quill and it had feathers of its own. An arrow.

The guard fell on his face, a heap of dead feathers.

"Are you goin' to stand there gawkin' all day," snapped Mudge as he notched another arrow into his longbow and tried to see down the tunnel, "or do you think it'd be too much of me to ask that you move your bloody aggravatin' arse?"

VIII

"Mudge!"

"Oi, I know me name and you know yours." The otter was starting to back toward the exit. "Now, if your legs are still connected to your feeble brain, I'd appreciate it if you'd get the latter t' movin' the former."

Mudge led him outside, then down the tree-choked slope to the water's edge, where their raft was beached. Jon-Tom had been disappointed when he'd called it up, but now it was as beautiful as a forty-foot motor yacht. They pushed off and began rowing furiously with the paddles.

From time to time Jon-Tom could see several shapes rise from the hollow interior of the island only to dive back inside.

"Beginnin' to think I'd never run you down, mate," Mudge was saying.

"Why'd you bother, after what you were saying the last time we talked? There were plenty of good reasons for you to forget about me, and none for coming after me."

"Well, let's call it curiosity and leave it at that, mate. If I think on it much I'm liable to get sick. Maybe I was just interested in seein' if you'd ended up as bird food or wotever. Or maybe I'm crazier than a neon worm."

"I don't care why you did it, I'm just glad that you did."

Mudge jerked his head in the direction of the rapidly shrinking island. "Wot 'appened in there, anyways? Never 'eard a screekin' and yowlin' like that in me life. You put a spellsong on 'em?"

"Not exactly. I just sort of convinced them to engage in a dialogue aimed at preventing the spread of injustice while maintaining equality among themselves."

"Cor, no wonder they was 'avin' a bloody mess of it! The poor flap-faces. Think they'll come after us after they get things sorted out among themselves?"

"Not right away, if then. If their leader survives this little debate, he's going to be too busy trying to put his organization back together again to worry about my whereabouts for a while. It probably wouldn't be a bad idea to keep a close watch on the sky for a few days, though."

"I follow you, mate. We won't be surprised from above like that again."

"Damn right we won't." He turned thoughtful. "I'm hoping that Gyrnaught... that's the eagle who snatched me... finds out what happens to the kind of system he espouses, finds out that it's doomed to self-destruction. I hope he learns that power corrupts absolutely. That greed quickly overtakes loyalty in the minds of supposedly obedient followers."

"Why 'e grab you anyways, mate, if not for munching?"

"He needed a musician."

"Tch. All 'e 'ad to do was ask, and I'd 'ave told him as 'ow 'e was wastin' 'is time." He grinned. "Sounds like a fowl business all the way 'round, mate."

If he hadn't just saved his life, Jon-Tom would have pushed him overboard.

The further south they rowed, the more relaxed Jon-Tom became. Clearly Gyrnaught had his wings full with his newly enlightened flock, and even if he did find the time to wonder where his musician had gone to, he had no way of knowing which way Jon-Tom had fled. As days slipped by, he was more and more convinced he'd seen the last of the eagle.

His relief was tempered by their surroundings, which grew thicker and more humid than ever. Clothahump's "pleasant tropical country" was closing in on them with a vengeance. The trees of the Wrounipai towered above their frail raft, supported by labyrinthine root systems which sometimes choked off their chosen route, forcing them to detour to east or west. Occasionally the roots themselves grew so tall it was possible to paddle beneath them. Shelf fungi and toadstools clung determinedly to the bases of the smaller trees.

What little dry land they did encounter was so thickly overgrown with brambles and thorn thickets that they had to hunt carefully to find campsites for the night. Mudge insisted they do this because the regular evening concert of eerie squeals and groans made him leery of anchoring out on the water.

Man and otter would huddle close together in front of their small fire for a long while before drifting off into an uneasy, disturbed sleep. But while both found the nocturnal noises unnerving, nothing slouched out of the muck to devour them as they slept.

Still, the dark, dank gloominess was all-pervading. Not quite as Clothahump had described it.

Mist clung to them day and night, rising from the steaming surface of the water. When it rained, which was often, the heat abated somewhat, but it became almost impossible to judge direction. This forced them to seek shelter beneath the towering roots of the larger trees. After a couple of weeks, Jon-Tom was certain the morning growth that covered his face was more mildew than beard.

Everything in the Wrounipai was slick with moss or rough with fungi. The intense humidity threatened to rot the clothes off their backs. It also seemed to penetrate to work on their minds, disorienting them and making identification of the most ordinary objects difficult.

They had beached the raft on a sand bar beneath the natural roof formed by several interlocking air roots, sharing it with freshwater crustaceans and other inhabitants of the brackish environment. Their campfire crackled fitfully, the flames struggling against the cloying atmosphere. It was a pitch-black night. Trees blocked out the clouds, and the clouds shuttered the moon. Their only light came from the fire.

But he could still hear, and something sounded very peculiar indeed.

Jon-Tom roused himself, his eyes heavy from lack of sleep. Nearby, Mudge lay rolled up in his thin blanket, snoring on, oblivious of the strange rushing noise which had awakened Jon-Tom.

The spellsinger listened for a long time before donning his cape and walking to the edge of the water. The sound was an unnatural one, steady and moist, like a rushing in a vacuum. He put his hand out into the rain, jerked it back as if he'd been stung, then slowly extended it a second time. He stared at it in wonder, shook his head to clear it. The phenomenon persisted. So he wasn't crazy.

Water beaded up against his extended hand. It felt like normal rain. It looked like normal rain. He drew back his hand again and tasted of it. A pungent, salty flavor that wasn't normal. He was relieved for that. It meant his senses were functioning properly, and he was relieved that it was the precipitation that was deranged and not himself.

He watched it until he was completely awake, then walked back to wake Mudge.

"Huh . . . wuzzat, wot?" The otter blinked up at him. Jon-Tom's face must have presented a less than pleasing sight, lit only by the feeble glow of their campfire. "Wot is it, mate? Cor, 'tis black as a magistrate's thoughts out."

"It's still night. The sun's not up yet."

"Then why," asked a suddenly irritated Mudge, "did you wake me?"

"It's raining, Mudge."

The otter paused a moment, listening. "I can hear it. So wot?"

"It's not raining right."

"Not right? 'Ave you gone daft?"

"Mudge, it's raining *up*."

"Gone over the edge," the otter muttered. "Poor bugger." He slipped free of his blanket and staggered sleepily toward the water's edge. A paw reached out into the rain. Water beaded up against the back of his hand while the palm stayed dry.

"I'll be corn'oled, so it is."

Jon-Tom's hand reached out parallel to the otter's. "What does it mean?" It was fascinating to watch the droplets strike the back of his hand, crawl around the fingers, and shoot up into the dark sky.

"I guess it means, guv, that 'is wizardness wasn't kiddin' when he told us this part o' the world was tropical. My guess is that the land 'ereabouts gets so wet from the 'umidity that it 'as to give back some o' the water to the sky from time to time. Not such an improper arrangement, if you thinks about it. Keeps everythin' in balance, wot? Up, down, up, down: a body could get confused."

"I can see what it's doing, but what does it mean?"

Mudge pulled his paw out of the upside-down storm and licked the fur on his wrist to dry it as he strolled back toward his makeshift bed.

"It means that the world's a wet place, mate."

Jon-Tom watched the up-pour a while longer before rejoining his friend. He curled up underneath his cape but lay wide-awake, staring out into the storm. The steady rush of sky-bound water was soothing.

"Actually, it's kind of neat. I mean, there's a wonderful symmetry to it, a kind of meteorological poetry."

"Right, mate. Me thought exactly. Now go to sleep."

Jon-Tom turned to him. The otter's silhouette was barely visible against the fading fire. "You live too fast, Mudge. Sometimes I don't think you have the slightest appreciation for any of the world's natural wonders."

"Wot, me?" He blinked sleepily at Jon-Tom. "'Ow can you say that, mate? Why, this upside-down drizzle, it revises me 'ole estimation o' 'ow the world's constructed."

"Does it? Then maybe there's hope for you yet, if it enables you to appreciate the strangeness and beauty of nature, the astounding surprises that it has in store for all of us. There is magnificence in a slightly altered natural phenomenon like rain."

"Actually, mate, I see it a little differently. See, I always thought the world was a toilet. 'Tis nice to learn that it can function as a bidet also." Whereupon he rolled over once more and went back to sleep.

Jon-Tom resigned himself to the fact that his companion was, aesthetically speaking, a primitive. He contemplated the upside-down rain thoughtfully. It was disorienting, but lovely and not at all dangerous. If naught else it was a welcome change to their monotonous surroundings.

It continued to pour upward for a good part of the early morning. Standing on the raft, they remained clean and dry as they paddled through a sheet of rising precipitation. The raft was a little cube of dryness sliding across the plant-choked waters of the Wrounipai.

Eventually the humidity fell below a hundred percent and they left the region of constant rain behind. The water had become a narrow, lazy stream, one of many cutting through parallel ridges of upthrust granite and schist. It was an improvement over the country they had crossed, but not the balmy paradise Clothahump had described. Dense undergrowth still crowded for space among the stone and water. They found themselves paddling down a green tunnel lit by intermittent sunlight.

On one rocky outcropping Mudge located bushes which produced delicious green-black berries shaped like teardrops, and the two travelers spent a whole afternoon gorging themselves. The stony island provided a clean, dry resting place as well, and they decided to spend the night.

Jon-Tom awoke the following morning, stretched, and was awake in an instant. They were surrounded. Not by Gyrnaught's minions, nor by the faceless demons of Markus the Ineluctable.

There were thirty otters staring back at him, and every one of them looked exactly like Mudge. Jon-Tom had experienced his share of oddities recently, but nothing to match this.

"Good morning, Jon-Tom!" the thirty chorused in unison.

He tried to rein in his panicky thoughts. Was he seeing some kind of multiple mirror image fashioned by someone well versed in the wizardly arts? No. If that were the case, they should all move as well as talk simultaneously. But some were bending over in laughter, others talking to their neighbors, still others doffing their hats by way of greeting. Each moved independently of the other.

There was a simpler explanation, of course. This world had finally sent him over the edge.

One similarity stood out on careful inspection. It was enough to convince him he hadn't tumbled down some metaphysical rabbit hole. While each duplicate of the otter moved independently of the others, displaying different expressions and making different gestures, every one of them stayed in one spot. None retreated and none approached.

Until one stumbled into him from behind and nearly scared him to death. He grabbed this sole mobile by the shoulders and shook it violently.

"Mudge, is it you?"

The otter's eyes were glazed. "I ain't sure no more, mate. I used to think I were me. Now I ain't so sure. I was out gatherin' breakfast berries when I came back to see this lot." He gestured at the circle of Mudges enclosing their campsite. "Maybe I ain't me. Maybe one o' them is me."

"We're all you," said the otterish chorus, "every one of us."

"Yes, but I'm a better you," insisted a pair of Mudges off to the right.

"Not a chance," argued three across the circle. "We're the best Mudges, we are."

"Oi, you couldn't fool your own real parents," declared a quartet of Mudges from the right flank.

"There has to be an explanation for this," Jon-Tom said quietly. "A sensible explanation."

"Sure there is, mate," said the Mudge standing next to him. "I've been 'angin' around you too long, and now I'm as loony as you are."

"Neither of you is loony," said the two Mudges directly in front of them.

As Jon-Tom blinked, or thought he blinked, the Mudges disappeared. They were replaced by something much worse: a pair of six-foot-two-inch-tall, indigo-and-green-clad Jon-Toms. He stared at the perfect duplicates of himself.

"A trick, it's a trick of some kind. An optical illusion." Sure it was, but who was doing it, and why? They'd heard nothing during the night, and the sensitive Mudge would surely have been alerted by the encroachment of so many intruders. He turned to the otter.

"You haven't heard anyone on the island besides us?"

"Not a soul," the otter assured him. "But we sure 'as 'ell 'ave acquired some company."

"There has to be more than one of them at work here," Jon-Tom muttered. "There's too much happening simultaneously for a single creature to be responsible."

"You're right there." He turned on the voice, only to see three more Jon-Toms chatting amongst themselves. One leaned against his ramwood staff, another pointed, while the third studied his hands. But they stayed rooted in three spots. In fact, it seemed as if... yes, he was positive. The three new Jon-Toms occupied the same locations as three now-vanished Mudges. The otters had turned into Jon-Toms.

"I don't know who you are or what you are, but if you're trying to frighten us, you've failed."

"Speak for yourself, mate," Mudge mumbled under his breath.

"Frighten you? Why should we want to frighten you?" inquired a trio of Mudges off to their left.

Once more Jon-Tom's mind underwent an unsettling shift in perception. The Mudges vanished, to be replaced by three trees. Each consisted of a trunk which topped out in a weaving, flexible point. Flowers grew from the base of the trunk. In the center of each was an indistinct, puttylike face. Jon-Tom could see eyes and mouths but no nose or chin. An ear protruded from each side, and a single thick, tapering vine grew from the top of the tree. Or maybe the trunk became the vine; Jon-Tom couldn't tell where one ended and the other began. Maybe there was no tree: just the single tall vine.

"We don't want to frighten you. We're just practicing our art. It's rare that we get an audience." Jon-Tom turned and looked behind him. Three more Mudges had disappeared. They had been replaced by another pair of trees and a single giant butterfly. It fluttered but didn't stray from its fixed position.

"That's so true," the butterfly declaimed. "Our audiences are few and far between."

"Your art?" Jon-Tom murmured.

"We're mimics, imitators, mimes," said one of the vines. "It started as a defense against the plant-eaters. Our trees are actually below the surface." So these *were* vines he was looking at, Jon-Tom mused. "We protect our buried trees by imitating things the plant-eaters are scared of."

"It works very well," said a giant caterpillar. "It's hard to try and eat something that looks like you. Personally, being into photosynthesis, I never could understand the motile digestion cycle."

"Anyways," said a couple of Daliesque nightmares, "it gets dull just sitting around waiting for something to try and dig up your tree. So we stay in shape by practicing different duplications. That gets boring, too, unless we get a new audience with a fresh perspective." The nightmares vanished, were replaced by twenty pairs of applauding hands.

"Come now," said something like a small dinosaur, "what would you like to see us mimic? We're the best, on this side."

"Not quite the best," insisted a quartet of upside-down birds across from the boaster. "You could never do this."

"Fertilizer!" snapped the other vine, immediately becoming an astonishingly colorful assortment of dangling avians.

"The feathers don't run the right way."

"They do too!" The reversed birds all stared at Jon-Tom. "Tell us, human, do they look right to you?"

He was slowly repacking his kit. "It's hard for me to say. Not really my area of expertise. I guess they're okay, for feathers." He started toward the beach where they'd left their raft the night before. Mudge was right behind him.

"Oh, you don't have to be an expert." Three vines interlocked to block their retreat. "All you have to do is bring a fresh perspective, to be a new audience. You're the best we've had in a long time. Much too long. We can't let you go now. We have so *many* imitations stored up. We need someone new to evaluate them for us."

Jon-Tom eyed the intertwined vines and took another cautious step forward. The vines sprouted clusters of six-inch-long, poisonous thorns.

"What do you think, Mudge?"

"I don't know, mate. I 'aven't judged any contests in a day or so."

"It won't take long," several other vines assured them.

"Our repertoire isn't infinite."

"We should finish in a couple of years," said four giant rats.

The rapid changes were making Jon-Tom slightly queasy as his brain struggled to keep up with his eyes.

"We'd love to watch you perform," he said slowly,

"but we have important business of our own to attend to, and I'm afraid we can't quite spare a couple of years."

"Oh, come on," said two versions of himself, using their ramwood staffs to push him back toward the center of the circle, "you'll enjoy it. Be good sports. We'd go hunting an audience if we could, but we can't. We're stuck to our trees."

"Yeah, don't you sympathize with us?" said something Jon-Tom couldn't even give a name to.

"Sure I sympathize," he said quickly. "We just don't have the time to spare, that's all." He spoke politely, while wishing he had a family-sized bottle of weed killer in his backpack.

"Just sit back and relax," said five startlingly voluptuous naked ladies from off to one side. "You'll get used to it after a couple of months and then you'll be with us in spirit as well as body."

"Be with you in spirit?" Mudge squeaked.

"The spirit of the performance."

"Oh." He let out a sigh of relief.

"I'll start, I'll start!" declaimed one of the women. It became, quite remarkably, three fish swimming in empty air. This was only the first of countless astonishing imitations, as the stage shifted from one vine or group to another, the duplications traveling around the circle in dizzying profusion.

If either Jon-Tom or Mudge showed signs of boredom, they found themselves rudely jostled back to attention by shouts or smells.

Morning became afternoon and afternoon wore on into evening. When night crept over the island, the mimevines turned to mimicking creatures capable of bioluminescence.

"This is all very entertainin'," Mudge commented to his companion, "but I'd rather not make it me career, mate."

"Me neither. There has to be a way out of this."

"'Ow about makin' a show o' inspecting one of their bloomin' imitations close-up-like and then makin' a break for it between 'em? They're stuck 'ere. Once past 'em, we ought to be able to make it easy to the raft."

"I'm not sure what they'd be capable of if agitated," Jon-Tom muttered. "Maybe they can imitate things that throw toxic darts. I don't want to find out. Not that it matters. They're watching us too closely, and I don't think we could surprise them as you suggest. Actually, they're pretty decent folks, for a bunch of art-obsessed vegetables, but I think this is what's meant by a captive audience.

"They're going to keep us here, judging their work, until they've run through a couple of years' worth of imitations."

"We won't be much use as judges if they let us starve."

"I don't think they'll let that happen. But we're stuck here, unless..."

"Unless wot?" wondered Mudge, flinching as a huge luminous crustacean materialized behind him.

"That was a good one, wasn't it?" asked the eight-pincered crab-thing. The vines flanking it opted to become delicate orange anemones.

"Unless I can get them to imitate a certain something." He climbed to his feet and found he was the center of attention. Ghostly glowing things eyed him intently.

"Okay, everybody, listen up!" The vines swayed toward him. They'd been nothing short of polite, in their childlike fashion, but he didn't think he'd get a second chance at this. Better get it right the first time.

"You claim you can imitate anything?"

"That's right... that's right...!" they chorused back

at him. "Anything at all. Just name it. Or describe it." They rippled and flared in the darkness, displaying everything from gymnastic feet linked to long arms to a talking rainbow.

"Not bad." Jon-Tom showed them his duar. "But how are you at reacting to a musical description instead of a verbal one? How are you at listening and imitating what you hear?"

"How's this?" said a giant, fleshy ear.

"That's not exactly what I mean. Can you mimic only what you hear in the music? Pure music, without descriptive words? Can you imitate feelings, for example?"

"Try us, try us!" urged a chain of worms.

So Jon-Tom sang the song he'd selected, a gentle, easygoing, relaxing song. He'd sung it once before, and it had put an entire pirate crew safely into the arms of Morpheus.

It seemed to work here, too. The vines slumped, resembling for the moment nothing more complex than vines. When the song ended, he shouldered his backpack and nodded for Mudge to follow.

They were almost to the edge of the clearing when two vines suddenly rose to interlock in front of him. They formed a very authentic-looking wall of giant razor blades.

"Nice try," said a couple of sarcastic Mudges from nearby. "We thought you might try and trick us. It won't work. We're as alert and aware of what's goin' on around us when we're imitatin' as we are when we're not."

"So you might as well relax and enjoy the show," four Jon-Toms told them. "When you're hungry we'll bring you berries. Real berries, not imitation."

Jon-Tom and Mudge reluctantly returned to their seats of honor in the center of the clearing. The kaleidoscopic procession of imitations resumed.

Mudge leaned over to whisper to his companion. "I like those berries, mate, but if I 'ave to eat 'em for the next two years, I'll turn into a bloomin' berry meself. Unless I go bonkers first. You're goin' to 'ave to try some stronger kind o' spellsingin'."

"I don't know," he murmured. "Next time they might take my duar away." He made placating motions, raised his voice.

"Okay, okay, you've convinced me we can't get away, just as you've convinced me that we're in the presence of the all-time masters of mimicry." Mutters of appreciation came from around the circle. "But so far everything I've seen you mimic has been alive. Almost everything, anyway."

"Live things," said a three-foot-tall cornflower, "are much harder to mimic than not-live things. There's no challenge in imitating dead things."

"Then you haven't been properly challenged. For example"—he bent to pick up a piece of feldspar—"can you imitate this? Not just any chunk of rock, but this specific piece, perfectly?"

"He asks if we can imitate it," said an irritated moose. Instantly Jon-Tom and Mudge were surrounded by a wall of feldspar slivers.

"I have to admit, that's pretty good." Jon-Tom rose, tossed the fragment of rock aside. "Though I do see a little movement here and there. You're all supposed to be rock-steady. So you think mimicking not-live things is easy, do you? Here's a tough one for you." He paused for effect. "Let's see all of you imitate *water*."

This generated a flurry of uncertainty from the encircling vines, mixed with excitement at the prospect of a real challenge. They twisted and jerked, struggling with the necessary physical and mental contortions demanded by the request, until applause sounded from behind Jon-Tom.

He turned. Several of the vines were applauding one of their colleagues. This vine had vanished. In its place was a stable, very narrow waterfall. The water never touched the earth, but the illusion was remarkably real.

"Congratulations! That's more like it." Mudge gave him a nudge.

"'Ere now, mate, let's not go gettin' too interested in this business, wot?"

Jon-Tom ignored him, spoke to the rest of the mimics. "Come on, surely that's not the only one who can do it!"

The vines continued to struggle. Soon he and Mudge were surrounded by waterfalls, bits of lake and pond and swamp.

"I didn't think you could do it," he told them. "I'm impressed, I admit it."

"Don't stop now," said several of the vines, caught up in the spirit of the moment. "We can go back and finish our stored illusions anytime. Challenge us again."

"Yes, something harder this time!" said another.

"I'll try." Jon-Tom rubbed his chin and tried to look intense. He already knew what he was going to say, but he didn't want his captors to know he'd thought it out carefully beforehand. If this was going to work, it had to appear spontaneous. Even to Mudge.

"Okay," he said, as though the idea had just occurred to him. He turned a slow circle, gesturing eloquently with his hands as he spoke. "You thought water was hard? Try this. I want you all to imitate..." and he let it hang tantalizingly for a moment, "*emotions.*"

That froze the vines. Then they began contorting and jerking as they launched into vigorous discussion among themselves. Jon-Tom heard whispers of "Can't be done... never been tried" interspersed with more positive assertions such as "Can we mimic anything or can't we?... Can't let the human think he's stumped us... Sure it can be done... Just takes a lot of work..."

"And to make it worthwhile," Jon-Tom went on, "no more of this hanging around waiting for one of your companions to come up with the solution. You all take a chance on it simultaneously or it isn't fair. Otherwise you're just imitating the first one of you to be successful." He indicated the initial waterfall. "You've got to try and do it together."

One of the vines fluttered toward him. "Fair enough, man. Go ahead and try us!"

"Right. First emotion is... anger."

A brief hesitation, and then the vines began to darken. They turned deep, violent shades of crimson and yellow and orange. Some sprouted barbs and thorns that twitched and cut at the air.

"Good. Very good," Jon-Tom complimented them. The vines relaxed, congratulating themselves and conversing as they faded to their normal green hue. "No time to relax. I'll go faster now and make it harder on you. Next emotion is laughter."

Vines ballooned, drifting in the air like pennants despite the fact that there was no breeze. Some displayed polka dots, others were checkered, some boasted stripes like barber's poles, and one enterprising vine turned plaid.

"Sadness!" Jon-Tom barked.

The laughter vanished as the vines immediately went limp and stringy, turning deep pea-soup green or mauve or lavender. They began to drip false tears, swaying plaintively to an unheard dirge. They were getting better with practice and Jon-Tom changed emotions with increasing rapidity. Surprise, fear, elation, suspense, uncertainty...

"'Ere now, guv," said Mudge, "this party's lots o'

fun, but don't you think we ought to—?" Jon-Tom put a hand on the otter's shoulder and squeezed hard, continued to shout suggestions.

Faith, hope, charity, insanity...

He spoke the last in the same tone as all the others, with the same inflection. The effect on the primed and responsive mimevines was shocking.

For the first time, there was no rhyme or reason to their imitations. Colors shifted wildly. Some vines expanded while others bulged. A couple shrank all the way back down into their underground, hidden trees. Two flailed the earth until they came apart, beating themselves to pieces on the hard ground.

He didn't have time to observe all the damage his challenge had caused, however, because he was running like mad for the beach where their raft lay.

He had to pull Mudge at first, but the otter caught on quickly enough. This time no imitation steel materialized to block their retreat. As they crossed through the circle, Jon-Tom looked back. Those vines that were still intact were slamming into each other, beating the air, the ground, whistling and moaning and shrieking. The noise was worse than the sight.

"I had to get them going," Jon-Tom explained as he ran panting toward the water. "Had to get them to doing their imitations fast, one after the other, bam, bam, bam! Had to get them working without thinking, acting reflexively on my challenges, so that it would become a point of pride for each individual to keep up with its neighbors.

"I didn't think my earlier lullaby was going to work, but it was worth a try. They'd probably been watching out for just that kind of trick on our part, so I figured the worst that could happen was that they'd get to show us we couldn't escape. I let them believe we were resigned to our fate and then tried to make it look like I was caught up in the spirit of the contest."

They were on the raft now, pushing hard on the paddles, sliding out onto the water of the Wrounipai and putting some distance between themselves and the floral asylum they'd left behind.

Mudge glanced back toward the island. "You think they'll ever come out of it, mate?" Distant shouts and moans could still be heard, though they were fainter now.

"I think so. Gradually one of them will realize that they're doing it to themselves and cure itself. Then the others will imitate its return to sanity. Those who aren't too far gone. I could've left them with that thought, but I'd rather they discover it on their own, after we're safely on our way."

"Right. You sure 'ad me fooled, mate." He frowned. Jon-Tom's expression had turned sorrowful. "Hey, wot's wrong now?"

"Oh, I don't know." He turned back to concentrating on his paddling. "It's just that...this is silly, I know...but while we were trapped back there I had thoughts of...you remember Flor Quintera?"

"The dark-'aired lady you brought over from your own world? The one who went off with that smooth-talkin' rabbit?"

"Yeah, that's her. I thought for a minute back there about asking the mimevines to imitate her. That would have been an interesting sight, thirty perfect copies of that perfect body all dancing around us."

"Blimey," Mudge whispered, "now, why didn't I think o' that? Not to do up your ideal, o' course, but some o' me own favorite fantasies."

"Too late now," Jon-Tom said with a sigh. "Unless you'd like to go back. I could wait for you on the raft. Maybe the same trick would work again."

"Not bloody likely. No thanks, mate, but I've 'ad more than enough o' vegetables that look like your Aunt Sulewac one minute and somethin' out o' a bad dream the next. I wouldn't go back there even for thirty perfect females. Me, I prefer me paramours with all their imperfections intact."

IX

After the tidal wave of variety provided by the mimevines, the monotonous regularity of the Wrounipai was a welcome change. But as they floated further south, the terrain, if not the climate, began to change. Tall stone spires cloaked with thick foliage began to thrust skyward from the water. Instead of granite, the rock was mostly limestone. Creepers and bromeliads found footholds in the pitted stone, cracking and eroding the towers.

"A semi-submerged karst landscape," Jon-Tom murmured in wonder.

"Just wot I were about to say meself, guv," said Mudge doubtfully.

That night they camped on a sandy beach opposite a cliff too steep even for creepers to secure a hold. While Mudge hunted for dry wood, Jon-Tom walked over to inspect the rock wall. It was cool and dry, a comforting feeling in a land brimming with quicksands and mud.

Mudge returned with an armful of dead limbs and dropped them into the firepit he'd dug. As he brushed dust from his paws, he frowned at his friend.

"Find somethin' unusual?"

"No. It's just plain old limestone. I was just thinking how nice it was to find some firm ground in the middle of the rest of this muck.

"This was once the floor of a shallow sea. Tiny animals with lots of calcium in their shells and bodies died here by the trillions, fell to the bottom, and over the eons turned into this stone. As time passed the sea bottom was lifted up. Then running water went to work here, wearing away open places."

"Do tell," said Mudge dryly.

Jon-Tom looked disappointed. "Mudge, your scientific education has been sorely neglected."

"That's because I was too busy gettin' educated sorely in practical matters, guv."

"If you'd just listen to me for five minutes, I could reveal some of nature's hidden wonders to you."

"Maybe after we eat, mate," said the otter, raising a quieting paw. "I want to enjoy me supper, wot?"

Following the conclusion of a sparse but satisfying meal, Jon-Tom discovered he no longer felt like lecturing. His mood tended more toward melancholy. Lifting the duar, he regaled the unfortunate Mudge with long, sad ballads and bittersweet songs of unrequited love.

The otter endured this for as long as he could before rolling up tightly in his blanket. This managed to muffle most of Jon-Tom's singing.

"Don't be so damned melodramatic," the insulted balladeer said. "After all these months of steady practice, my singing must have improved somewhat."

"Your playin's better than ever, mate," came a voice from beneath the blanket, "but as for your voice, I fear 'tis still a lost cause. You still sound like you're singin' underwater with a mouth full o' pebbles. Or would you prefer me to be tactful instead o' truthful?"

"No, no," Jon-Tom sighed. "I thought I'd improved a lot." He strummed the duar's dual strings as he spoke.

Mudge's head emerged from beneath the covers. His eyes were half-closed. "Me friend, 'tis late. You can now carry a tune o' sorts, whereas a month ago your mouth wouldn't 'ave known wot to do with it. That's an improvement o' sorts. 'Tis not willingness you lack, but a voice. Be satisfied with wot you 'ave."

"Sorry," Jon-Tom replied huffily, "but I need to practice if I'm going to get any better."

Mudge made a strangled sound. He couldn't win. If he praised the man's singing, then he sang all the more enthusiastically, and if he criticized it, then Jon-Tom needed his "practice." Life kept dealing him jokers.

"All right then, mate." He burrowed back beneath his blanket. "Try and get 'er all out o' your system. Just don't wail on till dawn, okay?"

"I won't be at it too much longer," Jon-Tom assured him. He sang about days at the beach, and old mother earth, and friends he had known back in the real world. Then he put the duar aside and prepared to curl up next to the fire.

Something gave him pause. More than a pause: it was like an electric shock against his retinas. He sat up and blinked.

It was still there, and growing stronger. Or was it?

Leaning over, he shook the ball of fur and blanket next to him.

"Oh crikey, now wot?" The otter stuck his head out for the third time that night. "Listen, mate, you can 'ave the bleedin' fire. Me, I'll sleep on the raft. Hey"—he sat up quickly, suddenly very much awake—"you look like you saw a ghost."

"Not a ghost," he mumbled. "I saw... Mudge, I'm not sure what I saw."

The otter studied the darkness. "I don't see nothin'. Wot do it look like? Where'd you see it?"

"Over there." He rose and walked toward the bare white cliff. Mudge followed, eyeing the night uneasily.

Jon-Tom pointed at the rock. "There. That's where I saw it. And there was something else. Just the slightest quivering under me as I lay down. A tremor, like."

"Mate, this 'ole country's on shaky ground."

"No, this is solid rock under this sand, Mudge. It was an earthquake. I'm sure of that. There's lots of earthquakes where I come from, and I know what one feels like."

"I didn't feel anything."

"You were asleep."

"Right. So wot were this thing you saw up against this 'ere rock?"

"Not up against it, Mudge." He put his hand on the limestone and rubbed it. It was cool, solid, absolutely unyielding. Impenetrable. "It was *in* the rock."

A dubious Mudge also ran a paw across the solid stone. He spoke carefully, as if speaking to a cub. "Couldn't 'ave been nothin' 'ere, mate. There ain't a crack in this cliff."

"Not in the cliff," Jon-Tom corrected him firmly. "In the rock." He turned abruptly on his heel, returned to the campsite, and picked up his duar. He started to repeat the last song he'd sung.

Nothing. Mudge stood near the cliff looking angry, tired, and frustrated all at the same time.

Then it was back. Just the slightest trembling in the earth, hardly enough to disturb one's sleep. They would have slept right through it if Jon-Tom hadn't seen it as well as felt it.

This time Mudge saw it, too. Jon-Tom knew he did because the otter was backing quickly away from the cliff. The earth tremor faded and returned, but the thing in the cliff remained.

"You see it, too, Mudge. You do!"

"Not only do I see *it*, mate," the otter whispered, "I see *them*."

Jon-Tom continued to play. More and more of the wispy, ghostly creatures materialized. They were not slipping or crawling over the face of the rock: they moved easily through the unbroken limestone itself. Faintly glowing worm-forms about the size and shape of Jon-Tom's arm. Oversized, brightly luminous eyes showed against the front of each specter. Barely discernible designs flickered to life on glowing sides and backs, each different from the other, no two alike.

As Jon-Tom and Mudge stared in fascination, they linked together head to tail, forming a long line that snaked through the rock. The line gave a twist, and the earth underfoot trembled again. Then the line broke apart and they scattered, a bunch of insubstantial big-eyed flatworms swimming through the stone.

Jon-Tom stopped singing. They began to fade away, only that wasn't right. They didn't fade away: they dove down into the solid rock. He moved as if in a trance toward the cliff. There, a minuscule crack no wider than a hair, running through the rock and down into the ground. That was where they'd congregated when they'd formed the link and the last tremor had struck. They'd lined up along the tiny stress fracture and twisted, and when they'd twisted, the ground had convulsed.

"I wonder what they are," he muttered aloud.

"I don't know, mate, but they seem to be going on their way, and I ain't about to ask 'em to linger." The otter was retreating toward his blanket, his gaze fastened to the rock. "I've seen enough of 'em."

A few still swam across the cliff face. Jon-Tom

put his fingers on the duar's strings. "All right, I guess we've seen enough. I called them up, so I guess I can make the last of them go away."

"That is what you think," said one of the worm-shapes in a breathy, barely audible voice.

Jon-Tom's fingers froze halfway to the strings. "My God, they talk!"

"Of course we talk." The voice was like a distant breeze, a faint rustling against his tympanum.

Mudge was too mesmerized to retreat. "How can they talk," he asked, "when there ain't nothin' to 'em?"

"There's something to them, Mudge. Just not very much. But they're there, they're real."

"Of course we are real. Such conceit." The faint words were precise, very proper and clear, though Jon-Tom saw no movement of lips. Indeed, the spectral worm had no mouth. "As a matter of fact, we can talk quite well, but there is no reason to practice conversation with those who live on the world's skin."

"Then why are you talking to us now?" Jon-Tom wondered.

"Your singing fetched us forth from our homes in the crust. Most extraordinary singing." The shaped glow momentarily vanished, only to reappear seconds later at another place in the cliff. It moved easily, fluidly, as if traveling through water.

"We are sensitive to vibrations. Good vibrations."

"The last song I sang," Jon-Tom mused. "I'll be damned."

"We are also in the business of vibrations," it told him. "Normally we ignore those who inhabit the void above the earth, as we ignore the vibrations they make. But yours were pleasing and unusual, extremely much so. We came to feel your vibrations, and to return the favor to you."

"Return the fav—" Jon-Tom considered. "You mean you made the little earthquakes?"

"The vibrations, yes." The worm-light paused and linked itself to several of its kind. Once again they lined up along the hairline crack in the cliff. Once again they gave a sharp twist. The sand shifted under Jon-Tom's feet.

The chain dissolved and many of its component individuals fled back into the rock.

"But this is impossible. You can't live in solid rock."

"Solid? Most of what appears to be solid is empty," the creature told him. "Do you not know this to be so?"

It was quite right, of course. Matter was composed of protons and neutrons and electrons and far smaller bits of existence like quarks and pi-muons and all sorts of exotic almost-weres. In between them all was nothingness, bridged by forces with even more bizarre names like color and flavor. The planets themselves were largely composed of nothingness.

So why not creatures which would find such emptiness spacious and comfortable? Of course they would have to be composed largely of nothingness themselves.

"What do you call yourselves?" In his own world they would be called ghosts—frightening, rarely glimpsed creatures of luminous insubstantiality. They didn't look anything like dead human beings, but then, manatees didn't look much like mermaids, either, and look how many sailors had mistaken them for waterlogged sirens.

Why shouldn't these worm-shapes be responsible for the reports of ghosts in many worlds? Vibrations could call them forth, psychic in his own world, his spellsinging here. It made a certain sort of supernatural sense.

"We do not name what is, and we simply are," said the glowing nothing.

"Sing another song," whispered a voice in Jon-Tom's ear. "Sing another song about the earth we live in."

He did so, drawing on every tune he could remember that mentioned the earth, the ground, the rocks. The cliff came alive with dozens of the worm-glows, all cavorting to and delighting in his spellsinging and the vibrations the duar and his voice produced. From time to time they linked up to produce minute, no longer disquieting earthquakes.

"What a pity you cannot follow and sing always among us," the speaker said. "Such exquisite ripplings in the fabric of reality. But you cannot live in our world, just as we cannot exist in the void you call yours."

"It's not a void." Jon-Tom reached out and touched the stone. "There's atmosphere here, and living creatures."

"Nothingness," said the worm speaker, and before Jon-Tom knew what was happening it had glided into his hand. He stared openmouthed at his fingers. Mudge let out a little moan. "Nothingness, except for those few solid things that move."

His hand was on fire, radiating light in all directions. There was no pain, only the strangest trembling, as though the bones had fallen asleep. It traveled all the way up to his elbow, then slid back down to his fingers. He pressed them to the cliff and the light went back into the rock.

"That hurt," said the worm-glow, "and I could not do it for long. There is practically nothing to you, near vacuum. The earth is better, more compact, room to move about without losing oneself. Now it is time to go. Proximity to the void you are depresses us."

Only the speaker remained. The others had all vanished into the rock.

"Sing for us some other time and we will try to stay longer."

"I will." Jon-Tom waved. He didn't know how else to say farewell to something that barely existed.

The head went first, followed by the rest of the worm-shape in a continuous, sinuous curve. It melted into the cliff. Then it was gone. There was a last feeble earthquake, accompanied by a distant rumble. Analog to his wave? Perhaps. Then sound and shaking, too, had ceased.

"Good-bye. They were saying good-bye to us," he murmured, enchanted by the memory of their visitors. "What a world this is."

Mudge sucked in a deep breath. "I do so wish, mate, that you'd let me know in advance when you're planning on doin' some spellsingin'."

Jon-Tom turned from the cliff. "Sorry. I didn't know I was doing any. I was just singing."

Mudge sat down and pulled his blanket over his legs. It was starting to drizzle. "I ain't sure you can just 'sing,' guv." Raindrops sizzled into oblivion as they contacted the fading campfire.

Jon-Tom curled up beneath his cape, careful to make certain the duar was also out of the rain.

"I mean," the otter continued, "it seems you can't control the magic when you're tryin' to spellsing and you can't control it when you're not, wot?"

"At least I didn't conjure up anything dangerous this time," Jon-Tom countered.

"Blind luck. They were an interestin' lot, though."

"Weren't they? Kind of pretty too. I wonder how much of the earth they claim for their home. Maybe all the way to the molten inner core."

"Molten wot? Now that's a unique conception, guv'nor."

"Nothing unique about it." Jon-Tom pulled his

cape over his face to keep off the rain. "What do you think the center of the planet is, if not molten rock?"

"Everybody knows wot it is, mate. 'Tis a giant pit. The earth's nothin' but a ripening fruit, you know. Planted in infinity. One o' these days she's goin' to sprout, and then we'll all see some changes."

"Primitive superstitious nonsense. The center of the planet is composed of metal and rock kept molten under the influence of tremendous heat and pressure." That said, he rolled over and tried to go to sleep.

The rain trickled down his cape, drumming on its impenetrable exterior, spattering on the surface of the Wrounipai. A giant pit. What an absurd notion! As absurd as the presence of barely substantial creatures living within the rock itself. Wormlike creatures.

Didn't worms infest rotten fruit?

Nonsense, utter nonsense. He refused to consider it any further. It was ridiculous, insane, crazy.

Besides, the image it conjured up made him distinctly uncomfortable.

He tried to concentrate on the memory of their visitors instead. What could you call them? Earth-dwellers, rock people, stone citizens? Idly he wondered what would happen if thousands, millions of them joined together along a really big crack in the earth's crust. Along the San Andreas Fault back home, say. What lay beneath that ancient fracture? Merely different sections of continental plate rubbing against each other? Or was it occasionally lined with millions of the geological folk joined head to tail, all preparing to produce one sudden, convulsive twist every hundred years or so?

That thought wasn't conducive to restful sleep either, here or on any other world. Geologic folk brought to the surface of the earth by his spellsinging: how absurd! As were so many things in heaven and earth that were no less real for their absurdity. Geological folks. Geo folk. Geolks. Since they had no name for themselves, he'd call them that. In his memories, since it was highly unlikely he'd ever encounter them again. He drifted slowly off to sleep, wondering if he'd ever be able to go spelunking again without seeing luminous, insubstantial eyes all around him.

Jon-Tom had hopes that the karst landscape they were passing through was an indication of drier country to come. Several days of steady travel southward quickly dispelled such hopes. The rocky spires became smaller and smaller and were not replaced by spacious, dry islands. Once again they found themselves paddling through scum-encrusted stagnant water beneath umbrellalike, drooping trees.

As they progressed he came to at least one decision: if Clothahump ever asked him again to undertake another "pleasant little journey," he was going to insist first on getting an accurate, non-metaphorical description of the country he was going to have to cross.

But of course, that wouldn't matter, because he and this Markus the Ineluctable were going to become fast friends, and Jon-Tom was going to utilize their joint talents to enable him to return home. That exhilarating thought helped sustain him as he and Mudge slogged on through the relentless heat and humidity.

At midday they usually paused for a rest and a brief snack, and also to allow the steaming sun an hour or so to fall from its zenith. The little islet they chose was not particularly inviting in appearance—full of odd-shaped, inflexible growths and gnarled protrusions—but it was the only dry land in the unstable bog they were presently traversing.

Return home. Home meant Big Macs and Monday Night Football, throwing Frisbees at the beach and watching Saturday morning cartoons... the good old stuff, not the sloppy new crap... catching up on his back work and the movies he'd missed. If there was any back work for him to return to. As far as anyone at the university was concerned, he'd simply disappeared, dropped out, quit. He was going to have a hell of a time getting his active status restored, much less changing the incompletes he'd have received in class. Sure he was.

All he had to do was tell them what he'd been doing these past months. Sorry, counselor, but you see, I just happened to find myself yanked through to this other world, but if my friends Clothahump and Mudge were here to explain... Clothahump, see, he's a wizard. A turtle, sir, about four foot high. Mudge is taller, but that's because he's an otter and... excuse me, counselor, but who are you calling?

No, he'd have to concoct something a bit more believable than that. Believable and elegant. Maybe he could tell them that he'd become bored with the routine of studying and had gone off to South America to expand his mind. Professors always liked to hear that you'd been expanding your mind.

A light tremor made the ground shift slightly beneath them.

"Your ghostly friends again," Mudge suggested, his words garbled because his mouth was full of fish jerky.

Jon-Tom gazed down at the slick surface they sat upon. It was bright daylight and hard to tell, but he didn't see any sign of the geolks. Besides, he wasn't playing anything on his duar. Maybe they were just lingering in his wake, hoping he'd play again sometime soon.

He bent over, squinted. Very strange ground. Dead and dying vegetation, lichens and mosses, algae and crustaceans. "I don't think the geolks are around,

Mudge. Anything could shake this pile of humus we're sitting on. Maybe it was a passing wave."

The otter gestured at the stagnant water surrounding them. "Ain't no waves here, mate, except the ones you and I make with the raft."

A second tremor rattled their senses, much stronger than the first. Gingerly, Jon-Tom rose to a standing position.

"Uh, Mudge, I think it might be a good idea if we got back on the raft. Real quiet- and quick-like."

The otter was several syllables and three steps ahead of him. The shaking resumed and now it was constant as Jon-Tom half ran, half stumbled toward the raft.

The island was beginning to rise beneath them.

X

"Damn it, mate, move your arse!" Mudge yelled as Jon-Tom fell to hands and knees. The otter extended a paw out to his friend.

Jon-Tom tried to stand, but the surface under his feet was now shaking like Jell-O as it rose from the water. He gathered himself and leaped, landing hard on the raft. Mudge shoved frantically at the paddles, trying to push them back into the water.

Too late. The island had risen on all sides, and they found themselves ascending into the damp air along with the beached raft. Water rushed off the black hillside, turning to foam where rising mass met the swamp. Mudge lay flat on the deck of the raft, clinging to the vines that held the logs together, while Jon-Tom wrapped both arms around one of the paddle poles. They were surrounded by strange growths which seemed to be attached to the island's bulk even where it had rested beneath the water. They resembled the skeletons of dead cacti, hollow and light.

Shellfish, snails, and other inhabitants of shallow-water environments scrambled for the water as their homes were lifted into the air. Jon-Tom would have joined them, but they couldn't abandon the raft and all their supplies.

The section of island on which they teetered finally stabilized, but the black land ahead continued rising. This substantial tower of mud and swamp ooze didn't stop growing until it loomed threateningly over them. Innumerable bottom-dwellers, frantic fish, and trapped underwater plants dripped from the tower's sides.

Then the ooze opened its dozen or so eyes and stared down at the puny creatures marooned on its back.

Mudge let go of the vines, put both hands over his eyes, and moaned, "Oh shit!" while Jon-Tom continued clinging to the paddle nearby, staring wide-eyed up at the emergent mountain of swamp muck.

"Ho, ho, ho!" said the apparition, showing a dark, toothless mouth more than wide enough to swallow the raft and its occupants whole. "What have we here? Strangers!"

Jon-Tom tried to smile. "Just passing through."

"You scratched me." The voice was heavy, ponderous, and slow.

"We're sorry. We didn't mean to."

"Oh, that's all right. I liked it." It grinned hugely. Jon-Tom noted that the size of the vast mouth wasn't fixed. It expanded and contracted and sometimes tended to slide toward the side of the head. So did the eyes, which ballooned from tiny dots to globular bulbs the size of a car. The vast curving bulk blotted out trees and sky.

"I am," Jon-Tom replied carefully, "relieved to hear it."

"You're nice," said the ooze. "Different. I like different." Eyes indicated the surrounding swamp. "Nothing here is different. Everything's always the same. I like different."

Jon-Tom's arms were cramping. Slowly, he loosened his grip on the paddle pole. "You live here in the swamp?" Now, there, he thought, was a clever question.

The answer was not as self-evident as he believed. A slow, rippling laugh emerged from somewhere down in the depths. It sounded like distant drums.

"Sort of. I *am* the swamp. I am the ———" and it said something incomprehensible.

Jon-Tom frowned. "Sorry. I didn't get that last."

The intelligent ichor repeated the rumble, which sounded more like a volcanic belch than anything else.

"What do you make of that, Mudge?"

"Indigestion, or else its name is Brulumpus." The otter had recovered enough courage to peek out between his shielding fingers.

"Brulumpus," Jon-Tom muttered to himself. He kept his eyes on those of the swamp, which wasn't an easy task, considering how they tended to float in and out of the black goop. They moved about like marbles in oil. A queasy concept. He tried to think of something else.

"That is me, the ———" and it made the belching sound again.

Jon-Tom let go of the pole. Despite its size and bulk, the mountain of muck did not sound threatening. If anything, it seemed to be making an effort to be friendly. Also, Clothahump had once told him never to let himself be intimidated by mere size. That was not so easy to do when a potential threat completely surrounded you.

He tried to phrase his words carefully. The Brulumpus didn't seem especially bright. "Very pretty swamp you are. I'm glad we haven't bothered you." He gestured with his left hand. "We're on a journey south."

"That's nice," said the mountain.

Not very bright at all, Jon-Tom mused. "Now, in order for us to be able to continue on our way, we have to have our raft here back in the water. Could you"—and he described the action with his hands—"let us down so we can get back in the water to continue our journey?"

"Continue your journey." The sides of the Brulumpus shimmied and Jon-Tom had to steady himself with the paddle. "But you are different. You are a change. I like different. I like changes."

"Yes, and we like you, too, but we really do have to be on our way. It's very important."

It made no impression on the Brulumpus. "Change. A change," it repeated ponderously. "I want you to stay and be different for me."

"We'd love to, but we can't. We have to be on our way."

"Stay. I'll keep you close to me always and take care of you. You want food, I can give you food." A portion of submerged swamp rose. Trapped within the cuplike shape was a whole school of small, silvery fish. They fluttered helplessly for a moment until the swamp sank again.

"If you are wet, I can make you dry." Jon-Tom and Mudge winced as a thick shield of solid goo arched from the water to shield their raft from the clouds overhead. It hung there for several seconds before withdrawing.

"I will hug you and love you and keep you," announced the delighted Brulumpus.

"That's awfully sweet of you, and we'd love to take you up on it, but we really have to—"

"Hug you and love you and please you and pet you and..."

Jon-Tom was about to reiterate his protest when a

strong paw on his wrist made him hesitate. Mudge stood on tiptoe to whisper.

"Stow it, mate. Can't you see you're not gettin' through to it? Garbage you're tryin' to be logical with, and it with brains to match. It ain't goin' to let us leave any more than the mimevines were goin' to."

"But it has to let us go." The duar rested comfortably against his back. "I can always try singing us out."

"Don't know as 'ow that'll work this time, guv. I don't know if this pile o' shit is smart enough to be spellsung. 'Tis friendly enough now. We sure as 'ell don't want to do nothin' to upset the little darlin'. It doesn't move real fast and it doesn't think real fast, and it just might get irritated-like before your spellsingin' could 'ave any effect."

"Keep you happy and feed you and hug you." The Brulumpus kept repeating the paternal dirge over and over.

"Then what do we do, Mudge?"

"Don't look at me, mate. I'm just suggestin' caution, is all. You're the would-be wizard around 'ere. Me, I just copes with things as they come. Ordinary things, everyday things. I'll fight me way through any swamp, no matter 'ow filthy and disease-ridden. But I'm damned if I'm goin' to sit and argue with it."

"You're such a great help to me, Mudge."

The otter smiled thinly. " 'Tis all done out 'o gratitude for the wonderful opportunities you've sent me way, mate." He put his paws to his ears to try and shut out the Brulumpus's unbroken recitation of love.

"Touch you and hold you and feed you..."

"Wotever you're goin' to try, mate, try it soon. I ain't certain 'ow much longer I can stand listenin' to that slop."

"What do you expect from slop except slop-talk?"

Keeping Mudge's warning in mind, he tried to decide what to try next while the Brulumpus persisted with its affectionate litany.

It liked them because they represented a change in monotonous surroundings, because they were different. That couldn't last forever. Eventually it would grow bored with them. Given its low level of intelligence, however, that day might be a long time in coming. How long? No way to tell. The Brulumpus might continue loving and holding and petting them for a couple of decades. Or even longer. If the Brulumpus was indeed a part of the Wrounipai it might be extremely long-lived. It might not tire of them until they'd become a couple of desiccated corpses waiting to be shucked off like any other kind of boredom.

What did it find so different, so intriguing about them? Not their appearance, surely, for there was nothing distinctive about either man or otter. Their intelligence, perhaps? Sure, that had to be it! The Wrounipai wanted more than companionship and company. It wanted to listen to some new conversation, wanted what it couldn't get from a tree, a rock, a fish.

There had to be a way out, a way that would allow them to depart without alarming their benign captor.

"Want to hear something interesting?" The mountain of muck leaned forward, drenching one end of the raft with scum and swamp water. Jon-Tom and Mudge retreated hastily to the other end. "That's close enough. I'll speak up if you can't hear me clearly." Proximity to that gaping, bottomless maw was disconcerting despite the Brulumpus's avowed good intentions. Maybe one day soon, out of boredom, instead of hugging and petting and loving them, it might decide to taste them.

"Go ahead," it told Jon-Tom, "say something interesting. Say something different."

"Actually, we're not all that interesting." He tried to sound bored with himself. "We're really very ordinary, even dull."

"No." The Brulumpus wasn't that stupid. "You are very interesting. Everything you say and do is different and interesting. I like different and interesting."

"Of course you do, but there's something that's a *lot* more interesting than we are. Something that's new and interesting and different all the time."

The Brulumpus leaned back. Water sloshed against its flanks as it took a long time to consider this simple statement. "Something more interesting than you? Is it more lovable, too?"

Jon-Tom hadn't considered the last, but he was on a roll now and could hardly hesitate. "Sure. More lovable, more interesting, more different. More everything. It won't argue with you or confuse you or even make you think. It'll just always be there for you, interesting and lovable and changing."

"Where is it?"

"I'll bring it here for you to have, but in return, you have to promise to let us go."

The Brulumpus mulled the offer over. "Okay, but if you lie to me," it said darkly, "if it's not more everything than you are, then you'll stay with me forever, so I can hug you and pet you and..."

"I know, I know," said Jon-Tom as he swung the duar around. He practiced a few chords. These songs would be a cinch for him to spellsing. Not only were they as deeply ingrained in his memory as any lyrics he'd ever heard, they even had a compelling power in his own world.

"Wot the 'ell can you conjure up for this mess that fulfills all those requirements, mate?"

"Don't bother me, Mudge. I'm working."

The otter leaned back, glancing up at the thoughtful, expectant Brulumpus. "All right, guv, but you'd better satisfy this smothering pile o' crud real soon-like, because I think it's gettin' to like us more by the minute. Though if nothin' else, your singin' may change that."

Jon-Tom ignored the barb as he began to sing. Despite the threat posed by the Brulumpus, he was in fine form that day. Even Mudge had to admit that some of what the man sang actually bore some small resemblance to harmony.

The first item that appeared in a ball of soft light on the Brulumpus's back was a toy gyroscope. It held the creature's attention only for a few minutes. Next Jon-Tom produced a grandfather clock. This was more intriguing to their captor, but he noted that Jon-Tom could produce the same noise as the clock's chimes.

Jon-Tom tried to interest it in a game of Monopoly, but the Brulumpus wasn't interested in playing at real estate, being a considerable bit of real estate itself. With Mudge looking on warily, he produced in wild succession a food processor, a Fugelbell tree, and a performing flea circus. The Brulumpus had no use whatsoever for any of them. Mudge, however, made the acquaintance of the flea circus immediately, and dove into the water, digging and scratching frantically at himself.

"You'll drown the act," Jon-Tom leaned over to tell him.

"That ain't all I'm goin' to drown!" The Brulumpus boosted him back onto the raft, where he glared at the singer. "Let's endeavor to stay clear of performin' parasites, shall we?"

Jon-Tom sighed. "It didn't engage his attention very long anyway. Don't worry. I'm just getting warmed up."

"Huh!" Mudge sat down and began wringing out his cap.

The flea circus gave Jon-Tom the idea of trying to sing up something to infect the Brulumpus, but everything he could think of was more likely to afflict himself and Mudge than it was a mass of already corrupting ooze.

So he concentrated on continuing the cornucopia of randomly interesting objects. He produced a model ship that ran by remote control, a *clavier à lumières* from an old Scriabin concert, a stack of *Playboys*, a coal scoop, a rocking horse. None held the attention of the Brulumpus for more than a moment or two, and the space around the raft was beginning to resemble the back room of a Salvation Army store. Jon-Tom's confidence was starting to slip.

"Isn't there anything I can conjure up that will interest you more than we do?" he asked plaintively.

"Of course not," rumbled the Brulumpus. "How could there be, when I can have everything you can bring forth and still keep you?"

That sent Jon-Tom staggering. He hadn't thought of that. Slow the Brulumpus might be, but it also had an instinctive grasp of the obvious.

"Oi, we didn't think o' that one, did we, spellsinger?" Mudge taunted him. "We're so clever, ain't we, spellsinger? We ought to 'ave thought o' that one first, oughtn't we to, spellsinger? Now me, I finds you duller than a dead rat, but this 'ere blob o' barf ain't nearly so discriminatin' in 'is company. So it appears as 'ow we're stuck, wot?"

"There's still the first thing I thought of. Like I told you, this is all warm-up. Though," he admitted, "I never thought of that last argument. Now I'm not so sure it'll work. See, this thing I have in mind is designed to appeal only to a true moron, and now I'm afraid the Brulumpus may be more than that.

Anything too complex would go by him without having an effect, but anything too simple won't interest him as much as we do."

"Well, you'd better try it, mate, wotever it be."

"I'm going to," Jon-Tom assured him. His fingers touched on the strings of the duar.

Mudge had listened to some strange lyrics fall from the lips of his friend the spellsinger, but none as bizarre as those which now poured forth in a steady stream. They made no sense, no sense at all, and yet he could feel the power attendant on them. Strong spellsinging for certain, just as Jon-Tom had said. He waited anxiously to see what the music would bring forth.

Once more the drifting ball of lambent green light appeared before Jon-Tom. Yet again a strange new shape appeared in its center and began to take on solidity and form. It was utterly different from everything that had preceded it. It bore no resemblance to the grandfather clock, or the toy boat, or the rocking horse, though it did somehow remind Mudge of the thing Jon-Tom had called a food processor.

Only this thing wasn't dead. It was noisily, vibrantly alive. Or was it? Mudge blinked once and saw through the illusion. No, it wasn't alive. It merely cloaked itself with the appearance of life. It generated illusions of life, but in reality it was full of zombies.

The fascinated Brulumpus leaned forward to stare at it, kicking up small waves at its sides. Multiple eyeballs slipped round to focus on the thing Jon-Tom had called up. Jon-Tom had matched intelligence to materialization perfectly. The Brulumpus ignored them as though they were no longer there.

Mudge found himself gazing dazedly at the box full of cavorting zombies. He could understand the Brulumpus's fascination. This was *some* magic! He tried to make sense of what the zombies were saying and could not, yet somehow their shouts and cries held him as if paralyzed. He couldn't pull away, couldn't turn his eyes. It was locking onto him tightly now, taking him prisoner just as it had trapped the Brulumpus, those strange, soothing, challenging, frenetic zombies who at the moment were assaulting him verbally and visually. . . .

"Double your pleasure, double your fun, with doublegood, doublegood, Doublemint gum!"

Another zombie appeared, and his tone was as ponderous and lugubrious as that of the Brulumpus. All the weight of the world was on the poor zombie's shoulders as he stared straight out at Mudge and said, "Do . . . you . . . suffer . . . from . . . irregularity?"

Something was tugging urgently at Mudge's arm. He blinked, to see Jon-Tom staring anxiously down at him.

"A minute, mate," he said, not recognizing his own vioce. "Just a minute. I 'ave to listen to this 'ere message. 'Tis important, see, and I . . . I . . ." He paused, licked his lips.

"You what, Mudge?"

"I was just learnin' 'ow to save me kitchen floor from unsightly waxy yellow buildup. Blimey, and I don't even *'ave* a kitchen floor!"

"Come on, Mudge. Fight it, don't let it get to you."

He dragged the otter toward the raft. Mudge fought weakly.

"But, mate, wot about the ring around me collar?"

"Snap out of it, Mudge!" Jon-Tom slapped him a couple of times, then shoved him toward the other paddle pole. By pushing against the paddles, they managed to slip off the side of the now rock-steady Brulumpus and back into the water. They pushed and pulled on the poles for dear life, and the otter slowly regained consciousness.

"Bugger me for an alderman," Mudge finally

breathed, "wot were that 'orrible magic?" Behind them the Brulumpus was fading under the horizon. It lay utterly motionless in the water, staring at the screaming, cheerful, demanding box which had rendered it instantly comatose. From its back blared a few last energetic words of farewell.

"Youuuu deserve a breakkkk todayyyyy!"

"Jon-Tom?"

"What?" He continued to dig at the water, wanting to put as much distance as possible between them and the part of the swamp that called itself the Brulumpus in case, just in case, the magic failed.

"I'll never criticize your spellsingin' again."

"Oh, yes you will," Jon-Tom said with a grin.

"Nope, never." Mudge raised his right paw. "I swears on the best parts o' Chenryl de Vole, Timswitty's slickest courtesan." He eyed the trail the raft had left in the water and shuddered. "It 'ad me, too, mate. Sucked me right in without me ever knowin' wot was 'appenin'. Bloody insidious." He looked back at his companion as they both ducked some dangling moss. "Wot does you call the mind-suckin' little 'orror?"

"Commercial television," Jon-Tom told him. "I think that's all that it's going to play. Twenty-four hours nonstop 'round-the-clock."

"It'll be too soon if I never see anything like it again."

"I only hope it doesn't burn out the Brulumpus's brain," Jon-Tom murmured. "For a pile of ooze, he wasn't such a bad sort."

"Ah, mate, that soft 'eart will be the end o' you one o' these days. You'd smile on your own assassin."

"I can't help it, Mudge. I like folks, no matter what they happen to look like."

"Just keep in mind that most of 'em probably don't like you."

Jon-Tom looked thoughtful. "Maybe I should sing another few jingles, just to reinforce the spell."

"Maybe you should just paddle, mate."

"See?" Jon-Tom smiled at the otter. "I told you you'd start criticizing my spellsinging again."

"It ain't your spellsingin' I 'ave a 'ard time with, guv. 'Tis your voice."

The argument continued all the rest of that day and on into the next, by which time they were confident they'd passed beyond the Brulumpus's sphere of influence. Several days later they received a pleasant surprise. The landscape was changing again, and so was the climate.

As far as Mudge was concerned, the lessening of humidity was long overdue, as was the appearance of some real dry land. The Wrounipai began to assume the aspect of tropical lake country instead of near-impenetrable swamp. Islands rose high and solid above the water, from which accumulated scum and suspended solids were beginning to disappear. Instead of pooling aimlessly around trees and islets, the water began to flow steadily southward. Currents could become rivers, and rivers gave rise to commerce. Civilization.

They could not be too far from their destination.

And then, as had happened on more than one occasion, growing confidence was dispelled by an unexpected disaster.

On calm water beneath a windless sky, the world turned upside down.

Jon-Tom was thrown into the air, legs kicking, arms thrashing. He hit the water hard and righted himself. But as he started to swim for the surface, something grabbed him around the ankles. He felt himself being dragged downward, away from the fading light of the sky, away from the oxygen his burning lungs were already starting to demand.

He couldn't see what had ahold of him and wasn't sure he wanted to. The harder he kicked and pulled with his arms, the faster he seemed to be going backward. Down, straight down toward the bottom of the Wrounipai. His lungs no longer burned; they threatened to explode alongside his pounding heart.

The last thing he remembered before he started to drown was the sight of Mudge off to his left. A far stronger swimmer than himself, the otter was also being pulled bottomward by something powerful, streamlined, and indistinct.

The nightmare of drowning was still with him when he rolled over and started puking.

As soon as he'd cleared his lungs and stomach of what felt like half the Wrounipai, he sat up and shakily took stock of his surroundings. He was sitting on a mat of dry grass and reeds that had been placed atop a floor of tightly compacted earth. Diffuse light poured through the curved, transparent dome overhead. It looked like glass but wasn't.

Off to his left, Mudge stood examining one wall of the dome. In front of the mat was a pool of water which lapped gently at the packed earth. The water was very dark.

Sensing movement, the otter glanced in his direction. "I was beginnin' to wonder if you'd ever come around, mate."

"So was I." He climbed unsteadily to his feet. "I think for a minute there, there was more water inside me than out." He coughed again. His mouth tasted of swamp and his guts were throbbing.

"Where are we?"

"We are in somebody's 'ometown, mate," the otter informed him glumly, "and I don't think you're goin' to like the somebodies."

"What do you mean?" Mudge's words implied familiarity with their captors, but Jon-Tom had never been in a place like this in his life. At least, not that he could recall.

The otter beckoned him over. "'Ave a look at this stuff."

Jon-Tom moved to join him in inspecting the wall of their transparent prison. As he ran his fingers over it, he saw it wasn't glass, as he'd initially suspected. Nor was it plastic. Actually, it was slightly sticky, like a clear glue. He had to yank his fingers clear of the wall. A portion of it stuck to his nails and he had to rub the stuff off on his pants.

Something else: his pants were dry. That meant he'd been unconscious for several hours, at least.

The wall did not run or drip. As for the source of the dim, rippling light, that was instantly apparent. The dome rested on the bottom of the lake. The Wrounipai was overhead, and the surface, Jon-Tom estimated, was a good sixty feet out of reach. He couldn't be certain. He wasn't used to judging the depth of water from below.

He turned back to the wall. "I think it's some kind of secretion."

"You mean, somebody went and spit it up?"

"In so many words, yes." He waved his hand at the ceiling of the dome. "This is all organic, not manufactured."

A recent memory made him stare down at the otter again.

"You said this was somebody's home."

"Oi, that I did." Mudge led him across the chamber and had him look out the other side of their prison.

The dome rested on a gentle slope which fell off sharply just beyond the structure's outer edge. A profusion of similar buildings occupied the lake bottom another fifty feet further down. Their architecture was unfamiliar. All were simple in design and devoid of visible ornamentation. Shapes moved slowly through and among them.

Jon-Tom recognized a few of the shapes, and the small hairs on the back of his neck stiffened as some of the most unpleasant moments of his life came back to him in a rush.

"I told you, you wouldn't like it," Mudge murmured.

Jon-Tom moved as close to the wall of the dome as he could without making contact with the sticky material and stared into the depths. Despite the dim light there was no mistaking the identity of their captors.

Plated Folk.

XI

They didn't belong here, in these warm, tranquil waters so far from their stinking home in the distant Greendowns. The Plated Folk were the builders of the implacable insect civilization which he and Clothahump had helped to defeat at the battle of the Jo-Troom Gate not so very long ago. This wasn't the Greendowns, and Clothahump had said nothing about the possibility of encountering any of them on the way to Quasequa.

Therefore Clothahump himself knew nothing of their presence here. That was a disquieting thought. It meant that in all likelihood, neither did anyone else in the warmlands.

"This is crazy. What are they doing so far from their homeland? A colony of them wouldn't be tolerated by the locals."

"I agree, mate. Any self-respectin' warmlanders would run the 'ard-shelled bastards all the way back to that cesspool they call 'ome. If they knew they were settlin' in to stay in their own backyards, that is. But think about it: this 'ere's pretty empty country, and these oversized cockroaches are all underwater-dwellers. Ain't nobody goin' to raise the alarm over a bunch o' invaders they can't see."

"It's hard to believe that they haven't been seen by a few hunting parties out from Quasequa or some other town."

"Maybe they have been seen, mate." Mudge's words were short and clipped. "Maybe them that sees 'em ends up down 'ere like us, and maybe they never gets 'ome to tell anyone else about wot they've seen."

Silently, they turned back to the wall and stared out into the poisoned waters. Jon-Tom saw waterboatmen paddling along on their backs, their eyes cast forever downward. Dragonfly nymphs were nursed along by water tigers, and water beetles of every imaginable shape and size swooped gracefully above the buildings of the colony.

If it was a colony. They had no proof of that yet.

"You think they have any contact with the capital of the empire at Cugluch, or could this be an isolated, independent community?"

Mudge scratched at his whiskers. "I couldn't say for sure, mate, but while you were lyin' there 'alf-dead, a couple of 'em came in to check on us and did somethin' that doesn't make me feel any too confident about our future."

"What's that?"

"They took your duar."

That was bad, Jon-Tom mused, very bad. "Maybe," he suggested lamely, "they were just curious about it."

"Right," agreed Mudge sardonically. "They're just a bunch o' bug-eyed music lovers and they likes to collect instruments. Maybe they'll also want you to play a solo for 'em later, but I wouldn't count on it. They spent too much time examinin' it and starin' at you and whisperin'."

"What are our chances of breaking out of here?" Jon-Tom stared up at the faint, twitching point of light that was the distant sun.

"This bloody wall's as solid as iron, mate. There's only the one way in and out, and I don't think we'll be makin' a swim for it anytime soon." He drew Jon-Tom over to the pool of water that was visible just inside one section of wall. "See, I don't think we'd get very far."

Drifting just below and outside the entrance to the dome was a terrifying marine form. The giant water bug was at least eight feet in length. It hovered in place like an armored submersible, displaying open mandibles big enough to snap off an arm or leg with a single bite.

Jon-Tom nodded to himself. "So we don't take any casual baths." He looked past the guard. Something much smaller was moving toward them through the water. He found himself backing away. "What's that?"

Mudge didn't budge. "Air delivery."

The three-foot-long beetle had hind legs twice the length of its body, each covered with dense, flexible hairs. Upon reaching the entrance to the dome it pivoted in the water until its hind end was facing the opening. Between its back legs was a thin silken envelope full of air. It backed toward the entrance and kicked once.

The silk envelope split. There was a giant *blup,* water sloshed over Jon-Tom's feet and then receded, and a sudden wash of fresh air hit him like a spring breeze. The beetle swam away.

"They do that regular," Mudge informed him, "which is why the air in 'ere ain't gone sour on us yet."

"That's thoughtful of them."

Mudge turned and began nervously pacing the hard-packed floor. "Wish I could say the same for the rest o' their manners. I ain't so sure I'd prefer not to suffocate." After completing half a dozen circumnavigations of the dome, he stopped in front of the entryway again.

"Now I know I'm faster than that big bastard, if I could just get past 'im." He let the thought trail off. "Trouble is, I'd probably do it in pieces."

Jon-Tom moved back to the reed mat and sat down. "I never saw them hit us."

"Neither did I, mate, until it was too late." He pointed toward the giant water bug floating placidly outside their prison. "That hunk of armored vomit came up underneath us and dumped us in. His smaller relations were waitin' to drag us down 'ere." He looked over at his companion.

"When they dumped us in this 'alf bubble, your face was all swoll up like a lizard's bladder. I thought you were a goner for sure. They did a little dance on your back and pumped about 'alf a gallon o' water out o' you, then gave up and left. After a couple of minutes you started groanin', then fell asleep. I wiped the drool off your face and figured I might as well wait and see if you woke up. That was yesterday."

Jon-Tom nodded. "I figured I must've been out for a while. What happened to our raft and supplies?"

"Scattered all over the lake bottom," Mudge told him sadly. "What they didn't see fit to salvage. They've got all our weapons in a little dry storage area over there, to keep the water from ruinin' 'em. Exhibit A for the prosecution, I'd wager."

Jon-Tom went to the wall. Next to their prison and separated from it by only a foot of water was a much smaller, air-filled dome. It was crammed with weapons and personal belongings scavenged from an indeterminate number of similarly unlucky travelers to this part of the Wrounipai. The most recent acquisitions were clearly visible atop a wooden hamper: his ramwood staff and sword; Mudge's longbow and arrows and short sword; some of their food stock; and atop everything else, dry and apparently undamaged, his precious duar. If not for the intervening water and walls he might have reached out and grabbed it.

"Mudge, if we could just get ahold of my duar..."

"Then you'd charm 'em all with your sweet songs, mate. Unfortunately, there's only one way out o' 'ere, and I ain't about to try it unless that mobile butcher shop out there swims off to take a crap or somethin'. Uh-oh." He started backing toward the far wall.

Jon-Tom looked around nervously. "What is it, what's wrong?"

"Company."

Jon-Tom hurried to join him.

One by one, a trio of Plated Folk entered the chamber. Spend the majority of their lives beneath the water they might, but they still had to go up to the surface from time to time to breathe. Their bodies concealed lungs, not gills. So they built air chambers to live in, like the imprisoning dome.

Two of them looked like twins. They wore some kind of thin, unrusted metal armor. Jon-Tom thought it might have been tarnished copper, but he wasn't certain. Each was about four feet in height.

The third was a tall, reedy character who looked something like a hydrotropic walking stick but really resembled no insect Jon-Tom had ever seen before on this world or his own. It wore no armor and, unlike its two stocky companions, carried no weapons. Instead, in one set of pincers it held several thin sheets of metal thick with engraving.

This sickly seven-footer bent to confer with its aides. Together they appeared to discuss the contents of the metal sheets. Then it straightened to its full height and pointed an accusatory finger in Jon-Tom's direction.

"There is no question. He is the one."

"Is the one!" his two shadows declared loudly.

"Is the one what?" Jon-Tom asked innocently.

"The music wizard who called forth the fire horse and slew the Empress Skrritch at the Jo-Troom Gate. You are he."

Jon-Tom burst out laughing. "I'm *who*? Look, friend, I never heard of the Jo-Troom Gate or the Empress Skrritch or any of what you're talking about. My companion here and I are wanderers in this land. We're just a little while out from Quasequa, having ourselves a bit of vacation. I swear I don't know what the devil you're talking about!"

"But you do know about lying. That much is evident," murmured the tall speaker, "because you do it so forcefully. You are the wizard. There is no point in denying it."

"But I do deny it. Forcefully, as you put it."

The pair of shorter insects moved toward him, drawing their short, curved swords. Barbs protruded from the sicklelike cutting edges.

They lumbered past him and one put a sword against Mudge's throat. The otter made no effort to dodge. There was nowhere to hide.

The fixed chitin could not convey much in the way of expression, but the speaker's meaning was clear to Jon-Tom nonetheless. "Do you deny it still?"

Jon-Tom swallowed. "Maybe I did participate in the battle for the Gate, but so did half the inhabitants of the warmlands."

The sword pressed tight against Mudge's Adam's apple, trimming some of the hair from his neck. "And I have some faint recollection of perhaps possibly maybe participating in some small way in the casting of some minor spell," Jon-Tom added hastily.

The hooked scimitar withdrew and the otter breathed again.

"That is better," said the speaker.

"No need to take it so personal," Jon-Tom said,

but the speaker ignored him, spoke instead to his two aides.

"This is a great day for this outpost of Empire. A memorable day." The aides resheathed their swords. Their chitin was a rich maroon color, black underneath and marked by thick black vertical stripes across the vestigial wing cases. The speaker was yellow and black, with white spots on his cases. "There will be decorations for all, and the war council will be pleased. The Empress herself will commend us."

"The Empress?" Jon-Tom blurted it out. There seemed no harm, since they were certain of his identity. "I thought Skrritch was slain during the battle, as you just said."

"So she was. I refer to the Empress Isstrag, now reigning. She will preside over your deaths. A small measure of revenge will be gained for the destruction you wrought at the Gate. I shall turn you over to the Dissembling Masters myself. Our land-dwelling cousins will be most delighted."

"Your cousins? Then you didn't participate in the battle?"

"Distance precluded our lending aid to our cousins in the Greendowns, and in any case the battle was waged upon the land. We could have been of little help. We regretted our exclusion. Now you have provided us with a means to make up for it."

"If you didn't join in the fight, then you've got nothing against us, and we've got nothing against you," Jon-Tom argued desperately. "Why not let us go on our way? We've no quarrel with the inhabitants of Cugluch."

"Ah, but they have a lingering quarrel with you, wizard. Your dismemberment will bring much honor on our isolated community. All will gain in prestige.

You must be kept alive and well for your delivery to the Masters."

"Look, guv'nor," said Mudge, "I know I don't 'ave a 'ole lot o' leverage 'ere, but if you're bound and determined to deliver us to this new Empress and 'er private torturers, 'ow about turnin' us in dead?"

The speaker shook his head. "That would mitigate the delight of the royal court."

"Aw, gee, that'd be a shame, wouldn't it?" said Mudge saracastically.

The speaker missed it. "It speaks well of you that you should take such an attitude. That is commendable in a servant."

"Servant! Who's a bloomin' servant!" Mudge's outrage, like Jon-Tom's earlier disclaimer, was ignored.

"Perhaps the Empress will even allow this unworthy one to be present at the entertainment you will provide."

"Yeah, I'll wave good-bye to you," Mudge muttered sullenly.

"If not, there will still be ample glory in delivering you up into her presence."

"I'm curious about one thing," Jon-Tom said. "How did you know who we were?" He indicated the storage chamber outside the main dome. "You've obviously murdered dozens of travelers."

"Trespassers in our waters." Bulbous compound eyes focused on Jon-Tom. "As to the matter of identifying you, you underestimate yourself, man." The speaker's voice was hoarse, a rasping sound, due at least in part to the long, thin tube of a mouth from which his words emerged.

"Did you think we are so disorganized as to not take care to pass among ourselves descriptions of our greatest enemies? Do you think we would let them pass unnoticed among us? Great generals and great wizards among the warmlanders are well known to us. You should be proud to be among the notable, pleased that you should be so quickly recognized in a land so far from the place where you did battle."

Somehow Jon-Tom didn't feel flattered. "If you know that I'm a great wizard, then you must also know that I ask these questions only to gratify my curiosity before we leave this place."

"I do not think your curiosity strong enough to cause you to linger this long," observed the speaker cannily. "If you could leave freely, I believe you would already have done so. Indeed, were you capable of such sorcery, I do not think you ever would have been captured." He paused, and Jon-Tom had the feeling the tall insect was eyeing him curiously.

"There was known to be among the warmlanders during the battle for the Gate a great and strange spellsinger. To make magic, a spellsinger of any race must have an instrument with him." He gestured with a three-foot-long arm toward the storage chamber. "That instrument, perhaps."

Jon-Tom didn't look toward his duar. "Perhaps. Or perhaps this small flute I always carry with me." He reached inside his shirt.

The two stocky insects nearly broke their antennae diving for the exit, jamming tight for an instant before tumbling to safety in the water beyond. The giant water bug stirred uneasily, its massive front pincers flexing.

The tall speaker flinched but did not retreat. He relaxed when Jon-Tom's hand stayed concealed inside his shirt. "A small amusement. I understand." He turned his head to eye the dome's entrance. His two aides were peeking cautiously back into the air-filled chamber.

Jon-Tom didn't understand the phrasing, but it certainly sounded like a curse that fell from the speaker's speaking tube. A contemptuous curse. The aides slowly reentered the dome under the baleful gaze of their superior. Jon-Tom's interpretation of their expressions was not pleasant.

As though nothing had happened, the speaker turned back to him. "Tomorrow we will make a special conveyance for both of you. It will contain a small air chamber like this one so that we can travel safely to Cugluch underwater. There are many rivers and quiet lakes between here and the Greendowns, and we should not have to expose ourselves to the land-dwellers very often. There will be no chance of rescue for you. You might as well enjoy the journey. You will be pampered."

"Fatted calves," Jon-Tom murmured. "How are you going to cross Zaryt's Teeth?"

"There are rivers that tunnel through the mountains. We know them. You shall come to know them as well, though it is knowledge you will never be able to share. Now I have a question, man. What were you intending in this country, so far south of your own land, from the region backing onto the Gate?"

Mudge jerked a thumb in Jon-Tom's direction. "This one 'ere, guv'nor, 'e's a bloody tourist, 'e is. He likes to get out and see the wonders o' nature and all that crap."

"And what of you?"

"Me? That's easy. See, I'm barkin' insane, ain't I? I'd 'ave to be or I wouldn't be 'ere." With that he sat down on the reeds, a decidedly peeved look on his face, and refused to answer any more queries. The worst they could do was kill him.

"You must be an interesting person, spellsinger wizard," commented the speaker. "It is a long journey between here and the Greendowns. We may enjoy many a diverting conversation along the way."

"'Fraid not," Jon-Tom told him evenly. "I'm not much on small talk with casual killers."

"We are not casual. I am disappointed. I would have thought your reaction to your situation might have been more enlightened." It performed a gesture that might have stood for a shrug, or might have meant something else entirely.

"It will make no difference in the final judgment. You know your fate."

With dignity, the speaker turned and vanished through the watery portal, flanked by his stocky aides. There was respect in the giant water bug's movements as it swam aside to let the trio pass. Jon-Tom watched the speaker swim slowly around the dome, heading back down toward the buildings below.

There was a rush of water from the entrance. The giant water bug's head, with its massive mandibles, was even more impressive out of the water.

"YOU STAY," it grunted in a crackling voice, then pulled clear to resume its motionless patrol. Water surged in after it, making their humid prison damper than ever.

"Tomorrow, he said," Jon-Tom murmured, gazing toward the watery sky. Already it was growing dark inside the dome as the sun sank toward the horizon. "That doesn't give us much time."

"It doesn't give us any time, mate. We're doomed."

"Never use that word around me, Mudge. I refuse to acknowledge it."

"Right you are, mate. We're stuck." The otter turned away, bemoaning his fate.

In truth, there seemed no way out. Even if they could somehow manage to slip past their monstrous guard, their movement through the water could be detected and recognized instantly by any of the vibration-sensitive inhabitants of the underwater community.

As for the dome, if they cut a hole in it, water would pour in and prevent any exit. In any case, it would take at least a week to make an impression on that hard, sticky material with Mudge's claws and his fingernails. It was as if they were imprisoned in a cell completely encased in alarm wires. All they had to do was move to trip one.

That didn't keep him from thinking about escape, but by the time they'd finished the evening meal their captors thoughtfully provided, he was forced to admit that his usually fertile imagination could generate nothing in the way of a plan. Not even a suggestion of a plan.

Mudge was right this time. They were stuck. Maybe they would have a better opportunity to escape during the long journey to Cugluch. In that case, he'd only hurt their chances by not sleeping.

The mat was soft, but not reassuring.

"Where's the other one?" said an excited, rasping voice.

Jon-Tom opened his eyes. It was light inside the dome again, but barely. The sun was still rising. He shivered in the damp cold air.

The dome was alive with activity. Sitting up on the reeds, he tried to force his eyes to adjust to the feeble light. Busy water beetles scurried around, inspecting the walls, sniffing at the floor, tearing the reed mat up around him. All of them carried six-inch-long knives.

He counted at least a dozen of them. Two ran past, still shedding water from their recent entry. As his brain began to clear he saw that they were not merely active; they were downright agitated.

Standing close to the entrance was the speaker. His maroon aides huddled close to him. Their swords were drawn and they, too, were searching the interior of the dome anxiously.

Then the speaker's words, filtered through his half-asleep thoughts, struck home.

"Mudge?" He got on all fours, feeling through the reeds where the otter had been sitting last night. "Mudge!" The otter's musk was still strong in the enclosed chamber. That, and the impression of his body in the reeds, was all that remained of him.

When Jon-Tom rose, he was immediately surrounded by three of the sword-wielding water beetles. He put their edginess and Mudge's apparent absence together and reached an inescapable conclusion.

The otter had split.

As the rising sun shed more light on the search, his smile grew wider and wider. The Plated Folk were already repeating themselves. After all, there were only a limited number of possible hiding places within the dome. Somehow Mudge had made it to freedom without waking his companion or alarming their giant guard.

He wasn't angry with the otter for not alerting him. Obviously, whatever avenue of escape he'd followed wasn't suitable for the gangly Jon-Tom, or Mudge would have gotten both of them out. Sure he would. Jon-Tom refused to believe otherwise.

He wouldn't allow himself to believe otherwise.

Besides, it was only justice. Only fair that having been unwillingly dragooned into this expedition, Mudge should be the one to escape with his life.

Then there was no more time to bask in the success of the otter's chicanery because the speaker was towering over him.

Bright compound eyes gazed down at the single remaining prisoner, and that raspy voice repeated the question it had asked of its minions only minutes earlier.

"Where is the other one? The short furry slave?"

"He's not a slave," Jon-Tom said defiantly. "As for your first question, why don't you go screw yourself and see if it brings forth enlightenment?" He derived unexpected pleasure from the vehemence of his reply.

It had absolutely no effect on the speaker. "Tell me or I will have your limbs removed."

"What, and deprive the Empress of so much delight?" Jon-Tom grinned up at the speaker. "Not that it matters. I don't know where he is any more than you do. Your folks woke me out of a sound sleep. You were here and Mudge was gone. Where to I couldn't say, and I don't care as long as it's far away from here."

"I do not think you are telling the truth, but as you say, it matters not. You are here and he is gone. You are the important one anyway. You are the one they will greet with joy in Cugluch. The flight of the other is irritating. That is all." He gestured with a long arm. The chitin flashed in the light.

Several short laborers were bringing something long and rectangular through the entrance. It looked uncomfortably like a coffin, for all that Jon-Tom knew it was designed to preserve his life, not his corpse.

"The means by which you will be transported safely to Cugluch," the speaker explained unnecessarily. "The escort is ready. Now you will be made ready."

Jon-Tom tried to take a step backward, only to find himself hemmed in on all sides. He was much taller than every one of the Plated Folk with the exception of the speaker, but they were stocky and strong.

"What do you mean, 'ready' me?"

The speaker elucidated. "One as clever and well versed in the arcane arts as you is always a threat, even without your magic-making instrument. I will take no chances on you working mischief during our journey, or on suiciding at the last moment."

Long arms pushed. Jon-Tom felt himself shoved to

one side. Looking past the speaker he could see something like a five-foot-long cockroach waiting patiently near the portal. An air-filled ovoid was strapped to its back. Within, he could see his ramwood staff, duar, and the rest of the supplies that had been salvaged from their raft. The laborers were strapping the air-filled bier onto the back of another.

Then the speaker stepped aside, revealing the ugliest speciman of Plated Folk Jon-Tom had ever seen. It walked on all sixes instead of fours like the speaker and water beetles. Its body was long and thin and flattened from head to thorax, while the abdomen swelled into a grotesque globe. In color it was muckledедun except for the comparatively small eyes, which were bright red.

As it moved toward him, it raised its two front arms. Tiny vestigial wings began to vibrate excitedly against the thorax, which was very narrow. It was also the smallest of the Plated Folk in the chamber, barely three feet long. So was the tightly curled ovipositor-like tube which protruded from the base of the bulbous abdomen. It curved up over the insect's back and head. The hypodermic tip quivered in the air a foot in front of the creature's head.

Jon-Tom found he was breathing fast as he searched for a place to hide. There was no place to hide.

"Listen, you don't have do to this," he told the speaker, his eyes following that wavering point. "I'm not going to give you any trouble. I can't, without my duar."

"This is a reasonable precaution, particularly in light of the disappearance of your companion," said the speaker. "I do not want you to vanish one night when we are almost to Cugluch."

"I couldn't do that, I couldn't." He wasn't ashamed of the hysteria rising in his voice. He was genuinely terrified by the approach of what in essence was a three-foot-long needle.

"There is no need to struggle," the speaker assured him. "You can only hurt yourself. The Ruze's venom has been used on the warmblooded before. It knows exactly how large a dose to administer to render you immobile for the duration of our journey."

"I don't give a damn if it's been to medical school. You're not sticking that thing in me!" He jumped to his right, hoping to clear the surprised guards and make a run for the water, not caring anymore whether they used their swords on him or not.

They did not have the chance to react. As soon as Jon-Tom moved, the Ruze struck. The stinger lashed down like a striking cobra. Jon-Tom felt a terrific burning pain between his waist and thighs as the stinger went right through his pants to catch him square in the left gluteus. He was surprised at the intensity of his scream. It was as if someone had given him an injection of acid.

The Ruze backed away, its work completed, and studied the human with interest. Beetle guards spread out. Jon-Tom staggered a couple of steps toward the entryway before collapsing. One hand went to his left buttock, where the fire still burned, while he tried to pull himself forward with his other hand.

The coldness started in his legs. It traveled rapidly up his thighs, then spread through the rest of his body. It wasn't uncomfortable. Only frightening. When it reached his shoulders, he collapsed on his stomach. Somehow he managed to roll over onto his back. His elbows locked up in front of his eyes, then his wrists and fingers.

The long, thin, bug-eyed face of the speaker came within range of his vision and gazed down at him from a great height. Jon-Tom fought to make his vocal cords function.

"You . . . lied . . . to . . . me."

"I did not lie to you," the speaker replied calmly. "You will not die. You will only be made incapable of resisting."

"Not that." It took a tremendous effort for him to speak. His words were weak and breathy. "You said it . . . wouldn't . . . hurt."

The speaker did not reply, continued to regard him as it would something moving feebly beneath a microscope.

Jon-Tom wondered how long the effects of the injection would last. How many times between here and Cugluch would he be subjected to the Ruze's fiery attentions? Once a week? Every morning? Better that he find some way of killing himself quickly. He couldn't even do that now. His paralysis was their security.

It was difficult to tell if the speaker was pleased, apologetic, or indifferent. As for the Ruze, it was only doing a job. The dose it had injected had been delivered with a surgeon's skill.

Satisfied, it nodded its absurdly small head and indicated that the task of immobilizing the prisoner had been completed. The speaker turned to a group of unarmed water beetles waiting patiently nearby. Jon-Tom felt stiff, uncaring hands turning him. He wanted to resist, to strike out against his tormentors, but the only things he could move were his eyes.

Then they were placing him in the oversized glass coffin and preparing to load it onto the back of the waiting cockroach-thing. Inside the water-tight container it was peaceful, silent, warm. He fought against falling asleep: that was what they wanted him to do, so he stubbornly resisted doing it.

The speaker was nearby, giving orders. Jon-Tom was lifted into the air, and thin straps were passed over and around his container. He could tell he was being moved only because he could see movement through the transparent material. He could feel nothing.

Then he was falling. The coffin had slipped, or been dropped. There was a rush of new activity around him, but the cause of it remained foreign to his senses. His vision was starting to blur from the effects of the Ruze's toxin. Soon he would be asleep despite his best efforts to stay awake.

Staring straight upward he thought he could make out a vast dark shape coming toward him. It was blocking out the sunlight. For an instant it appeared to linger near the apex of the dome, and then the dome came apart. It did not crack or split like glass or plastic. It simply imploded.

An explosive influx of water sent his coffin spinning, along with the bodies of his captors. With his perception already distorted, it was impossible to tell which direction he was tumbling.

He was alone, a pebble in a bottle, a tiny human marble being bounced between floor and walls. Something had shattered the dome. That much he was certain of. He wanted to cry out as the water spun him in circles, but his tongue and vocal cords were paralyzed now. It didn't matter. There was no one to hear him.

The wall collapsed, and the swirling currents threw him outside the broken enclosure. The angry waters quieted. It was peaceful outside the boundaries of the ruined dome, though stirred-up sediments clouded the pristine water of the lake. Or was the darkness only in his mind?

It seemed as though he was falling now, still tumbling over and over, bouncing down the side of the underwater hill on which his prison had been constructed. He fell slowly because of the water and because of the air within his coffin. The latter was already beginning to smell stale. When he started to black out, he suspected it was due not to the aftereffects of the injection he'd received but to the depletion of his small air supply.

In his drugged fashion he was elated. He would not have to suffer repeated visits from the Ruze, nor some slow and painful dismemberment in distant Cugluch. He was going to die here and now. He would have smiled if his paralysis had permitted it. The Plated Folk were going to be cheated of their ceremonial revenge.

Then the darkness came to him, and he welcomed it.

XII

After an eternity it occurred to him that the temperature around him was rising. Not so surprising in death, perhaps, but it did surprise him that he could sense the change.

He tried to open his eyes. The muscles protested. It was as though he were not completely dead. He tingled all over, an excruciating sensation.

Since his eyes weren't functioning, he tried to move his lips. They worked, but fitfully. He forced them to. He badly wanted a swallow of air.

When he finally managed that complicated series of movements, he tried to scream. The air went down his throat and into his lungs like a chunk of raw liver. The next swallow was easier, however. Long-dormant glands generated saliva, and this helped even more.

Possibly he was not dead. He argued the point with the rest of his body, which insisted he was. He had drowned or suffocated or both, but he certainly wasn't alive.

Exhibit A for the defense: he could breathe. The prosecution faltered in its argument, and then the case for his demise was in tatters. Nothing like introducing a surprise piece of evidence at the critical moment, he mused. But now he would have to prove to the court that he was capable of consciousness.

First witness for the defense to the stand. I call...sight! Open one lid and swear on your optic nerve. Do you solemnly swear to see, to perceive, to provide a view of the world arould this not-quite-corpse? I do.

Someone was staring down at him, a fuzzy moon of a face. It wore an anxious expression. There was a black nose; a lot of brown fur; bright concerned eyes; and whiskers that twitched.

"Mudge," he mumbled. Someone had filled his mouth with glue.

The face broke out in a scintillating smile and looked away from him. "Now, ain't that interestin'. 'E thinks I'm 'is friend."

A calming, reassuring, confident voice. Only problem was, it didn't belong to Mudge. It was too high-pitched.

Jon-Tom put a hand to one ear, delighted that he was able to do so, and did some plumbing.

"Take it easy, man," the voice said. "You don't look so good."

"That's appropriate," he mumbled. Strength was flowing back into him along with consciousness. "I don't feel so good either."

The otter leaning over him was definitely not Mudge. In place of the familiar green felt cap and feather, this stranger wore a leather beret decorated with glass buttons. The face was slimmer than Mudge's, the features more delicate. Instead of a simple vest it wore a complex assortment of straps and metal rings. Lower than that he couldn't see. Changing his line of sight would have meant raising himself up on his elbows. He didn't feel he was ready for that yet.

"Hi," said the otter. "Me name's Quorly. You're cute. Mudge told me you were cute, but not very bright. I thought a spellsinger was supposed to be bright."

Maybe it was the curled eyelashes, Jon-Tom told himself. Or the streaks of paint above the eyes themselves. Makeup? Or war paint? He couldn't decide.

Another otterish face hove into view and smiled hesitantly down at him. Still not Mudge. This one was too wide, almost pudgy. Somehow the idea of a fat otter seemed like a contradiction in terms, but there was no denying the new arrival's species, or corpulence. He wore a wide, floppy chapeau that drooped over his eyes.

"This is Norgil," said Quorly.

"Hiya!" The new arrival frowned over at the female.

Female. Quorly was a she, Jon-Tom decided. So the face paint was makeup, then. Or maybe it was makeup *and* war paint. With otters, according to what Mudge had told him, you could never be sure.

"Think 'e can 'ear us?" Norgil asked.

"I can..." Jon-Tom was startled by the croaking sound that issued from his throat. He tried again. "I can...hear you. Who are you?"

"See?" Quorly beamed down at him as she spoke to her companion. "He's alive. That Mudge chap was right. He's just a little slow." She spoke to Jon-Tom. "I just told you. I'm Quorly, and this is Norgil." She looked to her left and gestured. "When you feel up to it I'll introduce you to Memaw, Splitch, Frangel, Sasswize, Drortch, Knorckle, Wupp, and Flutzasarangelik...but you can call him Flutz."

The names all ran together in Jon-Tom's brain. He'd have to try and sort them out later.

At the moment, all his energies were concentrated on the difficult task of sitting up. When he failed at that, he settled for turning over on his left side. This operation he accomplished with some success, save for throwing up effusively and compelling his two attendants to jump clear. Despite his bulk, Norgil proved himself as agile as any otter, moving with a kind of high-speed waddle.

"'E's alive, all right," said Norgil disgustedly.

They were on an island, Jon-Tom knew. He could tell it was an island because he could see the water of the Wrounipai off in the distance. Of the Plated Folk there was no sign.

He glanced past his feet and was rewarded with a view of lean-tos, more elaborate temporary shelters, and a couple of crackling fires. Two unfamiliar, outrageously attired otters were broiling several huge fish on a long spit over the larger of the two blazes.

Several others were sliding spitted, cleaned fish on long poles and setting them out to dry in the sun.

"We're a 'unting party," Quorly informed him. "'Tis a lot easier to make a good 'aul when there's a bunch o' you all workin' together. 'Tis also more fun. We do right well. Usually don't come this far north, but 'tis been a long time since anyone tried to tap this district, so we thought we'd give 'er a looksee. Lucky damn good thing for your arse that we did."

Another shape was approaching. Norgil moved aside to give the newcomer room. And at last, a familiar face and voice.

"Top o' the mornin' to you, mate!" Mudge pushed his cap back on his forehead, gave Jon-Tom a quick once-over, and put an affectionate arm around Quorly's waist. She leaned back into him, grinning.

No wonder Mudge was smiling so broadly, Jon-Tom mused. It had been a while since he'd been with any of his own kind. He struggled to smile back.

"Hello, Mudge."

"'Ow you feelin', mate?"

"Like a reused tortilla: pounded flat on both sides."

"Don't know wot that be, but you look beat-up for sure. 'Ad a bad moment or two down there." He nodded to his right. "Couldn't find you nowheres. Old Memaw spotted the box they'd stuck you in slidin' down the side o' the embankment. If she 'adn't o' seen you when she did, it'd been too late for you by the time we'd o' found it."

Jon-Tom nodded. "I believe I'd like to try sitting up now."

"Think you're up to it, mate?"

"No, but I'm going to try anyway."

Strong, short arms helped support him. For a minute he thought he was going to throw up again. His friends looked alarmed and he hastened to reassure them.

"No, I'm better now, it's okay. It's the aftereffects of the shit they shot into me. My insides are still on a roller coaster."

"Wot's that?" Quorly asked.

"See? I told you 'e were a strange one, even for a 'uman," said Mudge.

She looked sideways at Jon-Tom. "Yes, but 'e is cute."

"Don't you go gettin' any funny ideas, luv. Besides, 'e 'as funny ideas 'imself." Mudge nodded at Jon-Tom. "'As a phobia or somethin' about stickin' to 'is own kind. Don't care much for variety."

"Oh." Quorly looked solemn, then shrugged. "Well, 'is business is 'is business."

Jon-Tom paid little attention to this casual dissection of his sexual preferences and tried to massage some feeling back into his cheeks and forehead.

"What happened? How did you get away?"

"Well, mate, after you fell asleep last night, I stayed awake rackin' me brain and tryin' to think o' somethin'. 'Tis easy to think in the darkness, and it were damn dark down there once the sun went down. Some o' them creepy-crawlies 'ad their own glow lights, but they didn't come up around our jail. Don't need much light when you're used to gettin' around by feelin' the vibrations in the water.

"Anyways, I was fresh out of clever notions when our delivery bug with the 'airy 'ind legs showed up to make 'is regular air drop. That's when it 'it me, mate. The only thing comin' into our cell regular and unquestioned was air, and the only thing takin' its own sweet time leavin' was the bug that brought it.

"So I gets this idea in me noggin, see, and I kind of roll over toward the exit like I'm movin' in me sleep. The next time delivery bug comes back and dumps 'is air I'm restin' quiet as an undertaker right close to the water, and I just sort o' rolls out behind 'im when 'e leaves. Didn't even try to swim, just let meself float up behind 'im so as not to upset our 'ammer-'anded guard with any undue movements. 'E never even turned to 'ave a look, I'm 'appy to say. The big 'ard-shelled ugly bastard.

"Delivery bug never even knew I was 'auntin' 'is 'eels. Too busy with 'is bloody job, I expect. Anyways, I went up like a bubble, not movin', until we got near the surface. Then I just let meself drift along like an old log. After I'd floated for a while, I started swimmin' real slow-like, ready to break all records for the ten-leaguer if anythin' showed up behind me. Nothin' did. Got away clean. Didn't really start movin' till I was sure I was away safe and unnoticed. Then, well, you never saw anythin' move through the water that fast, mate."

"I was thrilled you escaped, Mudge, but I never expected you to come back after me."

Mudge looked a little embarrassed, didn't look at his friend directly. "Well now, mate, to be perfectly practical about it, I found meself thinkin' that there weren't a whole lot I could 'ave done for you all by meself, so I kind of bid you a tearful 'ail and farewell and it were nice knowin' you and struck off back northward in a big curve. 'Adn't gone too far when I got 'ungry and found a deep pool full o' fish. After that little swim I was more than a mite starved.

"Wot 'appened was I got meself good and tangled up in this big net. Thought those bleedin' bugs 'ad some'ow followed me and caught me all over again. Wasn't so much scared as angry with meself.

"Come to find out when I were dragged into the daylight again that it weren't our old bulgy-eyed buddies at all that 'ad caught me, but a swell lot o' distant cousins." He patted Quorly on the derriere and she giggled.

An extraordinary sound. Jon-Tom had never heard an otter giggle before.

"You should 'ave 'eard 'im as we were untanglin' 'im from our net," she told Jon-Tom. "'Im all tied up in there with our fish and water reeds and bait and all. Wot a mouth!"

"I'm just the expressive type is all, luv." He turned back to Jon-Tom. "Anyways, findin' meself among this 'ealthy bunch o' the clan forced me into one 'ell o' a battle with me conscience, mate. I couldn't decide wot to do. So I decided to leave it up to them as to whether to take the risk o' goin' back and tryin' to spring you from the chitinous jaws o' death, as it were. And wouldn't you know that every one o' the bloomin' fools opted to do the dumb thing and go back?" Mudge shook his head sadly. "You've been rescued by a lot o' certifiable crazies, mate."

"I am grateful," Jon-Tom said with feeling, "for your collective stupidity."

Quorly blinked at Mudge. "Wot did 'e say?"

"Don't pay 'im no mind, luv. 'E just talks like that sometimes. 'E don't mean nothin' by it. See, 'e were studyin' to be a solicitor and 'e can't 'elp 'imself. It's kind o' like a disease o' the mouth."

She eyed Jon-Tom appraisingly. "I thought you were a spellsinger."

"That too," Jon-Tom told her.

Mudge leaned close and whispered. "'E's a bit confused about everything, see?" The otter tapped the side of his head.

"Oh." Quorly looked properly sympathetic.

Jon-Tom endured everything in silence, partly because he was used to Mudge and his brand of humor and partly because he was too happy to be alive and safe to quibble about being subjected to a little casual abuse.

"How did you finally get me out of there?" He rubbed at his forehead. "All I remember is something dark and wide blotting out the light and then the dome breaking."

Mudge managed the difficult task of strutting while standing still. "Me sainted mother always told me that if I ever found meself in a fight with somebody bigger than me, to find meself a rock big enough to make things equal. So the lot o' us did some 'untin' until we found a really nice 'unk o' stone lyin' loose on one o' the larger islands 'ereabouts. No easy job in this muddy slop, it were.

"We wrestled it into the toughest fishin' net they'd brung with 'em, and then the bunch o' us swam over with it this mornin' and dropped it square on top o' their precious dome." He grinned at the memory. "Busted it all to 'ell."

"It could have crushed me, too," Jon-Tom murmured thoughtfully.

Mudge shrugged. "'Ad to take a couple o' chances, mate. As soon as they saw us comin', which was mighty late, for which I'm grateful, the Plated Pricks started organizin' a defense. But the last thing they expected were an attack, and they didn't make a very good job o' 'andlin' it. For one thing there ain't the bug alive that can outswim one o' us otters. Ain't much o' anythin' that can, especially when we put our minds to a specific job.

"And if we'd caught you accidentally under our little gift, well, you wouldn't 'ave been any worse off than if we 'adn't dropped the rock at all."

"True enough," Jon-Tom had to admit.

"We were a little worried," Quorly told him, "that it might not be big enough to break your prison."

"Sure made a mess o' it," said Norgil with satisfaction. "It was fun! We swam circles around 'em, though we did 'ave that bad time when we couldn't find you inside."

"The surge of water when the dome collapsed pushed me over the side," Jon-Tom explained.

"Right, mate," said Mudge. "Memaw spotted you and then we lowtailed it out o' there before those bugs we didn't crack on the 'eads could get their wits together. Oh, and you remember our charmin' 'ost, the speaker? I 'ad the distinct pleasure o' seein' 'is 'ead caught under our rock. As 'e were the only one o' that lot who seemed to 'ave any brains much, I don't think they'll be comin' after us anytime soon."

Jon-Tom digested this, nodded. When he finally stood, the movement prompted waves and shouts of greeting from the rest of the band. "You really think we're safe here?"

"Ought to be," Quorly told him. "Besides them losin' their leader, as Mudge just said, we took a roundabout ways back to our camp and 'id our scents well. And we're a long ways from their town." She shook her head, her words full of disbelief. "Plated Folk, right 'ere in the Lakes District. Who would 'ave thought it possible?"

"Lakes District? Then we're not in the Wrounipai anymore?"

She gestured northward. "Boundary kind o' wanders about, but we're right on the edge."

"How do you tell where one stops and the other starts?"

"Use our noses," she informed him. "When it smells clean we know we're in the Lakes. When it starts stinkin' we know we're in the Wrounipai."

Jon-Tom considered this, said almost inaudibly, "I don't know how we can thank you for what you've done."

She shrugged. "No big deal. Like Norgil says, it were kind o' fun. Got to do somethin' once in a while for excitement or life gets downright borin'."

Jon-Tom shook Norgil's hand, then Mudge's, and moved to do the same with Quorly. She ignored his outstretched palm, threw both paws around his neck, and yanked him down with surprising strength to plaster a couple of dozen short, sharp kisses on his face. He fought to pull clear. It was like being attacked by a wet machine gun.

Mudge thoroughly enjoyed his friend's discomfiture. "Now, don't go gettin' all flustered, mate. That's just the way we otters is. Real friendly- and affectionate-like." He hugged Quorly to him. "Ain't that right, luv?" She generated that exceptional giggle again and Jon-Tom eyed her warily lest she ambush him a second time. He tried to visualize her giggling as she rammed one of the Plated Folk through the thorax with her fishing spear.

"Come on then, mate, and meet the rest o' the gang." Mudge put one arm around Jon-Tom's waist and guided him toward the camp, kept the other locked securely around Quorly.

It was more like dumping him into a blender full of nuts, Jon-Tom mused as he tried to sort out his mob of new friends. The hyperkinetic fishing party swarmed over him, prodding, poking, hand-shaking, kissing, and asking questions at a rate only slightly this side of supersonic. Over the past months he'd finally managed to learn how to cope with one otter. Trying to deal simultaneously on a coherent basis with eleven of them was beyond the capability of any sane being. So he finally gave up trying and let their inexhaustible energy and excitement wash over him in a flood of fur, faces, and emotion.

Some were taller and thinner than Quorly; none were as heavyset as Norgil. They were divided evenly between male and female. Everyone mixed freely, and while several shared obvious bonds, none were joined in a formal relationship akin to marriage.

Leader of this anarchistic amalgam was an elderly silver-tinged female named Memaw. She examined the resurrected human with a sharp eye.

"Well," she finally declaimed in an elegant tone, "you are a bit short of fur and long in the leg, but then, I'm long in years and short of tooth and I get by." She grinned up at him, her mouth displaying an alarming absence of the full complement of otterish orthodontics. Jon-Tom doubted if it slowed her down. Watching Memaw, he doubted much of anything would slow her down.

"You're welcome to join us."

"I appreciate your offer, ma'am. Mudge and I, we..." He broke off, staring past her. Stacked neatly against the inner wall of one of the lean-tos, dry and apparently unharmed, were his ramwood staff; his backpack; and most important of all, his irreplaceable duar. "You saved our stuff!"

"Naturally, mate," said Mudge. "Or did you think I went lookin' for you first?" Appreciative laughter rose from the assembled otters.

"No wonder you get along so well with this bunch," Jon-Tom shot back, "they even laugh at your execrable jokes."

"Wot'd 'e say?" Knorckle asked Splitch. He was the biggest and strongest of the band, barely half a foot shorter than Jon-Tom. Splitch, on the other hand, was the picture of petite furred femininity.

"I don't know. Mudge says he was studying to be a solicitor."

"Oh," Knorckle grunted, as though that explained everything.

Mudge stepped in Jon-Tom's path. "'Old on a minim, guv, let's not practice any singin' now, wot? We just made friends 'ere. Don't want to go drivin' 'em off already, do we?"

Memaw wagged a warning finger under Mudge's nose. "Now, you be nice to your human friend, even if he is a bit slow at times! He's had a more difficult time of it than you have, he has, having nearly been killed by those dreadful Plated Folk." She turned and smiled maternally up at Jon-Tom. "Don't you worry none, young one. I'll see that this other youngster minds his tongue while he is around me."

"It's all right, Memaw. I'm used to it. It's just Mudge's manner. Sarcasm's as natural to him as breathing."

"Humph. Sharp teeth I don't mind, but I can't stand a sharp tongue. Nevertheless, if you don't mind, then I will stay out of it."

"Look, about what you said about us joining your hunting party, that's real nice of you, and I like fishing as much as the next guy, but I'm afraid we can't accept." There were a few moans of disappointment, none of which came near to matching the anguished expression that came over Mudge's face.

"Aw, mate, can't we at least stay with 'em for a little while? It's a pleasant change to be among friends and safe for a change." He stepped forward, took Jon-Tom by the arm, and led him away from the cluster, making him bend over so he could whisper in his friend's ear.

"There's food 'ere for the askin', guv. We're safe from the Plated Folk, and there's plenty o' good companionship, laughter, and song; and besides"—he lowered his voice to a conspiratorial murmur—"the three youngest ones—Quorly, Splitch, and Sasswise—they're as hot as that pool you busted the Mulmun in. I'm tellin' you, mate, all we 'ave to do is—"

Jon-Tom rose, stared coldly down at the otter. "I might have known that your reasons would all derive from your baser instincts, Mudge. You're acting on the advice of your glands instead of your brain."

"You bet your arse I am, mate, and if you think you're gonna drag me away from this crowd o' willin' lovelies so we can go parley with some ill-dispositioned magician in a strange city, you're sadly off."

"Maybe they'll come with us, show us the way."

Mudge shook his head violently. "Not a chance. This is a 'untin' party, remember? They move all over the country, only go into the smaller towns to trade. Never make it into the big cities like Quasequa."

"Never?" Jon-Tom turned and strolled back to his milling, chattering saviors. Mudge trailed along behind him, hurrying to catch up and tugging anxiously at his friend's sleeve.

"Now, wait a minute, lad, wot be you goin' to say now? Just that they're friendly-seemin' now don't mean you can't make enemies o' the lot o' them with a misplaced word 'ere and there. Listen to me, mate!"

Jon-Tom ignored him, halted in front of Memaw. "Your offer is beguiling, but we really can't go with you. You see, we are on the final leg of a vitally important mission."

Mudge put both hands over his face and fell

backward with a groan. "Oh, blimey. 'E's goin' to tell 'em everythin', 'e is . . . the bleedin' idiot!"

The spellsinger proceeded to do precisely that. His audience listened raptly until he finished.

". . . And so," he concluded, "that's why I'm afraid we can't take you up on your offer. We have a job to do, much as I'd love to exchange it for a few months of hunting and fishing."

The otters immediately fell to arguing and discussing among themselves. The vehemence of their debate took Jon-Tom a bit aback, but all the ear-pulling and nose-biting and cursing seemed, remarkably enough, to eventually produce a consensus free of dissension.

Drortch spoke first, fiddling with her necklace as she did so. It was fashioned of some heavy, silvery braid which shone in the sun. "Wot can the two of you do against the rulers o' Quasequa?"

"Whatever we can. Whatever we must. There may be no danger at all, no problem to deal with if this Markus the Ineluctable and I turn out to be on the same wavelength. If we can communicate with each other and reach an understanding, then we can do all the fishing we want."

"I wouldn't count on that," said Frangel slowly. "Not from wot I've 'eard o' this bloke. Word is this Markus 'as been 'avin' taxes raised not only in the city but in all the outlyin' districts as well."

"That would mean the tax on our catch would be raised," muttered Wupp angrily.

"Well, we ain't never paid no taxes to Quasequa and we ain't never goin' to!" declaimed Flutzasarangelik.

"Right . . . yea! . . . never . . . !" The rest of the band took up the first cry of defiance.

Memaw raised a paw for silence. "Where'd you hear of all this, Frangel?"

"When we were leavin' Quasequa the last time we were in for supplies. Couple o' blokes on a street corner were reading the paper aloud."

Jon-Tom pursed his lips as he stared down over his nose at Mudge. "So they never go into the city, eh?"

The otter offered up a wan smile by way of reply, hunted for a hole big enough to crawl into.

"What else did you hear?" Memaw prompted the younger otter.

Frangel licked his lips. "I 'eard that this Markus is goin' to demand assurances o' allegiance. Not to Quasequa, mind you, but to him direct."

"Wot an outrage!...Never 'appen...got a snowball's chance in the Greendowns if 'e thinks 'e can force that on everybody...!"

Memaw turned to Jon-Tom and the cries died down. "You have still failed to properly answer Drortch's question, young human. If you are not on the same 'wavelength'—whatever that may be—as this Markus the Ineluctable, how do you propose to convince him to stop his activites should he prove unresponsive to your initial entreaties?"

"Naturally, our response will depend on his. If he proves stubborn and uncooperative, well, I have a mandate from the great wizard Clothahump, my instructor, to do whatever I think is in the best interests of the people of Quasequa. As Mudge has told you, I am something of a spellsinger. The Plated Folk knew that, which is why they wanted me so badly."

"Bugs ain't got no taste," Mudge grumbled. He stood off to one side, looking surly and refusing to participate in the discussion.

"Assuming your powers are functioning, you truly believe you can overcome this magician? It is rumored he is extraordinarily powerful. He defeated the famous Oplode the Sly."

"Like I said," Jon-Tom told her, with a quiet confidence he didn't feel, "we'll do whatever's necessary."

He moved through them to pick up his backpack, slung it over his shoulders, did the same with the duar, and gripped the ramwood staff. Then he looked significantly toward a solitary figure standing away from the others.

"Mudge?"

"Wot!" the otter growled, not looking back at him.

"It's time we were on our way."

The otter shook his head sadly. "Ain't it always?" He let out a sigh, moved to follow as Jon-Tom started toward the beach.

Behind them the hunting party congressed intently, heads sticking together in a circle, looking for all the world like an undersized rugby scrum.

Frangel stuck his head up first. "'Ang on there, 'uman! We're comin' with you."

Jon-Tom paused, turned. "That's damn decent of you, and we'd sure like the company; but this isn't your fight, and you're not operating under the kind of obligation that I am."

"Screw your obligation!" said Quorly. "We're not gonna stand 'ere and let ourselves be taxed like that."

"That's the spirit," Jon-Tom told her. "No taxation without representation!"

"And we don't want none o' that neither!" Sasswise said angrily.

Jon-Tom swallowed and let his simile go down in flames. Quorly sashayed over to him.

"Anyway, you're not goin' to do anythin' without our help, Jonny-Tom."

"And why not?"

"'Cause you ain't got no boat anymore."

All that bouncing around must have caused him to bump his head a few times, he reflected. That was one minor fact he'd managed to overlook.

"I admit we could use a raft or something. The Plated Folk made a mess of ours. Could we borrow one of yours?"

"Don't be a fool." She winked at him and joined the scattering of her companions.

Jon-Tom watched dizzily as they broke camp, packed, and prepared to depart. The entire process took about five minutes. There was only the one craft in any case, a large, low-gunwaled boat that bobbed at anchor on the other side of the island. Gear was stowed neatly below the single deck. Jon-Tom followed them aboard, already out of breath. And he hadn't done anything but watch.

"But why?" he asked Quorly. "Why risk yourselves to help us?"

"Lots o' reasons," she told him, "the principal one bein' that we're bored. Even catchin' fish can get old, you knows."

Jon-Tom tried to adopt a serious mien as he stepped on board. "This isn't a game. If I can't get along with this Markus, it could be dangerous for all of us." He remembered Pandro's description of the attack by faceless demons almost certainly sent in pursuit of him by the magician. "I know he's capable of using violence against those he thinks mean him ill."

"Tough titty." The delicate little Splitch spat over the side. "If 'e gives you any trouble, we'll just 'ave to show 'im the error o' 'is ways, won't we? A little danger'll add some spice to the visit."

Jon-Tom could only look on admiringly as they pushed off from shore. There wasn't a concerned expression in the bunch. On the contrary, they acted and sounded excited, as if they were looking forward to the coming confrontation.

"I don't know what to say."

"Save your breath for this Markus the Ineluctable," Knorckle told him as he settled himself behind an oar. Muscles bulged in his short arms. "From wot Frangel says, you'll be needin' it. This magician bloke sounds like a thoroughly disagreeable person." Murmurs of agreement sounded from his companions.

Jon-Tom searched the center of the boat. There was no mast and no means for raising one, only the two sets of oars. He hunted for an unoccupied bench.

"Now what are you about, young human?" Memaw had taken up a position next to the stern rudder.

"I like to pull my own weight."

"Kind of you, but I'm afraid there aren't any empty places. Each of us knows what to do. So just make yourself comfortable until we get to Quasequa."

"All right, but I won't like it."

"You don't have to like it." She smiled cheerfully at him. "Now, sit down, stay out of our way, and behave yourself."

"Yes ma'am." He did as he was told.

Everyone except Splitch, who was lookout, bent to their oars. Turning neatly under Memaw's guidance, the boat began to move south. Jon-Tom sat and fidgeted for as long as he could stand it before muttering to the helmsman.

"I don't want to rock the boat, Memaw, but I *can't* just sit here and let the rest of you do all the work. I wasn't brought up like that."

"Nonsense. There's nothing you can do in any case. There are only eight oars."

Jon-Tom considered, then said brightly, "I know." He moved his duar into playing position. "I can sing some rowing songs."

"Yeah!...great...good idea!...let's 'ear 'im sing...!" the rowers chorused enthusiastically.

"No, no, no!" Mudge rushed to restrain Jon-Tom's fingers. "You might magic us back to the 'ome o' the Plated Folk, mate, or even worse."

"Relax, Mudge. I'm just going to make a little music, not magic."

"I've 'eard that one afore, I 'ave." He took his argument to his brethren.

"'E's a spellsinger all right. Trouble is, 'e 'as this sort o' scattershot effect that..."

Jon-Tom was drowning out the otter's pleading, singing cheerfully with the mass control on the duar turned halfway up. No way could Mudge be heard over that volume. The otter finally gave up and moved as far away from the singer as he could get without abandoning ship. He squatted down against the bow and waited. His eyes never left his friend's instrument as he waited nervously for catastrophe to strike.

Jon-Tom modified an old Dionne Warwick standard and started off with a lilting little ditty newly titled "Do You Know the Way to Quasequa?" then segued into "By the Time I Get to the Quorumate." As the boat continued to slide through the water without being obliterated, Mudge finally allowed himself to relax. Quorly helped him.

The words didn't rhyme but that didn't dampen Jon-Tom's delight. Traveling songs were always fun to sing, and sailing songs even more so. Occasionally the otters would join in, their high-pitched squeaky tones gathering in strength as they picked up on the lyrics. It didn't seem to matter that no two of them could harmonize. That blended in nicely with Jon-Tom's erratic tenor, which is to say, not at all. But what they lacked in talent they made up for in enthusiasm. Somehow the boat stayed on course.

By the time Jon-Tom wrapped up a final chorus of "We Were Sailing Along on Moonlight Bay" and launched into "Row, Row, Row Your Boat," Mudge was prepared to spend the rest of the cruise tied to the stern with his head underwater.

"There's one consolation for me in all this, mate," he told Jon-Tom shakily between verses.

"What's that?"

"There ain't no torture too cruel, no 'orror too vile to contemplate, no death so slow that Markus the Ineluctable can inflict on me that'd be any worse than 'avin' to endure this terrible tintinnabulation."

"Why, Mudge"—Jon-Tom let loose with a couple of fresh riffs—"anyone would think you were some kind of music hater."

"'Ow could they think that, mate, when there ain't no music around for me to 'ate?"

Quorly traded places with Splitch and put both arms around the otter's neck. "Why, Mudgey-Wudgey, don't be such a sourpuss." She brushed his whiskers with hers and he was forced to relent.

"Aw, well," he allowed, "maybe there is a kind o' music on this boat."

Pinching fingers made Jon-Tom jump. He turned to see Sasswise grinning at him from her bench as she pushed steadily on her oar. "Quorly was right about you, Jonny-Tom. You *are* cute."

Jon-Tom thought of another song very quickly.

XIII

As the days passed and the miles accumulated beneath their keel, the character of the land they were passing through began to undergo a drastic change. The huge emergents dripping with moss and vines gave way to rust-colored palms and house-sized bushes erupting with rainbow-hued flowers. The water grew clear enough for them to see the sandy bottom fifty feet below. Even the sky changed as fog and mist fell behind them. The humidity dropped to a tolerable level and the light of midday became bearable.

They began to encounter communities constructed on stilts, and clusters of small fishing boats. The otters waved at the inhabitants and they waved back. The dark cloud that hung over this beautiful land was thus far only metaphorical. Everywhere Jon-Tom looked he saw signs of abundance and cheerful, busy people. There were even a few human beings.

Gradually, much larger islands replaced the smaller outlying ones. Buildings of reed and palm gave way to more permanent structures of wood and stone. Smoke curled from the chimneys of structures that climbed steep cliffs, while the homes of avians clung precariously to the topmost crags.

Clothahump had been vindicated. This was a magnificent, prosperous land. He told Mudge so.

"Oi, 'e was right about this much," the otter reluctantly conceded. "All 'is wizardship did was neglect to tell us about that little stretch o' filth and slime we 'ad to slog through to get 'ere. A triflin' oversight, wot?"

Jon-Tom stared over the bow. "I just wish I knew more about this Markus."

"Still think 'e's come over from your world, mate?"

The expression on the spellsinger's face reflected his uncertainty. "I don't know what to think anymore, Mudge. I'm not as certain as I once was. I'd feel better about it if we could hear someone say something nice about him." He took a deep breath. "Well, we'll know all about him soon enough."

Around him the otters were still singing, booming out all the songs he'd taught them during the past days with a vocal ferocity that was beginning to wear even on their instructor. His fingers were too tired for him to accompany them on the duar anymore, but that didn't seem to matter.

"Don't they ever slow up? Don't they realize how serious this business could turn out to be?"

"They know 'tis serious, mate, and they're actin' as serious about it as they can be. See, one otter can be serious. Two otters can't look at one another without crackin' up. Get three or more o' us together in one place for more than two minutes and you've got a nonstop party. Don't worry about 'em, guv. They're 'ell in a fight."

"I can believe that. I've seen you fight."

"This lot ain't no different."

"It is nice to have allies. Surely they'll quiet down when we reach Quasequa. We don't want to make a spectacle of ourselves when we pull into town."

"Don't count on gettin' any quiet or decorum out

of this lot. And remember, you're the one who talked 'em into this."

"I didn't talk them into it." Jon-Tom sounded defensive even to himself. "They volunteered."

"Sorry, mate. You don't get off that easy."

"It's just that if they don't quiet down some, we'll attract a lot of attention. I don't want this Markus to know I'm around until I'm ready to meet with him."

"Oh, I wouldn't worry too much about that, guv. From wot sweet Quorly's been tellin' me, Quasequa's a mighty big place, and plenty rowdy when 'tis on its good behavior. So we're likely to blend right in."

"You don't care what happens anyway, do you, Mudge? Not so long as there are a couple of compliant ladies around."

"Now don't go gettin' on me case because o' that, mate. Just because you 'ave this peculiar puritanical streak in you that keeps you from enjoyin' the attention o' others and because you ain't 'ad much luck with your favorite red'ead."

"Talea's just taking her time before making a commitment," Jon-Tom replied frostily.

"Lad, lad, she's a free spirit, that one. Maybe she'll come back to you and maybe she won't. You might know about spellsingin', but I knows about females. That's a special kind o' knowledge all its own."

"You know how to talk, anyway." He lapsed into silence for a while, found himself watching Memaw steer the boat, her paws steady on the rudder as she led her friends in the umpteenth rendition of "Anchors Aweigh."

"As for this mob, I don't guess I could get rid of them now even if I wanted to."

"Not bloody likely," Mudge agreed. "I keep tellin' you to quit worryin' about 'em. Remember, they didn't 'ave no trouble stealin' you away from the Plated Folk."

"I know, I know. It's just that I'd feel really guilty if any of them got hurt on my behalf."

"This ain't no bunch o' cubs on this ship," Mudge said somberly. "They know wot they're gettin' into."

They were interrupted by Splitch's shout from the front of the boat. "Quasequa!" Jon-Tom and Mudge rushed toward the bow as the rest of the otters pulled harder.

If Clothahump had underestimated the travails of their journey, he'd also underestimated the beauty of their destination. Three of the five main islands that composed the city proper were visible dead ahead. Multi-storied buildings built of quarried white limestone climbed the sides of each island's central peak. Palm trees rustled in the gentle wind, and here and there a copper-clad roof showed bright bronze in the sun.

They were traveling among heavy traffic now. Most of the boats were smaller than theirs, a few with sails bulked larger. The Isle Drelft lay off to port, Isle Sofanza to starboard, and the central island called Quase where the Quorumate Complex was located loomed straight ahead. Massive stone causeways connected all three islands, their multiple arches high enough for the majority of boat traffic to pass freely underneath. Carved shells and animal faces decorated each.

Crowds filled the causeways, the constant hum of their conversation reaching out across the water. The babble bespoke a vibrant community, full of life and commerce. Quasequa certainly didn't strike Jon-Tom as a city about to fall under the domination of some alien tyrant. As yet, though, the citizens were not at war with their own government. As yet. If luck, skill, and charm were with him, the face of this exquisite metropolis would remain always as it was this morning.

Flowers. He'd never seen so many flowers in one place. There were blossoms floating past on the water that were the size of his hand, shiny lavender striped with yellow. He lifted one from the surface and inhaled deeply of its lingering fragrance: pure peppermint.

Smaller boats hove alongside. They were populated by the familiar extraordinary assortment of intelligent species, all hawking handicrafts, dried fish, fresh fruits and vegetables, drinks chilled by ice spells, erotic art, and ship's supplies. Memaw steered through them, ignoring the familiar pleas of the floating hawkers.

Flowers grew from the tops of trees, from the sides of buildings, out of neat green hedgerows that lined the streets, and even out on the open lake. Rubbery-looking lilylike pads slid past, their centers startling with clusters of tiny blue blossoms no bigger than Jon-Tom's little fingernail. Still-smaller blossoms hung from silk balloons that floated through the warm air. When the breeze stilled they would settle to the water, only to rise again on the next puff of wind. They made the sky look as if it were full of flying rubies.

Memaw leaned on the rudder, and the boat turned slightly to port, angling for the low quays that lined the shore of Isle Quase.

"There is an inn we frequent during our visits here," she told him. "A good place to eat and rest while digesting the newest rumors and juiciest gossip."

"Everything seems so normal," he told her. "The people look content. Maybe this Markus and I will get along after all."

"Sometimes healthy fur can conceal rotting flesh. We shall see. Regardless, it will be nice to sleep in a real bed again." She adjusted their course minutely and gestured at a two-story-tall rock edifice that lay dead ahead. It was built right down to the edge of the water.

"The chap who runs this place, Cherjal, is privy to just about everything that happens in Quasequa. He should be able to tell us whether there will be dangerous work awaiting you here or whether you can relax and enjoy the sights of the city."

As they drew near, the reason for the inn's location became clear. With its siting right on the lake, it catered freely to water- and land-dwellers alike. They tied up to an empty slip, and Jon-Tom's newfound allies ushered him inside.

The single large eating and drinking room had a low-domed ceiling and was crammed with chattering muskrats, beavers, nutrias, and capybaras in addition to unfamiliar otters. Water entered via an opening to the lake, permitting the easy entry of an occasional freshwater porpoise.

Thunder boomed outside. They'd arrived just ahead of a tropical thunderstorm. Through the openings to the lake, Jon-Tom could see the heavy drops churning the smooth surface and was glad they'd pulled in when they had. Inside the inn, all was snug and dry.

Memaw left them seated at several tables, returned a few moments later with the proprietor. Jon-Tom didn't rise to greet him. The ceiling, lined with shiny sea-green tile, was too low.

Cherjal was a large koala. He wore an apron, vest, the ubiquitous short pants, and a bright blue scarf around his forehead. He let out a tired groan as he plopped down in an empty chair and regarded his new guests.

Jon-Tom sipped at his sweet cider and waited patiently while Cherjal exchanged pleasantries with the rest of the otters. The floor was full of drains, and the dampness of the room reflected the inn's largely riparian clientele. There was no sign of mold or mildew, however, and he suspected the place was scrubbed clean every night. Still, he couldn't escape the feeling that he was sitting inside an enormous terrarium.

"So how go zee feeshing, Memaw?"

She shrugged and set down the dope stick she'd been puffing on. Jon-Tom had already taken one whiff of the pungent smoke and set temptation aside. He needed all his wits about him now, and half that stick would've laid him flat.

"Not bad. Our trip turned out to be full of interesting digressions, however, hence our early return. We happened upon this tall human chap and his friend and helped them out of a difficult spot. This is Jon-Tom."

"Hi." He extended a hand, was surprised by the koala's powerful grip.

"His friend Mudge is around somewhere. Well, no matter." She leaned across the table. "What does matter is something we stumbled across where the Lakes meet the Wrounipai: a complete colony of water-dwelling Plated Folk."

"Plated Folks?" Cherjal's eyes widened. "How shocking a discoveree thees be! How reemarkable. How frighteneeng."

"Yeah, it sucks," Frangel agreed.

"Indeed, indeed." Cherjal considered. "Sometheeng must be done about thees. These Plated Theengs cannot be allowed to colonize our waters. An expeedeetion must be mounted to wipe theem away."

"There is no need to panic, my good friend." Memaw crossed silver-furred arms. "The colony is not that big, and we left them with sufficient to think about to keep them from causing trouble for a while." Mutters of agreement sounded from the rest of the band, except for Mudge. He was too busy stuffing himself with freshly broiled fish to care much about the conversation.

"So you come back to mee early. What can I do for my favorite lady, heh?"

"Always the flatterer, Cherjal." She smiled across the table at him.

It was raining harder than ever now. Jon-Tom could hear the drops drumming on the roof. The warmth from so many furry bodies and the thick scent of their mixed musk was making him sleepy. It would be so nice just to find a warm bed and lie down and sleep for about two days.

Unfortunately, he couldn't do that. Not just yet.

"We need to know what this new advisor to the Quorum is like, what his plans are, and what he's been up to," he asked Cherjal.

"So. You weesh about Markus the Ineluctable information, heh?" Right away the koala lost some of his good humor. "I have plenty I can tell you, yes, and not much of eet much nice.

"Nobodies took much notice of eet when he defeated Oplode the Sly. The cheef advisor spends hees time mostly advising the Quorum. Very leetle of what hee do treeckles down to us ordinary ceeteezens. Then thee rumors up-started. Steel nobodies pays much attention. As long as it don't much affect their lives, thee people preety much ignore what thee government gets up to." Cherjal lowered his voice and took a moment to check the inhabitants of the tables nearby before continuing.

"They say thees Markus setting up hees own network of spies. Eenformers in Quasequa, can you imagine?" He shook his head in disbelief at his own revelation. "Theen last week eet finally happening. At first nobody believe it. Thee shock steel not settled een, I theenk. That's why everything look so normal around town."

"Believe wot?" Sasswise asked him.

"What thees new weezard he done. He dissolve thee Quorum. Temporarily, hee say, unteel a new one can be chosen. Meanwhile he running Quasequa all by heemself."

A new voice interrupted loudly. "I knew it!"

All eyes turned. "You knew what, Mudge?" Jon-Tom asked.

"I knew we should've stayed 'ome."

"Calm down." He looked nervously over the otter's head, but none of the other patrons appeared in the least bit interested in the conversation taking place at the far side of the room. Of course, a good informer wouldn't reveal his interest. "We're still not sure who's done what," he told the otter softly.

"No, eet ees certain not yet who is completely altogether responseeble," Cherjal admitted. "But thee rumors they say also that thees Markus has put all the members of the Quorum who don't support heem into the dungeons beneath the Quorumate. Seence nobodies can get een to see heem or them, thees can't be verified, and the members who come and go as they please, like Kindore and Vazvek, won't say what they must know."

"When's all this supposed to have happened?"

"Only a few days ago." Cherjal rubbed his flat black nose, sniffed. "Nobody really knows nothing. When asked, word come back that thee members of thee Quorum are engaged in long and deeficult deescusions about the future of the city. But that what they always say when they want to have private party and geet smashed."

"So the government of Quasequa is either overthrown or drunk," Jon-Tom decided.

Cherjal nodded. "About thee size of eet that ees. Those of us who fear thee first worry that Markus may solidify his power on the Quorum with thee help of those who support heem until eet ees unbreakable becoming." He stared up at Jon-Tom. "You gots strong eenterest in thees even though you not coming from Quasequa, man. Why?"

"I think it's also rumored that Markus claims to come from another world." Cherjal nodded. "I think he may come from mine. If I can meet with him, I may be able to straighten a lot of things out."

Cherjal glanced at Memaw. "Is true? He from another world?"

"Who'd lie about a thing like that?"

"Maybe a magician," Cherjal suggested.

"That's exactly why I need to talk to him," Jon-Tom said. A paw came down on his shoulder.

"'Ere now, mate," Mudge mumbled, "if this 'ere bloke's the type to go around deposin' rightful governments, it don't sound to me like 'e's the kind who'd be ready and willin' to 'elp you find your way 'ome."

"I admit it doesn't sound promising, but we don't know anything for certain yet and we won't until I meet this Markus. Like I said before, if he is doing these things, he may be doing so to protect himself because he's in a strange place and he's afraid for his safety."

"So hee protect heemself by taking control of everybody else?" Cherjal made a disgusted sound. "Doesn't matter no ways. No ways you can meet heem. Hee sees nobodies. Lots of people have tried to see heem. Nobody do it, and those who try too hard disappearing."

"Isn't there an appointments secretary for the Quorum, or something?"

"For thee Quorum, there is. For Markus is nothings. Only Quorum members themselves have seen heem. Appointments secretary will tell you to lost be getting."

"I see." Jon-Tom considered for a long moment

before saying, "Then we'll just have to make our own appointment. Where is Markus staying?"

"Een a private apartment in the Quorumate Complex. So the rumors saying."

Jon-Tom leaned as close to the koala as he could. "You wouldn't happen to know of a service entrance that's lightly guarded, would you?"

Mudge broke out in a broad grin. "Bugger me, mate, can it be that you're finally comin' 'round to seein' things the way the world is instead of 'ow you'd like 'em to be?"

Jon-Tom replied primly. "I am always pragmatic, Mudge."

"Oi, is that wot you calls it? I always thought it were called breakin' and enterin'."

"We're not going to break anything," Jon-Tom snapped, leaving the second half of Mudge's definition uncommented upon.

"There are several serveece entrances," Cherjal informed them, "but all are being guarded."

"Who does the guarding?"

"Eet vary from place to place."

Quorly spoke for the first time, grinning over at Jon-Tom. "Don't you worry none about the guards, luv. You just leave that little problem to Sasswise, Splitch, and meself."

"I don't know—" he began uncertainly, but she cut him off.

"We'll handle things...so to speak." Twin giggles came from the table nearby.

"I wouldn't ask anything like that of you if this wasn't really important, Quorly. I wouldn't want you to do anything that's..." Mudge leaned over, his nose inches from Jon-Tom's.

"Now, you shut up, mate," he murmured, "or you're goin' to make the ladies feel bad. They're volunteerin' for this little caper and they damn well know wot they're about. Might even 'ave themselves a good time doin' it."

"We always 'aves ourselves a good time doin' it," Sasswise commented from the neighboring table.

Not for the first time since he'd fallen in with this remarkable gaggle of otters, Jon-Tom blushed.

"It could be very dangerous."

"Now, didn't you already say that?" Quorly sounded exasperated. "That were 'alf the point in our comin' along."

"That is right, dear." Memaw looked over at Jon-Tom. "We shall help you gain entrance to the Quorumate so you may meet with Markus the Incomprehensible."

"Ineluctable," Jon-Tom corrected her. "But why?"

"We already told you, I believe. We do not care for this new wizard's politics. We stand ready to fight anything that infringes on our freedom, including each other. Can't just allow this sort of thing to slide by."

"Not bloody likely!" snorted Knorckle.

"Damn right on!" Norgil agreed.

"Then it is settled," she finished, smiling warmly at him.

"We thank you all from the bottom of our hearts. Don't we, Mudge? Mudge?"

There were more giggles from the other table, indicating that at the moment, Mudge was more interested in getting to the heart of somebody's bottom.

XIV

A slivered moon helped to conceal their approach as they paddled toward the Quorumate. The complex was constructed on a narrow, rocky peninsula that extended like a crooked finger out into the lake. This made it nigh impossible to approach without being seen, hence the decision to sneak up on it via the water.

It was a much more impressive edifice than Jon-Tom had imagined, rising some six stories above the lake. Numerous towers and walls had been enlarged over the years until the original buildings had merged in a single rambling structure that covered nearly all of the Quorumate grounds. Flying buttresses braced several towers from the outside. These were capped by flagpoles from which fluttered pennants signifying the main islands which composed the city.

The boat they'd borrowed from Cherjal drifted toward the single pier. Several other small craft were already anchored there, bobbing like metronomes in the gentle swell.

Quorly, Sasswise, and Splitch adjusted their feath ered hats as they slipped out of the boat. All three were dressed to kill, so to speak. Making no attempt to hide their presence, they staggered straight toward the guard station, giving a perfect imitation of three drunken, carousing ladies of the evening out for a good time. Meanwhile Jon-Tom and the others lay low in the boat and waited.

Half the night seemed to go by. Jon-Tom found himself staring at the moon. It looked like the same moon he used to watch set over the Pacific. There was the same pattern of mares and mountain chains. How could that be in this world, so different in so many other ways from his own? There was so much he still didn't understand.

The sounds of running feet interrupted his reverie. Hands on ramwood staff, he tensed, as did his companions.

But the face that peered down at them, hat askew over one eye, was a familiar one.

"Come on then!" Quorly whispered urgently at them.

They piled out of the boat and ran up the pier. Jon-Tom was something of a runner, but already he saw he was going to have a hard time keeping up with this bunch.

Quorly led them up a succession of steep stone steps until they reached a circular patio that overlooked the pier. Lying side by side were an unconscious wolf and weasel. Their armor was stacked haphazardly off to one side. Sasswise and Splitch stood over them, daintily readjusting their attire.

Sasswise was swinging a weapon in circles. It looked something like a cast-iron nunchaku. She gestured with her free paw at the weasel.

"Belongs to 'im, this does. After we got acquainted I asked 'im if I might 'ave a look at it. He was afraid I might 'urt me delicate self with it, but I promised 'im I'd be careful." She put a finger to her lips and assumed an innocent look. "'Pears I wasn't careful enough. Wot a shame."

"Right then, let's hop to it." Memaw directed Knorckle, Drortch, and Wupp as they bound the two guards. They snored on peacefully, dreaming perhaps of happier moments. They were going to be more than a little upset when they came to and realized what had been done to them.

"We can't just leave them here." Jon-Tom peered carefully through the open doorway into the building. "Another patrol might come along and find them."

"Right," said the petite Splitch in her little-girl-cub voice. "Let's dump 'em in the lake."

"No, no, I want to try and avoid any unnecessary killing."

"Told you 'e was weird," Mudge whispered to Quorly.

"We can put them in the boat," Memaw suggested.

Jon-Tom waited anxiously while half the otters proceeded to dispose of the guards. The hallway which led invitingly inward remained empty.

Several minutes passed. He was startled to see their boat moving slowly away from the pier, its sail raised. Sasswise gave him an explanation when she rejoined the others.

"We compromised, Jonny-Tom. Nobody'll find 'em now. The wind'll carry 'em out into the lake proper."

"What happens if they run into another boat? Fishermen or something?"

"Won't make no bit o' difference," Splitch assured him. "I mean, if you were told to guard an important place and somebody found you tied up and sailin' away from that place with your pants missin', would you be in a 'urry to report it to your superiors?"

"I guess not." He turned his attention inward. "Let's find this Markus." He called down the hall, where Memaw had stationed herself behind a table. "All clear?"

She nodded and waved. They crowded in, commenting on the elegant furnishings and marble floor. The ceiling was impressively high, which meant that Jon-Tom could move without having to walk hunched over. His oft-bruised head was grateful for the clearance.

They trotted down the long hall and turned left. Cherjal had provided them with what was generally known of the Quorumate's floor plan, but no one was certain of the location of the residential rooms where Markus was likely to have his headquarters. They'd have to find that themselves.

Everything went smoothly until Sasswise leaped into the air grabbing at her backside. When she came down she started haranguing the innocent Norgil.

"Will you watch wot you're doin' with that damn sword!"

"Now, look 'ere, m'lady, I'm just keepin' it 'andy in case we're attacked . . . if you don't mind." Norgil gestured with the stubby but sharp offender. "Why don't you give a body a little room to move about?"

"Move about? I'll give you room to move about, you fat slob. I'll move you . . . !"

"Quiet!" Memaw said sharply. "Be quiet, you two!"

Already too late, Jon-Tom saw despairingly. A pair of halberd-wielding foxes had crossed their path a safe distance down the corridor. The noise brought them back to investigate. Now they were staring straight at the tightly packed clutch of invaders.

"You there, where did you come from?" one demanded to know.

"Cur's cockles!" Memaw muttered. She glanced right, then left, and led them up a side corridor. Not knowing what else to do, Jon-Tom followed. Shouts and yells rang out behind them.

"So much for the element o' surprise," groused Mudge.

"It'll be all right," Quorly assured him. "You'll see. We'll lose that pair of fools quick enough."

Mudge skidded to a stop. "Righty-ho, but wot about this new lot o' fools?"

A whole platoon of soldiers had appeared in the hall directly ahead and were now charging toward them. The platoon was an interesting mix of species, varying in size from armed rats and mice to two great cats and one ape.

"Listen," Jon-Tom said innocently, "can't we talk about this?" The ape stabbed at him and he jumped aside, bringing down his staff on the other's spear. Instead of listening to reason, the ape reversed his weapon and tried to shove the butt end through Jon-Tom's teeth.

He ducked and the blow passed over his head. A swipe with the ramwood took the ape's legs out from under him. The sound of fighting was deafening in the narrow corridor. The otters found themselves at a disadvantage in such confines, where they couldn't make use of their quickness. But the guards' reinforcements couldn't get at their quarry and kept bunching up against each other in the corridors. Superior numbers couldn't be brought to bear against the invaders, but neither could they escape.

Jon-Tom saw Mudge cut a tendon in a vizcacha's leg, saw blood spurt, and watched as the stripe-faced soldier went down, too stunned to scream. Then something whacked him on the back of his neck and he staggered. He whirled, hunting for his assailant, and saw nothing but stars before his eyes.

The stars grew brighter as he was hit again. He blinked and shook his head. As he did so he leaned slightly backward, and saw his attacker. An armored possum hung by its tail from one of the rafters. Iron weights were strapped to its waist and it was taking its time picking out targets among the otters below.

Nobody could reach him and Mudge was too busy defending himself with his sword to unlimber his bow.

The possum wasn't used to fighting someone as tall as a human, however. Jon-Tom tried to knock the dangling fighter loose with his ramwood staff but couldn't quite reach him. For its part, the possum decided to stop playing around. The next iron ball it selected was lined with short, sharp spikes. It struggled to draw a bead on Jon-Tom as he bobbed and dodged below.

Jon-Tom thumbed the concealed switch set in the staff, and the ramwood lengthened by six inches of sharp steel. A sudden jab pierced the possum's throat. It looked very surprised, hung for a moment longer from the ceiling, and then dropped like a stone.

The otters fought well, but no matter how many they cut down, there were always more soldiers to take the places of the fallen. By now the whole complex must be alerted, Jon-Tom thought grimly.

Still, it was Memaw who finally called a halt to the fighting when she saw the twisted form of poor Norgil lying limp against the marble. The otter had taken half a dozen sword thrusts and his life was leaking out on the floor. Already blood made the footing treacherous. That would take away the otters' one advantage: their quickness.

So Memaw put up her sword and said, "Enough. We surrender."

"Surrender? Wot's that mean, surrender?" said Quorly, panting hard. Her fine clothing had been shredded by sword cuts but otherwise she appeared unharmed.

"No, Memaw's right, she is." Knorckle tossed his sword aside. "Better to gather strength and wits in jail than to perish here."

The guards moved among them, collecting knives

and scimitars and searching briskly for any concealed weapons. Jon-Tom prayed they might leave him his duar, but they confiscated it also, along with his backpack.

When this was done, a massively muscled jaguar shoved his way to the fore. His leather armor was streaked with sword cuts.

"Explain this outrageous intrusion," he growled.

Jon-Tom stepped forward and growled right back at him. "Outrageous is the word for it. Here we arrive on time for our appointment and instead of receiving a courteous greeting, we are brutally attacked. What kind of troops do you station in here, anyways? Cutthroats and murderers!"

The jaguar's eyes narrowed and he stroked his chin. "An appointment, you say. With whom?"

"Markus the Ineluctable," Jon-Tom told him defiantly. "And is he going to be pissed when he hears how we've been treated."

"Markus, you say?" The officer pushed his helmet back off his ears. He looked tired. "Next I expect you're going to tell me that this is all a misunderstanding and that it'll easily be straightened out as soon as I take you to the advisor?"

"Of course," Jon-Tom replied easily.

The jaguar seemed to consider. "The master is sleeping and would not wish to be disturbed. This casts something of a shadow over your story, tall man. It may be that the appointment you seek will be with the Chamber of Official Torments... but that is not for me to decide. The Great Markus will do that."

"Fine with us. If you'll just take us to him, I imagine he forgot all about our visit tonight. He'll straighten this out fast." Jon-Tom glared at the soldiers bunched together behind the officer. "When he learns what's happened, heads will roll."

"I prefer to bounce them myself," said the jaguar evenly. "As a point of interest, some bounce nicely for a while, while others just go smash. I wonder which yours would do."

Jon-Tom went slightly weak in the knees, but didn't let it show. "Why not ask Markus?"

"Why not, indeed?" replied the officer surprisingly. "As I said, only he will know the truth of your words. If you'll be so kind as to follow me?" He gestured with a paw.

"That's more like it." Jon-Tom strode confidently past the jaguar, continuing to glare at the guards.

They descended several levels until the air began to grow thick and moist. They were below lake level, and moisture seeped relentlessly through ancient stonework.

"Markus the Ineluctable lives down here?" he asked their guide.

"No," rumbled the jaguar. "As I told you, he sleeps and would not wish to be disturbed. I will notify him of your arrival. As he's expecting you, I'm sure he'll be right down. Meanwhile, I thought you would enjoy explaining yourselves to the leading members of our government, who are at this moment awaiting your presence in their new conference chamber."

"We've heard that some members of the Quorum weren't getting along too well with their new advisor."

"Is that so? A vicious, unfounded rumor. So much gossip in the city marketplaces these days. You really shouldn't pay attention to such idle chatter. Ah, the Quorum doorman. You there!" he roared at a dozing javelina. "Visitors for the Quorum!"

Tusks flashing in the dim torchlight, the javelina roused himself and led them forward. Jon-Tom balked at the sight of the iron grille, but there was nothing to be done about it now. They were herded toward the open cell.

"There you go. Enjoy your conference," the officer said smoothly as the cursing, complaining otters were shoved through the opening. The javelina locked it from the outside.

Jon-Tom glared through the bars. "You're a real smart-ass, aren't you, fuzz-brain?"

"My, my, such language from those who are friends of the Great Markus," the jaguar said mockingly. "I will inform him of your arrival. Meanwhile, do make yourselves comfortable. I must see to the preparations for your evening meal. Swill is served in a couple of hours." He turned and stalked off toward the stairway, laughing uproariously at his subtle wit. His soldiers clustered tightly around him.

Turning, the otters found themselves sharing the cell with half a dozen surprised and rudely awakened elders. Here were those members of the Quorum who'd refused to countenance Markus's bid for power . . . and one other. The robed salamander stepped forward and introduced himself.

"I greet you, fellow sufferers. I am Oplode the Sly, former chief advisor in matters arcane and mystic to the legitimate Quorum of Quasequa and now chief advisor in those same arts to the deposed Quorum of Quasequa."

Jon-Tom wasn't ready for conversation with Oplode or anyone else. Failing to find an empty corner, he sat down in the center of the floor.

"My fault, dragging all of you into this. I should've come by myself."

"Let's not 'ave none o' that, Jonny-Tom," said Quorly.

"Right." Drortch put a consoling paw on his shoulder. "You didn't 'ave no choice in the matter. You couldn't 'ave made us stay behind if you'd tried."

"Right . . . that's so . . . better believe it . . ." agreed a chorus of otterish voices.

"'Ow come nobody ever asks me wot I wants to do?" Mudge found a section of empty floor to sulk on.

Memaw laid a maternal paw on Jon-Tom's head. "Norgil's time had come, that's all, my friend. Perhaps time for all of us. We have no regrets."

"But I do, damn it! You shouldn't be here with me."

"Damn right, mate," snapped Mudge. Memaw wagged a warning finger in his direction.

"Now, Mudge..."

"Don't 'Mudge' me, water-elder," the otter snapped back. "I've earned the right to 'ave me say, I 'ave. You've only 'ad to deal with this spellsingin' shit'ead for a few days. Me, I've 'ad to put up with 'is sorceral muddlin's for months. All I want is to live an ordinary life. An ordinary life, mind. And 'e keeps yankin' me off to join 'im on 'is bloody bloomin' bleedin' inexplicable quests and wotever. Well, I'm sick of it." He spat the words in Jon-Tom's direction. "You 'ear me, mate? Sick of it!"

Quorly stared at him in disbelief. "Mudge! I'm surprised at you."

"'Ell, lúv, I'm surprised at me, too. Surprised I'm 'ere, but not surprised at 'ow this 'as turned out. 'Twas only a matter o' time, it were. That senile old turtle went and spun the wheel o' fate one time too many, and now the odds 'ave finally caught up with us. Only thing that's surprised me is that I've survived 'is rotten company as long as I 'ave." He turned his back on them all.

"Turtle?" The elderly salamander wiped at his face. "Can it be that you are the help the great Clothahump has sent to us?"

"Not us," Memaw corrected him. "We are sort of along for the swim." She indicated Jon-Tom. "You need to talk to the young gentleman."

Oplode turned an amphibious eye on the uncomfortable Jon-Tom while one of the deposed Quorum members voiced the thought that was in all their minds.

"Just him? Him, and the noisy otter? They're our salvation? They are the strength Clothahump sends to us?"

"I fear it may be so." Oplode hesitated as he spoke to Jon-Tom. "Unless you and the otter are simply the advance scouts. That's it, isn't it? Clothahump and his mystic army are encamped not far away, awaiting your report, aren't they?"

Jon-Tom sighed as he turned to face the advisor. "Sorry. I'm afraid we're it. Me, Mudge, and our recently acquired friends. We're your help, and we haven't done a very good job of it so far. My plan was for us to slip in here quiet-like so that I could have a face-to-face meeting with Markus before anyone got excited. We didn't quite manage it."

"Now, there's a snappy news bulletin," Mudge muttered from his corner.

"An interesting stratagem," Oplode murmured, "but what good would it have done had you succeeded? You would still have ended up down here with the rest of us who oppose his bid for absolute power."

Jon-Tom tried to summon up some of his battered confidence. "Not necessarily. If he didn't listen to reason, I was prepared to fight him. I'm a spellsinger, and a pretty good one."

Oplode slumped. "A spellsinger? Is that all?"

"Hey, now, wait a minute. I've accomplished some pretty impressive things with my spellsinging."

"You do not understand. I do not mean to impugn your modest talents. But you must know that I am a wizard of no small stature, yet I was unable to counter the magic of this Markus. It is as unpredictable and peculiar as it is effective. No mere spellsinger, however voluble, can hope to deal with that." The salamander strained to see behind Jon-Tom.

"Besides which, you have no instrument to accompany you."

"They confiscated it along with our weapons and supplies."

"It does not matter," said Newmadeen sadly. "It's obvious this one wouldn't stand a chance against Markus anyway."

"I'd hoped to find a little more support here," Jon-Tom told them. He was starting to get a little peeved by all the criticism. "None of you have any idea of my capabilities. You don't know what I can do."

"Perhaps." The elderly squirrel who spoke was clad in rags. The bandage around his forehead indicated he hadn't accepted his deposition and subsequent incarceration gracefully. Several pieces of his tail were missing.

"But we do know what you can't do, and that's get in to see Markus. No one sees him anymore except his closest associates—Kindore and Asmouelle and the other traitors. And that dim-witted mountain of a bodyguard of his, Prugg."

"I *have* to see him. We have to meet. It's the only way to resolve things."

"Things will be resolved soon enough, as soon as he has consolidated his power," said the squirrel, whose name was Selryndi. "Markus will resolve his embarrassments by having them skewered, weighted, and dumped in a deep part of the lakes." He looked bitter. "We are at fault. We ought never to have allowed him to compete for the post of advisor."

"It was the law," said Oplode.

"Aye, but you warned us against him afterward and we didn't listen."

"Now is not the time for recriminations or for the

laying of blame. We must try to get word to the population. A general uprising is our only hope. Or we might try to bribe one of those close to him to attempt an assassination."

"That will not be easy and could hasten our demise," said old Trendavi, "considering how carefully he guards himself."

"Nevertheless, we must try. In matters both magical and political he grows stronger by the day. We dare not waste a moment in trying to unseat him. I do not intend to end up as fish food. If only Clothahump had seen fit to send us some real help."

"All right, mates." Mudge climbed to his feet and sauntered over. "That's just about enough. I admit we 'aven't made much of an impression on this Markus or anyone else in your bloomin' community, and we did kind o' botch our intended nocturnal visit to this Markus's bedchamber, but don't blame your problems on Jon-Tom 'ere. We were doin' a bit o' all right until somebody put a sword accidental-like in the wrong place and tempers got out o' 'and for a minim. Jon-Tom's done the best he could for you sorry lot. We didn't get you into this mess, you know.

" 'Ere we are, come down 'ere out o' the goodness o' our 'earts"—Jon-Tom gaped at the blatant falsehood but said nothing—"to try and 'elp you folks out o' a tight spot, and all you can do is moan and bawl about wot you didn't get. Maybe we ain't done so good so far but from wot I sees we ain't done any worse than you 'ave. So let's call a halt to the mutual name-callin' and see if we can't work together to figure out a ways to keep our skins intact, wot?"

It was silent in the cell until Jon-Tom said softly, "Thank you, Mudge."

The otter spun on him. "Shut your bleedin' cake-

'ole and start thinkin' of a ways out, you bloody interferin' twit." He stalked over to the bars in a huff.

"Charmin' friend you got there," Quorly told Jon-Tom.

"He is unique, isn't he?" Feeling a little better about himself, he turned back to the Quorum. "All right then. We're still alive and we've still got our wits about us. Oplode, if you're such a great wizard, how come you haven't magicked your way out of this prison?"

"Do you not think I have tried, man? The first thing Markus did after we were placed in this cell was to ensorcel it with some kind of containment spell. My powers are useless here. Not that I think he fears my magic, as he has already defeated me in contest, but he is very careful and takes no chances with any who oppose him."

Jon-Tom nodded, eyed the stone walls surrounding them on three sides. "What about digging our way out?"

"With this?" Cascuyom held up a spoon and a dull-bladed knife. "Even if we could cut into this old rock with our eating utensils, we don't have enough time."

Jon-Tom was about to make another suggestion but was interrupted. Footsteps sounded on the stairs outside their cell. Everyone turned to look.

The jaguar who had overseen their capture strode down the steps, leading a group of heavily armed guards. He approached the bars and peered through. The prisoners glared back, their expressions running the gamut from defiance to contempt. The officer ignored them.

"Which one of you is the leader here?" He grinned nastily. "And I don't mean you, Trendavi. The only thing you lead anymore is the procession to the urinal." The deposed premier said nothing. He had retained his dignity if not his position. "Come on, speak up."

"'E is," said Mudge suddenly, pointing toward Jon-Tom.

"Thanks," Jon-Tom said dryly.

Mudge shrugged. "You always said you wanted to lead, mate. No reason to be bashful now."

Memaw stepped forward. "I am the leader, you young hooligan. I will go with you." The javelina opened the grate.

Jon-Tom pushed her gently aside. "No, Memaw. It's all right. I'll go." He turned to face the jaguar. "Where are we going?"

"The Great Markus wishes to know why you have infiltrated his home and how many other traitors lie in wait outside to cause him further mischief."

"Ain't no other traitors but us," said Knorckle.

Memaw turned and swatted him up the side of his head, knocking his hat off. "Aren't we clever today, Knorckle. Tell me, are you going to help them pull the lever when they hang us, too?"

"Sorry, mum." The abashed Knorckle bent to retrieve his hat.

"Markus," the officer continued, "would also know whence you came, whether any of you escaped, and what the intentions of your allies on the outside might be." This time none of the prisoners was inspired to comment. The jaguar returned his gaze to Jon-Tom.

"I advise you to cooperate and reply truthfully to any questions Markus may ask." Jon-Tom's heart gave a little jump but he held his silence. "Master of the dark arts that he is, he possesses means of making you tell the truth that are both slow and painful."

"Then I'm to be taken to Markus?" The jaguar nodded.

Jon-Tom could hardly believe his luck. That was just what they'd been trying to achieve all along. He didn't say that, of course. Instead he tried to look defiant. "I'm looking forward to the meeting."

"Then you're either braver than you look or dumber." The jaguar gestured. The guards formed a semicircle around the cell entrance while the javelina pushed the gate inward. As soon as Jon-Tom had been pulled out, the gate was slammed shut again. The noise echoed through the dungeon.

"There is just one thing." Jon-Tom spoke offhandedly.

The jaguar eyed him impatiently, paws on hips. "Don't waste my time, man, or I'll have you dragged into Markus's presence. He won't like that."

Jon-Tom leaned close, whispered conspiratorially. "I'm not really the leader of this bunch. I'm a wandering minstrel, see, and I was forced to join them. Now, I know you probably think I'm making this all up"—the jaguar nodded sagely—"but that's why I'm not afraid of meeting the great Markus. He'll know the truth. Only thing is, I'm afraid he won't believe me unless he hears me sing, and I can't sing without my duar. The one your troops took from me."

The officer considered, eyeing Jon-Tom intently. For his part, the prisoner assumed the blandest expression he could manage. Finally the jaguar glanced toward his subofficer.

"What of what he says?"

The fox replied in a gruff voice. "Aye, there was a duar among the supplies we inventoried."

"Was it thoroughly inspected?" Jon-Tom couldn't breathe.

"It was, sir. Appears to be a perfectly ordinary instrument." Jon-Tom breathed again.

The officer nodded absently toward Jon-Tom. "A peculiar encumbrance to carry into battle. Yet you say you came to talk and not to fight." He grinned. "Well, you can't have it back."

"But it's only an instrument," Jon-Tom pleaded, seeing a last chance slipping away.

"Tough. Personal property of all you traitors is confiscated. There is one way you could regain possession, however."

"What do I have to do?"

"Convince Markus you're innocent." The jaguar's laughter boomed through the dungeon. "Let's go, and let there be no more talk of what *you* want!"

The otters crowded against the bars, shouting encouragement, while the deposed members of the Quorum hung back near the rear of the cell and looked on sadly.

"Chin up, Jonny-Tom! . . . stiff upper lip, old boy . . . don't let 'em get to you . . . show 'em wot you're made of, Jon-Tom! . . . give 'em 'ell, mate!"

Jon-Tom turned and rewarded his friends with a hopeful smile as he started up the steps. A trio of alert guards preceded him while three more followed. The officer stayed close to his side at all times. No chance to break free.

They climbed half a dozen flights of stairs until they finally emerged onto a stone parapet. After the heavy damp of the dungeon, the cool night air was a shock to his system. Several stories below, the water of the great lake glistened in the moonlight.

As they marched him toward a tower, he thought of making a break for it, of diving over the side to freedom. Two things restrained him. For one, if he happened to misjudge his leap, he would splatter himself all over the stones below. For another, he was a much better runner than he was a swimmer. No doubt Markus had his own allies among the aquatic species. Armed beavers or muskrats could recapture him in seconds.

Besides, it might cost him his chance to finally meet this mysterious Markus the Ineluctable. He'd rather have gone to the meeting with his duar nestled reassuringly under his arm, but at least he was going to see what their nemesis was made of. He wondered if the officer paralleling him sensed his nervousness.

What would Markus the Ineluctable be like? Human, yes. He already knew that. But what kind of human, and from what world? His own, this one, somewhere else? Was Markus nothing more than an ambitious local wizard who'd concocted his story of coming over from another universe solely to frighten and intimidate his opponents? Or did he come from some mysterious unknown dimension where evil held sway?

What was "human" and what was not? Couldn't something with horns on its head and a barbed tail be described as human? And if the latter description proved to be nearer the truth, what concern would such a creature have with the petty problems of one Jonathan Thomas Meriweather?

The tower they were marching toward could only be approached by a single narrow walkway. Elsewhere, the stone walls fell sharply toward the water far below. The guards flanking the entrance were the largest Jon-Tom had seen. Both lions stood half a head taller than six feet and were armed with massive metal axes.

The jaguar exchanged greetings with his oversized cousins, and the party was admitted to a hallway beyond. Once inside, Jon-Tom couldn't help noticing that his escort abruptly lost a lot of its boldness. They exchanged anxious, uneasy whispers and searched the torchlit corridor with darting, nervous eyes. Their words and reactions showed they didn't want to proceed any farther down that singular passageway, but the jaguar bravely led them on.

Until they halted ten feet from a last door. The officer took Jon-Tom's arm and pulled him forward. Stopping before the door, he rapped three times on the wood with one paw. The door opened slightly. Putting the other paw in the middle of Jon-Tom's back, the officer gave him a shove and sent him stumbling inward. The door was pulled shut quickly behind him.

The room was not large, with a high ceiling and open wooden beams from which dangled wired-together skeletons. Whether they had belonged to the subjects of arcane experiments or to unlucky supplicants, Jon-Tom had no way of knowing. The room was softly lit, and the source of the illumination was a shock.

In place of the familiar torches or oil lamps or, for those wealthy enough to afford them, globes containing light spells, were several battered but serviceable-looking fluorescent light fixtures. Though he searched hard, he couldn't see any cords or sockets. Nevertheless, the lights shone efficiently.

The furnishings were of local manufacture. Many were decorated with gold and pewter. There was a large table with chairs, many sculptures and wall hangings, and several tall crystal vases full of jewels. Of more interest than that, than even the fluorescent lights, were the three two-foot-long model airplanes ensconced neatly in alcoves in one wall. There was a Fokker biplane painted red, a Cutlass WWII dive bomber, and a miniature Beechcraft Bonanza.

"You may approach," declared a voice.

Jon-Tom whirled and stared toward the poorly lit far end of the room. The voice was heavily accented. Was this Markus the Ineluctable? He moved toward the voice, ready to retreat as best he could if the wizard reacted with blind rage.

As he crossed the room he made out a large

wooden throne resting on a dais several steps higher than the rest of the chamber. Small tables held silver candlesticks. Leaning up against one leg of the throne was an exquisite, bejeweled, and quite functional sword. Jon-Tom was cheered by the sight. It hinted that the Great Markus didn't have total confidence in his magical abilities.

Markus the Ineluctable slouched on his throne and regarded his prisoner imperiously. Resting by the wizard's right hand was by far the strangest object in the room. Jon-Tom couldn't take his eyes off it.

"I am," the inhabitant of the throne announced grandly, "Markus the Ineluctable, Markus the Great, Ruler of Quasequa and all the Lakes District and all the lands that conjoin them. Soon to be Emperor of the World."

"Yeah," Jon-Tom replied evenly, "I know who you are. What I want to know," he said, pointing at the alien intrusion lying next to the wizard's right hand, "is if that's a pastrami on rye. It looks like a pastrami on rye." He sniffed. "It smells like a pastrami on rye. It's got to *be* a pastrami on rye!" His mouth was salivating. He could smell the mustard ten feet away.

Markus's eyes widened as he stood. Jon-Tom had a clear view of him for the first time. He wore a strange black suit backed by a dirty white shirt and black bow tie. The tie rode the collar slightly askew. There was a moth-eaten black top hat on his head. In his left hand he held a stick or cane of black plastic tipped with white at both ends. A black cape trailed across the throne behind him.

All in all he presented a moderately impressive appearance, except for one thing which the inhabitants of Quasequa would tend to overlook. Markus's shoes were brown brogans.

"How dare you digress in my presence!" he snapped,

but there was evident uncertainty in his accusation. It lacked conviction.

Five six, maybe five seven, Jon-Tom decided. In his late forties and not in real swell shape. In fact, despite the wizard's strenuous efforts to suck it in, a substantial paunch kept creeping out over his belt line. There didn't appear to be much hair beneath the black top hat. Bushy brown eyebrows framed deeply sunk, dark eyes. Bags sagged beneath. The nose was flat and almost triangular. Jon-Tom couldn't tell if the shape was natural or the result of having been broken several times.

The mouth was thin and delicate, almost girlish. Frizzy sideburns exploded from both sides of the head. An enormous fake diamond ring glistened on one finger.

"Excuse me. It's just that the last time I saw a pastrami on rye was in the Westwood Deli on Wilshire Boulevard. If you knew what I've been eating these past months, you'd understand my reaction."

Markus the Ineluctable descended from his throne and found himself in the awkward position of having to stare up at his prisoner.

"Where'd you hear that?"

"I've heard it all my life." He was no longer afraid. Still not too hopeful, but no longer afraid. "I'm a graduate student...I *was* a graduate student...in law at UCLA until I found myself yanked over here."

"UCLA," Markus mumbled. "Well, I'll be damned." He circled his visitor slowly, inspecting him as carefully as would a museum curator who'd just unwrapped a newly arrived statue. "You aren't putting me on, kid? You're for real?"

"Damn right I am. The question is, who the hell are you?"

At this the wizard straightened slightly. "I'm Markus the Ineluctable, that's who. Ruler of Qusquoqua." He shook his head. "Damn. Never can get that right. Ruler of Quasequa."

"Can the bullshit and tell me who you are and how you got here."

Markus nodded up at him. "All right." He removed his top hat, set it on a nearby table. Jon-Tom saw that he was bald all the way to the back of his head.

"But first you tell me how you got here, kid."

"I don't know," Jon-Tom told him truthfully. "A local wizard needed help, and for some reason I got picked on. It was a mistake, but that hasn't made me feel a whole lot better. He can't send me back, at least not for a long time. So I'm stuck here. I've been stuck here for quite a while. How about you?"

"Well, you know, kid, it's the damndest thing..."

Jon-Tom found a chair and settled down to listen.

XV

"See," Markus told him "I'm a professional magician." Jon-Tom chose not to comment on this. Hear him out, he told himself. Markus was more than willing to talk; indeed, he seemed eager to do so.

"Markus the Ineluctable's my stage handle. My real name is Markle Kratzmeier, from Perth Amboy, New Jersey. I've been doing the same schtick for years, all up and down the East Coast. I mean, I knew I'd never get rich, but it was better than pushing lettuce around in the market, and you can work your own hours. And you never know when some agent might see you and ask you to go out to Vegas.

"Haven't made it yet, though. Once played a nice joint in Manhattan and a couple of times a real sharp club in Atlantic City, but usually I ain't that lucky. I do the usual gigs: private parties, bar mitzvahs, kids' birthdays." He made a face. "God, I hate doing kids' birthdays. Little snot-noses always crawling all over you, throwing up and begging for candy. I've also worked most of the bump-and-grind joints from Jersey City all the way down the coast to Surf City. I've seen a lot of life, kid, and not much of it pretty."

He took a deep breath and leaned on one of the tables for support.

"So anyway, there I am in this Con Edison power plant. Bunch of the guys who run the place are throwing a stag party for their foreman because the sap's getting married the next day. They don't have enough money to rent a hall, so they get together with the night shift and decorate part of the plant on the sly, see? Wasn't so bad. I've worked in worse dumps. It was noisy in there, but at least it was clean.

"I'm doing my stuff, building to my big finish, and it's going pretty good because they're all smashed or stoned anyway."

"Big finish?"

"Yeah." Markus beamed proudly. "I saw one of the gals or one of the guys from the audience in half."

"That's original."

"Hey, don't knock it, kid. Maybe it's an old trick, but it still buffaloes the marks. Anyway, I have to do one more thing before I get to go home. There's this big cake, see?"

"I get the picture," Jon-Tom said, nodding.

"Yeah. They hired this bimbo from one of the local topless joints." He paused, thinking, and those bushy brows drew together. "Merill, or Cheryl, I think her name was. Anyway, she's gonna pop out of the cake in her swimsuit. The trick is I'm going to wave my wand after the guys get through moaning and make her suit fall off. Pretty neat, huh?"

"Very witty," Jon-Tom admitted carefully.

"So I'm trying to do it up right, give these guys their money's worth. I'm waving my wand all over the place"—he demonstrated by fluttering the cheap plastic wand—"only I don't look where I'm going. Suddenly everybody's shouting, and the broad is screaming, and I feel myself going ass-over-backwards, and I think, okay, that's it, you dumb schmuck, you finally bought it. Had to overdo it for a couple of extra tips. I'm falling over and over and the damn cape's in my eyes and I can't see a thing except I get just a quick look at this big dynamo or generator or whatever the hell it was.

"Then I hit it. Tell me something, kid. When you were little, did you ever get real clever and stick your finger in a socket?" Jon-Tom nodded. "Well, for about ten seconds there I felt like I'd done just that, only with my head. I'm shaking all over before I black out.

"When I wake up, I'm lying in a room in this rockpile and there's this big dumpy character leaning over me asking me if I feel okay." Markus's tone was earnest. "Kid, I don't mind telling you that this is a little tough to take, coming off a stag party where I didn't have a damn thing to drink. I swear, not a drop! Couple of beers maybe, one shot of rye. Pretty good stuff too. But I know I ain't drunk.

"So I try to keep cool even though this refugee from a horror flick is standing over me, and I get the idea to wave my wand and make with a few magic words to try and scare it away, and what do you think happens? Something picks the big jerk up and throws him across the room." He paused to take a long drink from a pewter tankard. "Local booze ain't half-bad, kid. Anyways, I see that this mass of talking meat is more scared of me than I am of him. So I start fooling around with the old wand"—he conducted his words with the plasic as he spoke—"and what do you think I find out?"

"What?" asked Jon-Tom guardedly.

"That all those cheap tricks I've been practicing for twenty-five years, all the junk I've been doing for spoiled brats in Westchester and their tight-assed mothers who wouldn't give me the time of day, they all work here. For real. I can do real magic. Not only like the stuff I've always done, but new stuff, too. Ain't that a pip?

"So I talk to this big dummy who found me and see that he's long on muscle but slow upstairs, and I get the lay of the land. I find out that there's another magician here who kinda runs things from an advisor's post. I feel my way around, introduce myself real nice, and finally meet up with a couple of the guys who sit on this Quorum or Mafia or Congress or whatever you want to call it. Some of them see which way the shit's flying and some of them don't, and with a little magic and the help of the ones who see right, I take over the whole damn city." He spread his hands and grinned.

"Just like that. Me, Markle Kratzmeier from Perth Amboy. Now I'm the advisor, the chief, the head honcho. And this is only the beginning, kid. Only the beginning. These hairy rubes think I'm the greatest thing to hit them since chopped liver. And you know what? I am. There's got to be stuff I can do I ain't even thought up yet. Me, Markle Kratzmeier. After years of eating dirt and yessiring and no-ma'aming and putting up with you wouldn't believe what kind of shit, I'm on top. You know what? It feels good!"

"That sounds swell," Jon-Tom agreed. "You know what else? I can do a little magic myself."

"Izzat so?" Markus suddenly looked wary.

"Oh, nothing big, nothing like what you've done," Jon-Tom hastened to reassure him. "Just small stuff. Entertaining, like that." He took a chance and moved nearer. Markus didn't back away from him.

"Now, what I was thinking was that with the two of us working together on the problem, maybe we could figure out a way for both of us to get back home."

Markus eyed him in disbelief. "Get back home? Why the hell would I want to get back home, kid? I mean, look at the setup I've got here. Tell you what, though. You play your cards right and don't screw up and maybe I can use you. It'd be nice to have somebody to talk with about back home. But go back?" He waved at the lavishly decorated room. "You want me to trade this in and go back to doing bar mitzvahs and weddings and working crappy clubs up and down the Jersey coast? You got to be nuts, kid.

"Anyway, I wouldn't know how to start getting home, even if I cared to try it. No way. See, these rubes know what money is, and what power is, even if most of them do look like they came out of the local zoo or dog pound. In other words, they know what's important in life. Maybe some of them have whiskers that grow sideways instead of down, and paws instead of palms, and fur coats instead of skin, but they're still people. And I can run the whole bunch of them. Hell, I *am* running the whole bunch of them! And like I said, this is just the beginning.

"Know something else?" He winked and Jon-Tom felt suddenly unclean. "There's even people like us here."

"I know."

"And some of the dames look pretty good. I've seen some broads around here who could've made it big in the big casinos except for what they all seem to be a little on the short side. That suits me fine since I ain't no center for the Knicks myself. They're all in awe of me, afraid of me." Markus's sunken brown eyes looked more piggish than ever, Jon-Tom mused.

"I like that. I like it a lot, kid. I like them all bowing and scraping and cowering in front of me. Go back home?" He laughed, a short nasty sound. "If I tried touching any broads who looked half as good as the ones here back in New York, they'd spit on me and call a cop. You, you're young and good-looking, kid. You never had that happen to you. You haven't the vaguest idea what it's like for a woman you idolize to spit on you.

"Well, nobody spits on Markus the Ineluctable!" he snarled. "Go home? I'd sooner cut my own throat right now. All my life I've gotten the short end of the stick. All my life people have cut me down. Well, no more. This is my chance to get back at them, and I ain't giving it up!"

Jon-Tom listened to Markus rave on and forbore from pointing out that the people of this world had never put him down. Jon-Tom was just old enough and had seen just enough of the world to know for the first time exactly what he was up against in the person of Markus the Ineluctable.

He was one of the faceless ones, one of the insignificant, uninspired, nameless persons whose only real purpose in life was to occupy a few bytes in a government computer. A number more than a reality, an organic something in the shape of a man who took up space. Someone who under normal conditions was incapable of doing good and too incompetent to do evil.

But a twist of space-time, a jog in the smooth procession of events, an irony of eternity had thrust him into this world and had placed him in a position to do damage all out of proportion to his naturally constituted self. In his own world Markle Kratzmeier would simply have faded away without making much of an impression on existence one way or the other.

But in this world, Markus the Ineluctable and his ability to work magic posed a terrifying threat to people who had never known of his history, his problems, his concealed envies and hatreds. That didn't matter to someone like Markus, who believed that all the forces of the universe were arrayed against him. He wanted to strike out, strike back against life, and it wouldn't matter to him who or what got in his way.

So Jon-Tom had been both right and wrong. The man who had usurped power in the city-state of Quasequa was indeed from his own world, but only in body. In spirit he was an alien, an evil import, and a danger to everyone who came in contact with him. The problem now at hand was not one of getting home, but of saving himself and his friends.

It was clear that Markus's only interest lay in gathering as much power to himself as possible.

Carefully. Jon-Tom was going to have to proceed very carefully. Markus wasn't stupid. He was no scholar, but he had street smarts, and those could prove more dangerous than real intelligence.

"I understand. I mean, you've got a helluva setup here. A couple of expatriates like you and me from the good old U.S. of A., we ought to stick together. Like I said, I've got a little talent myself. Nothing like what you can do, of course, but I can do small stuff. I know we wouldn't be equal, wouldn't be a team. I wouldn't expect that. But with my abilities augmenting yours, we could really show these dumb animals a thing or two."

"Yeah. Hey, you know what I'd really like?" Markus told him after he'd finished making his proposal. "I'd really like a couple of Big Macs, some fries, and a vanilla shake."

"I could go for that, too," Jon-Tom told him enthusiastically. "Why don't you let me do this one?" He looked around as if searching for something. "I do my magic better with some music, though. It's like with your wand. Kind of helps to set the mood, if you know what I mean. Your guards took my instrument away from me. If I could have it back I promise you a regular MacFeast." He pointed. "Right on that table there. Then we can make plans."

Markus stared at him for a long moment, then repeated his thoroughly unpleasant laugh. "What's the matter with you, kid? You think I was born yesterday? You think I've spent all my life poking through every dump on the East Coast without learning nothing about people?"

"I don't know what you're talking about," Jon-Tom said lamely.

"The hell you don't. You're too eager. Too eager to throw in with me, too eager to help, too eager to throw your buddies over, and you're sure as hell too eager to get your mitts on your guitar or whatever it was that my boys took off you." He smiled. It was no more pleasant than his laugh.

"Tell you what, though. I'm a fair guy. This buddy of mine I was telling you about earlier? His name's Prugg. Maybe I'll let you wrestle him for your duar. In fact, I'll go one better than that. You beat him and I'll take you on as my partner, fifty-fifty split, straight down the line. How's that, kid?" Before Jon-Tom could reply, Markus looked past him and whistled.

"Hey, Prugg! Come on out and join us. I want to introduce you to smart-boy here."

Something moved in the darkness near the back of the room. A section of wall pivoted on its axis, revealing an immense shape. It stepped out into the room. In one paw it easily held an iron club that looked like an Olympic barbell that had been melted to a stub at one end. A leather cuirass two inches thick covered it from chest to thighs.

The bear was nearly nine feet tall and probably weighed in the neighborhood of a ton and a half.

"Kill now?" it rumbled expectantly.

"No, not now." Markus looked back up at Jon-Tom. "How about it, kid? Can you take him?"

"Come on," Jon-Tom said uneasily, "this isn't funny."

"You bet your smart ass it ain't." Markus's smile vanished as he moved forward until he was standing right next to his prisoner. "You fucking college boys think you know everything, don't you? Mummy and Daddy paying your way through school, paying for your car and your dates?"

As a matter of fact, Jon-Tom had been holding down two part-time jobs to help pay his tuition, but Markus wouldn't allow him a chance to get a word in edgewise.

"Not me. When I was twelve I was hauling crates of vegetables to make enough money to buy shoes. Lettuce, tomatoes, cucumbers, squash; all that shit. You think I ever saw any of that money?" He shook his head angrily. "My old man took it away from me to buy booze with so he and my mother could go out and get drunk every Saturday night.

"If you dropped one of those crates and it busted, it came out of your salary. When the fresh stuff came in from the truck farms in central and south Jersey, the college boys used to come in from town to buy for the supermarket chains. One time I was watching one of the women who sometimes came in with them. Real slick broad, long legs and everything.

"Anyway, I had a whole crate of tomatoes on my back and I dropped it. Busted all over. Some of it got on this buyer's shoes, and they made me clean it up right there in front of everybody. All the other guys just laughed at me.

"I've never forgotten that, kid. Never thought I'd have a chance to do anything about it, until now."

"That wasn't me," Jon-Tom told him as calmly as he could. "I wasn't there. I probably hadn't even been born yet."

"So what's the difference? You intellectual schmucks are all the same. Think you know better than everybody else. I'm giving you a better chance than your kind gave me. I'm giving you a chance to fight your way out."

Prugg smiled thinly and let out a grunt that rolled through the room like thunder.

"At least let me have my instrument."

"Why, so you can work some magic maybe? Do a disappearing act? Huh-uh, kid, not a chance. This is my roll and I'm playing it for all it's worth. I'm keeping these dice unless fate jerks them out of my hands. I'm going for the whole ball of wax this time, and I don't need any wise punks from back home trying to muscle in on my territory. Tell you what I will do, though. I'll tell Prugg to go easy on you. Maybe he won't kill you. Maybe." Then he was looking toward the door as though Jon-Tom had ceased to exist as a human being.

"Hey, Thornrack! Get in here."

The jaguar who had conveyed Jon-Tom from the cell appeared. "Yes, Master?"

"Take this punk back downstairs and toss him in with his friends, but don't hurt him. I want him in one piece for later."

"Yes, Master." Thornrack entered the room and put a powerful paw on Jon-Tom's shoulder. "Let's go, man."

Markus's jeering followed Jon-Tom as he was led from the chamber. "What's wrong, kid? No snide remarks? No snappy comeback? I thought your kind had an answer for everything. Don't you? Don't you!"

The door slammed tight behind them, but as they rejoined the waiting escort and started out of the tower, Jon-Tom thought he could still hear Markus the Ineluctable ranting and raving furiously behind him.

He wasn't feeling very optimistic as they led him back down into the bowels of the Quorumate, down below the water line and into the dungeons again. Somehow he *had* to regain possession of his duar.

The only way to unseat the two-bit dictator that Markle Kratzmeier had turned into was with magic.

Certainly without the duar he wouldn't stand a chance against the bear-mountain named Prugg.

"Open it up," the jaguar said to the javelina turnkey. Jon-Tom saw his companions lined up against the bars. Clearly they read the expression on his face, because there was no cheering. Only Oplode eyed him with something approaching interest as the grille was opened and he was shoved unceremoniously inside. The grate closed with a metallic *clang* which echoed through the darkness.

Guards and turnkey retreated up the stairs, chatting conversationally. As soon as they were gone, the otters crowded around him.

"Well, mate, 'ow'd it go?"

"What did you learn?" Oplode asked curiously.

"He's from my world, all right, but I resent having to admit it. I didn't actually see him work any magic, but I don't doubt that he can. His living quarters were full of evidence."

"He proved his abilities to me in person," Oplode said softly.

"Well, wot do 'e want?" Mudge asked.

"The same thing every other tin-pot would-be emperor wants: everything. He's a dangerous, homicidal, frightened, thoroughgoing bastard, and that's giving him the benefit of the doubt. Oh, he did make one show of magnanimity. He said that if I could outfight his bodyguard, I might get my duar back."

"Prugg." Domurmur nodded knowingly. "I like you, man, but I'd put my wagering money on your opponent."

"So would I," said Jon-Tom grimly. "I've got about as much chance of beating him as I do of getting Thornrack to let us escape. Less, probably." He glanced down at Mudge. "Remember the bouncer at Madame Lorsha's in Timswitty? This one makes him look like a cub."

Mudge's whiskers twitched. "That don't sound none too promisin', mate."

"It isn't." He paused. Something had been troubling him since he'd reentered the cell, but he'd been too busy telling of his meeting with Markus to focus on it. Now he did, and it gave him a start. "Hey, I think I can feel a—"

Three pairs of furry paws slapped over his mouth and most of the rest of his face, muffling him completely. Memaw stepped close, put her fingers to her lips. Jon-Tom nodded slowly and the paws were withdrawn.

Taking his hand in her paw, she quietly drew him toward the darkest corner of the cell. The rest of the otters moved aside to let them through. There was a small twist and bend in the far corner where the cell curved around to follow the contours of the outer wall. It was there that Jon-Tom saw the source of the thing that had bothered him since he'd rejoined his companions.

A steady breeze.

It rose from a section of floor where the paving had been removed. The hole was rapidly being enlarged by the otters' best diggers. A pile of cracked and broken rock was stacked neatly against the far wall. Memaw pointed at it.

"Rotten, from age and the dampness. Quorly smelled the air coming in and we traced it back here to the floor. We managed to break the old stones away." She leaned forward and whispered anxiously. "How is it coming, my friends?"

Knorckle looked up at them. His face was smeared with wet dirt and pulverized rock. "There's somethin' else down 'ere, all right, mum. It ain't solid and it ain't water."

"Don't smell none too good," opined Mudge. He'd moved up to stand next to Jon-Tom, who reflected on the fact that the otter's shifts in mood were as fast as his fingers. "But 'tis air. Where's she comin' from?" He leaned over and tried to see into the hole. Flying paws and dirt made it difficult.

"Maybe a way out," murmured Memaw, hardly daring to hope.

Selryndi had walked over to watch. The squirrel drew his tattered cloak tightly around him, sniffed. "Can't be. This is the lowest level of the Quorumate."

"Not necessarily, my friends." Those who weren't digging turned to look at Oplode, whose expression for the first time reflected his nickname. That in itself gave Jon-Tom cause to hope. "There are... stories." His wise, shining eyes roved over the ancient masonry. "The Quorumate Complex is the largest structure in Quasequa, and the oldest. It is said that as it was built, the Lake of Sorrowful Pearls rose around it, so that the dungeon we are now imprisoned in once stood above the water line.

"It is, therefore, not inconceivable that there could be still older levels farther below."

The digging crews worked in relays while the rest kept a careful watch on the stairway. Their energy and determination was wondrous to behold, except when someone got in someone else's way. Then Memaw would have to step in and break up the fight. These were always brief and harmless, but they cost precious minutes. There was no telling when the turnkey or Thornrack might return and decide to make a cursory inspection of their cell.

Jon-Tom didn't much care what lay below the broken, sodden stones. Anything would be better than having to face Markus's bodyguard in combat.

"She's wide enough now." Frangel wiped his paws on his shorts. "Who's first down the bung-'ole?"

"I'll go," said Memaw. Sasswise pushed her aside.

"No you don't, mum. Beauty before brains."

"That's what I said, my dear," countered Memaw, shoving back.

While the two of them argued, Flutzasarangelik (but you can call him Flutz) jumped between them and disappeared through the gap in the floor. The soft thump of his landing was heard clearly by those waiting anxiously above.

"It's not too bad," he whispered up at them. "I'm in some kind of tunnel. There's a little water runnin' along the bottom, and I can 'ear it drippin' down the walls in a couple o' places, but she seems solid enough."

"How big is it?" Memaw called to him.

"Not very. Old drainage tunnel, I thinks. I 'ave to bend to clear the ceiling."

Jon-Tom went cold. He'd always been a little claustrophobic and had trouble enough in local buildings with low ceilings. If Flutz had to bend, that meant he'd have to go on hands and knees, or crab-walk. This through a narrow tunnel full of water, below the level of the lake beyond, toward an unknown destination.

And the tunnel might get smaller as they went, closing in around them tighter and tighter, pressing against his sides as well as his legs until...

A hand nudged him. "Hey, mate, are you all right?" There was genuine concern on Mudge's face. "You look a mite green."

Jon-Tom took several long, measured breaths. "I'm okay. Let's go."

Quorly followed Flutz, then Sasswise, then Frangel. Selryndi was next in line and pulled up short, eyeing the dark hole uneasily.

"Let's not be hasty. We don't know what's down there."

"But we do know what is up here," said Oplode, stepping around him. The salamander's tail twitched as he spoke. "Slow starvation and continued humiliation, or worse."

"Easy for you to say, wizard. You are as much at home underwater as a fish." He gestured at the otters. "To a certain extent, so are these industrious visitors. But the rest of us are strictly dry-land air-breathers. What if the water should rise to the ceiling?"

"What if the sun should fail to rise tomorrow?" said Oplode. "Remain here if you wish, and give our apologies to Markus the Ineluctable. The rest of us have an appointment with freedom." He turned and plunged through the opening, displaying an agility that belied his age.

Old Trendavi followed him, the pangolin's scales barely clearing the gap. The rest of the Quorum followed until only Selryndi remained.

Jon-Tom dropped through the hole and looked up at him. "I'm as much of a drylander as you are, Selryndi. If I can stand it, so can you."

The squirrel stood staring down at the tall young human. Then he muttered something under his breath, tucked his tail up against his back, and jumped. The rest of the otters brought up the rear. They took care to replace the floor as best they could. Any delay in discovering the hole would help to confuse pursuers.

Once the gap had been resealed, it was pitch-black inside the tunnel. Jon-Tom found he could still walk so long as he kept bent double. It hurt his back, but it was better than trying to crawl through the shallow, cold water that ran along the bottom of the tunnel. Still, he kept knocking his head against the ceiling, which fortunately had been worn smooth over the years.

It was anything but a pleasant hike. He kept bumping into furry bodies ahead and others stumbled into him from behind. Their only link and only guides were touch, smell, and anxious whispers.

They walked for what seemed like miles in the darkness before Frangel's voice echoed down the tunnel. "There's a branching up 'ere. Which way?"

"From which direction does the air flow most strongly?" Memaw inquired.

"From the left, mum, but the ceiling there is a bit lower." Jon-Tom cursed softly.

"Ignore it, mate," said Mudge from just in front of him. "You can 'andle it."

"I'll have to. If I go back to that cell, I'll have to go two falls out of three with a two-ton rug."

"Move on!" Mudge shouted toward the front of the line. "We're all okay back 'ere."

They pushed ahead until Frangel called another halt. "There's water comin' in 'ere pretty good."

The line shuffled slightly and Jon-Tom could hear the otters scratching around.

"Stone's loose," Memaw announced evenly. "We could probably break through. If the lake didn't come in too fast we could get out this way."

"Maybe you could," said Selryndi, "but what about the rest of us? We don't know how long we'd have to hold our breath."

"Is not the chance of freedom better than the sure death that awaits us all back in our prison?" Oplode asked him.

"Easy for you to say, gill-wizard."

"Memaw," Jon-Tom broke in, "does the tunnel go on?"

"Yes."

"Then I think we should keep going. Maybe we'll

find a better place. If not, we can still come back and try to break through here."

"My thoughts are the same, young man," she replied. "We are not abandoning anyone." A chorus of ayes rose from the rest of the otters and the line started forward once again.

As he stumbled past the place Frangel had found, cold water spurted over Jon-Tom's legs. The lake lay just beyond that feeble wall, ready to break in at any moment. If it gave way while they were further up the tunnel...

He forced himself to concentrate on the path ahead.

They seemed to be walking in a wide curve back toward the left, though the darkness had him completely disoriented. It didn't seem to bother the otters, though. He wondered if they would eventually arrive back at their starting point beneath the cell. Better the lake should break in.

Then Frangel's voice from up ahead, "It's opening up!"

Moments later they emerged from the tunnel into a vast open bowl. Jon-Tom's back protested as he straightened up. At first the big chamber seemed as dark as the tunnel, but as his eyes adjusted he found he was just able to make out dim outlines in the darkness.

The source of illumination was weak with distance: a tiny circle of light far above them.

"A well o' some kind," Quorly suggested, "inside the bloomin' Quorumate. That sound familiar to any o' you blokes?"

The Quorum members put their heads together and considered. None of them had taken much of an interest in the architecture of the rambling collection of structures they ruled from. Only Oplode had any ideas.

"In less civilized times condemned criminals were

rumored to have been thrown into such pits. It may be that this is such a place, long abandoned and only recently rediscovered."

"Damn!" Mudge shouted abruptly.

"What is it, what's wrong?" Jon-Tom asked him.

"Tripped over somethin', mate." He fumbled a bit in the darkness, lifted something for all of them to feel. Jon-Tom identified it immediately. It was a primate skull.

Oplode took it from Mudge and they could see his hands moving over the bone. "Cracked when the owner was thrown from above," he announced. Eyes immediately went to that distant circle of light.

It was quiet for a moment. Then Sasswise said, "Come on then, you lazy lot. Let's see 'ow big this 'ole is. Maybe there's another way in."

Everyone fanned out and began feeling along the wall. Climbing was out of the question, even for the agile otters. The damp stones arched to form a dome overhead. Only Oplode might have been able to manage it, in his younger days. Now he did not have the strength to cling to such a slick overhang.

"Got an idea," said Mudge. "Let's make a pyramid."

The otters discussed the proposal briefly, then settled themselves in the center of the chamber and proceeded to put on an astonishing display of acrobatics. They managed to stack themselves four high, but Splitch was still yards shy of the point where the vertical shaft of the well broadened out to form the curved ceiling.

The pyramid was collapsed and the otters brushed themselves off. "Wouldn't 'ave mattered if I could've reached the bottom," Splitch told them. "The shaft's as slick as a snowslide, and there ain't a 'and'old in sight. She's too wide to bridge." She eyed Jon-Tom thoughtfully. "You're long enough to do it, Jonny-Tom, but we've no way to get you up there."

"We had best find some way out," said Oplode. "This skull is fresh." Everyone shuffled about uneasily.

"Doesn't mean a lot," said Domurmur. "One of Markus's latest victims, no doubt."

"No doubt," agreed Oplode readily. "The question is, if the victim is a recent one, who or what has so efficiently removed the flesh from the bone?" Faint light glinted off his bulging eyes as he searched the darkness.

"If I only had my duar," Jon-Tom was muttering. "I might be able to sing up a ladder or rope or something. If only we—"

He was interrupted by noise from above. Voices, and the blare of ceremonial trumpets.

"Everyone, get back from the opening and keep quiet!" Oplode ordered them. They spread out quickly.

Sounds of a scuffle overhead, another blare of trumpets, and then a horrible high-pitched scream that increased rapidly in volume. It stopped abruptly when something struck the stone floor with a wet, sickening thud. The object bounced once and then lay still.

The sounds from above went away. Jon-Tom leaned cautiously into the light and saw nothing. Slowly, the refugees gathered around the thing that had been thrown down the well.

It was a small macaque, no more than four feet tall. A torn white lace ruffle ringed the neck above a green-and-blue jersey which was tucked into dark green shorts of bright snakeskin. Gold embroidery decorated the sleeves, and a belt of thin gold links circled the narrow waist.

The neck was twisted at an unnatural angle. One arm lay bent straight up behind the spine. Open eyes stared toward the well.

"Died instantly," commented Oplode softly. "Neck broke when he hit. Poor fellow."

Cascuyom pushed his way to the fore. "I know him. That is the honorable Jestutia."

"Yes, I know him also." Selryndi bent over the body. "One of our most respected citizens." He glanced up toward the top of the shaft. "Markus must be feeling very confident, to begin murdering such prominent individuals."

"Quiet, be quiet!" That was Mudge, snapping at them from somewhere far off to the left.

"Listen, otter, one of our colleagues and friends has just been foully slain, and I see no reason to—"

"Shut up, nut-eater, or I'll stuff that tail of yours down your throat." His voice dropped an octave. "There's somethin' else in 'ere with us."

A chill raced down Jon-Tom's back. Something had removed the meat from that first skull. "Mudge, we checked out..."

"There's another tunnel over 'ere, mates. A big one. And there's somethin' in it, and I think 'tis startin' to move."

"You are trying to frighten us," Selryndi said nervously.

"Oh, why sure, now, that's it, guv'nor," said Mudge sarcastically. "I've got nothin' better to do than make up scary stories, right?" He rejoined them and put a hand on the squirrel's back. "'Ow about you go and 'ave a looksee over there, guv, and prove me out to be the liar you say I am." Selryndi's feet dug into the floor.

"Listen, all of you," Memaw urged them. Mudge and Selryndi quit squabbling as something scraped against distant stones. This was followed by a heavy wheeze. Wind from another tunnel, Jon-Tom thought. Or something waking up.

Unconsciously, everyone retreated toward the drainage tunnel. "What do the old legends say about this?" Jon-Tom asked the wizard.

"Nothing," came Oplode's whispered reply. "There is not supposed to be anything down here. This is the place of the dead."

Chunk! Gravel shifted underfoot, followed by a vast exhaling and an odor like burning charcoal. Quorly clung to Mudge's arm.

"'Tis comin' this way!"

"Stay still, don't let it know we're afraid," Mudge told her, trying to edge behind Memaw and Sasswise.

Oplode raised a hand and muttered something under his breath, but it had no effect on whatever shared the chamber with them. It was moving nearer.

"It is no use. I am still constrained from working magic by the spell Markus laid upon me. I cannot break free."

"Get ready to run for the tunnel," Memaw told them. It lay close at hand, but it would take time for all of them to crowd inside the narrow opening, and a sudden rush ran the risk of stirring to action whatever was coming toward them.

There was a brief explosion of flame in the darkness, accompanied by a thick acrid smell. Then a low growl, rich and throaty.

"Try singin' somethin', mate!" Mudge urged Jon-Tom.

"But I haven't got the duar."

"Try anyway, mate. Try somethin'!"

"Sasswise," said Memaw, "you, Flutz, and I will try to divert its attention while the others file into the tunnel. The rest of you prepare yourselves." The otters scrambled to salvage old bones, rocks, anything that might be used as a weapon.

Jon-Tom began to sing. He had no plan in mind, no brilliant ideas, and he was certain the magic wouldn't happen without the duar's music, but he had to try. If nothing else, it might concentrate the thing's attention on him while the others fled into the tunnel. The first notes trembled, but his voice steadied as he sang on. He could hear his companions rushing for the tunnel entrance.

An immense outline turned toward him . . . and hesitated. Mudge called out to him.

"That's it, mate! Keep singin'. 'Tis workin!"

It couldn't be, Jon-Tom thought. There was no magic without the duar, none, no way! It couldn't be working.

Yet there was no question of it: the thing had halted in its leisurely approach.

A thunderous whisper filled the chamber then.

"Jon-Tom."

"Blimey," muttered Splitch, "it knows 'im!"

"It knows the spellsinger," Oplode observed aloud.

"Spellsinger," the voice echoed in the darkness.

Jon-Tom squinted, trying to see in the poor light as he took a reluctant step forward.

A blast of fire erupted over his head. Screams came from the otters and the Quorum members as they rushed in panic for the tunnel, running into each other and stumbling over the bones on the floor. But Jon-Tom didn't move. The fire had passed over him. Nor had it been directed at any of his companions. It had been aimed ceilingward, to generate light and not destruction.

The instant of brilliant illumination hurt his eyes, but not so badly that he couldn't recognize its source.

"Comrade Falameezar," he asked hesitantly, "is that you?"

XVI

A great clawed hand descended and picked Jon-Tom off the floor. He could feel the thick, leathery membrane that ran between the fingers. The hand lifted him until it paused in front of a mouth full of curving teeth. A single puff could incinerate him in a second, sizzle his bones and melt his flesh. There was heat and the smell of brimstone, but no hint of cremation.

"It *is* you, Falameezar! I'll be damned."

"We are all damned, comrade Jon-Tom," said the dragon somberly. "What are you doing here?"

Jon-Tom sat down on the slick, scaly palm and turned to his friends. "It's okay. He's a friend. This is comrade Falameezar, a good proletarian."

"What is the man talking about?" Memaw asked Mudge.

The otter strode boldly out into the chamber. "We know this bloke, we do. 'E 'elped us once before, on our way to Polastrindu. Though wot 'e's doin' 'ere I'll be buggered if I know." He looked back into the tunnel, which was filled with anxious faces. "Everyone, 'tis all right. You can come out. Only," he added more quietly, "wotever you do, don't say anythin' about makin' money." He fought to recall some of the confusing but effective conversations Jon-Tom had held with the river dragon as it had carried them up the river Tailaroam toward far Polastrindu not so very long ago. The dragon was . . . what had Jon-Tom called it? . . . a Marked Met. No, something more compact. Marxist, yeah, that was it. The dragon was a Marxist, whatever that was.

But he was certainly sensitive about it. Dedicated, Jon-Tom had called him. Mudge knew better. The dragon was nuts.

He spoke to his friends as they hesitantly emerged from hiding. "Just act collective," he told them.

"What does that mean?" Memaw asked him.

" 'Ow the 'ell do I know? Just make sure everybody does it."

Jon-Tom was patting the dragon on the snout. "Comrade Falameezar, it appears we are to be companions in misfortune."

"So it would seem." The dragon set him down gently, then looked around and opened his mouth. Another blast of flame spewed forth. The members of the Quorum cowered against the nearest wall, but Oplode and the otters edged forward.

Falameezar's well-aimed blast set a huge pile of debris on fire. It burned fitfully at best but provided enough light for everyone to see clearly for the first time since they'd fled from their cell. They gathered around while the dragon lay down on his belly, crossed his arms, and rested his head against them.

"How did you get here?" Jon-Tom asked him.

"I wasn't having much luck trying to raise the consciousness of the masses who live on the shores of the Tailaroam," the dragon explained, "so I determined to try to find a group of the oppressed who were more receptive.

"I'd heard much of this land, where the lakes are large and the fish plentiful. So I made my way here and, surely enough, found the workers badly in need of organizing." He sighed and a puff of smoke drifted ceilingward. "But as so often seems to happen, the people here were reluctant to listen to me."

"Can't imagine why," Quorly whispered.

"So I decided this time to try to convert the heads of state instead of the people."

"Uh-oh," said Jon-Tom.

"Precisely, comrade. I allowed myself to be deceived by the honeyed words of the local ruler, a strange human very different from yourself."

"Markus the Ineluctable."

"Yes. I did not know at first that he had deposed the rightful rulers of this place, nor that he was a powerful magician as well as a disgusting fascist whose only aim is the exploitation of the masses for personal gain. But by the time I learned all this he had rendered me sleepy. I vaguely remember being brought to the large room above. The floor was removed and I was dropped down here, and then walled up.

"I've tried to break out but the stone is solid and thick. It will not burn. So here I have remained, trapped by this evil imperialist. He does feed me well, though. The trumpet calls me when a meal is ready." Falameezar moved his head and sniffed at the body of Jestutia. "A banker this time. Markus is clever. He has learned that I will only eat capitalists."

"I'm surprised at you," Jon-Tom said accusingly. "Even a banker can be converted to the cause of the people."

"Not if he's dead." The dragon sniffed again. "Yes, a dead banker. I'm sure of it. I hate bankers, you know. Filthy robber-barons."

Near the back wall Newmadeen was hurriedly going through her pockets. Like the recently deceased macaque, she was also in the business of lending money. Until now she'd never had reason to regret it. Fortunately, Falameezar was too involved in conversation with his newfound friends to do any serious sniffing, and she was able to unburden herself of money, notes, and assorted usurious I.O.U.'s.

"Besides," he was saying, "a dragon has to eat." He extended his long neck and snapped up the unfortunate Jestutia in a single bite, chewed noisily.

"'Ere now," murmured Sasswise, looking at Newmadeen, "this one's gone and fainted."

Falameezar noticed it, too, sniffed curiously as he chewed. "What's wrong with your companion? If I didn't know better I'd . . ."

Jon-Tom hurried to distract the dragon. "It's the air down here. These are the legitimate rulers of Quasequa, by the way. They have no more love for Markus than you. They constitute the legitimate, uh, soviet that the magician has deposed."

"I did not realize that this government was so advanced," Falameezar replied in surprise.

"They're working on it," Jon-Tom assured him. "Aren't you?"

"Yes, yes, yes!" The conscious members of the Quorum managed to reply with enthusiasm, if a bit too quickly.

Falameezar looked pleased. "It is good to have right-thinking company in such sad circumstances. As it is good to see my old comrade again. You, too, Mudge, even if you did express the occasional reactionary thought." The otter allowed himself to be stroked by a single swordlike talon.

"If only I could get ahold of my duar," Jon-Tom mumbled. "Markus hasn't placed any anti-magic spells on me."

"That is so," admitted Oplode. "I would have sensed it if he had."

"Then there's only one thing left to try." He started toward the tunnel. "I have to go back to our cell."

"You're jokin', mate."

"No, Mudge. It's the only way. I've got an idea. Mudge, will you and Quorly come back with me?"

"Count on me, Jonny-Tom," she replied. Her ready agreement made Mudge's acquiescence a foregone conclusion.

"I'll be back in a little while, Falameezar."

"Good luck, comrade."

"Just a minute." Memaw stepped in front of Jon-Tom as he bent to enter the tunnel. She looked significantly past him. "What do we talk about with the dragon?"

"Anything you can think of. He likes to chat. The last weather we saw outside, jokes... Falameezar's great with jokes. Simple things. Just make sure nobody talks about how rich they'd like to be. Fame you can talk about, but not fortune. Tell him how much you all despise the capitalist bosses."

"What are those?"

"Never mind. Just do it. It'll please him."

Memaw was still reluctant to let him leave. "What are you going to do, work some strange magic on our behalf?" He nodded. "But I thought you told us you required your duar in order to work magic."

"There's magic, and then there's magic." He winked at her, then bent and began gathering bones. As many as he could carry. He directed Mudge and Quorly to do likewise.

"Oi, it works better when you use the duar, mate. There's less to carry." Staggering beneath his gruesome burden, he followed Quorly and Jon-Tom into the tunnel.

Making their way through the narrow tube had been difficult enough with their hands free. With the armfuls of bones it was twice as hard. But the otters never complained, and Jon-Tom was damned if he was going to be the one to call for a rest.

Eventually they found themselves beneath the entrance to their cell. They dumped their loads. Mudge went up Jon-Tom's back as lithely as he would have a tree, and listened.

"Dead quiet, mate. They 'aven't checked on us since we took our little walk. No need to, really. Wasn't likely we'd be goin' anywhere, now, was it?"

"Move those stones and let's get up there."

"Right, mate, but you'd better know wot you're about."

"You'll understand soon enough."

Sure enough, once their cargo had been arranged according to his instructions, Mudge knew just what his lanky, furless friend had in mind.

"What was that?" The javelina turnkey spoke to the fennec seated across the table. The fennec's oversized ears immediately cocked sideways.

"Beats me. I heard it too." He put aside his handful of odd triangular cards and shouted toward the stairway. "You prisoners be quiet or you won't get your next ration of slop!"

The eerie moaning which had interrupted their game grew louder.

"Don't sound like the otters," said the javelina, cleaning a nail on one upthrust tusk. He then used it to strip the bark from a piece of cane, stuck the clean pulp in his mouth and chewed thoughtfully. When the moaning continued he put down his cards, careful not to reveal them to his companion, and issued an irritated grunt.

"We'd better see what's going on down there."

"Maybe they're killing each other."

"They'd better not be. Thornrack himself ordered me to make sure they stay healthy until the new magician decides what's to be done with them."

He took a three-foot-long knife off the wall. The fennec opted for a long spear. This was excellent for poking at prisoners through bars.

Each grabbed a torch as they started down the stairs. Soon they were on the lower level, staring through the bars of the big cell. Staring hard.

"By the curl in my grandmother's tail!" the stunned javelina muttered. "What's happened to them?" His initial irritation had turned to panic.

"Dead," moaned a quavering voice from the back of the cell, "they're all deeeaddd."

"What do you mean, all dead?" the fennec stuttered as he struggled to locate the speaker. The voice responded with a moan.

"Open it up," he told the turnkey. The javelina nodded, used his keys and then his hands to swing the huge grate slightly ajar. Hefting the long knife, he entered cautiously while the fennec waited by the door in case any of the prisoners tried to make a break for it.

No one did. There was no one in the cell. Except...in the farthest corner he found the tall man sitting with his back against the wall. His hands half covered his face, and he was shaking in terror.

"What's the matter with you?" The turnkey's eyes roamed the deserted darkness nervously. "Where are the rest of them?"

"The wizard, it was the wizard who did it," Jon-Tom moaned feebly. He gestured with a shaky hand. "Did it to all of them."

"Did what?" The javelina's blunt muzzle twitched as he followed the pointing fingers.

A substantial pile of white bones lay nearby, heaped up in a jumble against the wall. Had the turnkey taken the time to look closely he might have seen that none of the skeletons belonged to otters, or a salamander, or a pangolin, but to entirely different species. It might not have mattered anyway. His knowledge of anatomy was pretty much restricted to knowing where the best place to stick a knife was.

"By the Ovens of Suranis!" he whispered fearfully.

"What is it, where are all the prisoners?" The fennec stuck his head into the cell, trying to see.

"Gone, all gone. Nothing left of them except their bones." The javelina swung his torch to illuminate as much of the cell as possible. "What manner of sorcery is this?"

"*He* did it. The salamander did it."

"Old Oplode?"

"Yes, yes, the slimy one! He said he was tired of this, tired of everyone and everything, and he did this. Only I was s-s-spared."

"A spell was put on him to prevent him from working magic. The new wizard did that himself. We were told," the javelina insisted.

"I know, I know, but the slimy one struck a bargain with the creatures of the dark, and now he's going to do *that* to all who oppose him." Jon-Tom pointed toward the pile of bones. "I saw, I saw him do it. He made the flesh run like butter from their bones, made it melt and drip..."

The fennec couldn't stand it anymore. His mind told him there was only one live prisoner left in the cell and his curiosity was killing him. He held his spear in front of him as he entered.

"What's this garbage this fool's saying?" he asked the turnkey.

"Look, they're all dead," stuttered the javelina. He pointed at the bones. "The wizard Oplode killed them. A great sorcery." There was fear in his voice now.

"I don't know about that," muttered the fennec, "but we'd better tell Thornrack." He started backing toward the exit.

As he did so, Mudge and Quorly dropped from the crevices in the ceiling where they'd been hiding and flailed away at the guards with the leg bones they'd been holding in their teeth. The javelina dropped his long knife, the man he'd been questioning underwent a miraculous transformation, and in seconds both guards lay dead on the floor of the cell.

Mudge hefted the fennec's spear while Quorly helped herself to the knife from his belt. "Now, that," Mudge said with ghoulish satisfaction, "is wot I calls magic!" He kicked the javelina in the side.

"I'm sorry we had to kill them," Jon-Tom murmured. "I don't like unnecessary slaughter."

"Oi, but this were necessary slaughter," Quorly observed. She glanced at Mudge. "Wot is 'e, squeamish or somethin'?"

"Or somethin', luv, but don't 'old it against 'im."

They crept out of the cell and started up the stairs. No one challenged them when they entered the deserted guard room, where they helped themselves to handfuls of weapons. Thus equipped, they took the place apart searching for Mudge's bow and Jon-Tom's duar.

"No luck," grumbled Mudge as he finished excavating the last cabinet. "Maybe further up. I thought I saw a barred storeroom on our right when they were bringin' us down 'ere."

Jon-Tom nodded. They climbed to the next level.

Where they found the storeroom Mudge remembered. They also saw a pudgy but alert hare standing in front of the half-open door.

At the same time, the rabbit saw them and turned to slam the door shut. Mudge threw his spear and the swinging grate slammed against it. The guard did manage a piercing scream before Quorly could cut his throat. Nothing can scream like a dying hare.

"Shit!" Quorly snapped, her eyes going immediately

to the stairwell leading upward. "That'll bring 'em down on us in a minute. I'll watch while you and Mudgey get your stuff."

Jon-Tom rushed into the storeroom. Tossed indifferently on a pile of spears was his ramwood staff. He grasped it like an old friend's proffered hand. But where was the duar?

"Right, mate, let's go."

He turned. Mudge stood waiting nearby. His quiver of arrows and longbow were slung against his back, and he was staggering beneath a load of metal and rock. Long links of gold coins were draped across his chest like bandoliers while necklaces of pearls and gems hung from his neck and wrists. His arms were full of gem-encrusted plates and goblets. Two tiaras rested askew on his crushed cap.

"Mudge, what the hell are you doing?"

The otter blinked, then looked embarrassed. He dropped his heavy load. Coins and gems went rolling across the floor.

"Sorry, mate. For a minim there I kind o' forgot where we are." Reluctantly, he unburdened himself of the rest of the treasure. "Couldn't we maybe take just a wee bit with us?"

"No, we could not." Jon-Tom snapped angrily.

"Will you two kindly get your arses in gear?" Quorly's shout reached them along with pounding footsteps from the stairs. There was a startled squeal and a four-foot-tall armored hedgehog went sprawling into the room, bleeding from a stab wound in the belly. "I can't hold this lot off forever."

Jon-Tom turned to search the room, but Mudge spun him around. The otter's eyes were wide as he pointed, not into the storeroom, but across the floor.

"There she is, mate!"

Jon-Tom fairly flew across the stones toward the crackling fireplace. He ignored the heat and the cinders as he yanked the priceless duar from the top of the fire. It was blackened in a couple of spots, but the strings were intact and so was the body. He tested it, was rewarded with a familiar mellow ring.

"That," he gulped, "was too close." He tried the tremble and mass controls. Everything worked. A slight shudder went through the paving stones as the music filled the room. "Let's get out of here!"

Only the fact that the stairwell was so narrow had enabled Quorly to hold off the guards. Mudge gleefully went to work with his longbow, and in a couple of minutes the passage was blocked by the bodies of the fallen. Those guards who hadn't been shafted retreated.

"That ought to 'old the bastards," Mudge said with satisfaction.

They plunged down the stairs, for the moment pursued only by confused shouts and angry cries. Jon-Tom had thoughtfully requisitioned the unfortunate javelina's keys. Now he used them to lock the cell from the inside. Arrows flashed past him. The guards had finally managed to bring up archers of their own.

Jon-Tom tossed the keys into the hole in the floor and followed them down.

"Wot about puttin' the stones back in place?" Quorly asked as she fell on top of him and slid off to one side.

"Take too much time," he told her. "They saw us come in here. As soon as they get the door open, the first thing they'll do is start checking the walls and the floor." He started running down the tunnel, cursing as he bumped against the unyielding ceiling while trying to juggle his burden of staff, duar, and extra weapons.

They weren't halfway back to the well chamber when excited yells sounded behind them. Some of

Jon-Tom's initial confidence evaporated and he tried to run faster, but it was hard to speed up in the confines of the tunnel.

"I didn't think they'd follow us down here," he yelled to his companions.

"I imagine they figure they can follow anyplace we can go, mate."

"You go on ahead. I'll catch up."

"Now wot kind o' cowards do you think we are?" Mudge replied, outraged. "Do you think that after all we've been through together, you and I, 'avin' come all this ways, that I'd for a minute think o' leavin' you behind to get your behind shot off? Wot do you take me for?"

Jon-Tom was gasping for breath now but still couldn't keep from replying. "There's also the fact that unless I can manage to do something with this duar, we'll all likely never get out of here."

"Well, yeah, that 'ad occurred to me, too," Mudge confessed.

Jon-Tom grinned, though he knew the otter couldn't see him. "Glad to hear it. For a second I thought the dampness might've addled your brain."

"Now, mate, you do old Mudge an injustice." But the otter didn't complain very strongly.

Meanwhile their pursuit continued to gain ground on them. Occasionally a flicker of light from closing torches would reach the refugees, spurring them to run still faster. The tunnel seemed to have stretched in their absence, lengthening like a rubber tube. The only advantage they possessed was the assurance of knowing their destination.

Even so, by the time the faint circle of light that marked the entrance to the well chamber appeared ahead, the guards were near enough for Jon-Tom to pick out individual voices. The three of them stumbled into the room, tripping and spilling weapons in all directions. The otters grabbed them up and waited for whatever might come.

Jon-Tom rolled over, discovered a pair of crossbow bolts protruding from the back of his cape. Once again he'd been saved by the thick leather. He plucked them out as several guards emerged from the tunnel mouth, only to find themselves confronted by not three but more than a dozen armed opponents.

Thornrack struggled to catch his breath, held his sword over his head. "All right, you've had your fun. You've led us a hard chase, but that's over now." He glared around until he located Jon-Tom. "We'll see how well you run with your calf muscles cut."

At that point Falameezar lifted his head, closed one eye, and spat. A small globe of very intense flame struck the jaguar's sword, which melted like taffy. Eyes bulging at the immense outline which was slowly rising behind the otters, Thornrack dropped the glowing metal and bolted for the tunnel. He ran into the guards who were clustered thickly behind him.

Falameezar sighted and went *poof* with his lips. Thornrack's tail burst into flame, and he redoubled his efforts to push past his own troops. They could hear him cursing and screaming halfway back through the tunnel.

"I don't think we'll have any more trouble from that direction," observed Jon-Tom dryly.

"No," agreed Oplode, dampening their euphoria, "but he will report what has happened back to Markus, and you can be certain the magician *will* do something. There are only two openings to this room: the tunnel and the mouth of the old well above us. Both could easily be plugged. We could be sealed in here to starve or suffocate, and no magic would be required to accomplish those ends. Somehow we must get out before Markus has time to react to our escape." Those salamander-slick eyes turned to Jon-Tom.

"Clothahump must have had confidence in you to send you by yourself in response to my request. If you are any kind of spellsinger, you must free us from this prison *now*. Even a wizard needs room to maneuver, and we have none of that here."

"'E's right, mate. We got your bloomin' music box back. Now show 'em wot you can do!"

Every eye turned to him. He was glad it was dark so they couldn't see how nervous he was. A song—what would be the right song?

Johnny Cash's "Folsom Prison Blues" created no openings in the stone walls, nor did any song of prisons or chain gangs. He started to sweat despite the coolness. Mudge sat down, looking resigned. He'd been through this before. Oplode looked disappointed and the rest of the party confused. It hurt Jon-Tom's recall, though his playing was as smooth as ever.

"Wot's wrong?" Quorly leaned over Mudge and snuggled close. "Nothin's 'appenin'."

Mudge ran fingers lightly over her fur. "'Tis just the way it works sometimes. 'E's a spellsinger for sure, but 'e's still new to 'is profession and don't quite 'ave the 'ang o' it quite. Sometimes the magic works and sometimes it don't. And sometimes you just 'ave to be patient."

"I'll try," she murmured worriedly, "but Oplode said we didn't have a lot of time."

Jon-Tom sang until he began to grow hoarse, and still the singing produced no results. Only a few idle gneechees, who didn't hang around long enough for him to finish a single tune.

More to cheer himself than out of any hope of doing anything, he launched into a spirited rendition of Def Lepard's "Rock of Ages." Still no magical escape hatches appeared, no stairways or corridors.

He got something else, though.

The otters stirred. Awed whispers rose from the Quorum members. Oplode's eyes narrowed, and he stroked his chin as he tried to analyze the meaning of this bizarre conjuration. Powerful sorcery it was, but of what kind, and what could it portend?

Only Mudge knew the origin of the shifting, glowing shapes that had appeared and now danced gleefully around the spellsinger's feet. He knew because he'd encountered them once before.

"Wot did you call 'em, mate?" he asked softly, staring along with the others.

The duar continued to produce thunderous, ringing chords. "Geolks," Jon-Tom shouted at him, "but what are we going to do with them?"

XVII

The exquisite phosphorescent worm-forms continued to multiply, until they occupied much of the floor and most of the walls. They twisted and flowed through the stone in a peculiar cadence all their own, sometimes in time to the rhythm of the duar, sometimes in time to one utterly alien. The chamber was alive with living rainbows.

Jon-Tom concluded a brazen chorus, kept playing as he spoke. "Hello! Do you remember me?"

"It is good to see you again, music-maker." The speaker might have been the same one who'd conversed with Jon-Tom back among the karst pinnacles in the Wrounipai, or it might have been another. There was no way of knowing for certain. Color was no clue. "Singing still, we see."

"Yes, but not freely. We're trapped in this place." He tried to alter the melody subtly, to substitute his words for Lepard's lyrics. "Trapped in this awful dark place."

"Awful? What is the difference between one vacuum and another?" the worm asked him.

"Freedom of movement. Something you take for granted. Can you help us out of here? I'll play whatever you like for as long as you want if you'll just help us get out of here. There's an opening higher up. Can you make something we can climb?"

"What is 'climb'?" inquired a coolly curious geolk. The other prisoners looked on in mesmerized silence. "What is 'out'? We like your emptiness but your movements concern us not."

There had to be something they could do, he thought desperately. What could the geolks do? They could move freely through solid rock, come and go as they pleased and...

They could make earthquakes.

"Find a crack in this wall... in the rock that surrounds us. Link together as I saw you do before. *Feel* the music."

"Nothing to do with us," the geolks insisted distantly. "To tremor we have to work together, and right now we do not feel like working together."

"Don't feel like working together?" a new voice said. Jon-Tom continued to sing while trying simultaneously to quiet Falameezar, but the dragon's political consciousness was up and he refused to be shushed. If anything, he looked inspired.

"Leave this to me, comrade. This is a matter of organization."

"But you don't understand, Falameezar," Jon-Tom said desperately. "These aren't your usual folks. They won't—"

"Workers of the world, arise!" Falameezar bellowed. "Join together in solidarity and nothing can stop you!"

"Nothing can stop us now," a bright blue geolk replied. "And we are not workers."

Falameezar would have none of it, continued to lambast the glowing shapes with the profoundest barrage of Marxist rhetoric Jon-Tom had ever heard. It made absolutely no sense to him, but it seemed to hypnotize the geolks.

"Make Vladimir Ilyich proud of you," Falameezar rumbled. "Show the world what true collective action can do!"

Whether it was Jon-Tom's music or the dragon's rhetoric or a combination of both, the geolks started to line up on the far wall, twisting and curling against one another.

"Get back, everybody," Mudge warned the onlookers. "And don't be surprised no matter wot 'appens. Be *ready*." He grinned at his friend the spellsinger. "Bugger me for a blue-eyed bandicoot if I don't think we're gettin' out o' 'ere!"

Still the geolks continued to gather, until the opposite wall of the well chamber was alive with blinding light. Jon-Tom had to close his eyes to shut out the intense glow.

Falameezar roared something about the worker's imperative at the same time that Jon-Tom and his duar thundered out the opening words of Quiet Riot's "Cum On Feel the Noize." The earth trembled as the huge rope of geolks convulsed. The concussion knocked Jon-Tom off his feet, and even Falameezar was tossed sideways.

His head rattling, he tried to keep playing, tried to do it as fluidly as Jimi or Robin Trower or Eddie van Halen would have. Finally he had to stop because the dust in his nostrils was choking him.

He opened his eyes to a different kind of light.

The geolks were gone, and so was much of the far wall. Light washed over the bottom of the well because the right side of the roof had collapsed. In place of wall and roof was a pile of rubble that reached all the way to the main floor above.

Falameezar shoved his way clear of the talus. "Free! Free from the imperialist neo-colonialist yoke!" He started pawing up the steep slope. "Where is he, lead me to him!"

"Easy, easy, comrade!" Jon-Tom struggled to catch up to the angry dragon. "If he sees you, he'll only put you to sleep again."

"No, he will not," said Falameezar decisively. "The people are awake to reality now, and nothing can put them to sleep again." Flame and smoke billowed from his jaws. "I'll reduce the fascist dictator to a cinder." He started climbing again.

"Don't underestimate him!" Jon-Tom shouted up at the dragon, but to no avail. Falameezar wasn't dumb, but he was more than a little impulsive, especially when the revolutionary fever was on him.

Shouts sounded from the floor above, and they found themselves looking up at Markus's guards. Their expressions were more than a little fearful as they stared down into the gaping hole that had materialized practically under their feet. If that wasn't enough to send them running, the sight of Falameezar climbing rapidly toward them finished the job. The floor cleared with gratifying swiftness.

"He'll keep the soliders busy," Jon-Tom muttered, "but I'll have to handle Markus. Somehow."

"You can do it, mate. You're the only one who can," Mudge said.

Jon-Tom looked grim. "Maybe I can convince the geolks to concentrate in his spine. Hell, we'll get him! I just managed a Marxist earthquake, didn't I?" He looked past the otter, waved to the others. "All right, let's go!"

Yelling and barking enthusiastically, the otters followed him up the slope. Oplode and the Quorum members trailed at a discreet distance. They were administrators, not fighters.

Falameezar was searching the intact part of the big room, hunting for fascists. Occasionally a guard or two would peer through a doorway, only to be sent fleeing by a ferocious blast of flame. Falameezer launched into a spirited rendition of the "Internationale." He was out of tune and had the words all wrong, but Jon-Tom wasn't about to correct him. The scaly Marxist was having too good a time incinerating capitalist dupes.

"We've got to find Markus as fast as possible, before he can get his wits together. Falameezar will keep his guards occupied." He looked at Trendavi, the deposed premier. "Can you show us the way to his tower?"

The aged pangolin nodded. "Without fail, my friends." He led them through a still-standing door.

Occasionally they encountered some of Markus's guards, but while the otters were usually outarmed and outweighed, they were never intimidated. Guards broke and ran without fighting. No doubt word of the escape was already racing through the Quorumate, and no solider wanted to risk the chance of encountering a bunch of hyperkinetic fanatics who might be backed up by a fire-breathing, if somewhat verbose, dragon.

"This way," Trendavi told them, turning to his left. Then they were outside, on the parapet Jon-Tom had been marched across not so long ago, racing toward Markus's sanctuary.

"He has outsmarted himself," Oplode commented as they slowed. The members of the Quorum were near collapse from the run, but not the salamander. His eyes glittered. "None can approach from three sides, but by the same token there is only this way out."

"I'm going in," Jon-Tom told them. "The rest of you stay behind me."

"I was about to suggest that meself," said Mudge.

They rushed forward. There was no sign of the

two armed lions who had flanked the entrance when Jon-Tom had been brought here before.

Actually, now that the final confrontation was at hand, Jon-Tom wasn't quite sure how to proceed. He didn't tell his companions that.

Attack. Always keep the opposition off balance. That was how he'd been taught and that was what he intended to do. The advice had come, not from a class on warfare, but on courtroom procedure. Jon-Tom didn't see why it wouldn't apply as well on the battlefield as in the courtroom.

Each inner door opened at their touch, until they confronted a door-sized slab that did not. Instead of moving aside, it leaned forward and growled. Black leather armor gleamed in the torchlight. Prugg gestured threateningly with his enormous club.

"You stop," the bodyguard growled menacingly.

Frangel tried to dart past the bear. The club descended with frightening speed and dented the rock where the otter had been a split-second earlier. Only Frangel's exceptional quickness saved him. Anyone slower than an otter would have been smashed to pulp.

That was the signal for the rest of the band to charge. Dodging Prugg's lethal swings, they darted all around him, poking and prodding with their spears and swords while yelling encouragement to each other.

"Get 'im!...take 'is bloomin' 'ead off!...kill 'im!...get the ugly bastard down!"

"Knock 'im over, tear 'is throat out!" a solitary voice yelled from behind Jon-Tom. The spellsinger turned, tapped Mudge on the shoulder.

"Kill? Tear his throat out?" he said dangerously.

Mudge put his paws behind his back and tried to

smile. "I was just sort o' coverin' our rear, mate. Don't want to be taken from behind, we don't."

"Guarding our rear, my ass!"

"Oi, that's wot I said, weren't it?"

There were times when Jon-Tom could tolerate his friend's shameless displays of cowardice. This wasn't one of them. Not with petite warriors like Sasswise and Splitch fighting to make a path for him.

Actually, he went a little crazy.

"You rotten, smelly, no-good . . . !" Reaching down, he grabbed Mudge by the tail and the ruff of his neck. The otter's feet bicycled through the air as he fought to free himself.

"Hey, take it easy, mate!"

"Get in there and fight alongside your cousins, damn you!"

Jon-Tom threw the otter forward, harder than he intended. He was too mad to judge his strength. To his horror, Mudge performed a single somersault and landed neatly on top of Prugg's head. The otter's impact shoved the bear's helmet down over his eyes, temporarily blinding him. Seeing this, Quorly lowered her head and charged underneath a deadly but badly aimed swing to hit the bodyguard head-first between pillarlike legs. Prugg let out a low grunt, bent over, and tried to find Mudge, who was frantically retreating down the bear's back. The club fell to the floor.

Memaw, Knorckle, and Wupp immediately dropped their own weapons in favor of the club. Turning the business end toward their opponent, they rushed forward at full speed, short legs churning, and made loud contact with the leather helmet Mudge had so recently abandoned. The impact sent them tumbling.

Prugg let out a strange low sigh and sort of keeled

over, like a falling redwood. He hit the floor with a muffled *brrouummm!*, out cold.

Jon-Tom and the others raced past while the club-wielders tried to collect themselves.

The last door beckoned. Were they in time? Had they moved fast enough? Or was Markus the Ineluctable waiting just inside, prepared to strike all of them dead with whatever new evil he had drawn into this world?

Jon-Tom pushed on the latch. Somewhat to his surprise, the door was not locked. The otters crowded in around him.

At the far end of the Room, Markus the Ineluctable, née Markle Kratzmeier, sat waiting on his throne. He looked different somehow. He'd straightened his bow tie and his white shirt gleamed. He did not seem particularly upset by the intrusion.

"Heard what was going on, kid. Didn't think you'd get this far. Congratulations." He tried to see past Jon-Tom, out into the hall, searching for his bodyguard.

"Sleeping," Jon-Tom told him wolfishly. "My friends here took care of that."

"Let me at the bald bastard!" yelled Drortch. Jon-Tom had to put out an arm to restrain her.

"This looks easy. I don't think it's going to be."

"No, it ain't, kid," said Markus quietly as he rose. Standing there on the dais, silhouetted by torchlight, he did not look anything like the cheap stage magician from Perth Amboy that he'd once been. There was a dark radiance about his person, a palpable aura of evil. It poured down from the throne to cascade over the onlookers clustered in the doorway, and several of the otters reflexively shrank back.

Markus stepped off the dais. He was wearing white gloves now, Jon-Tom noticed, and his shoes had been polished to a blinding sheen. Still brown, though.

The spellsinger held his ground as the magician raised his plastic wand.

"Oops." Mudge did his own disappearing act, retreating back behind the door.

Markus lowered the wand and smiled. "See how fast your companions desert you."

"They're not deserting me," Jon-Tom told him. He turned and looked down at his friends. "All of you: this is between Markus and me. Wait in the hall." Obediently, they filed out, leaving him with words of encouragement and a promise to rush in no matter what the danger should he call out to them.

"That takes care of *my* friends. Where are yours?"

Markus lost his smile. "Wise-ass. You'll be sorry." He glanced at the duar. "So that's what you've been so keen to get your hands on. Weird-lookin' gadget."

Jon-Tom let his fingers fall casually across the duar's strings. An explosive note filled the room.

"Hey, pretty good trick!" Markus complimented him. "Here's one of mine."

He aimed the wand at Jon-Tom and mumbled under his breath.

Jon-Tom prepared to duck or sing, as the attack demanded. Instead he nearly broke out laughing. A steady stream of brightly colored scarves emerged from the magician's sleeve. It was exactly the sort of trick you'd expect to see someone like Markus perform at a neighborhood party.

Except that the scarves knotted themselves around his ankles and began enveloping his legs, winding steadily upward. Meanwhile the flow from the magician's sleeve showed no signs of slowing.

If he didn't do something fast, in a couple of minutes he'd look like a psychedelic mummy. But what songs did he know about clothing? About scarves, or ties? Suddenly the flood of silk didn't seem so funny. There was an old cartoon song about a Chinese laundry . . . no, that wouldn't work.

In desperation he tried some lyrics from Carole King's "Tapestry" album. The scarves quivered but didn't vanish. Instead, they began to unknot themselves, fold up neatly, and stack in piles according to color on the nearby table. They unwound from his thighs and calves, then his ankles, until they were twisting and folding and stacking themselves as quickly as they emerged from Markus's sleeve.

Furthermore, each one bore in its upper right-hand corner the monogram *JTM*.

Markus frowned, lowered his arm. The silk assault ceased. "You're fast, kid. Not fast enough to make it in Atlantic City, but pretty good for here." This time he raised both hands. "For this one we need an assistant."

Something began to coalesce in the space between them. A faint silvery glow that drew shape as well as substance from his wand and fingers. An hourglass outline traced in air.

It didn't have fangs or talons. Jon-Tom was enraptured by it.

She was tall, as tall as he was. Blond, alluring, clad in next to nothing. She was walking toward him and whispering through puckered, inviting lips; cajoling him, tempting him, pleading with him.

"Please, can I have a volunteer from the audience?"

Jon-Tom found himself stumbling forward, a step at a time. He couldn't be certain, but he thought he could see Markus through her. A single gold tooth flashed in the magician's mouth. He was smiling again.

Somehow Jon-Tom retreated, though the effort of will required to back away from that seductive vision was tremendous. And she was still coming toward him, one perfect hand outstretched to lead him, lead him up onto the stage. How could he resist her? She was obviously so beautiful, so innocent, so badly in need of this job.

He couldn't resist her. But he could sing to her. Sure, nothing wrong with that. What gentle, reassuring ballad could he dedicate to her?

Hesitantly at first, then with growing strength, he began to play "Killer Queen."

The blond houri contorted as the first chords filled the room. She shimmied and twisted in front of him, though not the way he wanted her to shimmy and twist. But as she spun he was able to see the knife she clutched in her other hand. With a cry she lunged at him. Maybe he should have raised the duar to absorb the force of the blow, but he just kept on singing, trying to match the notes perfectly, trying to imitate Freddie Mercury as best he could.

The instant before the knife started to come down toward his throat, it, the girl, and the conjuration dissolved before his eyes like a lump of sugar in a cup of hot tea.

He blinked. Markus growled something vile and looked past him, mumbling and gesturing with his wand. His black cape stood out behind him even though there was no wind in the room.

A snarl came from behind Jon-Tom, familiar and yet alien to this place. The sound of the faceless demons.

They leaped from their alcoves, their curved teeth aiming for his face. He ducked the Fokker and ran for cover behind a table as they soared and dove at him, thirsting for his eyes. He knew nothing about airplanes. The only tune he could remember that had anything at all to do with flying machines seemed insufficient to counter the threat, but maybe it would buy him some time.

So he sang, "'Up, up and awaaay, in my beautiful balloon.'"

They filled the room in an instant: hundreds of them. Thousands, in all colors and shapes and sizes. Dozens of pops and bangs made it sound like the Chinese New Year as Markus's metallic demons slashed through the brightly colored obstacles.

The Fokker's wing brushed Jon-Tom's scalp as it shot over him. Its sharp propellor, the same one that had nearly decapitated a raven named Pandro, was entangled in a hundred strips of thin latex. It executed a final desperate Immelmann turn before it crashed into the wall behind him. A minute later the second demon bounced off the floor and skidded to a halt, its engine gasping and completely jammed by dozens of broken balloons.

When the third and last demon flew out a window, sputtering and wheezing as it plunged to its death in the waters below, Jon-Tom concluded his song, sent a silent thank-you from the Fourth Dimension to the Fifth, and waited while the balloons evaporated to see what Markus might try next.

He didn't look scared. Not yet. But neither did he look quite as sure of himself.

"You were right, kid. You were right and I was wrong. You're not a punk. You know your stuff. Maybe we should make a deal after all." He started toward the younger man. "Here, a peace offering: okay? Better we work something out between us than we keep trying to knock each other off."

Jon-Tom eyed him suspiciously, but this time Markus's hand brought forth no homicidal houris, no mechanical assassins. Just a simple bouquet of flowers.

"Be more appropriate if you were a broad," Markus said, "but this is the best I can think of. Don't flowers say it all?" He waved the bouquet at his erstwhile opponent.

Jon-Tom grinned, found himself nodding in agreement. Only problem was, he didn't want to nod. Nodding he was, though. Maybe it was because the flowers smelled so beautiful, so fresh and relaxing. Relaxing. He hadn't been able to relax in a long time. The flowers told him it was okay to relax, to take it easy. A wonderfully reassuring, cloying miasma issued from the bouquet.

"That's it, kid. It's all over. Nothing else to fight about. We'll just kiss and make up. Hell, what's there to fight about? There's plenty here for us to shareeeeee...."

Somehow Jon-Tom backed away from that soporific spiel, until his back was against the near wall and he couldn't retreat any further. Did he want to retreat? The small part of him that hadn't been drugged by the bouquet's aroma was frantic. Sing something! Sing anything, the first thing that comes to mind, so long as it has something to do with flowers!

Van Halen didn't sing about flowers. Neither did Men With Hats or Motley Crue or Godwanna. Blooms and daisies weren't the stuff heavy metal anthems were made of.

Not every great new group was that heavy, though. In fact, there was one...

He started to sing, amazed at how appropriate the music was. So it would be better if he were a broad, would it? Somehow that fit too.

This time he didn't sing to Markus. He sang to the bouquet. "'Karma, karma, karma camelliaaa, you come and go, you come and go, oh-oh-oh.'"

It was hard for him to duplicate Boy George's smooth, slightly buttery sound, but he managed, and the duar spit out everything from the background guitar to the harmonica solos. As Markus stared in shock at his hypnotic handful of blossoms, they began to depart in time to the lyrics. Their petals spinning like the blades of tiny helicopters, they lifted from his fingers and, traveling neatly in single file, circled once around Jon-Tom's head before flying off in perfect formation through the nearby high window.

Leaving behind in Markus's hand a paper cone which concealed a five-inch-long stiletto.

Markus stumbled away from the spellsinger, retreating back toward the throne. His hat was askew on his head, and he'd lost a couple of buttons off his cheap white shirt. He looked less like Markus the Ineluctable and more like a cheap bum.

"You're through here, Markus," Jon-Tom told him. "Quit while you're ahead, before I really get into my music. It's over, finished."

Markus pulled himself together, seeming to draw fresh strength from his proximity to the throne and the power it represented. "You think so, kid? You think I've had enough? Hell, I've just been playing up till now. Kid stuff. I thought that would be enough, but I was wrong. It's over, all right, but not for me. For you."

His face was wild, his expression full of concentrated fury. Everything he'd built here, everything he'd taken from a world he'd been pulled into against his will, was slipping out of his grasp. He was hanging onto his sanity by emotional fingernails. No, he wasn't finished. He was Markus the Ineluctable, Emperor of Everything, and no skinny punk-rocker was going to take that away from him!

Removing the top hat, he held it in his right hand while whispering and passing the wand over the opening. Then he tapped the brim several times. At first nothing happened, and Jon-Tom found himself hoping that the magician had finally reached his limits.

Then something came creeping out of the hat.

The room darkened as the sickly green vapor emerged. It pulsed with inner evil, curling around the legs of chairs, clinging to the floor as it crept down the steps from the dais. It moved slowly, exploring the environment into which it had been summoned.

Markus eyed it uncertainly, and it occurred to Jon-Tom that his opponent, in his anger and fury, might have overextended himself, might have called forth something stronger than he'd intended to.

Certainly that expanding cloud of poisonous green sprang from a source of evil far stronger than perfumed bouquets and faceless demons. There was nothing even faintly amusing about it. Despite its apparent insubstantiality, it was real in a way none of Markus's previous conjurations could match.

The magician glanced down into his hat. Apparently he saw something he didn't like, because he dropped it as if it had burned him and stepped back toward the throne, never taking his eyes from it. The hat tumbled down the steps, rolling to a stop on the floor. The frightening cloud continued to pour forth from the dark opening.

You could see through it, but the effort was dizzying. Furthermore, there were shapes inside the cloud, shapes that wrenched and heaved in agony at their surroundings. They moaned softly as they fought to escape their nebulous prison. The sound was chilling.

Vapor reached the ceiling and began to spread out sideways. Jon-Tom wanted to run, to get out of that room. The threat that was Markus had been reduced to insignificance by the cloud. Markus no longer mattered. Only getting away, getting out of there, getting away from *that*, mattered.

But a wispy tentacle of ichorous green brushed his foot, and he found he couldn't move. It was just a tiny thing, an airy caress. It paralyzed him in his tracks.

And it was so *cold.*

Eyes in the cloud then, small and piercing, floating above a round oval of a mouth. They hovered within the fog, sleepy and indifferent. The shapes flashed and slipped around eyes and lips as they fought to escape.

The cloud spoke softly in a patient, irresistible voice. Jon-Tom felt a chill strike him with each word.

"I've come for you. It is good that you called me."

Green vapor filled most of the room now. It was starting to spread out along the wall behind him. Soon it would engulf him completely. He knew what would happen then. It would suck him up inside itself, to join those other helpless, moaning shapes.

Then he knew what it was that Markus had conjured up, had called forth out of the depths of his fury and frustration. Instinct told him.

His body might be frozen to the spot, but he found he could still talk. Maybe the vapor wanted him to talk. Maybe that was a final gift it gave to all that it swallowed up.

"You . . . you're Death, aren't you?"

An eloquent silence was his reply. Jon-Tom could feel the cold closing in around him, patient, irresistible.

"I didn't know you could see Death." The cloud was thicker now, an icy green cold that began to prick at his bare skin.

"Any man who cannot see Death approaching is blind." The mouth-oval drifted closer. It was going to touch his own lips. The kiss of Death.

Jon-Tom listened to his own voice and was terrified at how feeble it had become. "But . . . you said you came for me, and that I called you. I didn't call you."

For an instant oblivion retreated. The wisps of

green foulness drew back and the cold fell away. Jon-Tom found he was shivering, and it was the first time in his life he regarded it as a sign of health.

"You called me."

"No." He tried to raise a hand to his duar, but his fingers suddenly weighed a thousand pounds apiece. He tried the other one, straining with his whole being. It rose, slowly, but it rose. He moved it because he had to. He didn't try to touch the duar this time. There was no point. Here was an opponent his spellsinging could not defeat.

Fingers weak and trembling, he pointed through the cloud.

"*He* called you."

"No," came a quavering voice from far across the chamber. Markus cowered down on his throne, trying to hide. "No, it wasn't me. I didn't call you!"

The eyes didn't free Jon-Tom from their relentlessly peaceful gaze. Perhaps another pair appeared elsewhere within the cloud. There was a pause, a brief eternity while the room hung suspended in the void.

Then Death whispered, "Markle Kratzmeier, age forty-eight, of Perth Amboy, New Jersey. You fell into a dynamo. You were electrocuted instantly. You died."

"No!" Markus shook as he waved his wand errati cally toward the cloud. He was hysterical now, his eyes wide as the vapor moved to envelop him. "No, I didn't die! I came here. I *am* here."

"You died," Death insisted softly. "I came for you but you had gone. I couldn't find you. I do not enjoy being cheated."

Then there was another sound in the room, a sound that chilled Jon-Tom more thoroughly than the touch of that annihilating fog. It was the sound of Death laughing.

"And now you have called me back to you. And the *living* say that life is full of little ironies."

"NO!" Markus screamed. He fell to whimpering. "I didn't call you, I didn't. Go awaaay." The wand twitched feebly in the air. "I send you back to where you come from. I command you."

The cloud was pulling away from the shivering Jon-Tom, dragging itself across the floor toward the throne. As it left him he found that he could move again. He started to head for the door, slowed thoughtfully. If Death wanted him, no door was going to stop it. Somehow he didn't think that was going to happen. What had happened was that he had almost been the victim of a fatal case of mistaken identity.

He turned. The fog had surrounded Markus completely. He could still hear the unfortunate magician. The shapes inside the cloud reached out to welcome him into their company. The torches winked out and there was only the green light left to see by.

There were no dramatic shrieks or screams. The whimpering from the throne simply stopped. Then the cloud began to retreat, sucked back down into the hat from which it had been summoned forth. An innocent-looking black top hat that the late Markus the Ineluctable had probably paid no more than ten bucks for in some cheap magic shop in Jersey City.

Then it was gone. Fresh air hesitantly wafted into the room. All that remained of Markus the Ineluctable, the All-Powerful, Ruler of Quasequa and the Lakes District, was a piece of white-tipped black plastic a foot long.

Still shivering, Jon-Tom strode over to the throne and picked up the wand. He tapped it against the wood. It made a soft clicking noise. On the side was the legend Made in Hong Kong. Handling it gingerly, he descended to the floor and dropped it into the open hat. It vanished.

Then he took a deep breath and did the hardest thing he'd ever done in his life. He picked up the hat. Carrying it carefully in his right hand, he walked over to the window nearby and threw it as far as he could. It sailed out into the night and he watched it fall. When it hit the water it was too light to make an audible splash. Either it would sink or the current would carry it into the river that drained the Lake of Sorrowful Pearls, and the river would take it out to the Glittergeist Sea to sink in thousands of fathoms of sunless, specterless water.

He found himself feeling sorry for Markle Kratzmeier. But not for Markus the Ineluctable.

Something creaked behind him. He jumped.

"You okay, mate?" inquired a hesitant voice. Mudge's face peeped uncertainly around the rim of the door.

Jon-Tom relaxed. "It's all right, Mudge. It's all over. You can come in now." He swallowed. "Everyone can come in now."

"Right, mate." But Mudge made a thorough survey of the empty throne room before he entered. Weapons drawn, the rest of the band rushed in around him.

Memaw crossed her arms over her chest. "Brrr! Young man, it's freezing in here. What happened?"

"Markus unintentionally called up an old friend of his. They went away together." Suddenly he was very tired, searched for something to sit on. The throne was out of the question, so he chose a pile of richly embroidered cushions stacked in a corner.

Trendavi waddled over to him. "What of our city?"

"It's been restored to you. You got it back." Trendavi accepted this information solemnly. Then he bowed before Jon-Tom, who was too exhausted to tell him not to, and went off to tell the other members of the Quorum.

Oplode had paced the length of the room, sniffing

at the chilled air. Now he peered down at the spellsinger out of wise, knowing eyes.

"Death has been in this place. You called it forth?"

"No, not me. Markus did it. I don't think he knew what he was doing when he did it. See, he'd died in the other world. My world. He escaped by being thrown through to here. Death had been looking for him ever since."

"So in his anger and greed he called up his own fate," Oplode murmured. "Justice." He sniffed again. "There has been much magic worked here this night. Great magic."

"I don't know how great it was"—Jon-Tom rubbed his face with both hands—"but I feel like I've just had the shit stomped out of me by an angry elephant."

Quorly put a comforting paw on his shoulder. "'Tis done with, spellsinger. 'Tis all over now."

A voice from across the room drew their eyes.

"Hey, you lot, look at me!" Mudge was sitting on the throne, his short legs a foot above the floor, both arms resting on the carved armrests. "Oi, I'm Emperor o' Quasequa, I am, and you louts can all pay me 'omage." He grinned down at Splitch. "Ladies first, o' course."

Jon-Tom spoke casually. "That is precisely where Markus was sitting when Death itself took him."

Mudge's legs abruptly stopped swinging. "You don't say. If that's supposed to scare me, why, it don't." He hopped down from the seat. "'Tis a mite chilly up there, though. Not really to me taste." He retreated in haste.

"Then there's nothing more for us to worry about," said Memaw.

"Well, there is one thing," Jon-Tom mused. "You all seem to have forgotten that we have a revolution-minded dragon running loose in the Quorumate's lower levels."

"Is that a problem?" Domurmur frowned. "If he is your friend, can't you tell him to leave us in peace?"

"He'll leave you in pieces if he finds out what kind of government you're running. You're going to have to move to eliminate bribery and corruption, stamp out the blatant buying of public office."

Selryndi sputtered a reply. "But that's impossible! How else do you govern?"

Jon-Tom grinned up at him. "I should let Falameezar instruct you, but I'll talk to him and see if we can't work out some kind of compromise that will satisfy all the concerned parties."

"We thank you," a relieved Trendavi said humbly.

So Falameezar was permitted to run a political reeducation center on the shore of Isle Quase, and the citizens were taught not to run in fear from his presence. Before too much time went by he was no longer frightening them, only boring them to death with his droning recitations of Marxist ideology. Despite his threats they began to drift away, and even the city troops couldn't force them to stay and listen.

As Cherjal the innkeeper put it one day, "I'd rather bee fried than forced to leesten to that garbage anymore!"

So Falameezar swam off one evening in search of more willing converts, bidding Jon-Tom and his friends adieu, singing the "Internationale" as he disappeared into a sunset which was, appropriately enough that evening, bright red.

It was the following night that Jon-Tom was compelled to go with a group of grim-faced police to the end of an empty municipal pier. At the far end of the pier was a large pile of fur. The pile sported a bunch of eyes, many of which were closed or bloodshot, an indistinguishable clutch of arms and legs, and reeked of liquor.

The sergeant of police was a three-foot-tall cavy,

short and testy. He gestured at the pile. "These your friends?"

"Uh, yes sir."

"Well, do something with them. We had to shovel them out of the Capering Gibbon tavern. They were being drunk and disorderly and obnoxious."

"Is that so bad? They did help save your city from the rule of Markus the Ineluctable, you know."

"Aw, that was weeks ago," said the sergeant. "Since then they've busted up half of what they helped save, insulted most of the ladies and some of the males, partied until all hours in quiet zones, and generally made a spectacular nuisance of themselves."

One lump of fur wiggled out of the pile and focused rheumy eyes on the sergeant. "Who're you callin' a nuisance, you sorry-lookin', worm-infested lump o' snake crap?"

"Mudge, watch your mouth!" The otter twisted 'round to squint up at him.

"Hiya, mate! Say, where was you the other night? You missed a hell of a party."

The cavy looked up at the much taller Jon-Tom, its nose twitching in distaste. "This party has been going on for a month now, and the patience of the Quorum is at its end. So in gratitude for what you have done for the city of Quasequa, it was decided to send you safely on your way." He gestured at the pile of otters. "We dumped them here, more or less intact. See that they don't come back."

"I'm sorry if they've caused you any trouble," Jon-Tom told him apologetically. The cavy threw him a sideways glance.

"Trouble? Oh, no trouble, no trouble at all. At least three dozen of my best people are stuck in infirmaries all around the city because of run-ins with your friends here." He jerked a tiny thumb toward the pile. "You sort 'em out any way you want to. Just keep 'em out of my jurisdiction, okay?"

Jon-Tom waited until the police had left the pier. Then he gazed down at the pile of fuzz. "Aren't you all ashamed of yourselves? Aren't you disgusted? You win the gratitude of an entire population, and then you throw it back in their faces."

Sasswise appeared, waving her sword dangerously about. "Nobody better not throw nothin' at me!"

"Ow!" Drortch emerged, flaring at her cousin. "You stick me with that again, you sodden slut, and I'll pull your tail out by its roots!"

"You and wot army, bitch?"

The two of them went at it enthusiastically, biting and kicking and pulling fur. The distraction was energetic enough to bestir their companions to action. The hill unpiled. Knorckle crawled weakly to the edge of the pier and proceeded to vomit violently into the Lake of Sorrowful Pearls.

Jon-Tom stood and watched, shaking his head in despair. Then he said something he regretted more than anything else he'd said since he'd left the relative sanity of Clothahump's tree.

"What am I going to do with you?"

A drunken Memaw gazed up at him. "Now, don't you worry, young fan . . . man, because we've taken a vote on thish, and we decided that we couldn't possibly think of letting you make that nasty old trip all the way back up to these Bellwoodsies you come from all by yourselves."

"Oh, that's all right," Jon-Tom said quickly. "I mean, I appreciate the offer, but Mudge and I managed to make it down here by ourselves, and we can make it home the same way." He looked around wildly for support.

A head appeared. "More company the better, mate," declared a thoroughly sozzled Mudge.

Weaving, drunken otters gathered around the distraught spellsinger, cheering and waving their swords about with complete disregard for the bodily integrity of their neighbors.

"Aye, mate...We're with you all the bayway!...Glad to come along!...Three cheers for the spullspunger...!"

Jon-Tom dodged a sword stroke that came perilously near taking a chunk out of his thigh. He found himself being backed toward the otters' boat, which the police had thoughtfully tied up at the end of the pier.

Mudge lurched along in front, one arm around Quorly, the other around Sasswise. "It'll be fun, mate, to 'ave a little good company goin' 'ome. Besides, I'd like for me friends 'ere to meet Clothagrump." He leaned over to whisper to Quorly. "This 'ere wizbiz 'as got 'imself an apprentice name o' Sorbl who can conjure up the best damn batch o' 'omemade 'ootch you never tasted, luv. Burn the linin' right out o' your bloomin' throat."

Quorly pressed tight against him. "Sounds wonderful, Mudgey."

"No, no," Jon-Tom told them, pleading desperately, "you don't understand. Clothahump is a very serious, sober-minded sorcerer. It's important that he see me in the same light or he won't send me home someday."

"Then we'll get along fine, Jon-Tome...Tom," said Wupp happily, "because we're damn sure serious about not stayin' sober."

Paws reached forward and lifted the protesting spellsinger, carried him down into the boat. Hands bent to oars, and after some initial confusion, the boat began to slide out onto the Lake of Sorrowful Pearls. Drortch launched into a spirited if slightly sloppy rendition of "Row, Row, Row Your Boat!" The melody was quickly taken up by her companions and the boat was soon producing enough noise to attract every water-going predator between Quasequa and the river Tailaroam.

Jon-Tom lay in the bottom of the boat and wondered if maybe Markus the Ineluctable hadn't been the lucky one.